About the author

Eric Grounds is a former soldier, businessman, charity director and Olympic sportsman. He has lived in Northumberland for more than sixty years, having arrived there as a little boy with a crewcut and a pronounced American accent. British and French education changed the accent and the nationality, which allowed him to be appointed as High Sheriff of the County in 2006.

WILL TO WIN

Eric Grounds

WILL TO WIN

Vanguard Press

VANGUARD PAPERBACK

A CIP catalogue record for this title is
available from the British Library.

ISBN 978 1 784655 62 4

*Vanguard Press is an imprint of
Pegasus Elliot MacKenzie Publishers Ltd.*
www.pegasuspublishers.com

First Published in 2019

**Vanguard Press
Sheraton House Castle Park
Cambridge England**

Printed & Bound in Great Britain

Acknowledgements

Let me pay humble tribute to my wife and children, who have bullied me for thirty years to present this novel. I couldn't function without their eternal love and support.

Dedication

This book is dedicated to the late and greatly missed
Brigadier Charles Bond, CBE

Chapter One

1974

'It's late for someone to phone,' muttered Corporal Jim Balchin, as his hand reached out to kill the buzz of the external line.

'Don't worry, Jim, I'll get it.' The speaker nodded briefly at his Intelligence Corporal as he seized the telephone, which sat on a makeshift wooden platform swinging on a telescopic extension between the two desks. '241,' he said.

There was a pause, pregnant with expectation, hollow in the rasp of breath at the far end. The hairs on his neck bristled as Edward Davidson shifted on the acrylic seat of his chair. His biro sketched three lines linked by a curling loop. He stabbed the paper.

'Is that you, Davidson?' muttered a voice. Irish, almost English in accent, cultured but lilting, with a hint of some other European tongue. There was a tremor of – of what? Fear, intrigue, concealment, excitement? 'What was it?' thought Davidson. 'Joe?' he said.

His eyes glanced around the office as he called to mind his source. On the wall opposite his desk hundreds of small photographs jostled into weaving ranks, portraits of more than two hundred possible terrorists, each one marked with a coloured dot and sequential number. Beneath the mugshots ran three tables groaning with rectangular wooden boxes filled with cards, each card meticulously and painstakingly completed in manuscript by twelve generations of intelligence staff. Every photo was linked to a series of cards, with background files locked in cabinets along the wall behind the Corporal's desk. Davidson put his hand briefly over the mouthpiece of the telephone and mouthed the words, 'Space Invader – get me his file.'

Jim Balchin turned to the line of cabinets behind him, opened the second drawer of the nearest one and flicked briefly through the hanging folders. As he turned back to hand the documents over, the voice on the other end of the telephone caught and murmured, 'Yes, it's me. I have to see you. Tonight. Now. It's urgent.'

Edward Davidson paused before answering. Joe McCall's file was open now in front of him. Pinned to the top document in the file was the image of a thin, unremarkable man. Lank, dark hair curled over a narrow brow; a nose perhaps too long; a chin certainly too weak. There was something almost Levantine about him. He had come unprompted out of the night to give information two months earlier. Edward remembered vividly the hand shaking him from a deep sleep as Charles Matthews, C Squadron Leader, strove to waken the exhausted Intelligence Officer. 'Edward, wake up. This is important. We have to talk.'

They had gone to the Officers' Mess. Charles to have a glass of whisky, Edward to sip at another cup of coffee. An active and energetic sportsman, Edward Davidson drank only when it would be boorish not to. His exhaustion had left him as the excitement of his brother officer sparked between them on their brief walk from the living quarters in the Nissan huts of Fort George.

'I think,' said Charles, 'that we have a coup on our hands. I made some notes, but you will want to take your own. I'll try to organise my thoughts better as we go, but this is likely to take us half an hour at least.'

Edward leaned back in the leather armchair, thankful that the Army at least knew how to live comfortably on operations. For all that the Mess was just a tin hut, it could have been the ante-room in Germany. Silver statues on occasional tables and oil paintings of elegant cavalrymen, partially lit by three scattered standard lamps, stared from the walls at the two descendants of their regiment, both tall, one dressed in disrupted pattern combat kit, the other in blue jeans and black polo-neck shirt. 'OK, Charles, I'm ready for anything. Let's have it.'

It was a tale of fear and intrigue, a tale of personalities in conflict, doctrines questioned, loyalties changed. No average meeting this. The informant was a blend of the undreamed and the unexpected. Drugs, he had reported, had taken him on Provisional business to the Middle East. He spoke Arabic, his mother had been born in Egypt. His father, who had been brought up in County Donegal, had gone to sea as an engineer. The tale was too long to relate, but suffice to say that, as the Troubles continued in the Six Counties, Joe McCall felt the urge to play his part in re-uniting Ireland. Through his father's family, he had met some of the 'boyos'. His job as a salesman for an international plastics firm gave him natural cover. For the past three years he had dealt in drugs and weapons through Beirut, Tripoli and Cairo, transporting the goods in trawlers to ports in the South of Ireland.

The crisp, orderly and staff-trained delivery of Charles Matthews made it all easy to grasp. He had brought chronology and structure to a fragmented tale, whispered behind a concrete border check-point. 'Why you, Charles? Why did he choose to talk to you?'

'I'm not sure. He definitely chose to talk to me because Corporal Williams specifically called my Rover Group to ask me to go out to Buncrana. He didn't say why; he just insisted. I hazard a guess that this man has been watching for some time.

Like any other Squadron Leader, I spend most of the time cruising my patch and keeping an eye on the lads. I guess if I were a sniper I would have little difficulty in selecting this particular target. But he didn't know my name. He merely asked for "the head man". It could just as easily have been Colonel Martin he wanted.'

'This is a bit too big for both of us, Charles. I will have to share it with two people: Mark Collins at Brigade and Micky Burgess at Special Branch. I'll get onto it now. Although you will want to be at the debriefing with the Colonel, I'll give him the gist before anyone at Brigade has a chance to wind him up.' Glancing at his watch, Davidson was surprised to note that it was now 4.20 in the morning. Another night with too little sleep, but who cared? 'I promise I'll come back to you Charles, but thank you – thank you for your very clear report, and for helping me to do my job with so little hassle. God, how exciting.'

'But it's a problem,' he thought. 'Do I tell Brigade first and thereby strangle the way in which I can tell Micky, or do I tell Micky and risk the wrath of my military masters? Clearly, I can't phone this through. I'll trust to fate, drive over to Brigade, stopping at the Branch en route. If Micky is around, I'll tell him. If he isn't, the Gods will have spoken.'

And so, the Gods played their part, too. Micky Burgess, the ubiquitous, determined and fractious Head of Special Branch, was in his office. 'Don't you ever go to bed, Micky?' asked Edward, as he sat opposite the squat policeman at a quarter to five in the morning.

'I'm a little like you, boy,' replied Burgess.

The chemistry between the two men was as natural and cohesive as it was unexpected. One, a dedicated fifty-year-old policeman whose longest trip to England had been to attend the Bramshill Senior Officers' Course; the other, a twenty-five-year-old English cavalry officer playing at cops and robbers on turf which was normally protected by the police with jealousy and suspicion. They had sparred for ten minutes when they first met, the Irishman wary of the culture and enthusiasm which he had learned to mistrust, but attracted by the sporting reputation of this quiet soldier. Edward Davidson had not mentioned his appearance at the Munich Olympic Games, but clearly, they were well briefed at Special Branch Headquarters. Despite his wariness about the military short-term solutions to terrorism, Micky Burgess enjoyed the company of people who did anything well without fanfare.

Davidson had related the story with less detail than he had been given by Charles Matthews. Burgess knew of Joe McCall; his first reaction was dismissive, his considered opinion more positive. 'Why did you come to me first, Edward? Every other Intelligence Officer goes off to bleat to that fine Brigade over the water and I receive a version which has more of the Foyle in it than fact. You'll not be popular, you know.'

Edward gazed directly at the heavy-set policeman. 'I'm here for just four and a half months, Micky. My opposite number at Brigade is here for two years. Neither of us has to live with the problem, and neither of us has a gut feel for what is true and what is false. If this source is as good as he sounds, it needs professional management, not parochial possessiveness.'

There was a silence. 'Some Bushmills?' asked Burgess. Davidson grinned. It would be churlish to refuse, and it might take the conversation into more fruitful territory. Legend had it that no British Army Officer had ever been asked to have a drink in the office with Micky Burgess. 'How can I refuse you, boss?'

It was six-thirty in the morning. Sober, just, Edward Davidson parked the Intelligence Office mini outside Brigade Headquarters and strolled across the windswept car park to check in at the main reception. His call from the Special

15

Branch office on the west side of the Foyle had alerted Mark Collins, who was waiting for him on the first floor.

'Jesus fucking wept, Edward. What the hell do you think you were doing sharing this with Special Branch before telling me?' Collins, a short, red-haired and fiery infantry major, had never understood the bloody cavalry anyway. Pompous, arrogant and dumb was his considered opinion of almost every cavalry officer he had ever met. And now Edward Davidson, the one donkey walloper to ever undermine his determined antagonism, had re-affirmed his most fundamental convictions. 'Don't you realise that this makes us look like bloody amateurs? Can't you grasp that the Special Branch will steal this from under our very noses? Jesus! I cannot believe it. I can just predict what the Brigade Commander will have to say.'

Davidson kept his peace. It had been a predictable outcome to the night's work. Whichever way he played it, someone was going to be angry. He didn't have any particular axe to grind with Collins, and the man had been fairly helpful over the past three months. But it had been clear to Edward during the first week of his tour that Collins would never get on with the Branch, and the Branch would deliberately obstruct someone like Collins, who seemed hell-bent on trying to establish a reputation. That was the trouble with the Army: as soon as people thought their career was likely to prosper, they lost all sense of proportion.

'Well, I am sorry, Mark.' He could see Collins' indignation at the deliberate but normal informality of the cavalryman. An infantry captain would have called him 'Sir' under these conditions. 'The fact is that you and I are tourists in this contest. I considered the two evident options and decided that if Micky was in his office, I would stop and talk through the information with him. I urge you to see this in a more positive light. Special Branch do not dismiss the source. They know of him and, yes, they do have some hesitation about his influence and validity. But on balance they give it the weight which my own enthusiasm conveys. There is no point in shouting at me. What's done is done.'

'Well, you'll have to tell the Brigadier face-to-face. This is just too big an issue and you may be sure that I shall brief him in detail.'

'Fine,' said Davidson with a shrug. 'I've been up most of the night and I doubt the Brigadier will be in before nine. When do you want me back here?'

'Be here at nine prompt. And I strongly recommend that you wear something more in keeping with the occasion.'

Davidson sighed inwardly and turned to stride out of the office before he told the little red engine how to stop his boiler from exploding.

It had been two hours of frenetic activity before he reached Brigade Headquarters again. A shower, shave, shit and change of clothes led to one of Corporal Harvey's outstanding fry-ups in the Mess, shared with Colonel Martin at one end of the dining room. 'I'm sorry, Colonel' – the whole morning seemed to be one long apology – 'After Charles and I had finished talking, it seemed to me that I would be wise to share this with the Branch first. You know how hard I have worked to earn Micky Burgess' confidence, and some of that is now producing a dividend. We would not have been tipped the wink over Eamon Coyle and Gerard McNulty if it had not been for the liking which Micky has for the Regiment.'

Martin Baker smiled openly and with warmth. The liking was all for Edward Davidson and not for the Regiment, as both men knew. Eamon Coyle had been lifted on the one night he had spent in Londonderry in more than two months. Edward had done the homework, identified the likely houses, and discussed it with the Branch. But the timing was all down to Micky Burgess. The Head of Special Branch would have been content to let Coyle carry on as he was on the basis that the

17

enemy you knew was better than any other. But his affection for Edward Davidson had given the Regiment the coup of capturing the current Provisional IRA Brigade Commander red-handed with a weapon in the City. McNulty had been the icing on the cake ten days later. Newly appointed as Coyle's replacement, he had been lifted in a swift and surgical operation which emanated from a quiet Special Branch phone call to Edward just after dinner in the Mess.

'Don't you worry, Edward. I'll talk to the Brigadier before you get there. You have my total support and you are doing an excellent job. The spleen of Mark Collins has no real venom; just let it roll off your back.'

'Well, thank you, Colonel. I must say, it's a relief to have my judgement supported. I just hope the Brigadier feels the same way.'

Brigadier James Winstanley was a Highlander. Five feet and eight inches in his socks, he looked like a benevolent piglet. The MC he had won when on secondment to another infantry battalion in Korea endowed him with a reputation for fearless bravery and his methodical rise through the Army to the command of 8 Infantry Brigade showed all the signs of a career which would end with a place on the Army Board.

Mark Collins mixed irritation with anticipation in equal measure. 'Good, you're on time. The Brigadier will see us now,' he said, when Davidson arrived. Together, they strode towards the large office at the southern end of the Headquarters building. Outside, a watery sun tried to break through dense cloud, the threat of rain narrowly restrained by a driving wind. In offices on both sides of the corridor there were the varied sounds of typewriters, telephones and murmured conversations. A coffee percolator bubbled in the clerk's office which protected the Brigadier from stray visitors to the Headquarters.

'Ah, Mark, Edward, good morning.' The Brigadier pointed to two armchairs near the window and, taking the third chair for himself, plopped back and stretched his short legs in front of him. 'Mark is not entirely jubilant about your actions, Edward.'

'Um, yes, I know,' said Davidson. 'But I had reasons and I am more than happy to justify them, Brigadier.'

'OK, let's hear them.'

Quietly, now practised by two earlier recitals of the details, Edward relayed a concise summary of the morning's events. Every now and again the Brigadier interjected with a question or comment, before summarising the report. 'You had a difficult choice, Edward. From a military point of view, I have to acknowledge Mark's irritation. But from the point of view of a commander who has to nurture relationships with every other party in this parlour, I think you have handed me a valuable weapon. And, let's face it, the Security Service would have taken this source on anyway. No, there is no doubt in my mind that this has worked out rather well. Mark, I am sorry that some of your thunder has been dissipated, but we must all work together to make the very best of this. Thank God this man McCall decided he wanted to talk to Charles Matthews. Thank God Charles talked to Edward. Now, let's get on with the business in hand. When is the Security Service due?'

This was all news to Edward. The Security Service no less. Probably time to turn to the right and dismiss, he thought. 'Um, would you like me to leave, Brigadier?'

'Oh, don't be silly, Edward. How on earth can we wrap this thing up if the one man who knows what's going on shuffles off to have a kip?'

Mark Collins shifted uncomfortably in his chair. 'I expect the Five man from Lisburn to fly in by chopper in about an hour, sir. I am told that he may have one of the Friends with him. Micky Burgess will come over, hoping to arrive when the helicopter does.'

Davidson's quizzical look was mute testimony to his confusion about 'the Friends'. Narrowly avoiding a supercilious response, Collins said, 'MI6 is known in the trade as 'the Friends'.

'Well, well,' thought Edward. 'It seems that neither Micky nor I will have much to do with this if we are to have half of Whitehall latching on to it.' To Winstanley he said, 'How do you want me to play it, Brigadier?'

Seventy minutes later, as the roar of the Scout helicopter engine subsided on the tarmac square outside the Brigade Headquarters, a sombre group of military, police and professional intelligence men gathered in the secure conference room. Edward gravitated naturally towards Micky Burgess, who stood apart from the cluster around the coffee cups and biscuits. 'You were right, Micky, my military colleagues were not hugely chuffed with me talking to you first.' Davidson glanced towards Collins as he spoke, noting that the uniformed soldier was busy climbing into the pocket of the senior man from MI5. He scratched his chin thoughtfully as he continued, 'Are we out of it after this?'

'Oh, I wouldn't be so sure,' said Burgess. 'Five will want to have control; Six will want to seal him up and leech everything out of him. If the man doesn't want to be anywhere near them, it will come back to us. I suggest that you produce your version of events in the way that you did to me. They know it already, but they will want to test your report. Don't embellish it, and don't make any suggestions. If it comes to a fight, it will be between me and these Whitehall warriors. Use this as an opportunity to learn how inter-service politics are fought.'

'Gentlemen,' urged the Brigade Commander, 'I think we should get on with the business.' Chairs scraped as the eight people present shuffled around the central table to find a tactical position. The junior MI5 man dawdled to fill his coffee cup, before turning to take a seat next to his senior officer, whose rounded form and tousled hair suggested a bon viveur of some distinction. A lean, intellectual-looking man in a Prince Edward check suit slipped into place on the left of the Brigadier. It occurred to Edward Davidson that this man must have been the model for Peter Cook's sketch 'My brother Esau is a hairy man, but I am a smooth man'. A slim, grey pen appeared from his inside breast pocket. He fixed a pair of metal half-framed glasses to a nose which was slightly hooked, then peered over the top of the rim with a look that resembled a hen harrier hunting for young grouse. Opposite the Brigadier, Mark Collins adopted the role of official scribe, swiftly and neatly noting the names of those present, checking the time, then politely waiting for action to begin.

'I think you have all heard the basic detail of an incident which occurred last night. C Squadron Leader of the cavalry regiment based in Fort George was called to a meeting at Buncrana. He met there with an Irish civilian we now know to be Joe McCall. He took extensive notes of his meeting, then conferred with Edward Davidson, the Regimental Intelligence Officer. Although you, gentlemen,' here nodding his head to the men from Lisburn, 'may wish to talk to Major Matthews personally, I took the liberty of excusing him from attending this meeting. He has a significant job to do and I did not wish to distract him from it. It was clear to me that the distilled product which Edward has presented to me was a firm foundation upon which to build. I should add that I am grateful to Micky Burgess, who telephoned me at 7.00a.m. this morning to commend Edward to me.'

Startled, the young officer turned to glance at Burgess, who sat on his right. The Head of Special Branch did not acknowledge him, but continued to gaze thoughtfully at the Brigadier, his hands immobile on the white paper pad in front of him.

'Now, before Edward summarises his report, it would help us all if we could record who is present. Giles, apart from Edward, we all know you. Edward, this is Giles Heworth, who runs the Security Service cell at Lisburn. Perhaps you would introduce your colleagues, Giles.'

*****

'Yes, it's me. I have to see you. Tonight. Now. It's urgent.' Abruptly, Edward's mind came back to the present. There was something distinctly wrong here. He and Joe McCall had met twice since the high-level intelligence meeting at Brigade. Whilst there was tension and hesitation, they had been able to communicate easily, and it was evident that McCall was happy to deal with a dedicated intelligence operator. On the other hand, there was no sensation that McCall wanted to spend his life with a serving officer in the British Army. Up until now, Edward, guided by Giles Heworth in Lisburn, had arranged the meetings. McCall had the office number, but they had agreed that he should phone only if there was something extraordinary to share. It was hard to imagine how their business could suddenly become so urgent.

'Can you talk freely?' he asked. Was it his imagination, or was the delay just a little too long?

'I need to see you now. Can you get out to meet me in Rosewood Avenue?'

Alarm bells were ringing loudly now. Never, never go where the source wants you to go, and never allow him to dictate the time. But the contact was not that strong; the need to respond in a positive and helpful way must be a consideration.

'I can see you, Joe, but not now and not at Rosewood Avenue.' Edward swiftly quartered the regimental area in his mind. Somewhere secure, perhaps a patrol nearby. Close enough for both to get to, but not so far for him that it would give time for an IRA ambush. He needed space to manoeuvre the car, but not become a sitting duck. Decision time.

'Pennyburn Industrial Estate. Ten minutes. Can you be there, Joe?'

There was another pause. OK, he needed to think where it was, how long it would take. 'Fine, I'll see you.'

'OK, Corporal Balchin,' said Davidson, 'Space Invader has asked for a meeting. There's something not quite right. I don't like it, but I dare not let him down. I'll take the mini now,' he said, as he checked the magazine of his own, licensed P38 pistol. He drew back the slide, checked the barrel, then let it click forward with a solid thunk and pulled the trigger. He slid the magazine back into the handle and tucked the weapon into the front of his trousers. Reaching to the wall behind his desk, he grabbed a small black radio, switched it on and listened briefly, before pressing a button on the side to send a message. 'Hello, Zero, this is Acorn. Radio Check, over.'

'Zero OK, over.'

'Acorn OK, out.'

'Would you phone A Squadron and let them know that I am going to Pennyburn Industrial Estate? I don't want them to make too much of it on the air, but if they could kindly make sure that the nearest patrol gravitates that way in the next ten minutes or so, I might feel a little more comfortable. I'll pop into the Ops Room here on the way out.'

'Good luck, boss.' Balchin's laconic style suited Edward's own. Both of them frequently found themselves sharing the night in the Int Cell, checking, cross-checking, reading reports, testing theories, establishing relationships, chewing the fat. Balchin was methodical, meticulous and neat. He stored facts and detail in his brain and supported it on paper. He admired the way his IO had focused on achieving quality results and had thoroughly relished the genealogical pursuit which had neatly identified Eamon Coyle's likely safe houses. As

Davidson left the office, he picked up the phone and dialled A Squadron Ops Room.

The Regimental Ops Room was a haven of relative peace and tranquillity. Sean Lomax, the Ops Officer, was studying the huge map of Londonderry, chinagraph in one hand, curved Petersen pipe in the other. Only one of the watchkeeper's chairs was occupied. Tony Wilson, a direct contemporary of Edward's, was struggling to complete the Telegraph crossword puzzle; it was a constant battle of enthusiasm against ability, but everyone enjoyed it.

'You off out, then?' he asked, taking a few precious seconds out from the complexity of 14 down: 'Horse moves towards a grave situation in Kent; ten letters'.

Davidson's grin was perhaps a little tighter than normal. 'Yup,' he said. 'An unexpected call to meet an important source. I'm not entirely happy about it and have asked Corporal Balchin to let A Squadron know that I'm going to Pennyburn Industrial Estate. Don't make a fuss about it on the air, though.' Sean Lomax's head tilted to one side as he asked, 'Should you not be taking someone with you?'

Edward, who was peering over Tony Wilson's shoulder, shrugged as he turned towards the door. 'I haven't time. I've got only seven minutes to get there, and I want to be there before my man. But you could do me one favour, Sean. Could you please phone Special Branch and leave a message for Micky Burgess, just to say that our mutual friend has called me out.'

The door opened inwards. As he stepped through, Edward turned and said over his shoulder, 'The answer's Canterbury, Tony.'

The little green mini was a great little buzz bomb, when it worked. As Davidson folded his long form into the driver's side, he took the P38 from his waistband and laid it on the passenger seat beside him. The radio went beside it, carefully placed nearer the passenger door so that he could grab his pistol without interference. With a muttered prayer to the God of Motor Cars, he pulled the choke half way out and twisted the key in the ignition. Whirrrrr, whirrr; then, praise be, the vital spark. The much-abused engine kicked into life. He pumped the accelerator for twenty seconds, then jabbed the gear stick into reverse and, with some care in case anyone had appeared out of the night behind him, he reversed swiftly, left hand hard down to turn the car in a sharp loop, before changing his lock, easing into first gear and rolling forward to the twelve-foot metal wall which formed the gates to Fort George. A soldier was already there, one hand holding the right exit panel. As the mini slid to a halt, he pulled the gate wide and looked to the right and left down the Strand Road. With a friendly wave, he beckoned the mini out on to an apparently clear road.

Davidson darted out of the gates and turned right on the Strand Road towards the Shantallow and Carnhill, then left up Buncrana Road. Swiftly, he moved through the gears, acknowledging wryly that his timings were tight. The roads were empty, damp, but not wet. Yellow street lamps cast intermittent pools of light on residential streets. On the right a petrol station, closed for some weeks now after the fourth armed raid in as many months. Crossing below the Shantallow, second left, first left, short straight, one minute to go.

Ahead lay Pennyburn Industrial Estate. As far as he had been able to judge, all of the businesses were trying hard to make an honest living, although many of the workforce doubtless had strong Republican sentiments. No harm in political conviction, provided it didn't convert into illegal armed struggle, thought Edward. He checked his mirror: the road was still clear, nothing moved ahead. He changed down from fourth to third, double de-clutching to maintain revs. The Industrial Estate looked totally deserted. No lights, no cars, no people. He changed down again and accelerated through the left turn onto the broad concrete apron which ran along the north side of the site. There was an exit at the west end of the Estate leading on to Northland Road, and he decided to snoop along the serried avenues of buildings. The radio crackled into life. 'Hello, One Nine, this is One Three; please check licence number AIW 535. Over.'

'One Nine, wait. Out.'

The mini rolled westwards as Davidson peered down each lane of buildings. Nothing moved. Nothing unusual, nothing odd, just a sense of isolation. He reached the end of the Estate and glanced at his watch. It was fifteen minutes since the call. Joe was late, but there was nothing to worry about yet. He allowed the car to roll to a standstill, left foot pressing the clutch to the floor, first gear engaged, engine idling. It was the waiting which jangled the senses, he thought. Stay calm, lad. 'Lad' – what a term; everyone used it all the time. You could lend the word every nuance, convey so many different messages. I really must try to stop saying it, reflected Edward; it sounds so affected – and what was wrong with individual names anyway? On the other hand, there couldn't be many organisations, let alone a regiment, with thirty officers, of whom eight were christened Anthony.

Another minute ticked by. Nothing. He looked in the mirror to confirm that there was nothing creeping up from behind. Uncertain, he turned half in his seat to look over his right shoulder, then shifted in the other direction to look over the left. He slowly wound down the window, letting in the damp, brisk breeze. There wasn't a single sound. Eighteen minutes had now passed. He knew something was wrong, but this wasn't leading anywhere. Slowly, he eased his foot off the clutch and the car edged forward. No, it was no good waiting for twice the time. It increased the danger by more than a hundred percent. Time to leave.

Momentarily uncertain, Edward hesitated about returning along the formal apron of the Estate. The car had travelled sixty yards or so already. What if there had been someone lurking in the darker areas? With an abrupt decision, he pulled the wheel hard left and angled the car towards the western exit from the Estate. Eyes firmly on the rear-view mirror, he changed into second as he approached the main road. Still nothing there.

Heart beating a little more easily, he turned right onto the lateral road to go back the way he had come. The only trouble about this route was that there were not many side roads. It would be better not to repeat the outward journey exactly, he thought. By now he was in top gear, travelling at fifty-five miles per hour and nearing the eastern entrance to the Estate. There were three options: to take the left turn below Carnhill before joining the Buncrana Road; to join the Racecourse Road and go north; or to stay on the absolute reverse route until he could swing well south of the two residential estates. Despite the knowledge that there was a mobile patrol somewhere close by, it would be an unnecessary detour and risk to go into them, he thought.

Now certain about his return to barracks, Davidson slowed at the T-junction, glanced to the left and swung right to travel south along the Buncrana Road. Another junction and he turned left, swiftly picking up speed as he moved through second and into third. And... dammit... there was a car stationary, lights on, in the left lane. Indicating to overtake it, he changed down to second again, when suddenly both doors burst open and two men leapt out, facing him. They were no more than thirty yards away and he could clearly see both of them. More to the point, he could also see their weapons. Christ, it had been a set-up after all. How bloody stupid of him not to take a different route back. By now the engine was roaring its protest as his foot increased the pressure on the throttle. Two options, he thought: try to drive through, or attempt to head back in the direction he had just come from. The chances were that the closer he got, the more accurate their shooting would be. He grabbed the hand brake and yanked it up, at the same time pulling the steering wheel hard right. Jesus, was the thing going to turn over, he thought. The little car's tyres squealed as the rear swung in a sharp loop to the left, and Edward was aware of something popping in his left ear. Head down, right hand firm on the wheel, car slewing through one hundred and eighty degrees and beyond, a bump as he rode up over the opposite kerb, hand off hand brake and back onto the steering wheel. The little car surged forward, half on the pavement, half on the road; a lamp-post loomed out of the dark, jerk right, bump, bump, now firmly on the road with all four wheels. He risked a glance in the mirror. Bugger, the mirror had gone. Where was it? Change into third, change into fourth, distance from the ambush increasing, but still within range; keep going hard.

The radio was squawking, although he couldn't make out the words. Rational thought was returning to take over from animal reaction. He heard the thud as something struck the boot, and he checked his speedometer, noting with surprise that he was now travelling at well over sixty. It must be a record for this poor little machine, he thought. He judged that it was about eight seconds since he had turned, so he must be almost out of range of those jokers and their popguns. Phew, that was close – but it was not time to stop and mop the brow.

By now he was close to the edge of the urban area. He could either go left down into the relative safety of Rosemount, or keep on going to lurk in a country lane. There was a remote chance that he could help to catch the buggers, so better to find a spot to park in Rosemount. Changing down swiftly, he raced into the next left turn, changing back up through the gears. Beside him, the radio was still bleating; he would have to answer it. Still moving at sixty miles an hour, he scrabbled to pick up the radio with his left hand and fumbled it into position near his left ear. Awkward this: he always preferred to hold it to his right ear. There was a pregnant pause on the airwaves, so he thumbed the pressel switch and said, 'Hello, Zero, this is Eight Three, Acorn speaking. I just ran into a spot of bother. Over.'

'Zero.' It was Sean's voice, calm, reassuring. Edward could imagine the tension in the Ops Room. 'Are you secure? Over?'

'Eight Three, yes. I had just turned onto Inch Road to return to you when I was ambushed by a dark blue Ford with two gunmen. The vehicle was pointing east, clearly waiting for me. I think his registration was AIW 177, although I am uncertain about the first three letters. Both men were armed with pistols. Thank God they weren't Armalites. Over.'

'Zero.' A pause. 'Roger. And are you still in the immediate area? Over.'

'Eight Three, no. I was keen to return home in one piece. Over.'

'Zero, do that. Callsign One Three is now close to the scene of the incident and more callsigns are en route. Return to base and report here on arrival. Out.'

Chapter Two

'This has more holes than a colander,' laughed the MT Sergeant as he walked around the mini. 'What were you up to, sir?' he asked Edward.

'Just driving, Sergeant Davis; a little tour around the city. You know how irritated some drivers can get, though, and I came across two people who didn't like me overtaking them.' Despite his airy manner, Edward Davidson was horrified to see the damage to the car in the clear light of day. The rear of the vehicle had six bullet holes dotted around the boot. The back window had gone. 'That,' thought Edward, 'must have been the shot which removed the rear-view mirror.' Three of the bullets had been found in the sandbags which Corporal Balchin had put in the boot in order to make the mini a little more stable when cornering. Of the other three, there was no sign.

'Bloody hell, I'm going to have to find a new car for you, sir. There's no point in trying to conceal this one now. In fact, it will be pretty hazardous for anyone to drive it around Londonderry ever again.'

'Make it something really fast and slinky, will you. I can't stand chugging along at a snail's pace; and on the evidence of last night, I may need some acceleration in future. How long do you think it will be before you can find us a replacement?'

'To be honest, I have no idea, but I'll chivvy things along. You're something of a celebrity now and I'm sure that Brigade will do all they can.' With which, the amiable Sergeant saluted briefly and wandered back into his Nissan hut. Edward shoved his hands in his pockets and looked gloomily at his old car. He would have to hitch a lift down to Special Branch later. Due to see Micky Burgess at 11 o'clock, he first had to see the Colonel and then brief the assembled officers at Morning Prayers. Time to get back on the road.

Martin Baker greeted him warmly when he rapped on the Commanding Officer's door. 'Did you manage to get some sleep?' he asked.

'Thank you, Colonel, I did. Actually, I slept like the proverbial log and swear I didn't dream at all. I've just been along to MT to have a look at the car. Heaven only knows how those hoods missed me.'

'Well, we're all grateful they did. Inevitably, some people are going to think that you were out joy-riding. Don't let it get to you. Most of them will be jealous. What concerns me most, however, is your future.'

'My future, Colonel?'

'Yes. It is quite clear that you were set up last night. None of us can guess what happened to Space Invader, but it is my bet that he was under duress. It is going to take time to work out the how and the why. I find it hard to believe that he was a plant from the start, although I guess anything is possible. Whichever way it goes, the fact is that you are now very hot material. I have no doubt at all that your successes with Coyle and McNulty have created a desire for revenge in the Provisional IRA. The fact that they nearly succeeded is a strong warning to us, quite apart from indicating that other soldiers in plain clothes must be more at risk now. I cannot sanction any trips by you which are not absolutely vital to your work.'

'Um, I take your point, Colonel, but there are endless occasions when I need to go at a moment's notice, either to the Branch or to Brigade. I accept that I don't really need to go much further afield. Are you saying that I have to seek your authority before moving from Fort George at any time?'

'No. That would be bureaucratic and counter-productive. Nevertheless, I am making the point now that you must think doubly hard before sauntering off to gossip with Micky Burgess or Mark Collins. You are not to go up to see the Welsh Guards in the Creggan. We have four more weeks to complete on this tour and I would be much happier if I knew that we were taking you home with us.'

'No problem, Colonel. I want to leave with everyone else, too! Clearly, I am going to have to see the Branch and Brigade today. I have spoken on the phone to both and I'm expected for my first meeting at 11 o'clock. I know that Micky has been trying to find out where Space Invader is, so I will almost certainly have to see you again later today.'

'That's fine. Now, let's think for a second about Prayers. Everyone is agog with your escape. I intend to play it straight down the line, taking your report first, followed by A Squadron's summary of the follow-up. Thereafter, we will follow the standard routine. Let's go.'

The buzz of conversation ceased as soon as the Commanding Officer entered the conference room. Everyone rose. 'Do sit down,' instructed Martin Baker. Edward slid silently into the one available chair next to Sean Lomax and surveyed his brother officers. Every one of them was staring at him as if to confirm that he was the real thing. With a sideways nod of his head, he winked at Tony Wilson, who grinned cheerfully back at him. The Colonel cleared his throat and said, 'As you all know, Edward had some excitement last night. I intend to get that out of the way first so that we can all concentrate on other business once curiosity has been satisfied. I will then ask you, Gloria, to tell us about your squadron's follow-up. After that, we will revert to our normal daily agenda. Edward, let's have it.'

Following convention, Edward remained seated. With growing confidence, he succinctly related the sequence of events which had taken him out to Pennyburn Industrial Estate the previous evening.

'... And then I realised that the car was more sinister than I had assumed. When two armed men leapt out, I took evasive action and reported in as soon as I could.'

'That sounds like a gentle drive in the country, Ed,' commented Tony Walters, otherwise known as 'Gloria'. 'We all know that your car has bullet holes all over it. You have clearly had a narrow escape, so can't you give us a little more meat?'

'Not really. That's what happened. If I am honest, I can't remember the exact sequence of events because I was in too much of a hurry to get away.'

The Commanding Officer smoothed his hand over his cheek and mouth to conceal a wry grin. 'OK,' he said. 'Now, Gloria, what happened next?'

'Well, Colonel, Third Troop was not far away. Thanks to Edward's warning before he went out, we moved Will Harvey and his boys slowly towards the Industrial Estate. I was in the Squadron Ops Room and had just seen Fourth Troop depart for the northern end of Shantallow. Will reported gunfire at 1.32a.m. At that stage, we had no idea that Edward might be involved, although we more than half expected it. Amazingly, Edward reported in at 1.34. It was, perhaps, the longest two minutes I've known.' He looked across at the Intelligence Officer with real concern. 'The vehicle details allowed us to search with some focus, but for ten minutes we saw no sign of it. Then we couldn't miss it. The car was blazing away in Limavady Crescent and there was absolutely no sign of the former occupants. We scouted around for twenty minutes, but there was simply no clue of where they went. Since we saw no other vehicles on the move, it suggests that the boys came from Carnhill, but I wouldn't like to speculate who they may have been.'

'Ho, hum,' observed the Colonel. 'Well, we must congratulate Will Harvey's boys on their work, although it is absolutely maddening that we couldn't nab the culprits. Can we draw any more out of this?'

'Yes. Don't go for an evening ride with Edward Davidson,' quipped Tony Wilson. He had humorously given the same advice to one of Edward's decorative girlfriends in the past, little expecting to offer the same guidance for more serious reasons. There was a murmur of chuckles around the room.

'Right then, Gloria, you can carry on with less esoteric A Squadron business.'

An hour later, courtesy of a B Squadron rover patrol, Edward found himself at Special Branch Headquarters. Micky Burgess was in a supportive mood. 'It must be fifteen years since I felt at threat, boy. Are you all right after your fright last night?'

'I am, surprisingly so,' he responded. 'My real concern now is what became of McCall. Was it a deliberate set-up by him from the start? Or was he under duress?'

'I've had time to think about it,' murmured Burgess. 'We have moved a hell of a long way from the original contract. You operated in the most professional manner at all times and I have absolutely no doubt that the wealth of information gleaned from your two subsequent meetings with him were genuine. A man does not readily make admissions of that nature in order to set up a single murder attempt. Much as I hate to admit it, the management of the source rightfully belonged with the Security Service and Secret Intelligence Service. His contacts, method of operation and knowledge of high-level Provisional strategy were all well outside my normal bailiwick. Yes, I was interested, too, but neither of us would be able to make a case for local source handling.

'It was unusual that he was only prepared to work through you, though. I might have expected him to want to communicate through your colleague, Charles Matthews, but he took to you readily; we could all see that. Witness the fact that both of our Whitehall services fell in line without further ado. In sum, I judge he is genuine and therefore I must assume that he was under pressure in some way. That means that he was compromised, either by his own actions, or by ours.

'Now, if we study the handling in some detail, there is not much scope for a leak from our side. It is just possible that one of your crystal-clear reports fell into the wrong hands; but we are all so paranoid about classified information, that it is most unlikely. We have to assume, therefore, that something happened somewhere to alert the Provos.' Edward listened to the arguments with total concentration. There was no fault in the logic, he judged.

'So, the big question is what damage has occurred? Let us work on the basis that McCall was lifted. He will have been tortured. We know that he had fallen foul of his erstwhile associates anyway and they may well have been looking for an opportunity to exact revenge. Since he was in a mood for talking to us, I doubt he will have been able to withhold information about his relationship with us. The Provisionals know, therefore, that we have accumulated some valuable information about overseas contacts. They will almost certainly assume that we have analysed the current strategy and hierarchy as betrayed by McCall, but actually his information merely confirmed what we knew. Some of their foreign links are pretty secure, but they will warn the whole lot of a breakdown in security. I hate to say that there is very little chance that they will let our man live.'

'I have to tell you, Micky, that I really do not enjoy the notion that we may have been responsible for his death,' Edward murmured.

'It is not your problem, Edward. McCall initiated the contact. McCall followed it up. His argument with the

Provisional leadership was already an established fact. They don't like dissenters and both we and McCall knew that he was involved in the most dangerous liaison. I think he was almost certainly under observation. Truthfully, we want to be thankful that they didn't attempt to lift him when you met with him in London.'

'At least I was protected,' said Edward. 'It was straight out of a James Bond film: two-way mirrors, hidden cameras and sound equipment. I found it hard to keep a sense of proportion.'

'Well, here's a thought. You are the one person who received all the information face-to-face. That is very different from looking through a mirror or studying a film. Your perception of body language, tone, eye contact is still unique. You are now the most valuable asset for Five and Six.'

'Oh, do come on, Micky, I'm just an ordinary soldier. Fine, all this spook business is absolutely thrilling, but it's not my career. At the end of this tour, I'll revert to being a normal regimental soldier and try to get my eye back in for the next Games.'

He glanced at his watch. 'I must get across to Brigade,' he said. 'So awkward having no car. If I could use your phone, I will call the regiment to ask them to come and get me.'

'Don't be silly. One of my boys will take you, but you'll have to make your own way home after your meeting.'

*****

The reflection of the hills rippled along the surface of the loch far below. It was hard to see everything clearly now that his eyes were swelling so much, but it was a relief to be out in the fresh air, to feel the breeze, to hear a bird chirrup. Odd, really, how heightened the senses were under these conditions. His knees were getting wet, but that was a small penalty to pay for the beating to end. The past twenty-four hours had been hell on earth. The shock of being picked up by McDaid's bruisers was bad enough, and he had known immediately what to expect. But it had been worse than even he had imagined.

They had gathered three of the Council to interrogate him. It had started easily enough, but their anger had been so intense that they couldn't stop themselves. With the benefit of hindsight, the beating had stiffened his resolve. Had they continued to talk like sane human beings, he might well have told them almost everything. It was a shame to have been forced into telling them about the young British Army officer, and he wondered if he had died quickly. You never knew, though; he had been an intelligent and alert individual. That dreadful phone call, having to talk with a weapon stuffed down the left ear and the phone down the right. Davidson may have felt some of the fear, so he might just have covered himself.

But despite the beating, despite the torture with cigarettes and electric prods, despite the fear and the degradation of peeing in his pants, he had not told them everything. It was the one small strength he could retain. His three interrogators did not know the detail of his operations; they had not received his reports. He had given them something to chew on, and they may well assume that he had betrayed more, but they did not know. It was a solace in the final minutes of a man's life to grasp at small successes.

His head had dropped down onto his chest, so he lifted it again to study the hills. God, it was beautiful, Donegal. What a cracking land to live in. After the few short years of travelling around the world, he couldn't wish for a better place to end up. Shame it had to be like this.

He never felt his executioner close up behind him. His soul, his body, his mind were all focused on the broad vista of hills, water and rolling clouds. The shot, when it came, was straight into the nape of the neck, angled upwards to send the few ounces of lead into the brain. He was dead before his body hit the ground.

In silence, the three men standing around the body bent down to grab an arm or leg. In unison, they heaved it into the shallow grave. Then each man picked up a spade and steadily spilled earth over the final remains of Joe McCall.

Chapter Three

November 1977

In the four years since their last Ireland tour, the regiment had been lucky to stay in Germany. Most other regiments had been back to Ulster at least once, and some of the infantry battalions had been twice. The only trouble with being a long-term resident in Germany was the difficulty of getting back to England to see or chase women.

Colonel Martin Baker had moved on, elevated at a faster rate than he had imagined to take command of 20 Brigade in Detmold. Now Sean Lomax's period as Commanding Officer was itself drawing to a close. The future of his officers was one of his final acts of influence whilst in command.

'Edward, thank you for coming to talk. We need to discuss your future.'

It was always hard to think of calling Sean Colonel, reflected Edward. He had been such a good chum, easy to get on with, properly demanding, but human in his professional life. An outstanding host and blessed with a wife who didn't try to command the regiment herself.

'I have been talking to AG17, the officers' posting authority. We seem to have two options. You are just a little too young to go to Camberley yet, so we have to place you in a job away from the regiment for a while. There are competing factions. Your A Grade on the Gunnery Course at Lulworth has persuaded the Royal Armoured Corps that you must go to teach. Frankly – and I can see the confirmation in your eyes even now – I am sure that you would not enjoy that. Moreover, it is not going to give you a Grade Three staff officer qualification. On the other hand, it would allow you to spend more time training for the Moscow Games. On balance, unless you have a strong objection, I propose to say thank you but no thanks.'

'Thank God,' interjected Edward.

'The other job is curious. I must warn you that it will paint you as a specialist. It comes about because Brigadier, now Major-General James Winstanley strongly recommended you for an appointment of this nature. You may not be aware that he fought quite a battle to secure you as his G3 Int in Londonderry after Mark Collins. Between him and Micky Burgess, your files now hold the strongest possible recommendation for a high-level intelligence job. And we have been offered a real corker.'

Edward leaned forward. If it had to be a job away from the regiment, it might as well be an interesting one. 'They propose that you should be seconded to the Cabinet Office. Normally, the Army has one or two Lieutenant-Colonels on the Assessment Staff there. They are unaccustomed to mere Captains being there, and that is your substantive rank, even though you have now commanded a squadron for eighteen months. The good news is that you will retain your acting rank of major, and I have no doubt that you will secure the substantive rank at the proper time.

'The job is to work with the Assessment Staff. Your primary role will be to serve as the desk officer for all matters to do with Ireland – North and South. You will be expected to know all there is to know about the politics, economics, trade, industry and agriculture. Terrorism is an important, but not overwhelming, part of the brief. In preparation for this august appointment, we are to send you on the long intelligence course at Ashford, and then you will spend some time with the other Whitehall departments interested in Irish affairs. So, what do you think?'

'Frankly, Colonel, I am utterly gobsmacked. That means I will be living in London, does it?'

'Yes. I don't suppose it will do the bird stakes any harm. You will also have to spend quite a lot of time in Ireland, so be bloody careful! But, overall, I understand that your role will be to act in concert with the Northern Ireland Office, the Foreign Office, the Metropolitan Police, GCHQ, the Security Service and MI6. You will almost certainly meet former associates, since it seems that all those departments had some say in the plan to offer you the job. It is quite an accolade.'

The months had flown by. A bucolic farewell to the regiment was followed by three months as the most junior officer on a long course at the School of Military Intelligence. Theory was backed by practice, which included several fascinating lessons on how to break in to any building, how to interpret aerial photography and some excellent afternoons working with professional actors, who played their roles in the interrogation suite. Gossip in the Mess offered deeper insights into the life and experiences of the placements from other Whitehall departments. There was no doubt that the opportunity to live and debate with civil servants with no military experience was good for the mind. Most pleasurably, some of them were female, thereby adding a new dimension to the working environment.

Four other Army officers were on the same course. Henry Roberts had started his military life as a 10th Hussar and had been on the same Young Officers' course as Edward twelve years earlier: he was a kindred spirit in every way, and in no time at all the two found themselves enjoying evenings of playing bridge with much more experienced players, who found it immensely difficult to cope with the flair of two officers whose lack of attention to accepted conventions, combined with generously poured measures from a decanter of port, generally swung the contest in favour of the Cavalry.

Hamish Innes was a few years older and much more reserved. He was a Queen's Own Highlander with an agreeable Scottish burr to his voice, an independent mop of fair hair, fierce blue eyes and an unfortunate determination to play the bagpipes late into the night.

Tommy Makin was an infantryman from the Cheshire Regiment, blessed with an interesting career which had taken him all over the world because of his flair for languages. Even at this relatively early stage, it was clear that this was a man who would spend many years on the attaches' circuit.

The fourth soldier was already a Lieutenant-Colonel in the Gunners. Richard Braithwaite was about to take up a role with the Defence Intelligence Staff and had little or no experience of the intelligence world. He was encouragingly unstuffy, but there was little doubt that he saw himself as a cut above his younger colleagues.

Over the course of three months, the soldiers worked together and in opposition in syndicate exercises designed to open their minds to the practices, procedures and performance of good intelligence teams. Along the way, each had to submit to the positive vetting process, which generally involved a two-hour interview with a specialist whose mission was to uncover lurking skeletons in their background. Edward's view was that there was nothing to hide, so nothing to fear, but he was interested in the depth of detail that he had to explore with his interrogator. At this stage, he was still not aware that his own vetting would undergo a second, far more exciting level of investigation because of the nature of his future employment.

Without time to catch his breath, Edward found himself issued with a special laminated pass, a room number and a bank of telephones in a small office located on the first floor of the Cabinet Office, overlooking Whitehall. His colleagues from the course had been scattered to the four winds: Henry Roberts to Hong Kong, Hamish Innes to Northern Ireland, Tommy Makin to Paris and Richard Braithwaite closer to Edward's own parish in Whitehall.

'I take it you have never worked in Whitehall before, Edward.' The interviewer was a balding, paunchy sixty-year-old. His pin-striped suit was complemented by a waistcoat of the same material, with a heavy gold chain stretched loosely across the extended tummy.

'No, sir, this is the first attempt. I have a great deal to learn.'

'It might take you some time to acclimatise yourself to the language and style of the community, but you come highly recommended. We shall be patient with you and I hope you will be with us. You will be working closely with other desk officers with an overview of the remainder of the world. But because Ireland is such a hot potato, you are likely to see more of me than most people. You may also find yourself lining up to brief the Prime Minister. Does that worry you?'

'No, sir. I met him briefly when he came over to Germany and visited my regiment. I am perfectly comfortable briefing anyone – either individually or in groups.'

'Good. I would have been surprised if any Cavalryman had admitted to difficulty talking to people from any walk of life. But you will find this establishment is bureaucratic. I can tell you now that you may become frustrated by the way in which decisions are made. A lot of paper will cross your desk, and most of your energy will be devoted to analysing it, collating it and regurgitating it in a different style. You will receive information which comes from sources so secret that you will never be able to talk about it unless you know that all of the assembled company has access to the same sources. It is a small, intensely private world, incestuous in its friendships, parochial in its humour and arrogant in its superiority over those who do not have the right to meddle. You may be seduced by the secrecy, but I urge you to maintain your external interests, for, in due course, you will go back to normality.'

The Chairman of the Joint Intelligence Committee paused briefly to look out of his window overlooking St. James's Park. He removed his half-rimmed spectacles and rubbed the bridge of his nose with his left hand. His lower lip drooped slightly, making it look abnormally large in comparison to its superior mate, which sported a trim moustache of bristly white hairs. Outside, the drone of traffic could barely be heard as it passed along Horse Guards. 'I will have an unusual amount of work to do with you,' continued the Civil Servant, as he turned back to look Edward firmly in the eye. 'Ireland is at the top of our list of priorities in the intelligence world and you are about to become the most widely informed desk officer in the Cabinet Office. Let me amend that: you will be *the* most widely informed desk officer in the nation. You will have a right of access which is denied to everyone else. Do not abuse it, but do not be frightened to use it. Is that clear?'

'It is, sir,' said Edward promptly.

'Oh, for goodness sake, you soldiers tend to beatify people of senior rank and I cannot abide obsequiousness. When I was a diplomat, I made a point of reducing the formality of working relationships in the office. You must call me James. You will still have to call your generals 'General' and the Prime Minister 'Prime Minister', but everyone in this building is known by their first name. In my judgement, it does not minimise the sense of mutual respect for experience and professionalism.'

Ten minutes later, Edward Davidson was back in his new office overlooking Whitehall. A net curtain removed most of the natural light and added a sense of Victorian stuffiness to a room of minuscule proportions. 'Why the devil do all of the offices have these dreadful and smelly net curtains?' he asked his predecessor.

'Bombs.' William Caldicott was a man of few words. He had been the Irish Desk Officer for seven years and had adopted the mantle of his trade assiduously. Now that the time was coming for his departure, he found himself filled with an extraordinary mixture of emotions. Uppermost was a sense of dismay that his proximity to the Gods was about to vanish. He recognised irrational anger that this young whippersnapper – a Cavalry Officer, for Heaven's sake – was insolent enough to want to know everything that he knew. He could never do the job as well as Caldicott himself, and it was a mistake to appoint someone who did not understand the Whitehall network. Now that he had to hand over to someone else, he found it hard to marshal his thoughts and information succinctly.

'Bombs,' he said again for emphasis.

'How stupid of me,' Edward grinned ruefully. 'Here I am trying to learn about Irish terrorists and I overlook the evidence of their activity in London completely!'

'You must get used to the idea that terrorism is only a part of your remit,' Caldicott said ponderously. 'You will grow to know more about the Dail than you do about Parliament in Westminster. You will have to learn about agricultural policy, European trade, education, hurling and poteen. You should know as much about Irish politicians, Northern and Southern, as you do about your family, and you will read the *Irish Times* with a great deal more attention than you read the *Telegraph*.'

'I only read the *Telegraph* to do the crossword,' responded Edward, 'and I accept what you say. But for all that, the one thing which activates the politicians is a bomb behind Harrods. Terrorism drives their interest and, from what I have seen so far, it is the engine for our work in this office. Be that as it may, can we talk about the hierarchy here, because I still don't fully understand who does what?'

Caldicott nodded gravely, so Edward continued, 'Sir James Harrington told me that he used to be a diplomat, so how did he come to be the Chairman of the JIC here in the Cabinet Office, and, more to the point, what is his position in relation to the other intelligence Heads of Service?'

'Harrumph,' started Caldicott, reminding Edward vividly of some of the old buffers who could be found hibernating in the deep leather armchairs of the Smoking Room after a spirited lunch in the Cavalry Club. 'Sir James was indeed a diplomat, but he spent much of his life as one of the Friends.' His right eyebrow went up in equal and opposite proportions to the left eyelid, clearly begging a question about 'the Friends'. Edward sat mute, knowing perfectly well that this was the vernacular for the Secret Intelligence Service. 'In terms of ambition, those who follow a secret life in the Diplomatic Service often have to adopt a lower rank than their contemporaries in the mainstream of public life. It must be quite galling. But Sir James managed to bridge the divide without discomfort.' Caldicott paused to sip at one of his eternal cups of cold coffee. 'His intelligence record, if it were a subject for public analysis, would reveal a man of impeccable performance. Doubtless that is why he secured ambassadorial rank before moving to the Cabinet Office. They say that he was about to take over from Sir Clive Ottershaw as 'C' when the Joint Intelligence Committee decided that it would prefer to have him as its Chairman. As to his relationship with the other Heads of Service, I suppose it would be best to define him as first among equals. As Chairman of the JIC, he acquires the mantle worn by any effective Executive Chairman.'

'I found him refreshingly unstuffy,' said Edward.

'Don't be misled by the pussycat; it still has claws,' murmured Caldicott. 'He expects his staff to be better informed, more motivated, accurate and succinct than any other Whitehall warrior. If you don't know the answer, don't bluff.

But, equally, you should ensure that you can answer any question on that particular subject next time he talks to you.'

'Thanks for the tip. Tell me, though, what about the other Service Heads? Do we see them often and do they and their staff co-operate with us?'

'You will see the Heads whenever you brief the JIC in person. You won't find them dropping into the office for a cup of coffee. I suspect that you may, just may, be invited in to see 'C' when you go across to Century House for your first formal visit, but the Director General at Five is far too aloof. Frankly, the attitude percolates down through both Services. No-one is going to embrace you as a long-lost son, but on balance you will find that the Friends are brighter, friendlier, more inclined to share thinking. Over at the Box, you have to take a measured tread to gain any form of trust.'

Caldicott sipped at his coffee mug again and for the first time noticed that the liquid was stone cold. He shifted his bulk forward to the edge of his chair and tipped forward just enough to propel his body into motion. With a shuffling gait, he moved to the corner of the office and plugged in the kettle. Edward noticed that one of the buttons holding the back of his braces had disappeared, as Caldicott picked idly at his right nostril while the kettle element hissed into action.

'I won't be with you when you go around the other offices. It is better that you find your own feet. Technically, all of the people you talk to will have access to the same information that you do. But, clearly, they know much, much more about their own sources. So, you will learn about the content, but not the profile of human sources. In seven years, I have never met a defector or informant in the hands of Five or Six. The Met are fickle. They won't introduce you to their sources, but they will gossip. GCHQ is a different matter. Their information comes to each of us in the same form. Bear in mind that it is the most sensitive subject, and only the narrowest band of people has been vetted to receive HRT information.' Carefully, Caldicott wiped the tarnished teaspoon on a tissue pulled from the box on his desk. He measured two heaped portions of coffee into his cup and dropped in three brown lumps of sugar. Steaming water followed.

'It sounds as if we are all ladies of a certain age,' giggled Edward, but the joke floated off into the ether above Caldicott's head. A dedicated bachelor, he knew nothing of women's lives and cared not at all for their physical or medical condition. He simply would never connect the acronym HRT with Hormone Replacement Therapy. In his book, it only meant Highly Restricted Transmission, a term which was itself top secret, known only to the very few people who were cleared to read its material.

'The intelligence community is like a small village,' Caldicott continued, by this time armed with a piping hot cup of coffee. 'Some of the most unlikely people know everything, whilst others expect you to pay tribute to their feudal position. A direct question will not always deliver the right answer, and the answer you do secure may need further interpretation to make it worthwhile.' Once launched on his subject, William Caldicott became relatively animated and much more informative. 'For example,' he continued, 'your reputation for discrete and intelligent listening has passed through the police network from Londonderry. Jack Strong, who is the Commander in charge of Special Branch over at the Yard, is said to be quite looking forward to meeting you. Old whatshisname' – he paused – 'you know, whatshisname in Londonderry...'

'Burgess, Micky Burgess.'

'That's right, Burgess in Londonderry has told Jack to look after you. It seems they did a course together at Bramshill and have kept in touch ever since. If you were able to impress an Irishman on his home territory, you have a fair chance of rubbing along with Scotland Yard. Just remember that they respond to the same stimulants.'

Edward laughed. His capacity for Bushmills had expanded under Micky Burgess' tutelage, but he doubted that the Branch in London would like it quite as fervently.

The days flew by swiftly. Edward found himself immersed in files for much of each day, with brief visits to see his new working associates in their own departments. Caldicott never quite overcame his resistance to the evidence that his days in the Cabinet Office were coming to an end, but he never actively obstructed Edward's quest for information. And the information was endless. It took at least an hour to browse through all of the relevant newspapers each day. It could take another hour to go through the GCHQ material and another hour to soak up the information in the diplomatic telegram file. There were meetings, constant meetings, to discuss every aspect of the relationship between England and Ireland, between one ministry and another, between departments within Whitehall.

'How do you choose the subject of your weekly report to the JIC?' he asked Caldicott one morning.

'It's not so much the choice of subject as the length and depth of the report,' sighed his tutor. 'There is no point in tabulating a list of incidents because that is "Ops". You will find it hard to select the most relevant subject initially. Take this week. From a ministerial point of view, European subsidies are much more interesting in terms of cross-border farming issues than the bombs which went off in Dungannon and Portadown over the weekend. We have those interesting Sigint reports which give more than half a clue about the Agriculture Minister's strategy for the next meeting in Brussels. During the course of any week, you are unlikely to see a radical change in terrorist tactics, so you cannot labour the issue week after week in your report for the Red Book.'

The Red Book, Edward had learned, was the weekly digest of intelligence issues on a global scale. With copy number one going to the Queen and all the remainder of the copies limited to the closest circle of ministers and professionals, it represented the nation's opinion on the threat to British security in a concise but awesome form.

'So, what if I have nothing to say?'

'You will always have something to say, but you may not always see it published. Moreover, when it is published, you may find that it lacks the punch and conviction which you apply to your report, because some of the readers would be embarrassed if they ever learned where the information came from.'

'HRT?' queried Edward.

'Precisely,' said Caldicott.

*****

April 1978

Signals Intelligence was definitely a British strength. Thanks to the work of those early pioneers at Bletchley, the modern Government Communications Headquarters, GCHQ for short, was one of the most closely guarded public secrets. Everyone knew it was there, and some guessed what it did, but no-one – absolutely no-one – would ever talk about the product they received.

And Edward was now one of the *cognoscenti*. Daily, he read the words spoken by complete strangers who were apparently going about their legitimate business until some word, some phrase or even some technological error clicked the circuits into action to capture their conversations on tape. GCHQ collected and collated the information for desk officers to analyse in the context of all their other source information. And today, Edward was due to visit them in Cheltenham in company with four staffers from the Foreign Office.

'So how long have each of you been working with the Foreign Office?' Edward queried, as the train rattled through the suburbs of London at nine in the morning. The four, two men and two women, eyed each other before anyone responded.

'I suppose I must have been around longest,' said Edward Longstaff. 'I left Cambridge seven years ago and went straight into the FCO.' He had a very direct, level gaze and exuded the air of a professional diplomat. His suit was a muted King Edward check, the tie a masterpiece of geometrical balance, the shirt country rather than town. This man knew how to dress and made the soldier feel relatively young and gawkish, even though they must have been within a year or two of each other in age. 'I've just returned from three years in Bogota.'

'Columbia?' queried Edward.

'The very same. I was lucky to be able to travel around the rest of South America, but I grew to love Bogota.'

'Drugs and all?' persisted Edward.

'Drugs and all. We, um…' He paused to choose his words more carefully. 'We were quite interested in drugs.'

Despite his avid interest, Edward rightly judged that he could not press too hard. 'Well, ladies, what about you, then?'

The older one, Gail, must have been about twenty-five. Despite his apparent coolness, Edward found her physically attractive and more than half hoped that he would enjoy the brain as much. She was about five feet six inches tall, slightly rounded, but elegant, with long brown hair and eyes which seemed to have a touch of green. She grinned at him cautiously. 'I've only been with the Foreign Office for a couple of years. I wasn't keen to follow my father into diplomatic life because it all seemed too trite. I spent a bit of time in Paris. We lived there for a while when my father was in the Embassy, so

I knew a lot of people and wanted to brush up my French. But I guess that some professions are in the blood, and I soon realised that I wanted to follow Daddy after all.'

'And what about you, Jenny?'

'Oh, I joined at the same time as Gail, but came almost straight from university. 'I read History at Durham and the principal of my college nudged me fairly firmly in this direction. You know how it is.'

Edward, who had backed out of the university system in order to join the regiment as quickly as he could, did not know how it was, and for the first time wondered what three years at university might have done for him.

'And you, Terence?' he asked the remaining man. He couldn't quite work out if Terence was effete, gay or an exhibitionist. It came down to the bow-tie, he rationalised. In every other respect, Terence Williams looked unexceptional. Slightly above average height, he wore his charcoal suit comfortably, and the bow-tie gave him the air of a gallery owner.

'You have the edge over us, Edward. My colleagues have given you half their life stories, but we still don't know anything about you.' The others murmured politely in assent.

'Oh, heavens, my life is pretty ordinary; you won't want to hear about that. Come on, Terence, I asked you first, anyway.'

'And so you did, but I insist that we hear something about you first.'

Edward shrugged good naturedly. 'Well, I am a soldier, have been for eleven years. I still haven't worked out how someone decided to send me to London, let alone the Cabinet Office.'

'Oh, how wrong you are, Edward,' said Edward Longstaff. 'That makes you very interesting. After all, none of us work for the Cabinet Office, and we are all professional Civil

Servants. It is not often that one finds a soldier at the heart of Government affairs.'

'Well, it's hardly the heart. From where I sit, I have a closer acquaintance with the tea lady than I do with the Prime Minister,' laughed Edward self-deprecatingly.

'So what sort of soldier are you?' queried Jenny. 'My brother did a short service commission in the Royal Artillery.'

'Really?' said Edward with as much enthusiasm as he could muster. He had to acknowledge that he had a number of Gunner friends, but the civilised banter between Arms of the Service would normally have provoked him into saying something rude about anyone who was in the Artillery. 'Where did he serve?'

'Surprise, surprise,' Jenny said, 'he went to Germany and Northern Ireland. Isn't that where most soldiers go nowadays?'

'Come on,' said Terence. 'Do give us some background?'

'Well,' said Edward, 'I was only eighteen when I was commissioned and within six months of joining the Army I was a troop leader in Aden. That was quite exciting. Gun battles most nights, convoy escorts to the Radfan, but all relieved by a month in the Persian Gulf, where we did little but swim and sail. Then back to England to convert from armoured cars to tanks, before moving to Germany. Of course, all soldiers have been making four- to six-month tours to Northern Ireland since 1970, which has helped me to learn about Belfast, Londonderry and Armagh.'

'So, do you not find it a little frustrating to be behind a desk after all the action?' asked Longstaff.

'I guess the problem is that after a few years as a troop leader, seniority forces all soldiers to manage a desk. I spent almost two years as the intelligence officer and eighteen months as a Squadron Leader. I am quite used to being away from the coal-face of operational soldiering.'

'Tell us what a Squadron Leader is,' Jenny instructed.

'Cavalry regiments are different in shape and size from infantry and gunner regiments. We have squadrons of four or five troops. Each troop has four vehicles and each vehicle is manned by four men. There will be sixty-four to eighty soldiers in tanks, plus back-up staff like the Squadron Sergeant-Major and the SQMS, who deals with equipment and resupply. In sum, a Squadron Leader commands about one hundred men and is ultimately responsible for every aspect of their lives, including the social welfare of their families. As a result, we are very tight-knit, and that interaction is strengthened by tours of operational duty, when we depend upon each other for survival. There is no doubt in my mind that my closest friends for the remainder of my life will be the officers and men with whom I have worked.'

The civil servants looked at each other quietly. None of them had commanded more than a clerk and the notion of being responsible for so many souls in peace and on combat operations was an abrupt introduction to the versatility of soldiers. Here was one who seemed to have moved seamlessly into the operations centre of government to wage war with words and paper instead of tanks and soldiers trained to kill. Regardless of Edward's *laissez-faire* dismissal of his role, the four Foreign Office staff recognised that his appointment was no idle error.

The conversation became more general and increasingly relaxed as the team of five rode the rails to Cheltenham. Slowly, Edward learned a little more about each of the others and found good brains backed by very dry humour. It was clear that Edward Longstaff was the most experienced, but he was not aloof or supercilious. On the contrary, he was personable and warm. Perhaps Terence was the most difficult to get to know, and Edward could not work out if that was because he was super-intelligent, or merely a little bored with social chit-chat. The two girls were fun and Edward quietly acknowledged that he hoped to learn a lot more about Gail Ritchie. He hadn't enjoyed the company of a girlfriend for almost two years; this was the first person to appeal to him since the emotional break-up from Helen, with whom he had enjoyed a roller-coaster relationship.

At the railway station, they found a mini bus and driver waiting patiently with a small hand-written notice saying 'FCO/Cabinet Office'. They climbed in and trundled roughly westwards towards the large GCHQ site just off the A40. After a relatively informal signing-in process at the main reception, Edward was cut out from the herd. 'We need to talk in private,' said his guide, who turned out to be an equivalent desk officer working exclusively for GCHQ. Harry Martens was in his mid-to late-thirties and had the pale look of a man who lived his life in artificial light. 'Let's go to my office. We have got about eighty minutes before we meet up with some of my colleagues over lunch.'

They ambled down a corridor which stretched to eternity. Every now and again one door opened for someone to traverse the piste, before disappearing through another anonymous door. As they progressed, Harry proved to be an amusing and congenial companion.

'You heard the story about Sir Thomas Beecham after the piano recital?' he queried. Edward shook his head. 'Well, it was Mozart's Piano Concerto No. 21 – you know – famed in *Elvira Madigan*?' He didn't wait for a response. 'Well, the truth is that it didn't go too well, and after the soloist had left the stage, managers approached Beecham to ask if they could move the piano before the next item on the programme. With grave thoughtfulness, Beecham is said to have responded, "After that performance, I should think it will slink off on its own!"' Both young men brayed with laughter as Martens opened the door to his office. 'Welcome to my humble lodgings.'

For the next hour, Martens and Davidson beavered away at the task of bonding. Accepting that the serious work would occupy the afternoon, they exchanged thinking about their roles in the current climate and tripped lightly around their own backgrounds. Despite their hugely different experience and training, they found a great deal of common ground, and Edward was intrigued to study the subtle way that Martens approached problems. By his own admission, Martens was a bit of a geek. He was studious, not sporty. His work was not his life, but he was enthralled by the technology that allowed him to do his job. Of all the things that Edward did not expect, it was that Martens collected butterflies; he was quite pleased with himself for grasping the term 'lepidopterist' from the depths of his memory.

'Well, that's enough from me for the moment,' said Martens. 'Let's go and find my colleagues. We have rather a good restaurant here. I have arranged for my immediate boss and one of our analysts to join us so that you can put faces to names if you ever call.'

During lunch, Edward spotted the Foreign Office team, but it was clear that they were all on a separate mission and timetable. He, on the other hand, was pleasantly surprised to meet his new friend's manager, who was a dark-haired woman in her early forties, neatly dressed in a blue business suit with a white blouse. Mary Seymour proved to be a married lady with two teenage children. She had worked at GCHQ ever since graduating from Oxford twenty years earlier. The analyst, Bill Ogden, was quiet, reserved and offered little. Edward supposed that if you spent your life evaluating information from somewhere in the ether, you did not necessarily enjoy engaging with other people.

The afternoon was highly technical. Harry Martens made every effort to unveil the workings of much information for Edward to assimilate at a single sitting, and he rightly judged that he would learn more by listening attentively. Here was a world of which he had only read. He had hugely enjoyed RV Jones' book, *Most Secret War*, and he had worked assiduously on the files in the office to acquire enough information to have an intelligent conversation. Happily, it was clear that the two would be able to work together in harmony, even if the different tensions between Government departments was likely to produce occasional difficulties.

'I fear we will not meet face-to-face very often,' Martens stated, as they waited at reception for the Foreign Office team to appear. 'I resist going to London and, truthfully, most of what I provide is self-evident. Quite often I would not be able to say precisely how a particular report was obtained. Nevertheless, I do hope that you will call me whenever you feel you need to do so. I have greatly enjoyed today – it was almost like a holiday, being able to talk freely with someone from another world.'

They shook hands with friendly nods and Edward moulded himself to his travel mates, who had just signed out. The mood of the party of five on their way back from Cheltenham to London was thoughtful. Bound by a shared experience, they relaxed into murmured conversation. By common consent, open discussion about their visit to GCHQ was set to one side. Edward related Harry Martens' story about Sir Thomas Beecham, which kindled a response from Gail Ritchie. 'My father told me once that during the practice for a concert, Sir Thomas stopped the orchestra and pointed to the lady cellist, saying, "Madam, you have the most beautiful instrument between your legs, but all you can do is scratch!"'

The group heaved with laughter as Gail's eyes twinkled with delight. 'Here,' thought Edward, 'is a very naughty girl. What fun. And what a terrific man her father must be.'

Chapter Four

Knowledge and experience progressed by even steps as Edward fell into the life of a Whitehall warrior. William Caldicott had left for his well-earned retirement with a sanguine air and a murmured 'good luck'. For a few weeks, Edward struggled to create his own system for researching, drafting and honing his regular reports. The language was more stilted than he liked, and the decision about the focus and content was a constant challenge. He attended meetings in the Cabinet Office, the MOD, the Northern Ireland Office, at Box 500 and over the water at Century House. He was amazed to see that the headquarters of the Secret Intelligence Service was partially over a petrol station, which shouted about a vulnerability to terrorism that must surely concern the tenants of the twenty-two-storey building.

It was after his second Current Intelligence Group meeting that Commander Jack Strong loitered by the door of the conference room to intercept him. 'Come and have a cup of tea,' he offered.

The invitation was precisely what Edward had hoped for. Formal visits to the office never promoted confidences, and he was growing increasingly frustrated by the diplomatic dance which he had to perform with Civil Servant colleagues in other departments. 'Just let me drop my gear in the office. Why don't I meet you somewhere?'

'Yeah, OK,' said Strong. 'Just behind Cannon Row Police Station there's a nice little caff. I'll give you five minutes.'

Edward grinned amiably and walked swiftly to his office. 'Jim,' he said to his clerk as he popped his head around the door of the office next to his, 'I've just been asked to have a cuppa with Jack Strong. You'll probably be gone by the time I get back, so would you very kindly lock the safe in my office. I'm not sure if I'll be coming back anyway.'

'No problem.' Jim Shaw was a quiet, reserved man of about Edward's age. His overpowering interest in trains offered little scope for small talk with his office colleagues, but he was diligent and trustworthy, if lacking in humour. 'Good luck with the Commander,' he offered.

The tea was dark, sweet and steaming. 'Well, what do you think of Whitehall?' The Commander was the image of paternal interest. Edward recalled that his first impression of the man had been that of a cuddly, if overgrown and ragged teddy bear. Now that he was sitting with him one to one, the desire to confide was almost overwhelming. Mentally, he gripped himself: this man was in charge of the Metropolitan Police response to terrorism. He had seen more horror in his four years at Special Branch than most humans saw in a lifetime. His team was crisp, efficient, professional and dauntingly cynical. This teddy bear was really a grizzly, and must be treated with cautious respect.

'I admit that I find the bureaucracy tiresome. It seems that we spend most of our time composing and exchanging analyses of what's going on, rather than making things happen. I sort of hanker for some action.'

'They tell me that you are a man of action,' Strong murmured.

'Oh, that's nonsense,' said Edward, 'although I am more used to movement than immobility. I'm finding it very difficult to keep fit.'

'That'll be for your fencing, I take it?'

'Why, yes. How did you know I fenced?'

'I'm a policeman!' laughed Strong. 'I'm supposed to know what people do and what motivates them. In any event, I and my son enjoy the sports pages and he told me about your near success at the Olympic Games in '76. It must be disappointing to be within touching distance of a medal.'

'On the contrary. It's an incentive to improve. Yes, of course I was irritated with myself for failing to get into the medals, but it was my own fault. You can't afford a momentary loss of concentration at that level. I guess it's pretty much the same thing with you and your work: you can't afford to miss the clues and the difference with you is that you have the burden of protecting the public at large. When I am fencing, I have a duty only to myself.'

'Ah, well, lad, I've got a good crew to do the worrying for me. I reckon it's about time that you got to learn something more about us and I wanted to ask if you could spare a day to visit my team at work.'

The offer was as stunning and stimulating as it was unexpected. 'I, um, I don't want to be embarrassingly enthusiastic, but I could come now!' laughed Edward.

'Whoa, you'll have to slow down. We need to make sure that you don't sit in the office all day drinking tea, so I want a few days to plan something useful. Give me a call tomorrow and we'll set a date. We need to do it before the next CIG, when it would be nice to think we could make some of our colleagues discuss things instead of polishing their nails.'

Edward grimaced. 'I, uh, I don't think I've heard Charles Danby or Helen whatshername say anything at either of the meetings I've attended.'

'I doubt you will. The Northern Ireland Office and Home Office recruit mutes.'

'Newts?' queried Edward.

'No! Mutes,' laughed Strong. 'Newts no less. I used to play with newts as a kid. They were much more fun than our noble colleagues.'

'Sorry, Jack. I was pulling your leg a bit. The Army uses acronyms for everything and I thought it would be amusing to apply some of that thinking here. NEWTS would be something like Not Excited With This Subject, but it would have been more intelligent to have gone with the original. Let's think. Mutes. Um, Most Unreasonable To Expect Solutions?'

'Oh, you're learning, boy. You're learning. I like that.'

And so it was half an hour later that Edward finally made it back to his room in the Cabinet Office. As expected, Jim Shaw had left for the day, but on his desk, Edward found a note. 'Please phone Foreign Office Research Department. Gail Ritchie.'

A warm glow coursed through him. Gail Ritchie was a very fetching young lady indeed. He had resisted the temptation to chase her. After all, they had only spent a few hours together on a train and the truth was that he spent too much time in the office at present. His leisure hours were dedicated to reviving his fitness. But it would be very wrong to ignore a call. He glanced at his watch. 5.30p.m. She would probably be on her way home, but it was worth trying. He dialled.

'Research.'

'Is Gail Ritchie there, please?'

'Who's speaking?'

'Edward Davidson from the Cabinet Office.'

'Hang on, sir.' The line went dead, allowing Edward to conjure up a picture of the gorgeous Gail.

'Hello? Is that you, Edward?'

'Yes. Sorry I wasn't in, but I was invited out for a quiet cup of tea at Cannon Row. How can I help, Gail?'

'Mmmm. Are you a witness or the accused?'

'Neither. Unblemished record and, despite my training as a reconnaissance soldier, and thereby endowed with the benefit of keen observation, I am most unlikely to be called as a witness. Just doing my job by listening hard to associates in other departments. I enjoy Jack Strong's humour anyway. He comes across as a very solid, reliable and trustworthy man.'

'My! You move quicker than I thought you could,' she teased. 'The Police don't often open the door to ordinary mortals.'

'Well, I think he's taken pity on me. It does no harm to work with, rather than against. And how can I work with you, Miss Ritchie?'

The pause was just long enough to tickle the imagination on both sides. 'I'm having a few people around to supper next week. Tuesday. I wonder if you might be free?'

'That sounds wonderful. Hang on.' Edward flipped open his desk diary. Tuesday night was booked for fencing practice in Aldershot. 'No problem. I would love to come,' he said. 'Where do you want me, and in what dress?'

'I'm at 42 Prince of Wales Drive. Why don't you come at about eight? Be scruffy. The bell says "Baldwin and Ritchie", because I share with an old school friend, Jane Baldwin.'

*****

The ship was starting to tilt sideways and passengers seemed to be leaping from the rails all around him. He could see heads in the water and heard a woman screaming for her child. Someone was ringing a bell frantically. He knew he had to reach the bell if he was to help, but he couldn't make his way along the sloping deck. He started to grope his way along the rail and his hand struck something hard. Abruptly, consciousness returned and Edward fumbled for the telephone beside his bed. Through half-open eyes, he saw that the time was only just after three-thirty in the morning. God, he had been asleep for only an hour, but it had been so, so deep. 'Davidson,' he muttered into the mouthpiece.

'Edward Davidson?' a crisp, clear voice. 'Cabinet Office Night Duty Officer here. Sorry to disturb you at this hour, but I think you need to come in. We have a bit of an emergency.'

'Oh, God. Any clues?' Davidson said, as he rolled his legs out from under his duvet.

'Rather not say on the phone, old man. Just come as quick as you can. There's a good fellow.'

The ride through London on his small motorbike took Edward only twelve minutes door to door. As he drove, he reflected that four o'clock on a Wednesday morning was not the ideal time to be going to work, particularly after a good dinner party with the delicious Miss Ritchie. There had been eight of them in all: Gail, Jane Baldwin and himself had been joined by a young married couple who both worked in advertising. There had been a girl in her late twenties, Susan Hardcastle, who was developing a reputation as a wildlife photographer. Edward was unsure about his response to meeting Edward Longstaff again, because it hinted at something more than a professional relationship with Gail, but he was delighted to find that Henry Rawlings was Jane's beau for the evening. Rawlings and he had completed their Young Officers' Course together at Bovington almost twelve years earlier and, although they had got on well, they had not seen each other since Rawlings left the Army after extending his three-year short service commission for a second term. He had acquired a veneer of London sophistication and talked endlessly about his life in PR, but underneath it all Edward detected the same light-hearted and earthy humour which had drawn them together.

It was too early to resolve Gail's attitude. She was friendly, even warm, and had paid balanced attention to all of her guests.

Despite his heightened awareness, Edward was uncertain about her interest in either Longstaff or himself. Longstaff had left the party first, with Gail seeing him to the door. Evidently, he wasn't a resident, therefore. But the rest of them stayed on, quietly chatting as the empty bottles of wine accumulated.

Jane had attempted to draw out Edward about his life. After all, he was the one anomaly in the room: a serving soldier known to be working in the Cabinet Office. But Edward's gentle attempts to deflect attention were abruptly shattered when Henry Rawlings said that Edward was the only person he knew personally who had competed in two Olympic Games. The room went silent. 'Two Olympic Games?' queried Gail.

'Yes – they had to scrape the bottom of the barrel really,' muttered Edward. 'Munich and Montreal.'

'My God,' said Jane. 'Were you involved with that terrible incident with the Palestinians and the Israelis?'

'Well, I can't say that I was involved, but it affected the whole Games and everyone there. Ninety-nine percent of sportsmen don't want politics to be anywhere near sport. But our troubles were meaningless when you consider the outcome for the eleven Israelis who were murdered. And, if my memory serves me properly, five of the Black September terrorists died. It wasn't a very good outcome for either side.'

'And what sport takes you to international level?' Jane persisted.

'The sabre. By chance, officers of my regiment carry a sabre as their ceremonial weapon. It is very different from the sabre I use for sport, but the principles of fighting with a sabre are similar to both.'

'And are you a medallist?' Jane persevered.

'How embarrassing,' Edward shrugged. 'Well, the first time out was really the opportunity to groom myself for a second Games.'

'Yes, so?' urged Jane.

'He doesn't really want to tell you,' Henry butted in. 'The fact is that he missed the Bronze medal by the smallest whisker. Who was it that stuffed you, old mate?'

'Oh, the Russians. They took all three sabre medals in Montreal. I was beaten by Viktor Sidyak, who had won the gold medal in Munich in '72. There are no prizes for coming fourth.'

'Do tell us something about the whole atmosphere and experience,' Jane continued.

'Oh, well. Where do I begin? It is a shame that politics works its way into so many international sporting events. You may recall that twenty-two African countries boycotted Montreal. The activity was organised by Tanzania, who were protesting about the All Blacks rugby team playing in South Africa. I am sure that the protesters were gratified, but the poor old athletes, who had trained hard for so many years, had the holy grail snatched away from them at the last moment. That is very hard to bear. Frankly, such meddling undermines the whole Olympic principle and reduces the sensation that the competition is truly a world event. On the other hand, the atmosphere is always electric. One of the agreeable bonuses is that competitors can acquire free tickets to watch any event. I was really lucky to spend some time watching Nadia Comaneci in the gymnastics hall. She was totally incredible and aged only fourteen.'

'Is there any social life?' Jane asked.

'That is the surprise. Unlike a World Championship, where most competitors know each other from earlier competitions, an Olympic Games brings together the glitterati of all the sports. Some are well-known, some not, but you are all entirely equal and you can build good friendships in the brief fortnight that you share the Village. There is no alcohol, although you will find a fridge stuffed full of Coca Cola or Fanta at every corner. And the food is just superb. There is normally a ticket system which allows you to miss a meal but then bring in a guest to use the spare meal ticket. I have to confess that I am a total carnivore, so was able to eat two or three steaks at breakfast, lunch and dinner. We burn off all the calories by training vigorously.'

With a start, Edward realised that his hostesses were probably dying for them all to leave. Taking the opportunity to move on from Jane's interrogation, he leapt to his feet and apologised for breaking up a wonderful evening. He gave and received a peck on the cheek from both girls, before setting off on his trusted Honda 125 for his flat in Balham.

Parking in the MoD car park on the opposite side of Whitehall, Edward strode quickly across the road to the beckoning light of the Cabinet Office front door. 'Major Davidson, sir?' queried the night security guard.

'Yes.' Edward flashed his permanent pass. 'The Night Duty Officer called me about twenty minutes ago. Where does he want me?'

'If you just go up to the Signals Centre, you'll find him, sir.'

They half-recognised each other two minutes later. The problem with working in a large bureaucracy was that you never got to know everyone, so Edward had never met Richard Quinlan formally and their business lives had never crossed. Quinlan looked disgustingly fresh.

'Well done. You made that quite swiftly. Sorry to drag you out, but we've had a small excitement and the rules say we should involve desk officers in cases like this.' He half-turned to look down at his desk. 'Read this.'

Edward took the flimsy paper and scanned it rapidly. A naval rating of Greek Cypriot origin had been visiting his parents whilst on leave. He had been on his own in a bar in Limassol when he overheard strong Irish accents. Only half-interested, he listened in to the conversation at the table behind him. He quickly realised that he was hearing about the movement of weapons and, for whatever reason, the two men discussing it had not thought about anyone understanding them. He had left the bar as casually as he could and waited outside to see whether he could follow the men to try to identify them better. After some time, they had emerged and made their way to a small hotel near the port. The rating had telephoned his base. The MoD and Foreign Office were now laying on an operation to monitor the men and their activities, but time was not on their side, because it was suspected that a container-carrying vessel, which had left harbour that evening, was already carrying the weapons.

'I'm glad you woke me. This could be exciting.' Edward glanced at Quinlan. 'Does this sort of thing happen all the time?'

'Absolutely not,' laughed the older man. 'You should know, though. Don't you do Night Duties yourself?'

'No, I'm one of the lucky few who is judged to be on call all the time, so I don't have to undertake the routine duties. I guess I'm lucky not to have been called out before.'

Settled in his own office, Edward reached for his telephone list to find the number of Colonel Mark Humphreys, the colonel in charge of MO4, the department that oversaw global military operations. If intelligence was called to work, one could guarantee that operations would be there, too.

'Humphreys.' The voice was all that you might expect from a military man at work.

'Edward Davidson here, Colonel. I've just got in to work.'

'Ah, Edward. Thanks for calling. Do you think you could spare the time to pop across the road to my office?'

As he re-crossed Whitehall, Edward noticed that lights were on all over the MoD Main Building. Idly, he wondered if they all represented people at work, or energy being squandered. Four floors up, the corridor was relatively dark, although the light shining through the glass door to MO4's offices relieved the gloom.

'Morning, Colonel.' He noted that Humphreys was, like himself, dressed in casual trousers with an open-collar shirt and jersey. 'What goes on?'

Humphreys smiled wryly. 'We seem to have the makings of a Whitehall farce, and if we aren't careful, it will disintegrate into a disaster. All three Services plus three Government departments all scrabbling around to claim a coup. What it boils down to is one very bright and sensible naval rating behaving properly. I hope he earns promotion out of it.'

Humphreys rose to his feet and moved towards a large metal filing cabinet in the corner of the office. 'Drink? Coffee or whisky available.'

'I could murder a cup of coffee, but I'll do it and refresh yours while you talk.'

'Thanks. Well now, let's marshal our thoughts. We have two Irishmen who seem not to be totally security minded, one container ship registered in Antwerp, the hint of lots of weapons and the possibility that this is a blind. The objective is to confirm whether this is real and, if so, to grab the weapons along with the people who are due to receive them.'

'So who will run the operation? It seems pretty obvious that we will provide naval and air support, but we won't have any authority if the Weapons Intelligence Group at Box 500 want to manage it.'

'Absolutely. That's why you are such a vital cog. I don't belong to that Group, although I see their minutes. This is one of those rare occasions when the work of the Group will be fed principally by the Services. That gives us a little more authority and, since we have the resources to track the container ship, we have the strongest possible operational argument for being party to all of the planning. We both know how secretive they are at the Box, so don't allow them to sideline you. There is just one hiccup: we don't know for sure that any vessel, let alone this particular ship, has any weapons on board. Moreover, even if they are, we cannot be sure that they are aiming for England or Ireland. They may be destined for an operation against British forces in Germany, or they may be part of a wider terrorist plan.'

Edward gaped. 'So, what do we do? We could pursue an innocent vessel across half the globe and land up with some pickled herring. How on earth can we resolve whether it is a legitimate target or not?'

'It's a risk, obviously. We cannot guarantee that she will dock anywhere en route, so we cannot test whether the Irishmen are on board, or whether their weapons are there without them. But we do know already that this vessel is a long way from home, although there is nothing innately suspicious about a container ship registered in Antwerp finding its way to Limassol. I have called upon our naval colleagues for as much information as they can garner about the registration, ownership, movement and activity of the target. We may learn something about the pattern of its work. Lloyds may have insured it, so that's another source of information about ownership. In some ways we are hostages to fortune. We cannot afford to ignore the clues, so we are bound to follow them in minute detail.'

For the next half hour, the two men bounced ideas off each other. As the grey light of dawn sharpened to a clearer focus, Edward crossed Whitehall for the third time in an hour and rang the bell to the Cabinet Office.

'You again, sir?' commented the cheerful security guard. 'I hope you don't come to work at this time every day.'

'Nor do I intend to. What I need more than anything is a few more hours in my scratcher, a really hot shower and an enormous fry-up. I'll have to pop back to my flat for a shave, but I must write a few notes before going away to freshen up.'

The sun was sparkling on the river as Edward weaved in and out of the traffic on the way back to his flat. He was reminded of Wordsworth's poem, composed on Westminster Bridge in the early nineteenth century – 'Earth has not anything to show more fair: dull would he be of soul who could pass by a sight so touching in its majesty.' Magnificent, he thought. Those poets had the most wonderful gift, and, although he was attracted to almost any verse, he was particularly fond of Banjo Patterson and Kipling. They really knew how to drill down to the core of their subject. If anything was designed to make you weep, it must be 'The Last Parade', thought Edward, as he neared his digs in Balham.

Forty minutes later, he was freshly shaven, dressed in a charcoal suit with a plain blue shirt and a colourful Disney tie showing Snow White and the Seven Dwarves. This was his 'meeting' tie, because people, mainly women, felt that they had to say something to any man who brazenly revealed such a sense of humour. He leapt back on his faithful Honda 125 and set off back to the Cabinet Office.

Jim Shaw greeted him with a sardonic look and said that he was to turn around and cross Whitehall again for another meeting with MO4. Five minutes later, he was back on the fourth floor and walking towards the same glass door he had left only three hours ago. Mark Humphreys clearly had not been home, and Edward reflected that must be because he lived outside London. He ought to find out more.

'Good morning again, Colonel,' he said.

'Well, you've brushed up quite well,' said Humphreys. 'That tie is spectacular. Thank you for coming over so promptly. I just wanted to bring you up to speed on what we are doing, and it helps the whole team here if we have you at the same briefing. We need to go to the conference room, because the Navy and Air Force are joining us.'

The fourth-floor conference room was capable of sitting twenty people, so there was ample room for the four men from MO4, Edward himself, plus two naval officers and two airmen. Mark Humphreys had a reputation for doing all that he could to bring on younger officers, so he turned to Edward and asked him to outline the state of play. Over the next five minutes, he sketched the story of the naval rating on leave to the suspicion that a container ship which had left Limassol only a few hours earlier was carrying a consignment of weapons for the IRA. Questions flowed across the table as the sense of excitement and imminent action rose.

The Navy proved to be totally on the ball, providing information about the specific container ship. Owned by a Greek family, the company provided a weekly, fixed-day delivery service from Haifa to Ashdod, Limassol, Antwerp, Felixstowe, Rotterdam, Bremen and Hamburg. As a planning guide, the journey was almost 3,300 nautical miles to Antwerp and would take a little over ten days. The trouble was that nobody could predict where the weapons would be dropped, and there was no guarantee that they were on this ship in particular. If they were, it seemed likely that Antwerp was a viable destination, since it was the next regular stop. If they decided to dock somewhere else before Antwerp, it would send loud signals to anyone who might be watching.

Fifty minutes later the meeting broke up, with the Navy agreeing to task a submarine, and the Air Force undertaking to provide high-level reconnaissance. They resolved that the Navy would lead the project. Key objectives were to verify whether the shipment was real, on this specific vessel, and where the container was to be dropped. Planning beyond that had to be delayed until there was something tangible to do.

Wearily, Edward re-crossed Whitehall to his own office. He quickly told Jim Shaw about the overnight activity and then phoned Sir James Harrington's office to ask if he could drop by to brief him.

'Well done,' said Sir James. 'You seem to have sewn up all the loose ends. When is the Weapons Intelligence Group going to meet?'

'There is a meeting at 3.00p.m. I shall be there and have asked the Navy and Air Force to send their key men to help present the plan.'

'I would be grateful if you could summarise the discussions in a memo for me as soon as the meeting is over. Sadly, I have commitments all day and cannot be available for you for the rest of the day. We can catch up tomorrow.'

And with that, the fast pace of the past seven hours slowed to a crawl. Edward wandered back to his office, resisted another cup of coffee and delved into the piled in tray of routine paperwork.

Chapter Five

Edward glanced at his watch as he finished a ham sandwich at his desk. Two o'clock. Time to move to the Security Service office in Curzon Street. He quickly pushed all of the current files into his secure filing cabinet, closed the doors and twirled the dial to lock it. 'I'm off to the Box,' he said to Jim Shaw, picked up his briefcase and sauntered out into the passage to jog down the stairs.

Within yards of the front door of 70 Whitehall was the bus stop, where he waited for five minutes until the 159 arrived to take him to Piccadilly Circus. The traffic at Trafalgar Square was dire, so the journey took almost twenty minutes instead of the routine twelve. Alighting from the bus, Edward walked around the corner into Piccadilly and ambled past a tourist trap, an Italian restaurant and a clothes shop to wait at the next stop for a 38 bus. Ten minutes later, he stepped off the rear platform outside Green Park Station, waited for a gap in the traffic, then walked briskly to the far side and down Bolton Street. There at the end, looking entirely bland and uninteresting, was Box 500. It was 2.40p.m. Plenty of time to prepare for the meeting.

Edward was the first to arrive. He was never surprised by this, having been taught very early in his military career that there was no greater crime than being late. He found it intensely irritating when colleagues turned up after the appointed hour for a meeting. He carefully selected a chair half way down the table, right by the door, so that he could make a quick getaway. Ignoring the tea and coffee, he helped himself to a glass of still water, then removed his file, notebook and much-loved Waterman pen from the briefcase, shut it and placed it beneath the table by the left chair leg.

The only problem with meeting at the Security Service was that the rooms often had no windows. This led to rather slow, dreary meetings with people clearly wanting to nod off. In the very short time that he had been working with civil servants, he had formed a clear impression that they did not all have brilliant chairmanship skills. This was curious. After all, meetings were very much at the core of their professional lives. They should be absolutely excellent. Edward's own experience with the Army had been exemplary: he had never sat in a meeting which had lasted more than an hour; there were always definable outcomes and very clear information about what would happen next.

Minutes later, Captain David Blandy of the Royal Navy and Wing Commander Bill Moffat of the RAF, both of whom had been at the planning meeting in the MoD that morning, appeared at the door, led by a security guard. They greeted each other cheerily and Edward suggested that they should help themselves to tea or coffee. The colleagues booked their places on either side of Edward's chair as the next arrivals came into the room. Much to his surprise, one of the newcomers was Edward Longstaff, accompanied by another Foreign Office official, who introduced himself as Simon Avery. Longstaff shook Edward by the hand, saying, 'I hear you couldn't have got much sleep last night.' For a second, he thought this was a sly observation about the dinner party with Gail and Jane, but swiftly realised that the Whitehall bush telegraph would have kept Longstaff informed.

'You're absolutely right. They called me in at half past three this morning. That must be retribution for enjoying Gail's dinner party last night. It was good to meet you "out of the office", as it were.'

'Indeed, and when I phoned Gail to thank her this morning, she told me that you had been hiding your light under a bushel. Two Olympic Games, no less! I am impressed.'

'Oh, don't make too much of it. You must know that the Army is clever about keeping young officers away from soldiers. The interaction might ruin a soldier's potential, so the hard work of running the Army is left to the NCOs. If a new officer has any skill at all that they can develop, they send him away to pursue it. My regiment is particularly focused on sport, so we have had nine Olympians representing Great Britain in four sports since 1968, quite apart from boasting a range of internationals in every sport from rugby to field archery.'

They were interrupted by the arrival of James Stanton, the MI5 chair of the Weapons Intelligence Group. He brought with him a female secretary and was followed by individuals from the Northern Ireland Office, the Home Office, the Met Police and his new 'best friend', Harry Martens from GCHQ.

For a few minutes there was the general pandemonium of chairs scraping, coffee cups rattling and polite nodding at colleagues, before James Stanton brought the meeting to order. 'I think everyone is aware of the general situation, but I would be grateful if Edward Davidson could summarise the position as it stands now.'

Edward paused for thought, then crisply reported on the sequence of events. He turned to look at David Blandy and Bill Moffat, introduced them and asked each to rehearse the thrust of the meeting in the MoD earlier in the day, plus any update on subsequent activity.

David Blandy, a greying, woolly haired, weather-beaten man who did not look entirely comfortable in a pin-striped suit, confidently announced that they had added to the core of knowledge during the day. The Navy had checked on all the vessels that had left Limassol in the crucial twenty-four-hour period after their rating's report. They were now pretty confident that the ship that they needed to track was the MM *Callisto*, owned by a Greek family whose good reputation was beyond doubt. The company provided a weekly service from Haifa to Ashdod, Limassol, Antwerp, Felixstowe, Rotterdam, Bremen and Hamburg. As a planning guide, the journey was almost 3,300 nautical miles to Antwerp and would take a little over ten days. In his view, they were unlikely to divert to any port before Antwerp because it would raise too many questions with the owners and port authorities. But there was the remote possibility of a rendezvous with another vessel. Of course, that would implicate the captain and crew in a planned terrorist operation, and Blandy judged that was a step too far. The general consensus was that the ship, its owners and crew were ignorant of the contents of their cargo, although a question mark remained about their additional acceptance of two minders for their own shipment. The Navy's considered opinion was that the weapons, if they were on this vessel, were in a single secure container which would be put ashore wherever their contract directed. He proposed that the RAF should be tasked to find the ship, identify it formally, then the Navy would put a submarine on watch. By good fortune, there was one on patrol in the Mediterranean at present.

Bill Moffat confirmed that a Nimrod R1 was permanently based at RAF Akrotiri in Cyprus. The crew was briefed and ready to go.

James Stanton smiled thinly. 'Well, it seems that we have everything in place to follow our target; but are we totally confident that there are enough weapons on board to justify the effort and cost?'

Harry Martens cleared his throat. 'Chairman, I cannot give a guarantee, but we do have a chain of evidence about President Gaddafi's intention to support the Provisional IRA. Moreover, we know that a man called Patrick Mallon has been in Libya recently. He is one of the IRA's buyers. He has spent a lot of time in the USA, notably with Irish Americans in Boston. But he has also been known to work in the Middle East, and if this shipment has been organised by him, it will definitely merit our attention.'

'So what more can we do to confirm that the vessel, the MM *Callisto*, you said, is transporting a container of weapons?' asked the Chairman.

David Blandy was ready for this. 'My team is working on the ship's manifest. You will know that every container in the world has a unique numbering system, known as a BIC-CODE. This was devised back in the 1930s by the Bureau International des Containers (BIC). The International Organisation for Standardisation (ISO) adopted this system six years ago and delegated the exclusive management of the allocation of codes for international container transport to BIC. They also manage the publication of its official Register of owners' codes. Just to confuse matters a little, BIC-CODEs are also called ISO Alpha-codes. Thanks to the system, we should be able to trace the travels of any individual container. The problem for us is that *Callisto* is carrying 1,200 containers and we are going through the records manually to track the history of every one of them.'

'But you have no idea where the target container started its journey,' objected the Chairman. 'Surely it won't have started in Libya and travelled east to Cyprus to join a ship travelling to Europe?'

'You make a good point, Chairman, but we have to do this work methodically. And surely the point of this working group is to extend resources. I was hoping that other members of the group would be able to add insight. Someone, somewhere, will be able to find out how Gaddafi organised and delivered the weapons? For example, Mr Martens clearly has some ideas with his mention of Patrick Mallon. Good as we are, the Royal Navy doesn't have the wherewithal to evaluate President

Gaddafi's networks, nor can we master the travel itinerary of an Irish arms buyer.'

Edward Davidson stifled his grin, although he realised that Edward Longstaff had spotted the effort, giving a wry nod to cement their common thinking.

'Right,' said the Chairman. 'It's so refreshing having men of action at a meeting, and you are quite right to challenge us to perform. Mr Martens, I don't need to exhort you to squeeze your technology as hard as you can. My own service will devote a small team to evaluating Mallon, the buyer. I look to the Foreign Office to steer us on President Gaddafi's methods of operation to see if we can identify where the weapons will have started their journey. We don't have a lot of time; perhaps as little as nine days. We are grateful to the Navy and Royal Air Force. Please track down the *Callisto* as quickly as possible. I propose that we meet again in two days' time, on Friday 26 May at 11.00a.m.'

Edward Davidson slipped his briefcase on to the table and packed away his paperwork. 'That was terrific, Captain Blandy, thank you. What can I do to make life easier?'

'You're the glue, young Edward. We need you to keep the pressure on the other departments. I will let you know when we have distilled the vast body of information into something manageable.'

Edward realised that his plan to slip out quickly was optimistic. He really had to talk to James Stanton, who was still sitting at the head of the table talking quietly to the secretary. He moved towards them, attracting Stanton's attention in the process. 'Yes, Edward, what can I do for you?'

'I have to brief Sir James Harrington before the close of play. It would be most helpful if I could have the contact details of your team that will be looking at Patrick Mallon.'

'Of course. And don't hesitate to talk to me at any point. Helen will give you the details when you get back to your office, if that's okay?'

Edward retraced his steps to the Cabinet Office, arriving at his desk just as his clerk was leaving. 'I never seem to see you, Jim,' said Edward.

'Well, we have a special meeting of my railway group this evening. We have a visiting speaker who is going to share some of his photography.'

'Splendid,' muttered Edward. 'Do enjoy. I'll hope to see you tomorrow.'

Chapter Six

Edward sat at his desk, opened his diary and thought carefully for a few seconds. He had to go to see Sir James. He also had to phone Les Peters, who would be expecting him in Aldershot at 7.00p.m. for the training session which he had abandoned the previous night. Wearily, he pulled the phone towards him and dialled Sir James' secretary. To his dismay, the Chairman would not be available until 5.00p.m. With absolutely no alternative, he booked himself in for a ten-minute meeting, then double-checked his railway guide. Even if he ran the whole way to Waterloo, he wouldn't be able to catch one of the fast early-evening trains. The six o'clock took an hour and twenty-four minutes; add on the time from Aldershot station to the gym, and he wouldn't be able to get there before 7.40p.m. With a faltering heart, he dialled Les.

'Les, it's Edward. I don't know how to put this, but I am going to have to cry off again.'

'It's no good, Edward. You cannot expect to stay in the British team if you fail to put in the time. You are less fit than you should be, and I strongly suspect that your eye is not as good as it was. What's wrong with you? Have you lost the edge?'

'No. That's not it at all. But I am a soldier, paid to do a good job, and it just happens at the moment that I am at the very heart of an incredibly important military operation. I haven't talked too much about the nature of the work, but the reason that I am stuffed tonight is that I have to report to the Chairman of the Joint Intelligence Committee and he cannot see me until 5.00p.m.'

'Well, you have to make the decision, Edward. Either you commit to your sport or you don't. I do not want to lose my best fencer, but nor do I want you to be embarrassed by failing standards. We have done too much together to let this go to waste. Moreover, although we have two years until the Moscow Games, you need all the practice you can get. I don't want to miss out on the medals again.'

Edward nearly shouted at his friend, mentor and coach. But then his words struck home and he paused to reflect that the missed training session had been about having dinner with a pretty girl; it had not been about the security of the nation. 'Les, I am genuinely sorry. I have no desire to let you down and I am ambitious enough to want my chance once more. I guess my challenge is to do my day job and somehow create the time to meet with you. The irony is that one of the reasons I was given this job was to allow me more time to train. The killer is the journey from London to Aldershot, which takes up to two hours each way.'

'We are both complete idiots,' Peters interjected. 'We should be using the London Fencing School. They have two venues near Old Street and some very able permanent staff who could bring variety to your lessons.'

'But that means that you have to leave Aldershot, Les. I don't want to put you to more trouble than you need.'

'Listen. We both want the same result, which is your success in Moscow. If I have to make a few visits to London, so be it. And, to be honest, I like the way that the London Fencing School does business. It will be a much easier option for you and will keep your mind focused on your performance. I will phone them to see how they will accommodate us. Phone me tomorrow for a discussion about it, will you?'

Edward felt a weight lift off his shoulders. He desperately wanted to complete his career in fencing on a high note and he didn't think he could do it without Les's stern but humane approach. The mere fact of saving some four hours of travel on training days made sense. And, had he used his brain, he could have spent time at the school in the weeks that he had been in London.

The telephone rang. 'Edward Davidson,' he said.

'Mark Humphreys here, Edward. You have had a long day, but I need to see you and we have to brief DCDS(I).'

'Right, Colonel. Of course. I wonder when, because I am booked in to see Sir James at 5.00p.m.'

'Well, get your skates on. We can go to see the man as soon as you get here.'

As he walked across Whitehall, Edward reflected that there was plenty of fitness training on the pavements between the Cabinet Office and the Ministry of Defence. Seven minutes after putting his phone down, he walked into the office of MO4.

'I don't think you have met Sir William Horton?' asked Humphreys.

'No, Colonel. I am not even sure how he fits into the scenery.'

'OK. Quickly. The system is a little strange. The man at the top is the Director-General Intelligence, currently Noddy Willison. He is a retired Lieutenant-General and for the past twelve years the DGI has always been a retired serviceman. He reports to the Chief of the Defence Staff. His number two is the Deputy Chief of Defence Staff (Intelligence), currently an Air Marshal. Bill Horton is a good man. He enjoyed a full flying career and moved into the intelligence world only three years ago. This makes him a fresh set of eyes and ears, which is worth remembering, because he does listen.'

They left the office and strolled to the stairwell, climbing two levels to the sixth floor. 'Rather exalted surroundings,' muttered Edward, who knew that the territory was completely in the hands of the Chiefs of Staff. They walked towards the river, before turning right into a strangely quiet corridor. Roughly half way along it, Humphreys knocked lightly and opened a door into the room where DCDS(I)'s secretary worked. 'He's expecting us, I think?' The secretary nodded, rose from her desk and knocked on a communication door between her and her boss.

The Air Marshal proved to be the least stuffy of senior officers. Dressed in suit trousers, his shirt sleeves rolled up and a pipe in his mouth, he could have been at home in his library. 'Ah, ha. The Army has come to get me,' he joked. 'Welcome. Would you like tea?'

'No, thank you, sir,' said the two soldiers in unison.

'This is Edward Davidson, sir. He has been working in the Cabinet Office for the past three months while waiting to go to the Staff College. One of the reasons that he was posted to this unusual appointment is that he is an Olympic fencer of considerable note and needs to train harder for the Moscow Olympics. The posting authority, as ever, imagined that a posting to London would be a sinecure. He has also made a name for himself in the intelligence community, having impressed the Head of Special Branch in Londonderry some three years ago.'

Edward glanced sideways at Humphreys, who was far better informed than Edward thought. The Air Marshal put his pipe into an ashtray on his desk. 'I hope you make it to the Moscow Games, Edward. Just a thought. I know it sounds bureaucratic, but you should check the rules on the ramifications of going to a communist country when you have security clearances at the level that you must have. I have the niggling feeling that people may not want you to be put at risk.

Do me a favour, will you, and let me know, because if anyone wants to erect barriers, the earlier we deal with them, the better. Now, tell me all about the Irish arms.'

Edward briskly recounted the sequence of events and the actions taken, noting with care how very helpful the Navy and RAF had been. He elaborated on the Navy's detailed and methodical research into BIC-CODEs, the RAF's deployment of a Nimrod from Cyprus and the news that they had clearly established where the MM *Callisto* was. The Navy would be intercepting the vessel within the next two hours and would follow wherever it went. The Weapons Intelligence Group had been tasked to delve into Gaddafi's management of the weapons and the tracking and evaluation of Patrick Mallon. The Group would be meeting again on Friday.

'That's crystal clear. Thank you, Edward. Are there any operational issues, Mark?'

'Yes, but they are not really military ones. We don't know where the container with the weapons is to be landed. We are assuming Antwerp, so we will have to insert a surveillance team to maintain watch on the delivery. But it may be that they take the container to one of the subsequent ports. It could even be Felixstowe.'

'Well, that would certainly be easier for us to manage,' laughed the airman. 'Well, thank you both for making the time to bring me up to date. I look forward to hearing the story unfold. Don't hesitate to call me if you feel that I can help, Edward.'

Ten minutes later, Edward was back in his office on the other side of Whitehall. With half an hour in hand before his meeting with the Chairman, he turned to his address book and dialled Jack Strong's number at Scotland Yard. The Commander was out elsewhere, but his secretary noted that Edward had done what he had been instructed to do, which was to follow up Strong's offer of a day and night with his team.

She knew of the plan and said that there would have to be a little flexibility. While there was interesting activity for much of the time, Jack Strong felt that current operations were not going to be sufficiently instructive. Would Edward mind keeping a slot in his diary for the next two weeks? He said he was very happy with that, made a note in his diary, then rose from his desk and opened his secure filing cabinet, pulling out the routine correspondence that he had to deal with before it grew into an unmanageable mountain. As he rifled through the pile, his eye was caught by a diplomatic telegram, which was clearly doing the rounds of Whitehall's ministries, about the Foreign Secretary's desire to confirm that a piece of clarinet music was the correct rendering of the National Salute to the Sultan of Muscat and Oman. In the most beautifully phrased response, the Consul-General delivered an enormously funny account of his search for confirmation. This sort of humour, Edward realised, was fundamental to good writing and it was a joy to see how seasoned diplomats played their game.

With a start, he realised that he must trot along to see the Chairman, who proved to be in his office and ready to talk. For the third time that day, Edward related the state of play, ending on an upbeat note about the Navy's work on identifying the right container. Sir James seemed to be relaxed. 'Well done, Edward. You seem to have engaged with everyone who should be involved, and it's been a pretty long day for you. If I were you, I would shut up shop and go home, before anyone finds something useful for you to do.'

Chapter Seven

'God, I could do with being somewhere else.' Ivan Donnelly peered moodily out of the porthole of the Mess next to the galley. 'Who would ever want to be a sailor?'

Patrick Mallon continued to play Patience, without bothering to look up or respond. Donnelly turned and paced the width of the cabin, his hands firmly in his pockets and a cigarette drooping from the right side of his mouth. 'We've been at sea for a day and it doesn't feel as if we've moved an inch. They say it's going to take ten days to get there. The noise is really irritating, too.'

Mallon gathered the cards together, then dealt them out in another form of the game: Clock Patience. Donnelly sneered at him. 'Are you'se goin' to be playing with cards for the whole voyage?' Again, Mallon ignored him and silently worked his way through his twentieth game. 'Well, has the cat got your tongue, then?' Donnelly persisted.

Mallon took his hands off the cards, drank briefly from a tepid cup of tea and said, 'We just have a job to do. We are being paid. Actually, we are being paid quite well. We seem to be entirely secure. There is no threat to us, to the weapons, nor to our mission. I suggest you find a book and settle down. We cannot make the ship go faster.'

'Aargh. Bloody books. I haven't read one since… oh, since I left school. I want to be doing things. Killing the English would be a good start.'

'Well, there is nobody English on this ship, and if there were, we would be wise to leave them alone. Apart from the captain, who I think is Hungarian, most of the crew seem to be Filipino. Small wonder we cannot communicate with them; and, even if we could, what would we talk about?'

Donnelly shrugged, crushed out the remnants of his cigarette and tapped another one out of the packet which he took from his shirt pocket. 'I should never have agreed to come. You could have done it all by yourself, you and your fancy ways. I'm an active soldier in the Republican movement. I want to be in action doing what I do best. Sitting on a boat for ten days is going to drive me mad.'

'Well, all I can say is, grow up. You accepted a role – and I can't think why, if you hate it so much within a matter of hours of starting – but here you are. If you're so much the grand soldier, tell me about some of your exploits.'

Donnelly hesitated. 'Why do you want to know? Are you a spy or something?'

'For bleeding Christ's sake, I am just trying to take your mind off your problem. It cannot be solved. You have at least nine days more on this ship. If you want to talk, you have plenty of time to do so.'

'Well, then. I have shot soldiers and I have shot policemen. They haven't all died. But we did kill a lot of people at the La Mon House Hotel in February. It was gory, but we took out several RUC who were meeting there.'

'You were one of that gang, were you? Bloody butchers, that's what you are. From what I have heard, there were no RUC present and you blew up and burned a number of young people enjoying a dinner dance. That makes you brave men, does it?'

'Mind your mouth. It was a sanctioned operation. And we didn't actually intend to kill them all. We tried to issue a warning, but the telephone box had been vandalised. It took us ages to find a working phone.'

'So why boast about it to me now? That sort of blind atrocity does active harm to our cause which, I should remind you, is to push for the re-unification of Ireland. It is not to kill bright young Irish people going about their daily lives. And, as to being sanctioned, you and I both know that the Army Council subsequently banned all units from bombing buses, trains and hotels. It was a complete fuck up, that's what it was. If I were you, I would scrub that out of your personal history. You behave as if killing – killing anybody – is the objective. You are nothing more than a murderer feigning a political purpose to satisfy your gross behaviour.'

'My only mistake was to share that with you, Mr High and Mighty. I may not be able to make grand speeches, but I can deliver action. The end justifies the means.'

'Oh, ah? Well, I don't think it helps the cause of Irish union if we kill a dozen young Irish people at a dance. And it all sounds an easy cop-out if you blame a vandalised phone box for unintended casualties. You should have checked that before exploding the bomb.'

'You're so grand, man, aren't you? I bet you've never been on an operation, so. If you object to what we do in the field, why are you here?' Donnelly snarled.

'I certainly don't need to explain myself to you, but for the record, my job is to secure the weaponry that allows you to take action. Without me, we would run out of weapons in months. The Brits are far too efficient at finding our arms dumps. So the delivery that you and I are shepherding now was brought together by me dealing with Libya because President Gaddafi likes the way we cause trouble for the Brits.'

'And do you deal with the Americans, too?'

'I do. Good Irish Americans in places like Boston have a sentimental view of their homeland, although most have never been there. We do really well out of their fundraising activity and they provide some excellent weapons. Just last month I managed a delivery by trawler which included six M60 machine guns and a lot of Armalite rifles. That M60 is a real machine gun, a total killer.'

'Seems you've got it made, swanning around Libya and America with people giving you money and weapons.'

'It's not as rosy as you imagine,' said Mallon. I live life under cover, never go home, always sleeping in a strange bed. But I keep going because I have always been a staunch Republican. Ultimately, there will have to be a political solution. We just need to keep the pressure on the Brits by making life difficult. That's one of the reasons we organise bank robberies – on average we rob one bank every three days.'

'So, your grand design isn't so far different from mine,' said Donnelly. 'You rob Irish banks – I happen to kill some innocent and some not-so-innocent Irish men and women. And what weapons do we have now?'

'This is a useful load. At the top end, we have ten RPG-7 rocket launchers, five hundred Kalashnikov rifles, a ton of bullets and a lot of detonators. And for the first time, they have given us some Semtex. That'll make people's ears ring.'

'Well I just want to get back home and back to proper work,' moaned Donnelly. 'I'm going for a walk.' And with that, he opened the door that exited on to the high-level deck.

Mallon sat still, idly shuffling the cards. If he was honest, he couldn't really work out why the Council had insisted on both of them shepherding the weapons across Europe. Neither he nor Donnelly were armed, and what would they do if someone came on board and found the weapons anyway? Donnelly was a nasty piece of work. It had proved impossible for them to have a sensible conversation together; and, without being supercilious, Donnelly's intellect was very much at the low end of the scale. He was just a thug. That terrible incident at the La Mon public house exemplified it all. The perpetrators had tried to make out that they had evidence that there was an RUC meeting there. Clearly, they had not realised that there was a large party for young people and they had been entirely wrong about the RUC being present. It had been a ghastly slaughter of the innocents and had caused active harm to the Provisional IRA. This was not what republicanism stood for.

He thought quietly about the next ten to twelve days. Nine more days of reading books and playing cards, then arrival in Antwerp, where the container would be unloaded with others. They had been told that a Customs official would come to the ship to check the documents of passengers leaving the vessel. They would be able to catch a lift to the terminal. That left an unusual gap in the arrangements, because they would no longer have any observation or control of their container and its contents. Well, that was no longer his problem. The Council had made their arrangements and presumably a driver and tractor were booked in to collect the goods. He fanned out the cards again and started a further game.

Chapter Eight

The stack of newspapers on the desk was overwhelming: the *Times*, *Telegraph*, *Guardian*, *Belfast Newsletter* and the *Irish Times* had to be read daily. Edward had realised quite early on that the *Guardian* and the *Irish Times* were by far the most accurate reporters of Irish affairs. At last, some of the political issues were becoming clearer. The Taoiseach, Jack Lynch of Fianna Fail, had led his party since 1966 and was enjoying his second period of office as the Prime Minister. Only last year he had secured an overall majority in the Dáil. To his untutored eye, Edward could barely distinguish a difference in the style and content between the two leading political parties. Fine Gael seemed to argue pretty much the same public policies as their opposition, so perhaps success at elections boiled down to the character of the leadership. Dr Garrett Fitzgerald had taken over from Liam Cosgrave after their disastrous campaign in the previous year's election and, even though he was elected leader of his party by acclamation, he didn't seem to have the persona and high profile of Jack Lynch, whose sporting career before politics made him a national hero in hurling and football.

The phone trilled. 'Edward Davidson,' he said.

'Edward, this is David Wynne over in the MoD. Can I take a minute of your time?'

'Of course. What can I do to help?'

'Well, you may not feel so welcoming in a few seconds. We have had a contact from the *Daily Mirror*, who wants to talk to someone in the intelligence world about an Irish issue. It has bounced around the ministries and been rejected by the Police, Northern Ireland Office and Home Office. I have been instructed that the MoD should not engage with the Press… urm, let me rephrase that, we should not deal with them on this matter.'

'Heavens. What on earth is the problem?'

'Apparently, it has to do with a threat to the Brussels conference in November.'

'Surely the Foreign Office should be involved, then?'

'I don't argue, but it was put to me that we could cut short the whole board game by getting you to deal with it,' said Wynne with a laugh.

Edward thought for a few seconds. 'Well, we don't want Whitehall to be found wanting with the Press. I will consult our Press team and, subject to their advice, follow it up. Can you give me the contact details?'

'Indeed. The man is called Simon Harker. I can't tell you anything about him, but his number is 293 3831.'

Edward decided that it would be worth having a face-to-face with the PR team, so left the office in Jim Shaw's hands to go down to the ground floor. He had no relationship with them, but they always seemed to be quite cheerful. He knocked on the open door and walked in, to find a man of his own age tapping away at a typewriter. 'Can I take your advice, please?' he asked.

'Absolutely. You are talking to the guru.'

Edward snorted and introduced himself. 'I've been landed with a funny problem. The *Daily Mirror* have been trying to persuade someone in the intelligence community to meet and talk about a threat that they have uncovered. Nobody wants to engage, so the last ministry in the chain, the MoD, has dumped it in my lap. I don't mind meeting their man, who is called Simon Harker, but thought it would be wise to wave it past you first.'

'Fine. I'm Alan Smith, by the way. Just give me a sec.' Smith looked at an address book, picked up his phone and called the *Daily Mirror*. 'Alan here, Jane. Can you tell me about Simon Harker?' There followed an unintelligible muttering from the far end. 'Ah. Now that is interesting. Thank you, Jane, much appreciated.' He put the phone down and turned back to Edward. 'Simon Harker is a real character. He's bound to try to pump you for information, but it will do no harm to meet him. He is a giant of a Yorkshireman, smokes huge cigars, drinks like a fish and seems to act as a general factotum for the editor. If you do see him, would you let me know what goes on?'

Edward agreed readily and strolled back up to his office on the first floor to telephone Harker. 'Right, lad,' said Harker in a broad Yorkshire accent. 'I was beginning to fear that nobody was going to talk to me. As a reward, you can have lunch with me. Do you like steak?' Edward offered an acknowledgement. 'Right, there's a terrific steak house, the Guinea Grill, in Bruton Place, just off Berkeley Square. Can you meet me there tomorrow at, what, 12.45?'

As he put the phone down, Edward remembered the advice of Air Marshal Horton, who had expressed concern about potential bureaucratic barriers to him competing in Moscow. Unsure who to consult, he thumbed through his Whitehall directory to find the contact details for the man who had inducted him to HRT.

'Colonel Lewis? This is Edward Davidson in the Cabinet Office. You may recall inducting me to certain classified levels of access about three months ago?' The Colonel remembered clearly. 'Well, I have been given a piece of advice by DCDS(I), who learned that I am a candidate for the Olympic Games in Moscow in two years' time. I competed in the '72 and '76 Games as a fencer, and there is a reasonable chance that I will be selected for the '80 Games, if only I can train more. The question is whether my current security clearances would have an impact on that.'

He could hear the Colonel sucking his teeth. 'You have been given sound advice,' he said. 'Normally, we would say that people with the clearance you have should avoid going to communist countries, particularly if they cannot guarantee to be in the company of a fellow Brit all the time. The good news is that we have two years to work out a solution. Well done for coming to me so swiftly. Just give me your number, will you? I will do the due diligence on this and come back to you.'

With precision military timing, Edward entered the door of the Guinea Grill at 12.40. A waiter asked how he could help and Edward said that he was due to have lunch with a Mr Harker. 'Your host is here; follow me.' They sidled along a narrow passage, which opened into an intimate dining room with just eight tables covered in immaculate white tablecloths.

Simon Harker was indeed an enormous man. He must have been six feet seven inches tall and was blessed with a mop of ginger hair on top of a bespectacled, round face with a smattering of freckles. His huge paw grasped Edward's hand in a smothering grip. 'I am right pleased to meet you. Have a drink.'

Edward demurred. He still didn't drink too much, conscious of the impact on his weight and fitness; but his host was having none of it. 'Come along, lad. If you're going to have lunch on the *Daily Mirror*, you have to follow our culture and practices.' Wryly, Edward said he would love a glass of red wine to go with the steak.

'So, tell me something about you, young Edward,' Harker said.

'I thought I was here for you to tell me something, not the other way round,' Edward queried.

'Ah! You think I'm trying to pump you for information and intend to publish your life story in my newspaper?'

'It crossed my mind,' Edward acknowledged. 'But there is nothing of value for you and I can't speak about the detail of my work anyway.'

'OK, so I will tell you what I know. You are a soldier working in the Cabinet Office. You are also an Olympic fencer and competed in Munich and Montreal.'

'Oh, how embarrassing,' Edward muttered. 'Too many people know more about me than I care to reveal.'

'Well, don't be shy about it, lad. You're walking on water. But it is really interesting to have a soldier doing the job that you are doing.'

'It's not that complicated. The Army is rather generous about providing the opportunity for sportsmen to prosper. Someone thought it would be a cunning plan to give me two years in a London staff job, where I wouldn't necessarily be too busy. They were wrong, of course, but it does no harm to my CV.'

'And will you be selected for Moscow?'

'At present, I would say no. I keep missing training sessions and I am far less fit than I should be. But my trainer, a marvellous man called Les Peters, is going out of his way to simplify our training schedule, although he's an absolute devil when we are working together.'

The waiter arrived to take their orders. A rump steak for each of them, both cooked rare, with spinach and chips to keep them company. A bottle of Côtes du Rhone was ceremonially uncorked in front of them and Simon sampled a soupçon of the red nectar. Both glasses were filled.

'So, I must resist interrogating you. You'll want to know what we have on offer.' Edward sipped his wine and nodded.

'We have a number of informants littered around the world,' said Simon. 'Sometimes, they try a story on to see if we will pay, and sometimes they come up with information that we never expected. One of our really reliable people in

95

Belfast has produced a story about the European Summit conference in Brussels, and we think that you people ought to know about it.'

'OK. And?'

'The story is that when the Prime Minister flies in to Brussels, they are going to shoot his aircraft out of the sky with a surface-to-air weapon.'

'Oh, my God,' said Edward. 'That really is a story. And you trust this source completely?'

'Well, I wouldn't trust him with my wife, but when he tells us about the IRA, we tend to believe him.'

'And what prompts them to want to shoot Mr Callaghan down when he is engaged in an international event on foreign soil?'

'We think it's because he was the man who sent the troops into Belfast. It is a lower risk opportunity than it would be in England, and the chances of collateral damage will be limited if they fire when he is on his final flight path.'

'I am most grateful to you for making so much effort to let the authorities know,' said Edward. 'I am going to have to pursue some additional information to see if anyone, anywhere, has supporting intelligence. If they do, I will ensure that it reaches the people who make the decisions. How gratifying that you may be saving the British Prime Minister's life.'

'We may bollock the Government in the paper, but we are patriots, you know. I accept that you will go all quiet and shy with me, but if there is a chance after the event for us to print a story, so much the better.'

For the next half hour, the two men gossiped like two old friends, covering every subject from horse racing, which was a passion of Harker's, to the deployment of soldiers in Northern Ireland and the attitude of Irish Americans to the Troubles. Harker proved to be a fluent conversationalist, armed with a deep well of knowledge about world affairs. His probing into Edward's thoughts were gentle but perceptive, so Edward found himself thinking at least twice before saying anything which could be interpreted as a Cabinet Office opinion. And the steak proved to be succulent and tender, the wine light enough to take at lunchtime. He declined the glass of port which Harker accepted for himself.

Feeling somewhat the worse for wear, Edward left the genial newspaperman as he lit a cigar outside the restaurant. Walking swiftly, he made his way to Piccadilly to catch a bus back to the office, where he instantly started a series of telephone calls to his opposite numbers in the MoD, Security Service, Foreign Office and GCHQ. Within an hour, he started to accumulate enough information to write a brief for the Chairman of the JIC.

The potential for an attack was real. During the Vietnam War, the Americans lost or mislaid quite a range of arms and ammunition. Their Redeye missile, which they started to manufacture in 1968, was fired from the hand-held M171 missile launcher. Once fired, the missile would travel at Mach 1.7 within 5.8 seconds. A devastating weapon, although the early versions were less effective than the Mark 2, it had to be fired from behind the aircraft, because its homing device could only follow the hot exhaust of an aircraft engine.

There was also the Soviet 9K320 Strela, known in NATO as the SA7-Grail. It was less reliable than the Redeye and frequently failed to cause significant damage, even if it did hit the aircraft. There were some difficulties with the guidance system, and it was also much slower, reaching a maximum speed of about 600mph, although that wouldn't matter when an aircraft was coming in to land at a little over 200mph. A propeller aircraft on landing might well be a soft target. Britain's own Blowpipe, made by Short Brothers in Belfast, wasn't as effective as everyone hoped, but so far none had been lost or stolen, so it was less likely to be the chosen weapon.

Rather more humorously, David Wynne in the MoD reminded Edward that Bridget Rose Dugdale, the daughter of wealthy Devon parents, who had attended a good private school in Kensington, an overseas finishing school, and Oxford University, conceived a plot with her boyfriend, the Irish terrorist Eddie Gallagher, and hijacked a helicopter in Donegal in 1974, from which they dropped their home-made air-to-surface exploding milk churns on Strabane Police Station. The scheme failed because not one of them exploded, but it did not endear her to the authorities, and Dugdale was subsequently imprisoned in the Irish Republic, having been convicted in relation to the helicopter raid and the theft of millions of pounds worth of art from Russborough House in County Wicklow.

So much for the weapon. The question was whether the IRA had acquired one or more, or whether they were known to be hunting for one. Clearly, the matter should be discussed at the Weapons Intelligence Group, but there were some interesting reports from GCHQ, the Security Service and the Army which suggested that there was word on the street about surface-to-air missiles.

Edward realised that the Weapons Intelligence Group was scheduled to meet the next day. He pulled the phone towards him and called the Security Service, reporting directly to James Stanton with a request that the subject should be added to the agenda.

And, finally, he remembered that he had promised to tell Alan Smith about his lunch. Rather than telephone a man in the same building, he ran downstairs to find an empty office which was firmly locked. He scrambled back up the stairs two at a time in a modest attempt to maintain his fitness. The next thing was to write a brief report for Sir James Harrington. Now he thought about it, the passing of the buck to him in the Cabinet Office did have real merit. Any other report going through the other ministries would probably be sunk at the bottom of other detailed intelligence summaries. At least this one would go straight to the head man.

As Big Ben recorded 11.00a.m. on the other side of Whitehall, the Weapons Intelligence Group went silent in response to James Stanton's tap of his pen on the table. 'We have had five days to evaluate the main subject of today's meeting. Can the Royal Navy report first, please?'

David Blandy said that his submarine was lurking in the wake of the MM *Callisto* and was now close to entering the Atlantic. There was absolutely nothing of interest to report, and the ship had not had any contact with other vessels, nor had they looked like putting in to any port. On the other hand, his team had laboriously sifted through the records of the 1,200 containers known to be on board the target. They had quickly found groups of containers owned and used by clearly defined distributors. Not many were single units. They made one assumption, which was that anything produced by Gaddafi or his network would be likely to have a Libyan profile. This proved to be helpful, because only twenty containers demonstrated an overt Libyan link and, rather gratifyingly, Limassol had been the port at which these twenty converged from assorted starting points. You could argue that further time spent on researching them would reveal little more. There was no record in the public domain which would indicate what was in each container. Nevertheless, the ship's manifest did show one important fact, which was that the whole of the Libyan container shipment was due to be offloaded in Antwerp.

There was a community sigh of appreciation. This was promising and most helpful. James Stanton took the reins again. 'So it fell to me and my team to explore the man Mallon, and the Foreign Office to divine some hint of how Mr Gaddafi deals with this type of subterfuge.' He nodded his head towards Edward Longstaff.

Longstaff was already a seasoned Whitehall warrior. 'You will recall, Chairman, that in March of 1973, the Irish Naval Service intercepted a vessel called *Claudia* in their territorial waters. They forced it into harbour in County Waterford and discovered about five tons of arms and ammunition, together with Joe Cahill, a founder of the Provisional IRA and its Chief of Staff when arrested on *Claudia*. That operation was a disaster for the IRA. Cahill was far too senior to run a mission of this nature and had no special talent for moving weapons. With his profile and some very fundamental errors by the Libyans, the chances were that the operation would be spotted. The original plan was for the weapons to be loaded on *Claudia* at sea, but the arrangement was never completed. As a result, they took the vessel into Tripoli harbour. That caused some local discomfort, but they decided that it would be quicker and simpler to arrange the loading as quickly as possible in that very dock. Security was at an all-time low, really. *Claudia* was already marked as a vessel which engaged in illicit trading. Cahill himself had a public profile; the delivery and loading of the weapons were seen by many people. I imagine the chatter in Tripoli was far too public. Thanks to the good offices of the Royal Navy, we again had a submarine following them. Most curiously, Joe Cahill was made aware by the ship's captain of the high possibility that they were being tailed, but dismissed the threat.

'This experience taught Gaddafi and the IRA a lesson. They had all been far too casual about security. We strongly suspect – no, let me be firmer, we know that there must have been other Libyan arms deliveries. The nature of weapons recovered in Northern Ireland amply confirms it. But we have little solid information on how they have gone about their business. The container route does look a lot more secure, and so what if they have to take a roundabout journey. To be honest, I am impressed by the Navy's thinking, and it matters little that we cannot isolate the one or two containers with the weapons, provided we can monitor the whole batch.'

'Thank you, Edward. So, let us look at Patrick Mallon. There are many strands of information on this man. We do not believe that he was ever an active gun-carrying terrorist on the ground. He appears to have lived a blameless life, a traditional education, a degree in politics at Queen's University Belfast, then into the world of work. He has not been a commercial traveller, but he has travelled for commerce. He has worked in the pharmaceutical industry for almost twenty years, travelling frequently in North America, Europe and North Africa. It was thanks to stray bits of information that he came onto the radar. Proof positive came from sources in Boston, who confirmed that Mallon was actively involved in the buying and transportation of weapons. Effectively, he is perhaps one of three well-educated northern Irish Republicans who deal with overseas suppliers. Most importantly, however, thanks to the efforts of our American cousins and their satellites, we now know that he is on the *Callisto*.'

Edward Davidson sat drinking in the information. This was so different from soldiering, and a revelation about the ways in which the State could accumulate evidence for its own security. It was also quite impressive to see the collaboration between ministries, although he had not heard anything at all from representatives of the Northern Ireland Office at any meeting so far. And it was fair to judge that James Stanton had said more at this meeting than any Security Service representative he had met before.

'We believe that Mallon was in Libya three months ago. We know that he was in Limassol last week,' continued Stanton. 'Thanks to the police in Cyprus, we now know that Mallon and another Irishman called Donnelly were staying in a modest hotel off Franklin Roosevelt Road, close to the port. Donnelly is a nasty piece of work, and if we could arrest him, we might be able to tie down a number of incidents in which he could well have been involved. The two of them together in the right place at the right time strongly suggests that we are on the right track.'

The group paused for thought. James Stanton continued, 'It seems most unlikely that we will see any action in the next three to four days, but we cannot afford to lose the most helpful shadow of a Navy submarine. I hope that we can rely upon you?' David Blandy nodded.

'Very well. The next thing is to consider our reception committee. The Foreign Office has talked with our Belgian colleagues to seek permission for us to conduct an operation in the port of Antwerp. They readily agreed to a British surveillance team being inserted. The vessel would reach the port in the next three days, so the team will be on-site in two days. They will establish a good working knowledge of routes in and out; they know precisely where the containers are to be unloaded and where they will be stored. Superficially, everything is in order and ready to go.' Edward Longstaff said nothing.

'The next matter for discussion comes under Any Other Business, although I did intimate to your offices that we would need to discuss the potential for a surface-to-air missile attack on the Prime Minister's aircraft when he goes to Brussels for the European summit in November.' Stanton looked over to Edward Davidson, who promptly reported on the *Daily Mirror*'s advances and the generous lunch he had enjoyed at the Guinea Grill.

'We are treating this with a little caution,' said James Stanton. 'We have no specific intelligence about the acquisition of surface-to-air missiles, although we do accept that it has always been an IRA aspiration. What do other services think? Edward, you may be better able to summarise the Whitehall view?'

Edward thought for a second. 'Well, I can safely say that the whole network wanted to shift the meeting with Simon Harker to someone else. Maybe that was because he was from the *Mirror*?' He grinned, but nobody moved. 'On the other hand, nobody is denying the possibility. We are collectively accepting the potential, so I don't think that we can afford to ignore it. And we do have some latitude with time, because the conference is still a few months away.'

'And that is a fair point,' said Stanton. 'We do have time. It is as well to have it in our minds so that we can pursue further information actively. Edward, will you thank your man at the *Mirror* for his information, please?' Edward nodded. 'And will you all please actively study your sources for information about the potential of this attack.'

Chapter Nine

It was almost 1.00p.m. when Edward got back to his office in Whitehall after a meeting at the Home Office. It was always rather quiet on a Friday afternoon and it had been one hell of a week. Edward suggested to Jim Shaw that he could leave early, and Shaw readily assented. He was never going to work more hours than were needed.

Edward sat thinking about the week in general and, on the spur of the moment, picked up his phone to call Gail Ritchie. 'Foreign Office Research Department,' she said.

'Ah, ha, Miss Ritchie. Edward Davidson here.'

'Well, good afternoon, kind sir. Clearly the Cabinet Office doesn't have enough to do on a Friday afternoon.'

'Actually, you are right. It's been one of the longest weeks I have ever known, so I am trying to wind everything up for an early departure. I was hoping to kidnap you for supper tonight or tomorrow.'

'That's good of you. Tonight, is too sharp, I am afraid. We have some people coming in for drinks, and tomorrow I will be staying with my parents in Sussex. You would be very welcome to come and drink this evening, though.'

'That's really tempting,' said Edward with regret, 'but I simply must cut down on the booze, because it affects my fitness so much. Very boring, I know. I will just have to have a bowl of gruel on my own. And I guess it will be good for me to take exercise this evening, instead of sitting around having fun. What about next week? I hope I can tempt you out for a short supper.'

Gail hesitated as she flicked through her diary. 'What about Tuesday?'

'Done,' said Edward without pause. 'There's an amusing place in Shepherd Market, L'Artiste Muscle. It is French food – same menu for years, but utterly reliable. Mussels, snails, magret de canard, properly rare steak – all that sort of thing. Do you mind dining in Mayfair?'

'That would be absolutely super. Seven or seven-thirty?' responded Gail enthusiastically.

'Would seven-thirty suit you?'

Gail said, 'Of course. *A bientot.*'

As he put down the phone, Edward recalled that Gail's parents had been on a diplomatic posting in Paris a few years earlier. She probably spoke perfect French and knew Paris better than he did. Clearly, L'Artiste Muscle was an inspired choice. It would be cunning to do a piece of research on her father, Edward thought.

The restaurant sat at the corner of Shepherd Market and Shepherd Street. It was always buzzing with people, as drinkers spilled out of the King's Arms on the opposite side of the market and Ye Grapes at the northern end of the same short street. It was just too cool to ask to sit outside, so Edward arrived early to ensure that they could have the table in the corner window, where they were still part of the cheery community, but just secluded enough to eat alone. The joy about this restaurant was the agreeably casual way in which diners sitting at adjacent tables could and would butt in to your conversation if you looked ready to chat. Michel, who had looked after Edward on the many occasions that he had been to this restaurant since he was a newly commissioned young officer, greeted him warmly. 'Maestro,' he said, 'you have a pretty girl to entertain?'

'I do, I do, Michel. We will need your very best food, most agreeable wine and superlative service. I am trying to impress.'

Michel grinned and waved his arm towards the corner table, where Edward duly sat, sipping at a glass of sparkling water, trying to do the *Telegraph* crossword in his head. This puzzle had become the daily challenge for most of the living-in officers of the regiment, and was very hard to give up. He was quietly chewing over a fifteen-letter anagram when he caught Gail's scent.

'Is a girl allowed to interrupt the champion cruciverbalist?'

Edward leapt to his feet and leaned forward across the narrow circular table to offer a peck on the cheek. Gail accepted it with grace, pulled out the metal chair and slid into place. 'A drink?' said Edward.

'I don't want to lead you astray,' said Gail. 'If you are on a strict regime, I would hate to be the person who destroyed the plan.'

'Gail, you can lead me astray whenever you want. Special dispensation tonight. Les, my trainer, says that red wine taken occasionally with good meat is positively benign. Do you have favourite reds?'

'No, but I am interested. When we lived in France, my parents used to make a point of taking us on visits in the wine districts. I have been the length of the Loire, mainly to see those fabulous chateaux. We did Bordeaux quite thoroughly and had some of our most enjoyable holidays on the Lot near Cahors.'

'Aah!' said Edward. 'I think my good friend Michel would recommend a Cahors wine this evening. It suits the style of the restaurant.'

Gail took the menu off him and looked. 'Oh, yes, that Chateau Lamartine would be lovely, if you're happy with it?'

Edward raised an eyebrow at Michel, who was standing with his back to the kitchen, waiting for the signal. 'Lamartine, if you would, *mon ami*.'

'So, you must be very well versed with your wine?' he asked.

Gail looked slightly sheepish. 'It is all Dad's fault. He inspired my sister and I with the joy of such a widely grown, superlatively flexible drink. He introduced us to it before we were teenagers, but he has talked about wine throughout our lives and, had the world been different, I suspect he would have preferred a life as an oenologist instead of being a diplomat. Wherever he served, he built his travels around the vineyards.'

'So, where has the family been?'

'Well, he is now on the verge of retiring at the youthful age of 57. His last posting was as Ambassador in Belgium, and three years before that he was Ambassador in Portugal. We spent three years in Morocco and before that quite a long time in France, where he had two different roles, which kept us in Paris for almost six years, instead of the standard three. He's an able man, my old father, and I love him.'

'Daddy's girl?' asked Edward with a smile.

'He's the loveliest person, and my sister and I have been so lucky to have a father who always made the effort to be there for our big events, even when he was frantic at work.'

'So, your French is totally fluent?'

'To be honest, I should be better. I was educated at the Lycée in Paris and have attended French schools wherever it has been possible. I took the Baccalauréat instead of English A-Levels. But, yes, I do speak it fluently. And I have a smattering of Portuguese, all of which came from those vineyards on family trips.'

'What is he going to do when he retires?'

'We are all wondering. Diplomats spend some thirty years, most of it abroad, trying to find a community of interest out of conflict. He writes beautifully, crafted English and French. He loves his wines. I have told him to find a job which allows him to travel and write about wine. Mum isn't so keen. She has found her nest in Sussex, and after so many years on the road, she wants to make a garden which will always be hers, and cook delicious meals in a family kitchen, without having to worry about the quality of embassy food. I don't blame her. The wives of diplomats are rather like the wives of servicemen. No house is theirs exclusively, and in some careers, life is all about being under constant surveillance. I am so grateful that we never lived in the Eastern Bloc.'

'So, why did you go into the Diplomatic Service?'

'You conduct a great interrogation, Edward. I am giving away all my family secrets and haven't heard a word about you.'

'Don't be silly. I need to know something about you and, thanks to my old friend Henry, you discovered more than I normally publish. I can talk after I know as much as I can prise out of you.'

At that moment, Michel appeared with the Chateau Lamartine and withdrew the cork with an elaborate flourish. He tipped a mouthful into Edward's glass, who delicately pushed it across the table and suggested that Gail should taste it. Michel nodded in appreciation. A good diplomatic move with this very attractive young woman. She sniffed the wine, tilting the glass to two angles, explaining that the first was to capture the fruit and the second the alcohol. She sniffed deeply on both occasions, but didn't sip it. 'Perfect,' she judged. Michel poured enough into both glasses, placed the bottle on the table and asked if they were ready to order. They looked at each other and laughed.

'We haven't even looked at the menu,' said Edward. Seconds later, they resolved that Gail would have mussels followed by duck, while Edward said he could not resist the snails and a rare steak.

'The Diplomatic Service?' repeated Edward.

'I am sure that you have been tutored in much the same way. It is interesting how often children follow the careers of their parents. I have more friends who have gone into medicine because of their parents than I can shake a stick at. I admit I enjoyed my childhood and never felt the lack of a permanent home. We lived rather gilded lives, saw really interesting places, learned about the culture and language of unusual people. I will never forget driving with my parents over the Atlas mountains from Marrakesh to Taroudant on a shale road which snaked over a nine-thousand-foot pass with two-thousand-foot drops on one side or the other and no barriers. You would go round a hairpin bend to find a bus bulging with passengers, and it was obvious that it wouldn't be reversing. But it was really worth the experience, not only because of the dramatic wilderness, but particularly because, as you reach the southern slopes of the mountains, the road gets wider and metalled. The curves become more feminine. You hit the floor of the Sahara Desert and drive straight through orange groves which smell like the edge of Heaven. And the hilarious thing is that many of the trees have goats lying on their lower limbs.'

'Wow. That's quite a trip; and, if I may say so, a lovely tribute to your upbringing. By chance, I have been to Taroudant and stayed in one of those elongated hotels by the city walls. I remember lying half-awake as the Muezzin chanted his call to prayer as dawn was breaking at four in the morning. I have to say that I never used to enjoy that chant because, when we were in Aden, it seemed to be the signal for the evening gun battle. But the man in Taroudant had an absolutely stunning voice. It was not recorded, it was not harsh; it was like' – Edward paused – 'it was like a lover calling his bride.'

They both sipped their wine, before Edward went on, 'Does your sister feel the same way as you about the nomadic life you had as children?'

'Stop, Edward Davidson. I cannot tell you everything in a monologue. We really do need to have a conversation.'

''Kay,' Edward responded with a cheerful shrug. 'I was brought up in rather different circumstances, but admit that I share your view on the cultural impulse of family. Nurture beats nature, in my view. I was brought up by a man who was not a blood relative, but whom I called Uncle, and his mistress, who was my father's sister.'

'Oh, that is quite advanced,' gasped Gail.

'Don't worry. It does not imply an inherited instinct to live with more than one woman.'

'But why such an unusual arrangement?'

'My parents were travelling on holiday when I was at Prep School. They were on an autobahn in Germany when a truck broke through the central reservation. It took them out in a nanosecond.'

Automatically, Gail reached out to place her hand over Edward's. 'Oh, God! You poor boy.'

'I was eight years old. Of course, it was a shock. They had dropped me back at school only three weeks earlier. You sort of expect to see them at half-term or whenever. I recall my aunt coming to the school – it must have been within twenty-four hours – to see me. The headmaster and his wife were fully in the picture, but hadn't said a word to me, because Aunt Mary was so determined to deliver the news herself. Of course, she was shattered, too. After all, it was her brother, and they were very close. My mother got on with her famously. Perhaps it was a good thing that I was an only child.'

A tear glimmered in the corner of Gail's eye. 'I cannot believe that you seem so balanced.'

'Oh, heavens! Appearances are seriously deceptive. I am really very peculiar, wearing women's clothes on a Friday night and playing darts every Saturday.' Edward grinned.

'You idiot!' The tear disappeared with a quick brush of her right index finger. 'So, if I had agreed to dine with you last Friday, it would have been a girl's evening.'

'There's a thought. I love dressing up. Just give me half a chance and I will happily turn out dressed as a flapper. No, I am lucky, really. My Aunt Mary is a lovely, feminine woman who has never been able to embrace the idea of being a married lady. She has lived with Uncle James for more than twenty-five years, but resolutely declines to marry him. I have been extremely boring, pointing out that if he dies unexpectedly, she may not benefit from his Estate. They have no children, so I came as the perfectly formed ready-made son.'

'And what does Uncle James do?'

'He's a farmer, but spent a little time in the Army as a young man. In fact, I am in the same regiment: there's some evidence of the nurture factor.'

'Where is the farm?'

'North Northumberland. Terrific county: long and thin, with more sheep than people. It has the most beautiful coastline, many sturdy castles, splendid scenery and a real sense of community spirit.'

'Do you know, I have never been there. It seems so far away.'

'You can't say that when you have lived in places like Morocco. The train is quite efficient; much better than driving – and there are always spare vehicles at home. Maybe I could tempt you to come up when Uncle James has a shooting weekend?'

'Shooting? Are you a crack shot, Edward?'

'No, I wouldn't say that, but I first carried a weapon, a 410, unloaded, on a driven shoot at the age of ten. I was terribly proud to be allowed to hold a gun, and Uncle James did everything he could to instil good sporting instincts in me. People are always so generous. I have shot poor innocent little

111

pheasants all over the United Kingdom, and that practice improves your performance.'

The mussels and snails silently appeared in front of them. Edward insisted that Gail have one of his snails so that he didn't kill her with the smell of garlic. She chewed with appreciation and offered one of her enormous New Zealand mussels, which Edward declined.

'Uncle James proved to be a splendid father. He always tried to attend important matches, and he helped to steer me towards competitive fencing when my school reported that I had some talent. It meant giving up rugby, but I was never going to be an international.'

'I hate to admit that I have never sat through a fencing match. Isn't it awkward having yourself connected to an electric wire?'

'Actually, we don't have electronic scoring in the sabre. It is only the foil and épée. But I think that we will eventually be forced to adopt the electronic format, because sabre bouts are so quick and complex that referees have genuine difficulty understanding what is happening. Moreover, there is a trend towards poor-quality technique, because contestants try to bluff the referee with swift forward movement. I am sorry, Gail, I guess every sport has its funny ways, and we are all in a bit of a muddle about how to preserve the classic nature of sabre fencing.'

'So why fencing?'

'I was – I am a little boy. I was absolutely overwhelmed by Alexandre Dumas' book *The Three Musketeers*. There is romance, clear etiquette, good manners, physical ability, hand/eye co-ordination; it's got it all, really.'

'You are telling me that you are a romantic, Edward?'

'I am not ashamed of it. It is all about this nurture business. Aunt Mary introduced me to all sorts of wonderful books, and I have been buried deep in them ever since. She insisted that I extend my reading beyond the traditional British writers, so I read Goethe, Schiller, Jean Paul, initially in English translation, but then I started to learn German and re-read them in their native form. To me, German has become the romantic language.'

'And what about Hugo, Stendhal, de Balzac and Flaubert?'

'Ah, I would expect you to champion the French and, yes, I have read them. I read Madame Bovary as a teenager and was primly shocked by Emma's love affairs, although maybe she had some excuse.'

'You are shattering all my preconceptions about soldiers, Edward. I imagined that you were all addicted to breathing fire and killing people. Instead, I find a cultured romantic who is probably far better read than I am.'

'I am humbled by the assessment. We come back to the original premise about nature and nurture. I couldn't imagine going into any profession other than the Forces, but if I had been brought up by my parents, I might well have become an academic. My father was a don at Durham, and what I remember of him was a quiet, bookish man who loved to extol the beauty of literature.'

Gail was persuaded finally to talk more about her family, her face positively lighting up when she talked about her sister, who was two years younger and was working as a PA with a firm of head-hunters in Mayfair. Clearly, the two sisters thought the world of each other.

'Tell me about your home in Sussex,' Edward urged.

'I think one of the problems about the diplomatic service is that you rarely lay down roots in your own land,' Gail proposed. 'Mum's family came from the Surrey and Sussex general area. Dad's family were more Oxfordshire and Wiltshire. One of the major factors in their decision-making was to have good transport into and out of London, where they knew they could keep friendly tabs on us and, to be fair, where they could be readily accessible for us. The train from Victoria takes just about an hour, although a car almost always takes longer, because it's murder trying to get away from central London. So, in the final months of Dad's last appointment, Mum spent quite a lot of time hunting around Sussex, with a focus on the railway network. We've landed up between Forest Row and Colemans Hatch, in a neat little house with four bedrooms and a manageable garden. My folks absolutely love it.'

'I hope your father received a suitable reward for his years of service?' offered Edward, already knowing that Sir William Ritchie had been appointed KCMG in the New Year's Honours List.

Gail coloured. 'Yes. Yes. He was tickled pink, to be honest. I know that Mum is quietly pleased, but mainly for him. You don't earn a lot of money as a diplomat, so the handle of knighthood balances the books rather well.'

'And you still haven't told me what you read at university; nor, for that matter, which university it was.'

'I think that you are trying to embarrass me, Major Davidson. I read history at Oxford.'

'Well, I am honoured that you should have the time to gossip with a non-university man like me. I had the chance, but wanted to join a fighting regiment at the earliest opportunity. Your entry into the Diplomatic Service tells me that you must have secured a First-Class degree?'

Gail flushed again. 'My parents would have shot me if I had failed. I couldn't let them down, so probably drank less and attended fewer parties than many of my contemporaries. But I judge that it was worthwhile. We have the whole of our lives to live it up. Now, my turn. You said you specifically wanted to join a fighting regiment, and I remember that when we met on our trip to Cheltenham, you said that you had gun battles almost every night in Aden. Is it totally inappropriate for me to ask whether you ever killed anyone, or were any of your soldiers seriously wounded?'

'Will you think ill of me if I tell you that the answer to both questions is yes? Let me rephrase that. It is not inappropriate to ask, and I won't tell you any lies. My troop was in action countless times over some eight months. No holds were barred. We fought to survive, and even with the benefit of hindsight, none of us actively sought the opportunity to fire our weapons at real people. And as to the second question, we were extremely lucky, because we sustained heavy rifle, machine gun and rocket fire, but only one of my soldiers was injured when a sniper's bullet missed his head and hit one of the sights in his cupola. Glass fragments flew into his eyes and we feared he would lose his sight permanently.'

'Were you frightened?'

'You know, Gail, I was eighteen and nineteen years old. I was immortal. Intellectually, I accepted that I may be badly wounded or killed. Emotionally, I was untouchable. I guess there were a few butterflies in the stomach before an engagement kicked off; but, during the battle, my memory is that time moved a little slower than normal. We did not want to fire indiscriminately, and the .50 machine gun mounted in the turret of a Saladin is a very deadly weapon which fires more than five hundred rounds per minute. So, as the commander of four vehicles, each armed with that firepower and a main armament that could put down a high-explosive shell with devastating effect, part of my task was to ensure that we didn't behave like cowboys.'

'And in Northern Ireland?'

'Very different. Curiously, I have not been in charge of large groups of men in Ireland. My first tour there was as the Intelligence Officer. I know, I know. How unlikely is that?' Gail grinned. 'It's nonsense really. Soldiers stand out a mile. We tend to hold an upright posture, walk with a steady tread

115

and look people in the eye. The average citizen is much more physically relaxed. So it made little difference that I grew longer sideboards and hair, wore jeans and had a Mini as my transport. I looked like a British Army officer in mufti.'

'What a splendid term that is: mufti!'

'Typical of we Brits, really. I think we stole the term from the Arabs, for whom it means "Islamic scholar".'

'And were you shot at in Ireland?'

'Not often. There was one incident which could have been untidy. I was set up by a source who, it transpired, had been found out by his colleagues and was tortured then shot. We had agreed a place and time to meet. I set the parameters, so had a very small advantage. When he failed to appear, I gave it five or six minutes before deciding to make my way back to base. Two armed men intercepted me and very nearly achieved their objective. I had to do a hand-brake turn and get away as fast as the poor little Mini could go. They shot out my rear windscreen and rear-view mirror. The boot looked like a colander, but protected me, because it was full of sandbags. I was lucky.'

'Phew,' said Gail. 'You are the only person I have ever met who has been shot at, let alone been in action consistently for months on end. I don't think I have ever met anyone before who has admitted to killing another human being. I certainly didn't know that soldiers read romantic literature, and I have deduced that you speak three languages. And as if fighting for your life is not enough, you fight with a sword for sport. It's all rather overwhelming.'

'I hope not too overwhelming, Gail. I would be very sad if it deterred you from having more suppers in places like L'Artiste Muscle.'

'No, I assure you that there is absolutely no negative impact on me. But you are so different from the men that I have met as an adult. Yes, I am accustomed to people with excellent brains, and most are socially adept. Some are good at sports like tennis. I think the principal difference is that everything that you do is… what's the word I'm after? It's not "extreme", nor is it "intense". I am trying to find the antonym for "moderate", but that would imply that you are intemperate, which clearly you are not.'

'I can't help you, old sausage. To me, this is normality. And you have very cleverly turned the whole evening around by finding out much, much more about me than I have about you.'

As the conversation flowed, so too did Gail's duck and Edward's steak. The bottle was swiftly emptied, but Gail resolutely refused to have more.

'Thank you, Michel. Another excellent evening.'

Michel bowed with a flourish, and Gail said, 'So, you bring all of your lady friends here?'

'I don't have any lady friends, our Gail, just friends. I have spent at least half of my Army pay in this restaurant and will continue to do so. Our neighbours this evening left us alone, but ninety percent of my visits here end up with conversation flowing between three tables of complete strangers. It's a hoot.'

By good fortune, a taxi was dropping off a couple almost in front of the restaurant. Edward held open the door for Gail, then climbed into the left side of the vehicle. They were back in Prince of Wales Drive in fifteen minutes. Edward leapt out of the taxi, helped Gail to step down on to the pavement and escorted her to her front door. 'You could come up for a drink,' she said.

'No, that's jolly kind, thank you, but if Les knew that I was drinking so much, he'd go wild. I have enjoyed this evening so much. Thank you for being such good company, and let me apologise for telling you war stories. Unforgivable, really.' With which, he put a hand on each shoulder, leaned forward and enjoyed the intimacy of her scent, before he pecked her carefully on both cheeks and walked back to the waiting taxi.

Briefly, Gail felt a moment of rejection, but then shook her head and acknowledged that he was far too gallant to press any advantage so early in their growing relationship, and clearly, he was very dedicated to his sport. She resolved to find out a bit more about fencing in general and the sabre in particular.

Chapter Ten

For the first time, Edward felt that the Weapons Intelligence Group was working as a team. The close focus on a single target helped to create a sense of purpose. Now that the containers were ashore in Antwerp, the energy of creating a plan had been converted into impatience for the planned denouement.

'Moving on to a new subject,' said the Chairman, 'we now have convincing evidence that the Americans in Boston have provided some heavy machine guns – six of them – M60s. In some ways, it is surprising that the IRA have accepted them. They are cumbersome, belt-fed and heavy. The American Army would deploy them with teams of three, one person carrying and manning the weapon, an assistant to carry a spare barrel and ammunition, and the third person dedicated to carrying ammunition. I very much doubt that the IRA will commit three people to one weapon, although it is a very effective, hard-hitting tool. I cannot believe that they will be prepared to fire and forget; but, because of the weight, they will have difficulty moving it in and out of position for any attack.'

'Isn't it a little worrying that we are discovering so many arms deliveries in such a short time?' asked the Northern Ireland Office staffer.

'Indeed it is,' responded James Stanton, 'and it is an additional concern that we are seeing weapons flow in from both Libya and America; I find it hard to imagine a less likely team of collaborators. The good news is that we seem to be learning about the traffic quite quickly and the Army, in the shape of 14 Company, are remarkably adept at finding the weapons once they arrive.

'Before we break, I would like to know if anyone has any feedback on surface-to-air weapons being acquired.'

There was a brief pause, before Harry Martens piped up. 'I initiated a piece of work to collate relevant information. My view is that the IRA have actively sought to acquire such weapons for at least twelve months. As yet, I have no evidence that they have succeeded, but we all know that the intent is generally followed by success. I think we need to hear from sources on the ground, to be honest.'

The Chairman nodded slowly. 'You are right, of course. Once the goods have been sourced, there is unlikely to be a lot of signals traffic. It must fall to those of us with informers to ferret out the truth. We don't have many months left, and we will need to brief the Prime Minister promptly.'

As soon as the meeting ended, Edward hurried back to his office in Whitehall to telephone Mark Humphreys in MO4. 'Can I pop over to discuss something with you, Colonel?'

Seven minutes later, Edward was settled on a chair at the conference table in Humphreys' office. He reported the news about M60 machine guns arriving in Ireland, and it was clear that they had both come to the same conclusion. 'I think we might look for some help from DCDS(I),' said Humphreys, who then picked up his phone and rang to ask for time with the Air Marshal. Within ten minutes, Edward found himself back in front of the homely Sir William Horton.

'Do we know that the weapons have arrived?' he asked.

'No, sir, but I judge that we will hear confirmation soon. Although they didn't say anything, I believe that Five have a source close to the delivery team,' said Edward.

'So, I take it that you two want an M60 machine gun to play with?' Humphreys and Davidson grinned. 'I will just call my friend in the American Embassy,' said Horton.

The two soldiers sat quietly while Horton gossiped away with his contact. Clearly, relationships at this level were quite harmonious, judging from the chuckles. Horton replaced his phone. 'We are lucky. My friend is very enthusiastic about helping and is prepared to arrange for us to have an M60. The only impediment is that we have to collect it.' He paused. 'From Frankfurt.'

There was a moment's silence as they digested the information. Edward had an amusing brief image of someone walking on to a British Airways flight with a heavy machine gun. 'So, I will arrange with the Queen's Flight for you, Edward, to fly to Frankfurt. Be ready to go at a moment's notice.'

Edward was torn by the conflicting priorities, but realised that he could do nothing about it. The chances were that he would be on a plane to Frankfurt just as the containers from MM *Callisto* were emptied by the arms traders.

As he was shutting up shop in the Cabinet Office, Sir William Horton's PA telephoned to say that a staff car would collect Edward from the Cabinet Office at 8.00a.m. on Friday 9 June. He would be taken to Northolt, flown to Frankfurt Rhein-Main, where the US Army would greet him. He would sign for an M60 machine gun and fly back to Northolt, where he would be met by someone he knew from 14 Intelligence Company. He would have to make his own way home.

The drizzling rain persuaded Edward that he would not go to Whitehall on his motorbike, so he left his flat at 7.00a.m. and walked briskly to Balham Tube to catch the Northern Line to Stockwell. He had decided that he didn't need to be in a suit, so was in grey trousers with his blazer and a yellow tie with a pattern of blue fleur-de-lys. He double-checked that he had his passport, then bought a copy of the *Daily Telegraph* as he entered the station. Half an hour later, he walked out of Westminster Tube Station, turned right and then right again to walk towards the Cabinet Office. With almost thirty minutes to spare, he checked in at the front door and ran up the stairs to his office, where he left a note for Jim Shaw, who would be expecting him to be in the office today. The note was cryptic. 'On a mission for DCDS(I)... I probably won't be in until tomorrow.' You could never tell who might come poking around the office and he could hardly say that he was flying to Germany to collect a machine gun.

The staff car was five minutes early, which suited Edward fine. A smart RAF Lance-Corporal leapt out of the vehicle and saluted. 'Major Davidson, sir?'

Edward nodded. 'And you are?'

'Lance-Corporal Higgins, sir. I am to take you to Northolt.'

As they wove their way westwards, Edward chatted quietly to his driver, trying to find out about his family, service experience and interests. It took a little time to persuade him to open up, but as soon as they were on to the subject of sport, the Lance-Corporal became more animated. He was a dedicated Arsenal fan and seemed to know every statistic about the team and its performance. At Northolt, the sentry on duty at the gate directed them towards a hangar, outside which was a small twin-prop aircraft with the wings over the fuselage. 'Ah, ha,' thought Edward, 'if I am not mistaken, that's a Pembroke.' Folding his newspaper, he thanked the Lance-Corporal for delivering him safely and eased his long body onto the tarmac. Almost immediately, a Flight-Lieutenant appeared at the top of the four short steps into the aircraft. 'Edward Davidson?' he queried.

'The very same,' Edward replied.

'Come on board,' he was told.

'Don't I need to go through passport control?' Edward asked.

'Absolutely not. We are going on a training flight to Frankfurt and will not be entering the country formally. We fly to Rhein-Main, where I am told you will be met by an American officer who will do what he has to do with you, then we fly straight back. I'm afraid that this old kite doesn't go as fast as a British Airways Trident, which would get you there in an hour. Our flight time will be about two hours and twenty minutes, so I hope you have a good book to read.'

With a wry shrug of his shoulders, Edward shook the pilot's hand. 'I'm Michael Freeland,' he said, 'and my co-pilot today is another Michael, Michael Evans.' Edward shook him by the hand also and asked when they would depart. 'Now,' said Freeland. You have the entire cabin to yourself, so choose any seat. With the wings overhead, you will have an unbroken view of the countryside, but I regret we don't run to cabin crew, so you will find a bottle of water beside your seat. I will pop back to let you know how we're getting on once we are well across the Channel.'

A man could get used to this form of travel, thought Edward. No passport control, my personalised aircraft, no waiting for boarding. Maybe I should have joined the RAF after all. Moments later, the port engine started to turn, almost as if in the wind, before stuttering into action as the starboard engine went through the same routine. The door to the cockpit remained open and he could see his two pilots checking instruments and talking, presumably to the control tower. In less than ten minutes from driving through the security gate off the A40, the aircraft was roaring loudly at the end of the runway, waiting for clearance to take off. The noise was not unpleasant, but you wouldn't have been able to listen to a radio, thought Edward. He stared out of the window as the pilot released the brakes and they started to thunder towards the point of take-off. Seconds later, they were airborne and turning right towards Watford to circle London clockwise, presumably keeping well clear of the Heathrow flight paths.

Thanking his impulse to buy the *Telegraph*, Edward turned to the back page and started to work his way through the cryptic crossword. It was extraordinary that there were days when he would puzzle away without any success, put the paper to one side for a few hours, then come back and fill it in without pausing for thought. The brain was truly a miraculous machine. From time to time, his eyes lifted from the paper as he looked out of the window, and occasionally his mind drifted to the subject of the lovely Gail Ritchie. But he was so deeply immersed in the clues that he flinched when Michael Freeland tapped him on the shoulder and shouted, 'We are doing quite well and have passed Brussels. We may just make it in a little over two hours, so you can plan on us landing at around 11.30.'

Edward smiled his thanks and returned to the crossword, until he detected a change in the engine noise and felt the aircraft start to descend. Peering out of the porthole, he could see two large rivers, which he guessed were the Moselle and the Rhine. Twenty minutes later, he watched the wheels drop into position as the pilot feathered his wings and brought the aircraft down to the smoothest landing Edward had ever experienced.

They taxied for at least fifteen minutes. The airbase seemed to be enormous, with squadrons of American fighters and bombers littering the airfield in serried ranks. At last they arrived at a stand and pulled to a halt. Immediately, the engines were switched off and the pounding noise slowly disappeared. Michael Evans appeared from the cockpit and tinkered with the door mechanism, which opened readily, and steps were lowered automatically down onto the tarmac. 'You have a greeting party,' he said, as he turned to indicate that Edward could alight.

Edward jumped down from the cabin to find an American Colonel in uniform saluting him. Armed with nothing more than his newspaper, he pulled himself to attention to acknowledge the salute, then walked forward to introduce himself. The Colonel said that his name was Sam, Sam Wertenbaker. They shook hands. 'It is good of you to meet me, Colonel,' said Edward.

'We have to go for a short drive,' Sam said. 'I guess we'll be gone for about thirty minutes, if that's OK with your aircrew?'

Edward looked back at Michael Evans, saying, 'Do you fellows mind waiting for half an hour?'

The drive in a US Army Jeep was just five minutes to an open hangar, into which they drove slowly.

'I guess I don't know what you intend to do with this, but let me offer you one M60 machine gun with the compliments of the United States Army. Would you like to see how to dismantle it?' Thanks to his gunnery course at Lulworth, Edward was very familiar with the working parts of many weapons, but he carefully watched a soldier with chevrons running the length of his sleeve swiftly dismantle, then reassemble the weapon.

'May I have a go?' he asked. With a sly smile, the US serviceman stood back to watch the Brit make a mess of it. Edward paused for a second, then firmly started to take the weapon apart. In less than two minutes, it was in many pieces, neatly arrayed across the table top.

'You've done this before,' said the Colonel.

'Well, I have taken apart a lot of different weapons, and if I weren't doing my current job, I would be instructing gunnery at Lulworth, our principal armoured weapons training establishment,' said Edward; 'but not an M60. The principles seem to be similar to a Browning .50.'

With methodical precision, Edward then reassembled the weapon and grinned at the soldier who had demonstrated how to do it. 'Thank you for your excellent teaching,' he said. The soldier had the grace to look mildly embarrassed as he reassessed his evaluation of the British Army.

The Colonel produced two forms which stated in convoluted terms that he, Colonel Sam Wertenbaker, was formally handing over one M60 machine gun to the British Army for training purposes. Edward signed them with a flourish. The soldier lifted the weapon into the Jeep and off they set back to the Pembroke.

On reaching the aircraft, well inside the thirty-minute expected time-frame, they found the two pilots walking around the plane, checking that all was well. Edward leapt out, shook the Colonel warmly by the hand and lifted the machine gun from the rear of the Jeep. 'It's not light work,' he muttered, as he moved towards the aircraft steps.

The two pilots, who had been briefed only to serve as a taxi for a special mission, looked on with some amusement. 'Don't we have enough of these at home?' asked Michael Freeland.

'Oh, we have plenty of weapons, but this is an M60 and we need to study it carefully before the IRA acquire one. Do you mind where I put it?'

Freeland boarded the aircraft behind Davidson and moved towards the rear, where there was an open area with straps secured to the bulkhead. 'I think we should tie it down while we're in the air,' he said. Edward carefully placed the weapon beside the bulkhead, before Freeland efficiently wound the straps around the weapon and secured them.

'So, the time is now ten minutes after midday. With a little luck, we should be back at Northolt before three o'clock,' said Freeland, after which he turned, indicated that Edward should take a seat, and moved into the cockpit.

The Pembroke touched down lightly on the Northolt runway at two-fifty and taxied swiftly to the same hangar from which it had started. This time, however, they motored into the building. As the engines wound down, Edward saw an old friend, Sergeant Foxton of his own regiment, waiting beside a large Ford saloon.

'They said that I would know the person meeting me on my return. What a pleasure to see you, Sergeant Foxton.'

The soldier, dressed in casual civilian clothes, nodded his head. 'I admit I was surprised to learn that you would be my contact, sir. I thought you were working in Whitehall.'

'Absolutely, but I work for the Joint Intelligence Committee, and they needed someone who knew the ropes. In point of fact, I am sort of responsible for us acquiring the weapon, so it makes some sense that I should collect it. I just need to photocopy the American handover papers three times, but will you please sign this original before I do so?'

Sergeant Foxton took Edward's biro and scrawled his signature at the bottom of the form. Edward looked around to see if he could persuade someone to copy it, but Michael Evans pre-empted him, took the paper and marched quickly to the rear of the hangar, where it was clear that there was an office. While he was gone, Sergeant Foxton undid the straps and removed the M60 from the bulkhead. 'It won't fit in the boot with the barrel in place,' he said. Edward knelt down beside the weapon and swiftly dismantled it, much to Sergeant Foxton's amusement. The Sergeant picked up both pieces of the weapon, descended the aircraft steps, then placed the pieces in the boot of his saloon. Minutes later, Evans handed the original and three copies to Edward, who passed one copy to Sergeant Foxton and folded the other three documents into his right breast pocket.

'Any chance of a lift into London or to a Tube station?' he asked the Sergeant.

'Of course. I am actually going to Hereford, but I'll drop you at Northolt.'

Edward walked across to the two pilots, who were fiddling around purposefully with the outside of the Pembroke. He thanked them warmly for their slick service, shook each by the hand and wandered back to Sergeant Foxton's car.

'So, how are you enjoying the sneaky beaky work?' asked Edward.

'It has its moments,' the Sergeant replied. 'You know I can't really talk about it.'

'Don't worry, Sergeant Foxton. You don't have to tell me anything, because the formal monthly reports on 14 Company's work end up on my desk anyway. But I am interested to know if the coal-face soldiering is all that it's cracked up to be.'

The Sergeant relaxed. He knew Major Davidson well, having seen his work in Northern Ireland. He recalled that, as Intelligence Officer, he had caught two IRA Brigade Commanders during the 1973 and 1974 tour. Moreover, the evidence of the Major's involvement was sitting in the boot of his car. 'Well, I admit that it tends to be a lot more exciting than living on a vehicle park in Germany, but there are long periods of waiting around, hoping that something will happen.'

'Well, please keep looking after yourself. I know very well how close you are to serious danger. The Army is genuinely fortunate to have people like you who can do so much to frustrate the terrorists. How much longer will you be on this posting?'

'I've got at least eighteen months more,' said Foxton. 'I recognise how important it is to get back to the regiment to keep my name in the running for more senior appointments. But I will miss the cut and thrust of getting up close and personal with the bad boys.'

'I'll repeat my encouragement to stay alert. If you leave aside the young cowboys, the hardened professionals are very effective soldiers. Anyhow, here we are at the Tube station. Thank you for the lift. And look after my M60!'

The Tube was remarkably quick. It took just over thirty minutes to reach Oxford Circus, where he transferred to a Bakerloo Line train to Embankment. To the surprise of Jim Shaw, Edward walked into his office a few minutes after 4.00p.m.

'Now, Jim, I have three copies of a document here. We need to keep one for ourselves and send two copies to Colonel Humphreys in MO4. I imagine that he will pass a copy to DCDS(I).'

Shaw looked at the papers. 'An M60 machine gun? Where did you get that, then?' he asked.

'The American Army at Rhein-Main,' said Edward with a self-satisfied grin. 'But, more to the point, have we heard anything from MI5 about the *Callisto*?'

There had been no news, so Edward picked up the phone and called James Stanton in Curzon Street. He was put through immediately and was disappointed to learn that there had been no action worthy of report. The containers from the MM *Callisto* remained untouched. The surveillance team was in place. There had been no sign of Patrick Mallon or his accomplice. They had no alternative but to watch and wait.

Chapter Eleven

Inside the Port of Antwerp Terminal, between the main waterway of the Scheldt and the more intimate Kanaaldock B2, ten containers sat in their own island of sealed metalwork. Neat corridors between similar islands ran in grids going north to south and east to west. The whole terminal was humming with activity, although not in the immediate area of the surveillance operation. Here, all was quiet and empty, apart from two British soldiers lying in assorted places of concealment. For them, it was a long, boring exercise. They had to be alert at all times, day and night, because if someone moved any of the containers, they must be observed, photographed and, if necessary, followed. But nothing was happening. Inevitably, this sapped energy and concentration.

From this site, any container could be on another ship, a train or a trailer within minutes. The port was said to be the fifteenth busiest and also the largest in the world, covering more than twelve thousand hectares.

The soldiers were excellent at their job. They had been trained to lie immobile in uncomfortable locations for days on end. Every member of the team had earned his colours in the hedgerows of Northern Ireland. Rain, sun, wind or storm, they were invisible, untraceable. Once concealed, all they had to do was wait for their target to appear.

At the same time, in Northern Ireland, their colleagues were deployed on four different operations in Belfast, Armagh, and Londonderry. Those in power recognised that this was the strongest weapon that the British Army deployed against terrorism in the Province. Where most British soldiers in civilian clothes would stand out in a crowd because of their demeanour, walk and 'presence', these soldiers moulded themselves like chameleons into their landscape. When they had to work in public, they looked, sounded and behaved like locals. They were outstanding in concealment and they deployed cutting-edge technology to listen, to film and to photograph their prey.

Conscious as the IRA leadership was of Army surveillance, they had no idea about its sophistication. Innocent-looking, empty cars parked by the pavement could monitor conversations and take crisp video of activity nearby. Pin-head microphones and miniature cameras inserted in clothing, luggage, telephones or furniture chronicled meetings which those attending thought were totally secure.

Their skill at gaining access without trace was almost magical. Silent, patient, armed with all that technology could provide, the operators of 14 Int Company laid bare the internal workings of the Provisionals. So, when Seamus O'Heeney, Martin Laverty, Eamon McCardle and Billy Stevens met in an anonymous, brick-built semi-detached house in Berwick Road in the Ardoyne to discuss the plans of the IRA Council, they were unaware that their every word was being recorded and listened to in real time. Here was the solid evidence of the plan to shoot the aircraft of the British Prime Minister out of the sky as it was landing in Brussels for the European Summit conference in November. Here was an indiscreet conversation about the planned dispersion of the recently acquired M60 machine guns. Here, too, there was discussion about the loyalty of one of their own based in Armagh.

At the same time in London, Edward Davidson sat panting after a forty-minute session of circuit training under the direction of his coach. He had met Les Peters at 6.00p.m. at the

London Fencing Club in Norman Street, having not seen or worked with him for nearly three weeks.

*****

'We both know that the best training for fencing is fencing,' said Les, 'but you are less fit than you have been at any point that I have known you in almost eight years. Do you really think that you have the grit and determination to keep going, Edward?'

Edward hung his head, partly because he was so tired that he couldn't keep it up. His breath was ragged, his chest heaving, his legs on fire. He honestly didn't think he could do another circuit.

'Les, I am absolutely motivated and committed to this. I am desperate to have one more go in Moscow. On that score, I ought to tell you that the Services have already warned me that I have to jump through certain bureaucratic hoops before they will let me go.' He paused to gather his thoughts. He couldn't tell Les the detail of HRT clearance, but he had to make him understand that it was a very real potential impediment. 'I don't want you to think that this is some excuse for under-performance. My job has me at the very heart of the Whitehall machine. I am privy to sources of information with a breadth of knowledge which the security gurus cannot allow to be exposed. I have been told by two of the top men in the intelligence world that they want to help me achieve my goal, and they are glad that they have two years to work out a protocol, because they don't want me to be away from the company of at least one Brit at all times when I am in Moscow. The irony is that the Army sent me here specifically to give me the chance to qualify for and excel at the Moscow Games.'

'Well, I cannot affect that,' said Les, 'but I can affect your readiness. You won't need me to supervise your circuit and fitness training all the time. In fact, it would waste too much of our joint efforts. But you have to promise me that you are going to bring yourself back up to speed. I will sit down and plan your fitness schedule tomorrow. I want you to guarantee me that you will meet my milestones.'

'I do. I promise. I have never let you down in relation to fitness, Les. I will get back to the right level.'

'Very well. What we are going to do, Edward, is go back to basics with your technique. Do you remember John Curry, who won the figure skating gold medal in Innsbruck two years ago?' Edward nodded. 'He was already British Champion when he secured Carlo Fassi as his trainer in 1972. Fassi turned him into the European Bronze medallist in Zagreb in 1974 and European Silver medallist in Copenhagen in 1975. But he spotted a weakness in Curry's fundamental technique. This was a man who was already being promoted as the future World and Olympic champion, but even he acknowledged that there was other talent. He would do anything, simply anything, to achieve his goal. They put a hold on the extraordinary elegance of Curry's balletic style. Fassi forced his pupil to train in one square metre of ice. They practised every single basic figure skating movement in that small area. At first, Curry could hardly stand up. He kept falling over. And that was the point. He had become so artistic that he had forgotten the fundamental ingredients of his sport, and that would always have a negative impact on the judges' marking. In his sport, they were looking for perfection in every aspect of the performance, not just the artistry.'

Edward had recovered his breath, and was fascinated by his coach's lesson. 'In 1976, Curry won the European Championships in Geneva, the World Championships in Gothenburg and the Olympic Gold in Innsbruck. It was not a mistake. It was not a coincidence. It was the sheer guts, determination and desire of Fassi and Curry working as a team.

Now, you are my only chance, Edward Davidson, of producing an Olympic medal for Great Britain. We haven't won anything since Henry Hoskins got the épée silver in 1964 in Tokyo. He followed Allan Jay, who also won the épée silver in Rome in 1960. In fact, we have only ever won five Olympic medals in fencing, all of them with the épée.'

'I should know, Les, but where did we win the other three?'

'They were all team medals. London 1908, Stockholm 1912 and Rome 1960. I am offended that our wonderful sporting country has never won a foil or sabre medal. This is why I am so exercised by you, Edward. You have the most natural style, a real energy. I can see you with a medal, but I cannot do it for you. I can only do it with you.'

Edward looked at his coach and friend with a more thoughtful eye. 'Do you know, Les, that this is the very first time in our partnership that you have revealed the depth of passion and commitment. This evening you have lit a new fire in me because of your knowledge of Carlo Fassi's work with John Curry. Believe me, I am up for it. I perceive myself to be a weak vessel, but I will stop making excuses about my work commitments, although I will ask you to remember that I really do have to do my day job, too. If I can't crack the challenge of doing both, I will own up.'

Chapter Twelve

Edward enjoyed a leisurely breakfast in a café by St James's Park Underground station, quietly reading about the dreadful massacre in Lebanon where, bizarrely, Christians had killed Christians. The walk to number 10 Broadway took less than ten minutes. The all-glass-and-metal structure was some twenty stories tall and still looked modern after its eleven years as the Headquarters of London's Metropolitan Police. Nobody could be in doubt about the use of the building, which proudly displayed the name of the tenants on a tall silver pole topped by a triangular sign which announced New Scotland Yard on each of the three vertical faces.

Edward waited patiently at the reception desk while another visitor signed in. Reaching the head of the queue, he started to fill in his details and said to the receptionist that he was there to meet Commander Jack Strong. 'Ah, yes,' the man replied. 'Commander Strong warned us that the Army was going to invade. Good morning to you, Major Davidson. My colleague here is waiting to take you up to the eighteenth floor.'

The lift was large enough for at least fifteen people and was evidently dedicated to looking after the higher floors; no chance of getting on below the tenth floor. They whooshed up, to arrive in an anonymous foyer. 'If you would follow me, sir,' said the guide.

Jack Strong intercepted them before they reached the main open-plan office. 'Good morning, Edward. I am seriously pleased that you have been able to make the time to join us. I have a few of my officers waiting in our conference room. It

135

cannot be helped, but before we do anything, I have to give you the broad parameters of what we do and how.'

Four men stood as their Commander entered the room. 'Do please sit down. Let me introduce Major Edward Davidson, who is a cavalryman, sportsman, and now Whitehall mandarin. My old drinking pal, Micky Burgess, who is the Head of Special Branch in Londonderry, commended Edward to me when he learned of his appointment to work in the Cabinet Office for two years. As I have briefed you already, this is our chance to show the Army how we plods do our business.'

The team chuckled collectively. 'Edward, will you just give us a five-minute run-down of your career, please?'

He had half-expected this, so rose to the challenge. 'I hope I am not here under false pretences,' he started. 'I am a professional soldier and am coming up to the end of my twelfth year as a commissioned officer. I have seen active service in Aden and the Radfan, and for the past few years Northern Ireland. At various times I have been a Troop Leader of four armoured cars; I was the Regimental Intelligence Officer during a long tour which started in Belfast and ended in Londonderry, and I have commanded a Squadron with five troops and 118 soldiers to look after. It is a little bit of an anomaly that I should now be working in the Cabinet Office, where I have no soldiers, lots of paperwork and a civilian clerk whose only real interest in life is railways. I think my bosses are using this as a sort of holding ground before I go to the Army Staff College in Camberley.'

'And what he consistently fails to report,' Jack Strong weighed in, 'is that he has already competed in two Olympic Games and hopes to go to Moscow to retrieve the Bronze medal (or better) that he narrowly missed in Montreal. Of course, he has also had the vicarious experience of Palestinian terrorism at the Munich Games. Thanks to Micky, I can vouch for Edward Davidson's experience and skill in the world of terrorism. He will not betray our trust, so I ask you all to be open and candid with him.

'Now,' said Jack, 'let me introduce the team. First, this is Detective Chief Inspector Ryan Latham, who has been in charge of our surveillance teams for the past three years. He joined us shortly before the Balcombe Street siege. Next to him is Inspector Barry Gibbs, not to be confused with the much more famous Barry Gibb of the Bee Gees, because I am not sure that he can sing any note in key. He certainly can't do two. He is our intelligence lead. Sergeant Mike Jones is a really old hand with this team and is my very own living corporate memory, because he has been involved in everything since 1971. And last but certainly not least is Sergeant Alan Mason, who is one of my firearms specialists.

'We are going to spend an hour getting you up to speed on our activity. I promise it will be worth it. Later, we propose to link you up with Ryan, who will take you deeper into the world of surveillance. But we will start with Mike Jones, whose encyclopaedic knowledge of terrorism in this country is unsurpassed.'

It was immediately clear to Edward that Mike Jones was no ordinary sergeant. He was highly articulate, well dressed and comfortable with the task that his boss had dropped in his lap. Briefly, Edward wondered why he was still a sergeant, and filed the thought away to raise with Jack later.

'We tend to think of Irish terrorism to the exclusion of all else,' started Jones. 'Shortly after I joined the team in October of 1971, the Post Office Tower was bombed. Happily, nobody was injured, because it went off in the early hours of the morning, but the restaurant was closed for some time and eventually it was decided that it should be closed forever. Initially, we thought it was the IRA, and we even received a telephone call from a man who claimed that it had been planted by the Kilburn Battalion of the IRA. It turned out that it was a group of left-wing anarchists called the Angry Brigade, who carried out some twenty-five bombings which damaged property but injured only one person. This department was responsible for identifying the people involved, who almost all came from north-east London. The first person to be sentenced was actually a Lowland Scot called Jake Prescott, who went down for fifteen years. To his credit, he admitted that he had come to realise that he was the person who was angry, while his colleagues were 'just slightly cross'. Edward grinned.

'I use this as a helpful example because, over the past six or seven years, we have had terrorist incidents orchestrated by Black September, who were the people who interfered with you in Munich, the Popular Front for the Liberation of Palestine, an organisation working out of India that sent more than sixty letter-bombs to Jewish targets, and, of course, the IRA.

'Let me talk exclusively about the IRA. In 1973, there were fourteen bombing incidents in London, most of them minor in scale, although the events in March, September and December did injure a lot of people and caused serious damage to property. We were pretty sharp with the March bombings and I am still surprised that the IRA was so casual that we managed to arrest ten of them at Heathrow when they were trying to fly back to Dublin. You may remember the two sisters, Dolours and Marian Price, who were amongst those we picked up.

'There was an escalation in the number of bombings and shootings in 1974 and 1975, leading to the deaths of thirty-five people and injury to hundreds more. In 1976, there were only six days when the IRA sought to wreak havoc, but they had limited success. They turned their focus from buildings to trains, and in one incident in March, Vincent Donnelly seems to have got in a muddle and we believe that he was trying to rectify his map-reading error when his bomb went off. He survived, but shot a member of the public and a train driver, who died. Donnelly then shot himself, but failed to do so successfully. He is currently in prison. I don't want to diminish the impact of these events and I should remind everyone that more than seventy people were injured – some badly – when the IRA left a bomb in a litter bin at the top of an escalator in Earls Court.

'There were no IRA incidents in London in 1977, nor so far in 1978. The bad news is that we have had a number of incidents with a Middle Eastern flavour. In December 1971, the Jordanian Ambassador and a senior colleague were shot and wounded in the Ambassador's car. The culprits were from Black September. They managed to kill an Israeli diplomat with a letter-bomb in September, but twenty other letter-bombs were intercepted. There was a brief campaign of letter-bombs in September, with one Jewish gem dealer in Hatton Garden being wounded by a letter with an Indian postmark. Twelve more similar letters addressed to Jewish businessmen were intercepted in England, and a further fifty were found in India.

'The infamous Carlos tried to murder the President of Marks & Spencer in his home in December 1973. He was working for the Popular Front for the Liberation of Palestine.

'And you may well remember the shocking murder of a former Prime Minister of Yemen, together with his wife and an official from their Embassy. They were shot in their car outside the Royal Lancaster Hotel, and we still do not know who did it. It is probable that it was a political killing orchestrated in Yemen.

'Terrorist activity is not limited to London. There have been bombs and shootings in Aldershot, Birmingham, Coventry, Manchester, Guildford, Canvey Island and Caterham. And I should not omit the bombing of a military coach on the M62 that killed nine soldiers and three civilians.

'You may say that we have not been hugely successful if so many bombs and shootings have happened in our country over seven years. I put it to you that the limited number of incidents and the relative lack of casualties shows that we have been quite successful. We all know that it is impossible to protect the whole country all of the time, and a single terrorist has enormous latitude to operate in a way that suits them. What you don't hear about is the ones that fail, when we are on to them before they can do their business. The public doesn't hear about these quiet successes unless some politician tries to make capital out of them. We average between six and ten successful intercepts a year, which means that we foil multiples of that number of actual incidents.'

'Am I allowed to ask how you create the conditions for those intercepts?' Edward asked.

Jones looked across at Jack Strong, who nodded. 'We work hand in glove with the Security Service, and you will learn more detail about that when you study our surveillance performance. But I would say that there is good cross-service collaboration. The Irish problem looks set to go on for years, although we believe that there are fewer gun-carrying terrorists than there were five years ago. Perhaps our greater concern is international terrorism. You can see plenty of examples in the rest of Europe and the Middle East. Travel and communications are becoming cheaper and easier, so we have to assume that we will experience foreign interference more often.'

Jack Strong stood up. 'Thank you, Mike. As always, a crystal-clear summary of where we have been. And he is right to put down a marker about the future. The Red Brigades in Italy and Baader-Meinhof in Germany are not concerned about international borders, and there is evidence of them training in Jordan with PFLP and PLO guerrillas. Only a little over two years ago, the Baader-Meinhof group, working under the pseudonym the Red Army Faction, seized the West German Embassy in Stockholm. They murdered two of their hostages when the German Government refused to deal with them, but two of the six terrorists died when explosives that they had planted in the Embassy mysteriously exploded. The remaining four eventually gave up and are now in prison.

'We are devoted students of international trends. As yet, there is no world-wide central data of terrorist incidents. Nevertheless, from an informed estimate of some six hundred attacks annually from 1970 to 1975, there was a sharp increase in 1976 and 1977, when the number almost doubled. Indications are that this year the world-wide number of terror attacks is still rising. Something is going on, but it is far too early for us to evaluate what it is. What we can guess is that hate crime, religious intemperance, nationalism and bloody-mindedness will continue to manifest themselves with aggressive behaviour. And insofar as it affects this country, I and my team have to try to prevent it from happening.'

Edward had always understood where the burden lay, but he had no idea of the scale. 'So, you are looking for the proverbial needles in a haystack. Maybe fifty to a hundred malcontents operating in a population of, what, sixty million people?'

'That's exactly right. We have to rely upon every source that we can lay our hands on. We have to sift the information, evaluate it, find a way to access the targets, then build evidence to put them away. It is almost a moral crusade, and sometimes the perpetrators slide under the wire and achieve their goal. Thankfully, our relationship with the Security Service is fairly good. We both seek the same result. And from time to time we share our work with the Armed Forces. Most of the operatives at 14 Int Company spend some time training with us. One of the things they enjoy most is attending the Police Driving Course, where they learn how to handle cars in a way they had never imagined.'

'Is there any merit in talking about the Balcombe Street siege, or is it a distraction?' asked Edward.

Mike Jones cleared his throat. 'We were on to them. They were six men who spent about fourteen months making life a misery for everyone. The action heated up after one of the Active Service Unit shot and killed one of our colleagues, PC Stephen Tibble. The gunman was a man called Liam Quinn, whose flat we had identified. As we closed in to take him, he managed to get away. The flat itself was a bomb factory. But the chase was on. The gang had developed a habit of returning to previous attack sites for a second bite of the cherry. One of those sites was Scott's Restaurant in Mount Street, which they attacked in November 1975 by throwing a bomb through the window. It killed one person and injured fifteen more. We strongly suspected that they would come back, so we had a number of plainclothes officers littered around Mayfair. On 6 December, we saw a Cortina slow down outside Scott's and they started to fire into the restaurant. Happily, nobody was injured and the gang realised that we were on to them. If I am to be totally honest, the planning on our side was not a huge success, because we had no transport available. Two officers flagged down a taxi, which duly followed the gang to Marylebone, where both the terrorists and our officers abandoned their vehicles.

'The gang kept up regular fire against their pursuers and several officers received awards after the event, including Inspector John Purnell, who received a George Medal. The gang broke its way into the flat of John and Sheila Matthews at 22b Balcombe Street and used them as hostages for the six days of the siege. It was pretty intense stuff, but after the start of the siege, our role was complete. Everything had to be in the hands of the police negotiators.'

'Does history relate what became of the taxi driver, who must have loved living the cliché of "follow that car"?' asked Edward.

There was a silence as the police officers looked at each other. 'Do you know,' said Mike Jones, 'I think you are making a good point. I have no idea what became of him. He's probably still working as a cabbie, but his public profile is non-existent.'

'Now,' said Jack, 'time to move on to the surveillance side. Ryan and Barry will do a double act.'

Ryan Lambert stayed in his seat, looked Edward in the eye and asked, 'Can you tell me the principal factors that contribute to good camouflage?'

Edward laughed. 'I love it. I learned this in the Combined Cadet Force at school. Shape, shadow, shine, silhouette, spacing, sound, smell and movement.'

'Top marks,' said Ryan. 'You were well taught. Any of those factors can ruin the art of concealment. By and large, our targets have been taught the same mnemonic, and it is a crucial part of surveillance training to look out for frailties in their camouflage. All serious terrorists know the basics at least. The best know as much as we do. And I hazard the guess that your role as a soldier taught you how to hide seriously large objects like tanks, armoured cars and regiments of men.' Edward nodded.

'It will come as no surprise to you that we start with planning. We don't want to waste time following false trails, and we don't want to be caught out when we are on the track of a serious prospect. So, we accumulate as much information as we can before we set up any operation. The purpose of the exercise is to secure evidence that can lead to a prosecution, and life is magic if we can actually catch people red-handed. By definition, the work is covert and it may be conducted in a static position, or mobile on foot or in vehicles. The problem is that it is expensive in manpower and other resources.

'Quite a few of our current operatives are former military, and every person on the team is a trained police officer. This means that we can be confident about their knowledge of the law. We look for men and women who are intelligent, quick on their feet, fit, dexterous, and physically unremarkable. They have to mould themselves into the landscape to become invisible. If we are following someone by car, we always have at least three cars on the job, so that we can be in front, behind or beside the target. On foot, it is more complicated and I frequently deploy quite large teams if we are after a specifically important individual.

'We have an exercise in progress right now. I propose to put you into our operations room with Barry. You will follow the action from our control perspective. Later on today, one of my team will take you out on the ground to observe.'

'I will leave you now, Edward,' said Jack Strong. 'I think you will be enthralled by the next few hours. Towards the end of the day, the team will deliver you back to me, if that's OK with you?'

'This is so good of you all,' offered Edward. 'Please do kick me out when you get bored with me.'

For the next five hours, Edward sat glued to his seat in the operations centre, listening to the unfolding exercise in which a team of four officers played the part of a terrorist group preparing to lay bombs in the centre of London. No less than twelve surveillance officers made up the team that had to monitor what the 'terrorists' were doing. Having sat in many operations rooms himself, Edward was very much at ease with the environment, and quickly found himself in tune with precisely what was happening. He was struck by the professionalism and competence of the officers who were managing the exercise; it could just as easily have been RHQ on exercise in Germany. At some point, he was handed a plate of sandwiches and a Coca Cola, and was not allowed to pay.

Shortly after five in the afternoon, he looked at his watch and realised that he had probably outstayed his welcome. Ryan Latham, who had been present for the whole exercise, understood the signs and rose to his feet. 'I'll take you along to see the boss,' he said. 'One day we should get you out on the ground. I am sorry that it wasn't going to work for us today. The exercise is doing what it is supposed to do, which is to test the team's skills to their limits. Had we put you out there as an extra, it would have limited some of our ability to do the job thoroughly.'

'Ryan, I have rarely had a more interesting and informative day. Thank you so much for putting up with me and for giving me some insight into the incredible work that you do in defence of the nation. I have really enjoyed it. Moreover, it will certainly help me to understand what is going on when we have a real threat.'

Jack Strong looked faintly frazzled when Edward entered his office. 'The only trouble with becoming a senior officer,' said Jack, 'is that you lose touch with the coal-face and spend your life worrying about money, resources and policy.'

'That prompts me to ask you a question about police ranks and promotion. I was hugely impressed with Mike Jones. Surely he should be more than a sergeant?'

'You are bang on target. Mike is a very gifted man. He speaks English, French, German, Spanish and Italian. He has a degree in criminology and another in law. He is respected throughout Europe for his knowledge of terrorist groups and his very presence in my team lends me credibility. But he does not want to become a budget holder; he doesn't want to step back from the coal-face. And, to be honest, he doesn't see his rank as a limiting factor in his chosen career. I would promote him to Chief Inspector today, but he simply won't go along with the grand plan, and I do not want to lose him. One day, I hope that he will see that it will be worth his while to accept promotions so that he can retire with a proper pension.'

'How very admirable. Money seems to direct most of us mortals, so it is even more impressive that he is ready to work for far less than his potential. I hope you can persuade him in time. He's a good egg. Well, I must get out of your hair. I have enjoyed the most fascinating day, Jack. You have been really generous and your team has gone out of the way to make me feel at home. Thank you so much. I am not confident that I can ever repay the professional hospitality, but please believe that is my ambition.'

As they shook hands by the door to the Commander's office, Jack added, 'I tell you what you can do. Make sure you get to Moscow and secure your Olympic medal. And when you do, I want you to bring it here and show me.'

'Oh, heavens,' said Edward, 'it sounds as if my coach, Les, has got to you!'

Edward felt buoyant as he walked to St James's Park to catch the Tube to Westminster. After a day out of the office, he knew that he ought to spend half an hour going through the routine paperwork. In fifteen minutes, he was in his office, twiddling the dial on his security filing cabinet. Jim Shaw had left typed notes on top of the heap of paperwork in his in-tray. There was still no update from the Security Service about the container in Antwerp. Michael Richards in Century House had telephoned for a conversation. Harry Martens had called from GCHQ. Edward thought for a moment. The name Michael Richards rang a bell. Ah, yes, it was the SIS man who had attended that first meeting in Londonderry more than four years ago to discuss Joe McCall. That would be interesting. He flicked through the files: diptels, GCHQ reports, internal Cabinet Office papers, a note from Colonel Lewis about security and any visit to the Eastern Bloc. All of it could be dealt with in the morning. He glanced at his watch. It was just coming up to 6.00p.m. There was no training tonight, so it might be a good opportunity to try to kidnap Gail for an *ad hoc* supper.

He dialled Gail's number in the Foreign Office, but an anonymous male voice said that everyone had gone home. He turned to his address book and dialled her flat. Jane Baldwin answered. Gail was not home yet, but she urged Edward to drop in for a drink, because they would both be happy to see him.

With a spring in his step, Edward put away his files, locked the filing cabinet, left the office and jogged downstairs. He decided to take the Tube from Westminster to Sloane Square, then catch a cab to Prince of Wales Drive. In no time at all, he walked out of Sloane Square Tube station, walked to Lower Sloane Street and turned south. There was a Victoria Wine outlet just before the junction with Royal Hospital Road. He went in and found an agreeable bottle of Nuits-Saint-George for £4.50 and, declining a bag to put it in, he ambled down to the junction and waited for a taxi.

He rang the Baldwin/Ritchie bell at 6.40p.m. and was immediately admitted by Jane, who greeted him at the door to the flat. She looked a little guilty as she showed Edward into the sitting room, because sitting there, nursing a glass of white wine, was Edward Longstaff. Irritating as it was to have the competition there ahead of him, Edward was quietly pleased to see a man who, he judged, could become a good personal and professional friend. He smiled forgivingly at Jane, handed her the bottle of red wine and said that he would love just one glass of red.

As Jane disappeared into the kitchen, Longstaff half-whispered, 'Have you heard anything about Antwerp?

Edward shook his head. 'I haven't been in the office today, although my clerk left a note saying that there was a deathly silence. In fact, I have just enjoyed the most fascinating day with Jack Strong at the Bomb Squad.'

'My goodness. You do get around. GCHQ, Box 500, the Bomb Squad today. You must be super-efficient with the paper mill.'

Edward laughed. 'Although there is a hell of a lot to read, I find my daily assault by the newspapers is the most time-consuming activity. I read every Irish newspaper each day, plus the *Times*, *Telegraph* and *Guardian*, with the *Observer* on Sunday. I would never have believed it before starting this job, but the *Irish Times* and the *Guardian* are consistently the best informed.'

'Your burden is heavier than mine,' said Longstaff. 'I have rather a different type of brief.'

Jane came back into the room with a glass of red for Edward, the bottle of white to refresh the other Edward, and an empty glass for herself, into which she sloshed some white. 'Have you boys planned this visit?' she grinned at them.

'Clearly not,' Longstaff replied, 'but I am always happy to bump into the Major. You don't fit the image of a major at all,' he continued. 'Aren't they supposed to be blimpish and round, while captains are dashing and handsome?'

'I've never been unduly fussed about the rank, to be honest. Of course, it's helpful to have more pay, and mine went up by nearly fifty percent when I was promoted. I am now paid slightly more than a four-star general was in 1966. They didn't do too well in those days. But to respond to your question about planning, Jane, I have already told Edward that I spent today with the Bomb Squad. Absolutely riveting. One of the men who briefed me was a sergeant with two degrees and five languages under his belt. I asked his boss why he was still only a sergeant, and he told me that it was by choice, because he wouldn't be able to achieve so much if he were more senior. I thought he was the most able and admirable person.'

With that, they all heard Gail's key in the lock of the front door. She dropped several paper carrier bags in the hall and took a small step backwards when she spotted two men waiting for her with Jane. 'Goodness,' she said, 'you two are like London buses. You can't find one for ages, then a pair comes along at the same time.'

The men rose to their feet and grinned at each other awkwardly. 'I think that we both had simultaneous and spontaneous ideas about asking you out for supper,' said Davidson.

'Well, I am sorry. Tonight is not a good night. I am flattered, of course. Sometimes a girl just needs to stay at home, wash her hair and curl up on the sofa in front of the television.'

The two Edwards looked at each other. Clearly, nobody was going to win this contest. 'I tell you what,' said Davidson, looking at Longstaff, 'why don't you and I share a plate of something Italian at Como Lario?' The humour of this twist in plans made them both laugh. Gail briefly looked embarrassed, but decided that she was not going to change her mind. If the guys were going to be happy together, she ought to rejoice.

They bade the girls a fond farewell and decided that the warm evening should encourage them to walk. It was only a couple of miles and would take them twenty to thirty minutes. As they ambled along the east side of Battersea Park, they started to talk about the *Callisto* operation.

'It's been ten days since those containers were offloaded,' said Longstaff. 'I can't help wondering if we have a problem?'

'Well, I doubt that we can justify keeping the surveillance boys on the job for much longer. I think we are going to have to arrange for them to be "found" by an observant dockworker. I will talk to our operations people tomorrow morning. Mark Humphreys in MO4 is always on the ball. Are you content with that?'

Longstaff agreed. In some ways it was quite surprising that someone infinitely more senior had not been complaining about the prolonged operation. The surveillance team must be going nutty.

Como Lario was an intimate little restaurant tucked into the side street called Holbein Place, running north from Ebury Street. Always buzzing with people, it boasted white tablecloths and extravagantly energetic waiters. The food was always reliable and the drink relatively competitive. Despite a failure to book, they were slotted into a narrow table by the window, next to an earnest young man who was clearly trying to seduce the girl opposite him. They were not going to be able to talk about their work, so both were comfortable with talking about their background, hopes and aspirations and extra mural interests.

Longstaff was ready to be open about his family, which found its roots in East Anglia. His father had become an avid amateur genealogist and had been thrilled to trace the name back to Leicester and Norfolk in the thirteenth century. He had not managed to accurately link those early mentions with the modern-day family, but he was extremely happy to have traced a link to a multi-times great-grandfather through a will of 1666. Davidson listened carefully, first because he had no idea about any of his great-grandparents, and secondly because it was the first time that he had seen his companion so animated. His genealogist father had been a working accountant until last year and had welcomed retirement from a lifetime of numbers. He had a brother and two sisters, all gainfully employed in their chosen worlds, but none of them civil servants.

'So, what directed you towards the Foreign Office?' asked Edward.

'University,' was the immediate reply. 'I was reading PPE at Cambridge and my tutor gave me a very solid shove in this direction.'

'I seem to be surrounded by brainboxes now,' laughed Davidson. 'Of course, you all need startling results to get into your professions. I couldn't be bothered with it in the end and was very anxious to join my regiment, who I knew would be going to the Middle East. Truthfully, without diminishing the excellence of those of you that do go up to university, I am not confident that we all should.'

'I agree, although I am sure you would have enjoyed it and prospered. Remember that our universities have traditionally combined academia with athleticism. Many people have gone up solely to make the time to excel at sport.'

'Well, I don't regret it. I have enjoyed the very best of what the Army offers for twelve years now. I have been to places I would never have visited. I have had the encouragement and time to do sport and adventure training from the Atlas Mountains to the north of Norway. Actually, if I am strictly honest, my sport has taken me to more countries than my military commitment. I was really lucky to get into the team to take part in the World Championships in Gothenburg in 1973, Grenoble in 1974 and Budapest in 1975. Of course, Budapest was particularly fascinating for me as a soldier. We rarely get the opportunity to go behind the Iron Curtain.'

'And who dominates your sport?'

'Oh, the Russians have it in spades. They win all of the medals and continue to do so over the years. I would like to say that they have an unfair advantage because many of their sportsmen are technically soldiers, who serve exclusively to do sport. But that would be hypocritical in view of my own good fortune to be allowed to swan off to use my sabre. The only difference is that the Army gives me my pay, but do not pay the expenses. The Russians have it all thrown in.'

They realised that the restaurant was emptying. The young man and his girlfriend from the adjacent table had disappeared half an hour earlier. They swiftly split the bill, thanked the staff and moved out of the restaurant. Shaking hands with more than a comradely spirit, Davidson turned left to walk up Holbein Place to the Tube station. Longstaff turned right to Ebury Street.

Chapter Thirteen

Edward was in the office bright and early the next morning. Despite his disappointing failure to capture Gail for supper, he felt that he had really achieved a most useful rapport with his opposite number in the Foreign Office. His first call was to Mark Humphreys.

'Colonel, good day. This is Edward Davidson. I was hunting for some information about our operation, which seems to be dragging on.'

'You are absolutely right. I don't want to talk about it on the telephone. Have you time to pop over here for a quick chat?'

'If it's fine by you, Colonel, I will come across now.'

The tight little MO4 office was becoming quite familiar. 'We believe that we have been sussed,' said Humphreys. It is most unlikely that the Irish moved the weapons to Antwerp to leave them dumped there. We have tried to trace the movements of Donnelly and Mallon and can find nothing of any use whatsoever. I suspect that someone on the Port Authority tipped the wink to the Irish that we had a surveillance team on site. They couldn't have found out by themselves. And we cannot stretch our team by keeping them on site for any longer. Technically, we can pull the plug unilaterally, but it would be good management to engage with the other Whitehall partners to ensure their approval.'

'Would you like me to do that, Colonel? I can call James Stanton now, if you like. He can then disseminate the information. But before doing so, I ought to be able to sell him the Plan B.'

'Good plan. My thinking is that we want to make the discovery a spontaneous act, probably by one of the Port's security people. Our boys can create the conditions by opening some of the containers, not least because we want to know precisely what's in them anyway. The security people will then have the excuse to investigate. For safety, we will have to keep one or two guys on duty to ensure that the Irish don't slip back in when our backs are turned.' Indicating his telephone, Humphreys invited Edward to make the call.

James Stanton was more than ready to accept the Army recommendation. Irritating as it was that the target had slipped through the net, there was no point in wasting resources any further. He swiftly agreed to inform the members of the Weapons Intelligence Group and agreed to ask the Foreign Office to deal with the Belgian Port Authority to create a credible discovery.

Edward conveyed the decision to Mark Humphreys. They agreed that it would be good if the operation could be closed down completely in forty-eight hours. Edward then took the opportunity to leave, and reached his own office before 9.00a.m. He judged that this might be just a little early to return Michael Richards' call, so he phoned Colonel Lewis first.

'Oh, good. Thank you for returning my call so promptly,' said Lewis. 'I just wanted to let you know that if you were planning on going to Moscow today, we wouldn't let you. But thanks to your timely warning, we are all pretty confident that we will be able to work out a protocol for your trip if you do get selected to go there in 1980.'

'That's a relief,' acknowledged Edward. 'Had you said that it would be impossible, I would have been forced to give up my fencing. My coach will be relieved, too. Thank you, Colonel. What do I have to do now to ensure that this stays on the agenda?'

'Nothing, absolutely nothing. The bureaucracy now has you firmly in its sights. We have the time to create a workable plan and I fancy that we will be able to share that with you long before your selection is announced.'

The next call to Harry Martens was equally helpful. 'You will see your normal correspondence from my office,' said Harry. 'I am sending you some interesting and diverse information about the European Summit conference in November. I know I don't need to tell you, but this will be a useful distraction.'

They gossiped for a few minutes, with Edward inviting Harry to make the time to have lunch or supper with him if he could ever be persuaded to spend more time in London.

It was half past nine by the time that Edward managed to return the call to Michael Richards. It was swiftly clear that James Stanton had been on the phone to him already. 'I wonder if we could tempt you to lunch over here in Lambeth today?' he asked. 'I would like to keep you in the loop about the actions we are taking to close down the current operation.' Edward was thrilled. Although he had been to Century House on three occasions since he had started working in Whitehall, it still held a subtle attraction.

The morning flew by. The daily scrutiny of the newspapers, the mounds of routine files, the planning for regular reports all ate up the time without him hearing the minutes tick by. He was saved from embarrassment by Jim Shaw putting his head around the door and saying, 'You ought to be off if you want to get across the river in time for your meeting.'

Thanking him, Edward considered putting away his files, but instead asked Jim to be prepared to do so if Edward was delayed. He also realised that he ought to report developments to his boss, so asked Jim to talk to Sir Charles' secretary to arrange a brief meeting later that day, or the following morning.

155

He ran down the stairs, waved at the receptionist to say he would be back, and turned right in Whitehall to go towards Parliament, where he picked up a 148 bus, which would drop him almost outside Century House. At reception, he filled in his visitor's pass and said that he was expected by Michael Richards. Three minutes later, he was astonished to see Edward Longstaff walking towards him.

'You devious old fraud,' said Davidson. 'I genuinely thought you were quote Foreign Office unquote, not SIS.'

'Ah. Well. The sin of omission. I never intended to deceive. We grow rather circumspect in this job. Please don't take it amiss. My masters will be frightfully impressed that I have managed to keep you off the scent! Michael is my boss and we work on European terrorism.' They grinned at each other without malice.

Michael Richards greeted Edward warmly. 'I haven't seen you since we met in Londonderry five years ago. You earned high praise in the intelligence community by the way that you played the McCall operation. Such a shame that his own side latched onto him; but none of that was your fault.'

'I was genuinely sad about McCall's end. It nearly did for me, too, of course. You may know that the Brigade Commander tried to get me posted back to Londonderry to take over from Mark Collins?'

'Yes. I did know. We all had a real interest in your future. You may or may not know that, before your current appointment, the interested ministries and services were all consulted about your suitability. Thanks to that excellent Head of Special Branch, annoying as he could be to many soldiers, there was no dispute. I am certainly very pleased to have the chance to work with you.

'After speaking to James Stanton this morning, we talked to our opposite numbers in Belgium. They have kindly agreed to help us promote the small deception which leads to the discovery of the weapons currently sitting in a container in Kanaaldock B2 at the Europa Terminal. One of their middle-aged, long-serving security men will experience a life-changing epiphany and become a national hero tomorrow when, through diligence and observation, he will find insecure containers. As I understand it, this is the cunning plan hatched by you and Edward when you dined at Como Lario last night.' Richards' eyes twinkled.

The two Edwards grinned at each other. 'Actually, to be pedantic, it was as we were walking by Battersea Park before we reached the restaurant,' said Davidson. 'Clearly, we make a brilliant team. Now, I ought to telephone Colonel Mark Humphreys to confirm the action. He will want to know when our boys should access the containers.'

'May I suggest that we ensure that we put your Colonel Humphreys directly in touch with Stephane Timmermans, who works directly for Albert Raes, the Director of the State Security Service? They take their security very seriously and we want to ensure that they trust us. Here are his contact details.'

Edward nodded towards Richards' telephone. He dipped his head in agreement and Edward rang the well-known number at MO4. 'Colonel, this is Edward Davidson. I am with our friends in Lambeth. They have secured agreement for us to conduct the operation we discussed and have suggested that you may wish to liaise directly with their deputy in charge of affairs at their end. Let me give you the details.'

This was no time for further gossip. Humphreys acknowledged the contact details and rang off. 'Right,' said Richards, 'let's go upstairs for a little light lunch.'

The top floor of Century House seemed to comprise just one large open space, with windows looking out over London. Richards took the two Edwards across to the North West corner, which looked down on Waterloo Station. 'I am addicted to model railways,' he said. 'This view of Waterloo allows you to pretend that you are managing a miniature railway.' They stood in silence for a few minutes, enjoying, as most boys do, the sensation that they were in charge of the living activity below.

'You should meet my clerk, Jim Shaw,' said Edward. 'He is absolutely dedicated to the study of railways and their capital equipment.'

'We probably wouldn't get on,' said Richards. 'There is a huge gulf between the models and the real thing. And let's face it, I enjoy playing. They enjoy investigating. Now, let's have that lunch.'

The three men duly queued up along a counter which contained a range of dishes. None of them were inclined to adopt the healthy salad route, and all three went for the lasagne, without any additional vegetables. They gathered cutlery from a dispenser at the end of the counter and found a table.

'Edward tells me that you have already competed in two Olympic Games,' Richards stated. 'I myself was lucky to compete in the Biathlon in Innsbruck in 1964.'

'Good Lord,' responded Edward. 'You worked far harder than I do. I have tried langlauf skiing and find it quite knackering enough, even without the obligation to fire a rifle several times on the way round the circuit. Do you manage to keep fit still?'

'Evidently not,' replied Richards, looking ruefully at his own stomach, which, in all honesty, was like a washboard. 'Fourteen years is a long time, particularly when you are largely stuck behind a desk. But it was fun. There were a lot of soldiers in our team in '64. They competed in the langlauf, biathlon and bobsleigh.'

'Ah, that was the glory year for the bobsleigh: Tony Nash and Robin Dixon. I class them as the first true professional British Winter sportsmen, saving your presence, Mike. I am probably being unfair to all the other sports, but Nash and Dixon did things that the other teams did not. I met Robin at an Olympic reception a couple of years ago and he was telling me that they used to walk and run back up the track after every run. Nash did it in order to see the course from the other perspective and observe the competition's approach. Dixon did it to ensure that they were both fitter than any other team. And it worked.'

'I cannot argue with you. I have to say that I think that we cross-country skiers were super-fit; but, in comparison with other bobsleighers, Tony and Robin clearly had the edge. And it was no mistake that they were World Champions in '65.'

Edward Longstaff sat quietly listening to the two sportsmen trading knowledge and experience. It was far out of his worldly view and rather gratifying to observe that his boss and his increasingly interesting colleague were bound by their common performance on the international stage.

'My view is that we are missing a trick,' said Davidson. 'I guess that, as a club, there must be about six to seven thousand surviving British Olympians at any one time. If you think about it, that's quite an exclusive group. But we have no mechanism for that group to interact with up and coming sportsmen or the public at large, other than the BOA, whose focus naturally is on the management of British teams at contemporary Games. We could be doing so much to instil a sense of excitement in our people; we could be a major factor in leadership development; we could be educating the public at large about the benefits of elite sportsmen in their community.'

'You are absolutely right, Edward. It's idle old deadbeats like me that have failed to make that happen. I have no doubt that you will be at the leading edge of a British Olympian movement, but don't be in too much of a hurry. You need to work out the politics of sport. And, to be clear, you need to know precisely what you are trying to achieve. I don't want to deter you; I am just saying, be cautious. It could turn out to be a considerable weight around your neck. But when you are ready, and if you want support, do lean on me. I really admire your vision.'

After lunch, Edward made his way back to Whitehall for an afternoon with bureaucracy. The evening was dedicated to training at the Norman Street Club. Les's schedule was clear and challenging, and Edward had absolutely no desire to fail him.

Chapter Fourteen

Sergeant Serge Montagny idly scratched his tummy as he sat in the canteen, reading a copy of the *Gazet van Antwerpen*. His cup of tea was already cool, and his plate of carbonade flamande was totally clean. The chips had been perfect. He was not going to report to Celine, his round and motherly wife, that he had eaten them this evening.

After twenty years of working in the docks as a security officer, he had lost the youthful vision of a career full of achievement and publicity. In truth, he could hardly wait for the five years to retirement to pass. His dreams today were of happy evenings with male friends at any one of the three small estaminets that he tended to visit. Had he bothered to do the sums, he would discover that this evening's deployment would be his 4,889th mission to guard the security of the port. And during that time, he had never once seen nor experienced anything to justify the effort.

At the pre-deployment briefing, he had been instructed to cover Kanaaldock B3 from 8.00p.m. to 11.00p.m., then Kanaaldock B2 from 11.30p.m. to 2.00a.m., when he would be relieved by Thomas Peeters. There were no special instructions and no known threats. Life was entirely normal.

Looking at his watch, he sighed, finished his tea, folded the paper and left the canteen to go to the locker room, where he left the paper in exchange for his hat, his torch and his communication radio. Placing spare batteries in his jacket pocket, he locked the cabinet and walked out into the open air for the stroll to the northern end of the complex. Briefly, he called Control on the radio, received an acknowledgement, then set off.

At 11.00p.m., Serge made his way to the security hut beside Frederik-Hendrikbrug for a well-earned cup of tea. He would rest for thirty minutes, before moving to the second part of his night mission. At exactly that time, three soldiers of 14 Int Company started to gain access to the ten containers they had been monitoring for twelve days and nights. The locking mechanism on each container was virtually irrelevant and certainly no impediment to anyone who had been taught how to break into high-security buildings. The objective was to make it obvious that someone had tampered with every container in this block. The Customs seals had to be broken to emphasise the point. Within ten minutes, every container had been opened, and the Irish arms were found in the fourth one on the bottom row. There had been no attempt to camouflage or conceal. The boxes containing the weapons boldly stated what was in each one. The Corporal in charge made a note of the numbers: ten RPG-7 rocket launchers, five hundred Kalashnikov rifles, bullets too numerous to count and boxes of detonators. The bonus was a case marked Semtex1A.

The soldiers closed the containers, leaving two slightly ajar. The Customs seals were left on the ground in a heap as they withdrew into the dark to observe from a distance. They had to ensure that the security guard did his job.

Even the sleepiest observer would have spotted the evidence. Serge, to his credit, did not panic. After all, this was what twenty years of training and experience did for you. But how dangerous would the next part be? He could see one container with its door clearly unlocked. Perhaps the infiltrators were in the container? He quietly lifted his radio to his mouth and whispered 'Control, I have a problem.'

'Speak up, Sergeant, I can hardly hear you.'

'I have a problem,' whispered Serge. 'I have found a container and I do not know if the person who opened it is here. I need back-up.'

'Five minutes. Keep watch. The reserve will be with you in five minutes.'

Confident that their job was done, the three soldiers turned and walked off into the darkness. In fifteen minutes, they were in the car park at the Terminal Headquarters, where for the past fortnight their civilian car had been parked daily by one of their colleagues. The arrival and departure of a properly registered and logged vehicle was unexceptional.

Serge was hugely relieved when a Land Rover arrived with four other security guards. He affirmed that there had been no movement in or out. If someone was in the container, they would have him. As his partners fanned out around the mouth of the container, Serge pulled open the door and shone his torch into the depths. There was nobody there. He walked in and approached the first crate. *'Mon Dieu!'* he breathed. 'Thomas, Nicolas, come and take a look. This container is full of weapons. We must tell Control immediately.'

It had been a longer night than anticipated, but Serge could hardly contain himself as he slipped into bed next to the warm body of Celine. She murmured in her sleep, but these late arrivals home barely disturbed her. Setting his alarm for 8.00a.m., Serge rolled over and promptly went to sleep.

At 10.00a.m., Sergeant Serge Montagny reported to the Terminal Headquarters in his formal uniform. To his dismay, he was to be interviewed by the Deputy Director of State Security, Stephane Timmermans. He was even more bemused when he realised that the Deputy Director had marshalled newspaper photographers, reporters and senior staff of the Port Authority. The reception was totally unexpected and briefly awoke in the fifty-year-old a lingering memory of youthful ambition.

'I am very pleased to meet you, Sergeant Montagny,' boomed the Deputy Director. 'Your diligence, keen observation and professionalism are a tribute to the service. You have achieved a wonderful coup, which will clearly wound the terrorists whose weapons you uncovered. In due course, I know that the State will reward you in the most appropriate way, but for the present we, the State Security Service, want to pay public tribute to you.'

Montagny almost had the grace to blush: 'diligence', keen observation', 'professionalism'?

'Come, we will shake hands while the photographers do their business.'

There were some compensations, reflected Serge on Sunday. Celine, whose libido had been hibernating for several months, found a refreshing enthusiasm for her husband of twenty-seven years after reading of his exploits and poring over his photograph with the Deputy Director of State Security. The neighbours would be very envious of her small contact with fame.

Chapter Fifteen

In the month that had elapsed since the public discovery of the weapons in Antwerp, Edward had kept his nose to the grindstone at work and in the gym. He had tried to see Gail many times, but there were often good reasons why their diaries just did not match. But they did meet, once more for dinner at L'Artiste Muscle, twice for drinks after work, and once at a dinner party hosted by mutual friends. He was despondent because he simply couldn't get her out of his mind. He realised that he was becoming obsessed with her: her looks, her scent, her brain, her laughter. How on earth had she slipped so easily into his emotional sphere?

But Les Peters was definitely a happier man. They were doing what he had promised, which was to generate a fitness regime that brought Edward back close to the physical form he had enjoyed at the Games in Montreal, and they had cut back to the very fundamental basics of fighting with a sabre. They discussed the strategy, agreeing that everything started with movement on the piste. This meant that the first focus was on footwork for attack and defence, practising distance awareness and restructuring his stance. It was like being a total novice, but Edward knuckled down to do what his coach wanted, knowing that this was the only way that he would ever have the chance of a medal in Moscow.

Monday 17 July had been a standard day. Jim Shaw was away on leave, so Edward dealt with all of the incoming mail, registering the sensitive documents that needed a solid audit trail, and reading all of the information that might remotely impinge on his professional productivity. Now, almost five full months into his job, he was comfortable with the content and style of his regular reports, and he had established a good, humorous relationship with his boss, Sir James Harrington. For the first time, it seemed as if the factors which had coalesced to structure his posting to Whitehall were matching their intention.

He started to pack the papers into the secure filing cabinet shortly after 6.00p.m. He had left his Honda outside the flat in Balham, so decided to take the Tube to Sloane Square to shop at Partridges. They produced some wonderful ready-made meals, and he fancied some artichoke hearts and olives. Twenty-two minutes later, he exited into the bustle of Sloane Square, turned right, walked past the Royal Court Theatre and a bistro to cross to the north side of the square. Partridges was a few yards past the GTC on the west side of Sloane Street.

Lost in a world of his own, Edward spent some time gaping at the wine and spirits shelves. A bottle of red would go quite well with the meatballs he was planning to buy. He took his time, reflecting on what Gail might have recommended. Now, if the meatballs were quite spicy, it would be good to go for something Spanish: a Rioja, perhaps. He realised he was evidently getting too fanciful for, as he thought of Gail's selection, he swore he could smell her scent. And the genie popped out of the bottle when she said, 'Edward, you're not turning to drink, are you?'

For a micro-second his face revealed everything he had been thinking about Gail Ritchie. Short it may have been, but she recognised in that moment that he was infinitely more interested in her than she had imagined. She wasn't entirely ready for that, but it didn't repulse her, either. She laughed brightly and said, 'I thought I would hardly ever see you again after you and Edward Longstaff went off to have supper together.'

'Yes. Good male bonding. I like him enormously. He is bright, witty, articulate, well-informed and a dreadful nuisance, because he is as interested in you as I am.'

Gail blushed deeply. 'I didn't realise that I was part of a contest,' she said.

'Gail, you are an absolutely lovely young woman with brains, fabulous humour, and a sexy laugh. You will always be part of a male contest. Don't reject it. We all want to be part of your audience. Now help me to make a decision, please. I could buy a bottle of Rioja and the spicy meatballs that this shop produces with such consistency, or I could kidnap you and take you to Colbert, the bistro beside the Royal Court.'

'Oh, Edward, you are so forceful. I am supposed to be buying supper for Jane and me. I can't let her down.'

'I like your Jane, too, but she took just a little too much pleasure in the management of two Edwards and one Gail last month. You were as stumped as we were. She could see it coming and, if I am to be fair, may not have been able to avert any embarrassment, but she did enjoy it. Surely you have some supplies in the flat? And it is time for you to be kind to dumb animals. I have barely seen you for a month.'

She shook her head, as much in pity as good humour. 'Right, I must find a telephone box to warn her that she will have to fend for herself. Why don't you go across to Colbert to grab a table?'

With a much jauntier spring in his step, Edward carefully made sure that the shop staff knew that he was not absconding with their stock and walked briskly across Sloane Street to the bistro on the corner. Amazingly, the place was not packed. It was a lovely warm evening and some of the customers were outside, but there were tables free inside and out. It was almost like being in Paris. The Maitre d' spotted him immediately and Edward pointed to one of the exterior tables, then asked for the menu and wine list. By the time that Gail appeared, he had mastered the contents of both and was ready.

'I must say that you are looking in excellent condition,' said Gail.

'I should hope so. Les Peters has been beating me up. We have adopted a really arduous fitness programme, and he has forced me to go back to the very first fundamentals of my sport. I haven't been this fit for at least two years.'

'And what's this about going back to fundamentals. Have you forgotten the basics?'

'No, but Les told me all about Carlo Fassi and John Curry. It was – no, it *is* – entirely inspiring. So, we are trying to follow their example.' And when Gail asked what it was that Fassi and Curry had done, Edward explained.

'We have the menu and the wine list. I want to defer to your tutored judgement, Gail.'

She took the menu, swiftly recognised what she wanted for herself and said, 'Do you like oysters?'

'Love them. You are absolutely on the same track as me. I thought I would have half a dozen oysters, followed by moules.'

'Good, she said. I will fall in line with that, but will have only a small helping of the moules. May I suggest that we have the Gewurztraminer? It would be safer to have the Sancerre, but there is something wonderfully harmonious about having a mildly spicy wine with fishy food.'

Edward beamed. This was close to perfection. 'I learned about Gewurztraminer while I was in Germany. Two or three of us would bunk off on a Friday afternoon and drive to wherever. Once or twice we went up to Denmark. I travelled the length of the Rhine and the Tauber, following the Romantische Strasse towards Salzburg. But I loved a trip to Alsace, where we spent a happy weekend learning about Trimbach wines. On another weekend, we went to Wurzburg ob der Tauber, a beautiful medieval town with fortified walls, in order to try the Tauber wines, which are delivered in a bocksbeutel.'

'Bocksbeutel?'

'Yes, they are shaped rather like the Mateus Rosé bottles. The only trouble is that the Tauber is not a well-known wine river because, for some reason, the wine doesn't travel well. But drink it in the area and there is nothing to beat it.'

'Just humour me for a minute, Edward. My brain has slipped sideways to your sport. You say that your coach is taking you back to the fundamentals. Precisely what does that entail?'

'Hmm. I don't want to give you a lecture, but I have to set the scene a little bit. We fight on a piste that is eighteen metres long. We are required to fight in the central fourteen metres, so if one fighter is forced back to within two metres of the very end, the fight is stopped and the defender is put back on guard. The advantage is always with the person who is advancing, and he is given the priority, which we call a right-of-way. Where once the fighters were more stationary, today we often both set off at a run to meet up in the middle, hoping to secure the advantage. What Les and I are trying to do is to address the perceptions of the referees by ensuring that my footwork denies an opponent the advantage conveyed by a flèche.'

'A flèche? You use arrows?'

'No, actually I should have said 'flunge'.' It is a particular movement within a running attack. On the one hand, the opponent seeks a physical and a psychological advantage by speedy forward movement. Les and I feel that if we go back to the founding principles of the sport. We will demonstrate that we are fighting properly, according to the best traditions and with excellent technique. Moreover, I believe that it will give me an unassailable advantage, because it will surprise those who have not addressed the current issues affecting the referees.'

'OK, I can understand that. And when you have sorted out your footwork?'

'Ah, well. Thank heavens we have almost two years to prepare. We will conduct the same process with all of the other ingredients of the sport. There will be a great deal to do with elbow and wrist movement, and Les is investigating a specialist who can improve the way in which I use my eyes. Although we are looking directly at our opponents, we believe that there may be an advantage to be gained by training my ability to see movement at the edges of vision. There will be psychological training and long, deep discussions about the conversion of strategy into tactics and final performance.'

'Are all elite sportsmen preparing like this?'

'I cannot answer for them all, but I can guarantee that the majority are. We all want to win, you see. The only way to do that is to build up to the point at which your opponent cannot match you.'

'OK. I understand the thrust of it, even if I cannot perceive the detail. And all of this is going on against the background of a serious job in the Cabinet Office. How did that happen, and where will it take you?'

'Dear Gail, I am going to throw back at you an early statement of yours. We must have a conversation, not an interrogation.'

'I am on a roll. Please accept that I will tell you anything you want to know' – Edward's eyebrows arched and she giggled briefly – 'but I am just trying to arrange the package that is Edward Davidson so that I really do understand you.'

'I'm all for that. The Cabinet Office job came completely out of the blue. Back at the end of 1973, beginning of 1974, I was the regimental intelligence officer in Londonderry. I don't know precisely why, but I got on famously with the Head of

Special Branch, a man called Micky Burgess. It transpired that no soldier had ever managed to deal with him on level terms. He thought, with some justification, that the Army were doing more damage than good. He certainly wasn't going to share good intelligence with us. As always happens when communication is limited, the wall of antipathy between the Army and the RUC was unnecessarily high.

'I have always believed in trying to enhance communication. Curiously, that tends to happen more easily if you listen, rather than talk. So, I listened very carefully to what he had to say when I first met him. And then there came an opportunity with a walk-in source. I decided I would consult him before I consulted my more senior intelligence colleagues in the Brigade Headquarters. Of course, the Brigade intelligence man had a canary, but Micky was terrific. Unknown to me, he called the Brigade Commander to discuss everything before I managed to get over there to make my own report. Of course, the Brigadier was a much worldlier man and was delighted with Micky's overt transition from dogged unhelpfulness to cautious but enthusiastic praise.

'Phew. This is turning into a long story. Suffice to say, the Brigadier then sought to recruit me as his intelligence man when the incumbent, an infantry major, moved on. Again, I was sublimely unaware of the debates at our posting authority, where the Gunnery School at Lulworth had put in a bid to place me there as an instructor.'

'Why did they do that?'

'Oh, Gail. This sounds dreadful, but the fact is that when I did my long gunnery course, I passed out with the highest A grade that had been seen in a generation. In terms of the school, I walked on water.'

'There you go again, Edward. Everything that you touch seems to turn to that word I couldn't find at L'Artiste Muscle. Is it predominance?'

'No, I don't think so. I would never have achieved that sort of grading in signals or driving and maintenance. Gunnery suited me. Lots of barking of orders and stripping weapons down to their core components. If you enjoy doing something, you tend to do it well.'

'But you didn't land up in either Londonderry or Lulworth. You landed up in London.'

'Yes, it was a sort of compromise, I guess. Sean Lomax was commanding the regiment. We have always been good chums and I guess he knew me better than anyone. He knew that I would probably go mad at Lulworth, because there wouldn't be enough of a challenge. The Cabinet Office posting had two or three real benefits. First, it is a grade three appointment, so it ticks an important box in my long-term CV. Second, people imagined that it would give me more time to train for a medal in 1980; and third, Sean recognised that it never does any harm to work close to the seat of power. I would never have considered this last ingredient, but as Sean pointed out, I will spend two years with civil servants, politicians and senior officers who may well remember me if I return to Whitehall at some point in the future.'

'Bear with me. So, what happens after this posting?'

'The plan is that I go to the Staff College. You cannot expect to become a General without passing through that process. There are many options, because we have the Army, Navy and Air Force Staff Colleges, and there are opportunities to attend the staff course in places like Germany, Pakistan, India, Australia and the USA.'

'Your preference?'

'Golly. I should say Camberley. That's where the guys go who tend to get to the top. But if someone told me to go to Australia for a year, I wouldn't say no.'

'And after Staff College, what happens?'

'Probably a grade two staff job, maybe as a Brigade Major or DAA&QMG. Sorry, one is the operations man, the other is the admin one. Or it may be that I return to the regiment for two more years as a squadron leader.'

'So that takes us up to 1982. Are you going to be a general?'

'You are truly nailing me down, Gail. At this stage in my life, I aspire to become a general. If I thought that I was never going to make it, I would seek out an alternative career and...'

Before he could get the words out, Gail said, 'Reach the top of it.'

They stared at each other in silence for a few seconds. 'Yes,' he said.

'Well, I think that I have achieved my goal. I wanted to understand your view of the future. The desire to win is a considerable force, and I now know that it affects everything that you do.'

'Does that make me a terrible bore?'

She reached out to touch his hand. 'No, you could never be a terrible bore. On the other hand, I have described you as overwhelming once before. All that you do is intense, even though you come across as one of the most laid-back men in England. How does this manifest itself in your love life?'

Edward was unprepared for this. He should have seen it coming, because Gail was a very open, straightforward young woman. 'I don't have a love life at the moment, Gail.'

'Don't tell me that you have never kissed a girl.'

'I haven't said that. I just don't have a girlfriend at present, and haven't had one for some time.'

'Tell me about your most recent girlfriend. I hope she didn't go away because you were unsympathetic to female ways.'

'OK. She was called Helen. We courted for about two years. I think that we were appropriately fond of each other, but I cannot say that it was a love story. She was quite an emotional girl; there would be a lot of highs and lows. I am just a bluff old soldier and accept that I may not always perceive the intricacies of the female mind. She also had some difficulty with my dedication to my sport, which is part of me. I cannot just shrug it off. In the end, we agreed that we should not see each other for a time. That was almost two years ago, and I have not tried to contact her, nor she me.'

'Have you bedded many women?'

'That's the sort of question that I have never been asked, nor wanted to announce. I was brought up to the code that a gentleman should never kiss and tell. But I don't want there to be any secrets between us, Gail. If you want me to tell you, I will.'

She thought for a second. 'I realise that if I force the issue, it gives you the right to challenge me in the same way. I appreciate the gentlemanly code of conduct. I suppose I should have asked a slightly different question, which is: do you maintain more than one relationship at a time?'

'I am the complete monogamist. I haven't got the guile, energy or enthusiasm to chase after lots of different girls. In my experience, which is as a spectator with male friends, the guys who behave like rabbits tend to get found out, and it causes everyone lots of pain. That is simply not my style.'

'Your turn.'

'Very well. I am not going to interrogate you, and I certainly do not want to embarrass you. But in view of my propensity for enjoying combat which I always seek to win, I want to know if I should be viewing Edward Longstaff as a rival, because I am making it clear now that I have fallen for you and I want to win.'

She looked him straight in the eye. 'Edward and I have had a lot of fun. We have not got further than a rather chaste kiss. If I am honest, I don't think that his interest in me is physical. I see him as a very intriguing figure. His mind is like a bacon slicer. He has completed two fascinating tours, which are

174

magnetic attractions, because I like the subterfuge of intelligence work. And, of course, he is a spy. You knew that, didn't you?'

Edward laughed. 'Yes, I knew that. In fact, I had lunch with him and his boss not very long ago at Century House. Michael Richards was the SIS man who attended a conference in Londonderry four years ago when we discussed my new source. They sort of inducted me to the range of interests for which they are responsible. Edward and I get along rather well. I hope he will remain a friend long after I have moved out of Whitehall.

'Now, Gail. I have exposed my frailty. We have not known each other for more than five months and have not met as often as I wish. Nevertheless, I need to confess that I really want to get to know you much, much better. I see characteristics in you which, I believe, balance my strengths and weaknesses. For clarity, I admit that I could not imagine anything more magnificent than being in your bed, but I do not see you as a quick bonk. I see you as a much longer-term lover, friend and helpmate. As with all that I do, I am prepared to work at that, to earn your approval, to cement a solid, effective partnership. This is not the most romantic way of laying siege to your affections, but may I have your permission to start my campaign?'

She briefly looked down at her lap. He waited patiently, hoping that she would not turn off the tap immediately. 'Yes, Edward, you may start your campaign. Be patient with me, because I realise that I have much to learn. I will be honest. I have not been looking at a long-term relationship, but you are truly an extraordinary person. I may have looked under the external packaging, but I haven't seen the working parts.' They both roared with laughter, the allusion too close to the subliminal text to be ignored.

'Right. We don't need to start this with a parental beauty parade, but I have suggested to you before that you should come home to Northumberland when we have a shoot. It will give you an immediate insight to how my family works.

'You know that the grouse season starts on 12 August, which happens to be a Saturday this year. I have been asked to shoot by neighbours who have a wonderful, walk-up grouse moor in the Cheviots. It is hard work, because there is a lot of climbing up steep hills and tripping over heather and peat hags. But even if we don't shoot a single bird, the environment is fabulous. I propose that if you are available, we will catch the train from Kings Cross on the Friday, stay at home, shoot with the Ridleys on Saturday and leave after lunch on Sunday to catch the train back to London.'

'Goodness. This is so you, Edward. We are straight into action. It's only just over three weeks away.'

'So?'

'Well, of course I'll come. It would be absolutely lovely, and I am sure that I will learn an awful lot more about you from your Uncle James and Aunt Mary.'

Gail refused to let him escort her back to her flat, so Edward flagged down a taxi, gave the driver a £10 note and received his first light kiss on the lips from the lovely girl who had captured his heart.

Chapter Sixteen

'I think that wraps up the live intelligence,' said Edward in his weekly interview with the Chairman of the JIC. 'I am writing a report dedicated to political issues with the Dáil in advance of the Brussels summit, which will be on your desk next Wednesday, if that suits you?'

Sir James looked at his young staff officer and decided to test him in an unusual way. 'I hear that you are making friends with my god-daughter.'

Edward looked blank. 'Your god-daughter?'

'Yes, surely you haven't forgotten her already? Gail, Gail Ritchie. Her parents and I are very old friends, and it seems that Gail has been chatting to her mother about the interesting young man who is trying to take her by storm.'

Edward felt himself go a little pale. 'I wouldn't say take her by storm, but I candidly admit that I am completely entranced by her and she has given me permission to wage my campaign to capture her interest.'

'They are a wonderful family. Will Ritchie and I worked in the same mission in Berlin thirty years ago. 1948 was an exciting time to be in what remained of the city. He and Ellie met there and married in 1949. I was their best man and was thrilled to be asked to serve as Gail's godfather. She is a very bright, forward-looking young woman. I would not – indeed, could not – interfere, but you look after her, please, Edward. I had to tell Will some terrible half-truths about you to reassure him that you were not a wild cavalry officer who would have no thought for his daughter's welfare.'

'I imagine that this will sound defensive or pompous, but I am not that sort of man. Gail asked me if I maintained a portfolio of girlfriends and I hope she believed me when I told her that I am entirely monogamous. I simply don't have the ability to take on multiple emotional problems.'

'Well, of course you must have fun. That's the whole point of being young. I know that Gail has developed a real interest in her career, so you may find that it gets in the way. I understand that you are taking her home to meet your aunt and uncle for the Glorious 12th.'

'Indeed I am. Uncle James and Aunt Mary are the people who define me, and Northumberland is my playground. It seemed to me that if she had an early insight into what we are like on our own turf, she could make up her mind more swiftly about her level of commitment.'

'Good thinking. I hope it works out well for the pair of you.'

Minutes later, Edward was back in his office, dialling the Foreign Office Research Department. 'Gail Ritchie, please. This is Edward Davidson in the Cabinet Office.'

'Shouldn't you be working, Major Davidson?' said Gail.

'I am. I have just returned from my weekly briefing with the Chairman of the Joint Intelligence Committee, who told me that he is your godfather.'

'Oh, James. He is lovely.'

'You might have mentioned your relationship with him. He is my immediate boss.'

'Well, in fairness, you have constantly kept your precise role in the Cabinet Office off the agenda and you have never told me that you worked directly for him. I seem to recall you saying that you had a closer relationship with the tea lady than with the Prime Minister.' He could hear her giggling.

'Fair cop. But you wouldn't expect me to broadcast to all and sundry the full nature of my work.'

'Oh! So, I'm all and sundry, am I?'

'Gail! Heavens, you are going to be a handful. Well, now we all know. I understand that your parents have quietly checked me out with him. He told me that he had to tell your father a packet of half-truths to reassure him that I wouldn't behave like a caveman. Actually, to be fair, he said that I would not behave like a cavalryman, but in this context they both mean the same thing.'

'Oh, that is rather naughty of Daddy, but I can understand his instincts. I had a long conversation with Mum a couple of nights ago, because I had to explain why I wouldn't be going home on the weekend of the 12th and 13th. You can imagine how interested she was to hear something about you.'

'Well, I shall always be on my best behaviour. Are you still on for another visit to L'Artiste Muscle on Thursday evening?'

'Of course. See you then. *Adieu.*'

With something of a song in his heart, Edward turned back to his overflowing in-tray. He simply had to complete the brief on Ireland that he had promised to the Chairman, and that demanded much deeper reading of the piles of political comment in front of him. He started to make handwritten notes as he read the report of the European Council meeting in Bremen three weeks earlier.

'At their meeting in Bremen on 6 and 7 July 1978, the European Council agreed a realistic scheme for the creation of a zone of monetary stability by a fund of some forty-four billion European Units of Account (EUA). This would be in excess of the IMF and larger than any other European scheme ever discussed. All nine heads of government in the Council were present and agreed the measure.

'Nevertheless, the public agreement conceals some very interesting reservations in the Irish Government. They have considered the unusual position that they are in, being the only former sterling-area country to have maintained unchanged parity with the pound for more than fifty years since independence. The debate has grown in force since 1975, when sterling took a dramatic downturn against the US dollar and the countries of the European "Snake" linked to the Deutsche Mark.'

Despite himself, Edward realised that he was becoming increasingly fascinated with the financial discussions. He double-checked his source material and realised that the document would have to be classified HRT. Its distribution would be severely limited, because he was able to quote highly-confidential Irish decision-making.

His phone rang. 'Right, lad,' said a broad Yorkshire accent, 'you owe me some information.'

'Good day, Simon. How very agreeable to hear from you.'

'Aye, but I haven't heard from you. We spoke about a little problem two months ago. Is anything going down?'

'Simon, let me apologise for not staying in touch. As you might guess, nobody is going to make this a high priority when we still have almost four months to go before the next European summit. But I did report the matter in detail to my masters, who have "taken note", as they say in our bureaucratic circles.'

'That's probably fair. I think I am really just stirring your pot to ensure that you remember me with clarity and pleasure.'

'You don't mean claret and leisure?' quipped Edward.

'Well, that might be a very fair idea, not that you seem to take too much of the claret. Why don't you down tools and join me for a light lunch? I am thinking of a hostelry close to my next meeting; it's known as Simpson's Tavern, in Ball Court off Cornhill.'

'I can't keep on taking your hospitality, Simon, and I can't use my modest Army salary on long lunches with very amusing gentlemen of the Press.'

'Right, well, you sort out your own mental difficulties and just assume that I am the bearer of interesting tidings that I need to convey to the authorities. You have just one hour to get to Simpson's Tavern.'

Edward cast his eye over the scattered papers on his desk. It felt as if he would never make the time to deliver a coherent brief. But it was possible that Simon had something to add to the original report, and if lunch in the City was the price to pay, so be it.

He rose from his desk to explain the plan to Jim Shaw. He then stacked the paperwork in a pile that he thought he could unravel quickly when he came back, put it all in the secure filing cabinet, locked it, put on his jacket and double-checked his Tube map. He left the office and set off for Westminster to take the Circle or District Line to Cannon Street. The entire journey took forty-five minutes, so both he and Simon Harker were agreeably surprised when he walked into the chophouse well within the challenged hour.

'I don't think that you work for the *Daily Mirror* at all, Simon. On my relatively short acquaintance with you, I have discovered that you are a master of gastronomy, notably with regard to London's exclusive restaurants.'

'And why not? Newsmen traditionally source their news over food and alcohol. Look at those marvellous old pubs in Fleet Street. But I like this place. It's really old. Charles Dickens and Samuel Pepys used to dine here, and the establishment directly opposite was the very first London Coffee House. There are few better sites for people like us to exchange information.'

'You are a devil, Simon. A very agreeable one, but a devil for all that. I am sure that I shouldn't be here at all. But information is what it is all about. Do you, by chance, have any update on that original very helpful report you gave me?'

Harker looked mildly smug for a second. 'Reckon I might. But I'm not going to turn over and have my tummy tickled so easily. I want you to tell me something useful first. And I am not asking for State secrets. No, I just want to know how your coach is getting on with your training.'

'Simon. Really! This cannot be a legitimate newspaper interest. But it is good of you to ask. I could bore you to death on the subject, because in the past two months we have made enormous strides. Literally. First, my fitness, despite the best efforts of you and other friends, is improving radically. Second, we have made the decision to go right back to the fundamentals of the sport. If you like, I am learning about it almost as a beginner, but with the benefit of years of real, high-level fighting experience. Actually, this is quite exciting, because when you dissect what it is that the referees want to see, then apply it to best technique, you can quickly see how to counter some of the terrible practices that have crept into the sport. Where I was a bit despondent about my chances in 1980, I am now totally convinced that I will make it into the team, with a very honest chance of securing a medal. Gosh, that does sound cocky, doesn't it, but it's true.'

Harker clapped briefly but with enthusiasm. 'Different man. And there's something else about you, Edward. You have a brighter eye. I think you're in love.'

Edward paused. 'I had no idea that you were a seer.'

'So you are! That's marvellous. What's her name?'

'She is called Gail, Gail Ritchie. I met her five months ago and have seen her several times since. I should admit that I am completely lost. She is the most wonderful girl and I am having to use all my military, professional and fighting instincts to wage a successful campaign.'

'Have you met her mother?' asked Harker with a wink and a sombre expression.

'I know what you are thinking. I haven't, but I have had a most promising report from my boss, who has been a friend of the parents for over thirty years.'

'Who's he?'

'Now, now, Simon. I cannot tell you that. You may think that I am off-guard, but I do have to retain some notion of security.'

Harker laughed. 'I accept that. But check out her mother quickly. It always pays off. Now, we need to have some lunch.' They swiftly chose two lamb chops, spinach, roast potatoes and a bottle of red wine. The conversation wandered off down the road that they had travelled on their first meeting, with Edward thoroughly enjoying the robust analysis of his newspaper friend.

'So, I shan't keep you in suspense any longer,' said Harker, as he downed a second glass of Côtes du Rhone. 'Our source has come back to us with a more coherent view of the plan for November. I can give you two names of individuals likely to be involved.'

'That's absolutely wonderful. Do you impose limitations on how we use this information?'

'No. We asked the source, who is confident that he will be squeaky clean. It transpires that he is culturally against the idea of killing politicians of any hue. He has listened carefully to many conversations and made a number of deductions. We cannot fault his thinking. I leave it to you and your colleagues to decide how best to play it, but I am sure that you will be talking to the Garda.'

Edward slipped a slim notebook out of his jacket pocket, uncapped his pen and made a note of the names.

'Thank you, Simon. And thank you for another splendid lunch. I do assure you that I will come back to you with the outcome of all this. And I must take you to lunch at my Club. You will cause a sensation.'

'You don't need to do that, lad. The *Mirror* is your host, and it is always a pleasure to see you. But if you do offer to take me to your Club, which one is it?'

'The Cavalry Club, 127 Piccadilly. I will phone you with a prospective date by next Wednesday.'

With that, they shook hands, and Edward walked speedily to Cannon Street to get the Tube back to his office, where he found Jim Shaw trying to reconcile his files with the filing list. 'Did I make a foul-up while you were on leave?' asked Edward.

'No, no. You did fine. Thank you. I just seem to have got myself in a little muddle, and I don't want internal audit to chew me out because of it.'

Edward smiled and returned to his office, opened the safe and removed all of the papers that he had stowed there before lunch. First, however, he wrote a brief memorandum about the updated information on the IRA plan to shoot down the Prime Minister as he flew into Brussels. Although his instinct was to telephone the interested parties, he knew that the bureaucracy would only remember the information if he wrote it formally. To protect the source, he graded it 'Secret' and arranged to distribute it to the Foreign Office, the Met Police, the MoD, SIS and the Security Service.

Within minutes, he was drilling deeply down into European finance and monetary policy. The next three hours went without sound or distraction.

Chapter Seventeen

The crowds at Kings Cross were heaving. With the temperature at twenty-four degrees, most men were not wearing ties, and women were dressed in light summery clothes. There had been relatively little rain during the month so far, and the weather forecast for the North-East for the weekend was dry and fair.

Edward waited, as he had promised, slap bang in front of the electronic departure board, so that Gail could not fail to spot him. He had their return tickets in one hand, the *Daily Telegraph* in the other. True to her word, Gail appeared at twenty minutes to four, carrying a light bag. 'You don't have any luggage, Edward,' she remonstrated.

'I am going home. I don't need a bag, and I maintain doubles of my shaving gear and toothbrush both at home and in my flat.' He took her case. 'Come on. Platform five. I think the train will be stuffed full, but we have reservations. Coach E, seats five and six, which are at this end of the carriage.' They joined the surge of people struggling with too much luggage for an eighty-yard walk along the platform.

'People behave so badly when getting on a train,' Edward muttered. 'They push and barge, generally creating more of a ruck than they would if they just stood still.'

'You are turning into an old curmudgeon,' Gail giggled. 'Does travel always make you irritable?'

'No, Gail dearest. I just, I just… Well, I don't know what I just, to be honest,' he laughed. 'I am a little old-fashioned about giving people the space and courtesy to settle down.

Forgive me. I wish we could spirit ourselves to Berwick without the middle bit of actually travelling.'

On the dot of four, a whistle blew and the train slid gently into travel mode. Unbelievably, it was not over-crowded and there was only one other person sitting at their table, an older woman who looked as if she would far prefer to be sitting at home, and who announced that she was going to stay with her daughter, who lived outside Darlington.

Gail started to interrogate Edward. 'Now, I need to be much better informed about your family and home,' she said. 'You have told me the basics, but you should now brief me properly, so that I know the ropes in the Wood household.'

'Part of the idea is for you to see it with your own eyes – but let me sketch some additional stuff. Uncle James was a young officer in the regiment during the last months of the war. Although he was called up, he stayed for about four years; then his father was anxious for him to return home to take over the farm. I don't think that he resisted or resented that, but he didn't really have any choice in the matter. It seems pretty clear that he enjoyed the regiment enormously, and over the years I have met many of his contemporaries when they have come to stay for a shooting weekend, or on their way to fish further north. They impressed me sufficiently to consider the same regiment myself. Uncle James was pushing at an open door when he suggested it.

'He met Aunt Mary at the Berwickshire Hunt Ball, which was held at Duns Castle that year. She was staying with a girlfriend living in Swinton, which is a village north of Coldstream. I don't think that she was there as the girlfriend of anyone local, but it wouldn't have made any difference anyway. She has told me often enough that she set her cap at him that very first night.'

'So, this impetuous streak runs through the whole family, does it?' giggled Gail.

He smiled at her fondly. 'This isn't about being rash or impulsive. I think that the common ingredient is that, as a family, we are quick to know what we must do.

'He has asked her repeatedly and forcefully to marry him. I explained to you that she could never picture herself as a married woman. In her mind, remaining unwed is her declaration of independence. I have to say that I wish that they would marry. The State will take your money when you die by taxing you out of hard-earned capital. Ho-hum. Despite her intellectual approach, she has been a most loyal and devoted wife in all but name. They have never said that they regret not having children of their own, and they have served as my surrogate parents with all the affection and dedication I could desire.

'The farm is about six hundred acres, largely arable, but with a flock of sheep. We have two dogs, a Labrador called Hector and a terrier called Gimli. Hector is a real soppy date, but also a very effective gundog. I intend to take him with us tomorrow. Gimli will be furious with me, but he simply couldn't cope with the heather.'

'And is Uncle James shooting with us, too?'

'Yes. He is a very popular gun during the shooting season. An excellent shot, but not greedy. Not surprisingly, he taught me everything that I know about shooting. This is an annual event. There will be Harry and Michael Ridley, Uncle James and I, and normally one other shooting guest. Aunt Mary tends not to come out, but you won't be the only girl on parade. And her outdoor gear should suit you well.

'We have two couples coming for supper tomorrow night, and two more for lunch on Sunday. I hope you don't mind, but Aunt Mary is determined to give you a proper introduction to the county.'

Peterborough and York provided brief respites from the clickety-clack of the train, and their travelling companion, who

187

had been listening to the conversation discreetly as she pretended to read her book, bade them farewell with a nod to Gail, saying, 'Good luck. You should have lots of fun,' as she left them at Darlington.

They rattled over the Tyne into Newcastle absolutely on time. 'Only fifty minutes to go to Berwick,' said Edward. 'In some ways, I wish we were doing this in early May. There are two pairs of ducks who nest at the First Class end of the platform every year. It is quite extraordinary. They are totally unfazed by the trains and passengers, and the public leave them to get on with their lives. They turn the station into their own private nature reserve.'

Gail felt just a frisson of uncertainty as they pulled into Berwick. It was all well and good to start having an intriguing relationship with this tall, decisive man; but what if she couldn't get on with his family? She knew too many people whose mothers-in-law made life awkward.

Edward swung her case down from the rack, gave her a quick kiss on the forehead as she rose from her seat, and led the way to the exit. There was nobody waiting for them on the platform, which didn't surprise or deter Edward. They clip-clopped up the stairs, across an overhead walkway and down the stairs to the ticket hall. There, waiting, was a woman of Gail's own size with flecks of grey in her trim brown hair, slim, elegant, dressed in jeans and a pale blue blouse, with a thin necklace of pearls. She positively beamed at them and grabbed Edward in a hug, before standing back to look at Gail. Impulsively, she ignored Gail's hand and scooped her up into a motherly embrace which couldn't fail to melt a heart. 'Terrific,' she said. 'I would have recognised you at a thousand paces after Edward's description. You drive, darling,' she said, handing the keys to Edward. 'I want to chat to this young lady without distraction.'

The journey from Berwick to Duddo was only fifteen minutes along a road that begged to be driven quickly. With no traffic, it was straight but with four large bends to keep the driver honest. Gail had no idea where she was, although she could see big country with a backdrop of large hills which, she learned, were the Cheviots. Mary had put Gail in the front, placing herself behind Edward so that she could look at Gail side on. It took her no more than ninety seconds to have Gail chatting away about her family, her work and her history. This was interrogation as a high art, Edward realised. It had taken him several meetings to secure the same information, and he looked fondly in the mirror at the woman who had brought him up as her own.

'Home sweet home,' he said quietly, as they turned left down a narrow tarmac drive towards a four-square traditional Northumbrian farmhouse. The drive converted into a circle with a central grass lawn, in the middle of which sat a stone sundial. Two dogs raced out of the open door, barking and bouncing with the glee of animals that love to greet all visitors. So, what if it was family again.

'The Land Rover isn't here, so James must be somewhere out on the farm,' said Mary. 'Let me show you where you will be, Gail. Freshen up and join us in the kitchen. It's time for gin.'

Edward followed the two women upstairs and quietly dumped Gail's bag in her room. He ambled downstairs and walked out of the front door to enjoy the dogs for a few minutes, before turning round and going towards the back of the house, where an enormous open kitchen boasted an Aga, a large bare wooden table and solid worktops. The dogs followed and dropped into their beds, which were under a sideboard opposite the Aga. Seconds later, Mary appeared and touched his arm. 'Edward, you have the most marvellous young woman here. Don't blow it.' She grinned. 'Now, let's have gin, or are you being unhelpfully sober?'

'No, I could murder an ice-cold gin, thank you. Let me fix one for you, too. Les allows me to drink in moderation, so I judge that I can make the most of this weekend.'

'And you are looking terribly fit, Edward. Is Les giving you hell?'

'I'll tell you all about it later, but I have to admit that I haven't been this fit since Montreal. And we are doing some really interesting work. I told you the basics, all driven by the strategy that Carlo Fassi delivered with John Curry. We have started right at the beginning, doing foot and arm exercises that I haven't thought about since I started this sport so many years ago. Thanks to Les, we are using a much more intelligent approach to the art of winning. If we can't do it this time, it won't be for lack of effort.'

Gail appeared. She looked cool, relaxed and content. She couldn't have been happier with meeting Mary Davidson, who clearly adored Edward and was more than ready to welcome his new girlfriend. 'Gin?' asked Edward.

As he lifted another heavy cut-glass tumbler from a cupboard, Mary said, 'Supper is ready, but we need our drink, and I want to quickly show you the outline of the house so that you never feel out of place. Edward, you can prepare yourself for the return of our lord and master, who will need a drink, too. We girls are going on a tour.'

Edward presented the glass to her and Gail took a long, appreciative sip. 'Heavens, that's good. Why is it so much better in summer?'

'Lots more ice,' noted Edward.

'Right, come along, Gail.' Mary led the way out of the kitchen into the adjacent dining room. 'We normally eat in the kitchen, but we'll use this room tomorrow evening and on

Sunday. It just makes the dumping of dishes in the kitchen much less sordid.'

They moved across a corridor into what was evidently a drawing room. A room decked with three oil paintings and many watercolours, Gail immediately spotted family pictures on the grand piano which sat in a corner opposite the door. Unsurprisingly, she was drawn to look at the formal and informal photos, dominated by a colour portrait in a silver frame of Edward in blues. She looked closely. There were two medals, the inner one with a ribbon that had a vertical purple stripe bracketed by two white stripes. At the bottom was a simple silver cross. The other medal was clearly the General Service Medal with two clasps and, as she studied it more closely, she could see a bronze oak leaf on the ribbon. She stood back, looked out of the window to gather her thoughts, looked at the picture again, then turned to Mary. 'Is that what I think it is?' she asked.

'Oh, dear. This is so Edward. Of course, he hasn't told you, has he?'

'No. He hasn't. He is so self-effacing. I learned about his Olympic history only when a friend of his let us all know at a dinner party. I have to drag personal stuff out of him with a hook and chain.'

'Don't beat him up, Gail. He has always felt that he should not have received the award. He earned it when he was nineteen in Aden, where he and another young officer both got MCs. He has insisted to James and I that his troop were the heroes, not him. He is given to reminding us how these things work. If the organisation does well, the boss gets the prizes. As it happens, Tom Elliott, who was commanding at the time and put Edward forward for the award, was a troop leader with James at the end of the war. James interrogated him, because we couldn't persuade the boy to tell us about the action that led to the citation. Tom was perfectly robust. It was clear that

Edward really did deserve that medal. And to put his resistance into perspective, the first we knew of it was when the announcement was published in the papers and family friends telephoned to confirm that it was our Edward. He had known for almost two weeks. It was the same with his Mention in Despatches, which he was awarded after his last tour in Northern Ireland. He never said a word. To tell you the absolute truth, I don't think he ever reflects upon the incidents or the awards. The MC was won eleven years ago, and it is a racing certainty that he only ever considers it when he has to wear medals on parade.'

Gail snorted. 'I have told him several times that everything he does is so intense. He has to win, but then he is too reserved to say anything about it.'

'Between us girls,' Mary said softly, 'I put it down to the loss of his parents twenty years ago. Although James and I think of him as our son and, in fairness, he thinks of us as his only family, he has been on a lifetime mission to demonstrate to his long-lost natural parents that he is capable and resilient. You will find a depth of faith in a God, and a commitment to do the very best for all men. Of course, he is a man, and men are much more vulnerable than they like to believe. You and I need to have a longer girls' chat, because we both know that he has lost his heart totally and, whether you want it or not, you hold his emotional future in your hands. He would never do anything to hurt you. Already, in every small action, I can see how he is considering how best to impress and intrigue you. His failure to mention something which is, to him, so minor that it doesn't merit the report, is not a man being devious. In fact, if he ever did consider it, he would see it as unfair play to bring the award into the formula. Does that make sense?'

'Oh, yes. Of course it does. You know, I had no intention of developing a long-term relationship with anybody. I am focused on my career, and I have been having fun going out with lots of other young people merely to enjoy growing up. But, but… he is the most extraordinary person. He has a really good brain, he is magnificently well read, thanks in large measure to your support and direction, he does everything supremely well, he is the antithesis of us civil servants, but is successfully performing a role at the heart of government. And to back it all up, I discover by chance that he is a hero. What does a girl do?'

Mary smiled at her and put out her arms. 'This could be catching,' whispered Gail, as she enjoyed her second maternal embrace from Edward's aunt. 'I am going to give my father hell. I guarantee he knows about Edward's MC, because he rang my godfather, who is Edward's boss. And I only learned that a couple of weeks ago. Why are these men so secretive?'

More excited barking heralded the return of James, who, far from doing important things on the farm, admitted that he had dropped in on the Drakes in Etal for a quick Friday night gin. He looked at Gail carefully. 'I insist upon Droit du Seigneur,' he said, and put a hand on each of her shoulders to peck her firmly on each cheek. 'You must forgive an old man for insisting upon kissing pretty girls,' he chuckled. 'Welcome to Duddo. We need people like you to remind us about the wider world.'

Supper was convivial, noisy, warm and totally family. Gail participated as an equal member, but had the opportunity to listen, watch and enjoy. Edward was relaxed and open about his training and, to some extent, his work. He glanced at Gail and reported how surprised he had been to discover that his boss was Gail's godfather. 'She might have told me,' he said in mock complaint.

'Now that's not fair,' said Gail. 'You never told me exactly what you did in the Cabinet Office. How was I to know that you weren't the teaboy that you claimed to be?'

'And you have never told us what you do,' said James. 'Will you not give us a clue now?'

Edward paused. He was with the three people whom he valued most in the whole world. 'Of course I can. It's not terribly exciting. I am, if you like, the desk officer for Ireland. My remit covers North and South, and it looks at the economy, agriculture, politics, commerce and industry; and, of course, terrorism. But, because Irish terrorism is the government's top priority, I do spend more hours on that than I do on other facets of the work. I report directly to the Chairman of the Joint Intelligence Committee, Sir James Harrington, who was best man to Gail's parents when they married in Berlin in 1949.'

'Tell us a little bit more, darling,' said Mary.

'Well, I deal with the major departments of State: the Home Office, Foreign Office, Northern Ireland Office, Secret Intelligence Service, Security Service, GCHQ, MoD and Metropolitan Police. All of their summarised intelligence lands up on my desk, along with the detailed reports of 14 Intelligence Company, who are our most effective secret weapon against terrorism. I have a security clearance that most Whitehall warriors don't know exists, because some of the sources of information and their content are so very highly sensitive. Ninety percent of what I write can be read by fewer than one hundred people in the United Kingdom. Every week I write something that is published in the "red book", which is the government's intelligence report of what goes on in the world. Copy number one goes to the Queen.'

They all sat quietly reflecting upon this information, which was infinitely more than Edward had ever reported to his family in the past.

'So, you are a paper warrior?' asked James.

'Yes and no. Yes, in that I have to assimilate information from our global partnerships and reflect it in carefully honed bureaucratic reports. No, in that I do have the opportunity to help active operations. You are not to repeat this anywhere else, please, but I had a fascinating day a little over two months ago when I flew out of Northolt on a day trip to Frankfurt on an aircraft of the Queen's Flight to collect an M60 machine gun from the US Army. I brought it back and handed it over to a sergeant, who happened to be from the regiment, who is serving with 14 Company. The ultimate product of that trip will be the destruction of the terrorists who use the six M60s given to them by misguided patriots living in Boston.'

'Working closer to the tea lady,' giggled Gail. 'You old fraud, Edward Davidson.' She looked at her hosts. 'This man tried to persuade me that he was a sort of minor cipher clerk.'

The family relaxed comfortably. This was the right way to greet a new member to the team. Those that still had a glass of wine sipped carefully.

'Right,' said James. 'We have to leave at 8.30a.m., I regret. We will have breakfast at 7.30. You don't have to come, Gail, but I know that our hosts would love to see you. Perhaps you can try on some of Mary's protective gear before you go to bed. Are you going to manage Hector, or am I?' he asked, as he looked at Edward.

'I would love to. He can be on a lead with Gail, and I will manage the whistle.' Hector, hearing his name, lifted his head from the comfort of his bed. 'And I will give the boys a walk before we go to bed.'

James and Mary tactfully decided that they were off to bed, leaving Edward and Gail standing looking at each other. 'Will you give me a hug, please, Edward?'

'Try to stop me,' he said softly, taking her in his arms. She laid her head on his chest and he rested his head on top of hers.

'Do you trust me?' she whispered.

'Of course. What brought that on?'

'If you really do trust me, I want you to always be very honest with me. It was only as I was being shown around the house by Mary that I learned something about you that you haven't revealed. I find you intriguing because you do everything so well. You are extremely intelligent and well read, and you are the only Olympic sportsman that I have ever met. But I did not know that you had won a Military Cross. That is a very serious gallantry award, and you never thought to mention it.'

He hugged her a little tighter. 'My love, you would have thought less of me if I had trotted out the information over one of our few meals together. And I must tell you frankly that I have always felt like an imposter. It was my troop's action that created the conditions for some form of public recognition. Regimentally, we are not very good at putting people up for medals. Colonel Tom must have been pretty desperate for our tour to be capped with some metalwork.'

'Well, Mary told me that James had spoken to your Colonel Tom, who said that you had amply merited the award. Always be ultra-honest with me, Edward.'

They exchanged a tentative kiss. 'I will always be ultra-honest with you, Gail. I promise. Now, I had better take those two dogs for their late-night stroll.'

'And I will come with you. I need to see more of this farm.'

Edward went to the back door, took a whistle with a lanyard off a hook and blew it softly three times. Hector and Gimli were immediately ready for action. Gail said, 'It's amazing how light it is at this time of night. You don't need a torch at all, and it's after ten-thirty.'

'I once played tennis with friends at eleven o'clock at night,' responded Edward. 'And it is light before four in the morning. Marvellous time of year. But it is the absolute opposite in winter, when it gets dark at four in the afternoon.' He gripped her hand and they strolled out towards the farm buildings, with the dogs quietly sniffing for new smells.

As they returned to the house, Gail announced that she was going to have a bath. She would come to give him a good-night kiss later. A very happy Edward locked the back door, turned off the downstairs lights and climbed the stairs to his room, which had its own en suite loo and shower. Quickly, he stripped off, took a shower, dried his hair and popped on some boxer shorts, before slipping into bed with the book that he had been reading on his last visit home.

There was a tentative tap on the door. 'Are you decent?' Gail asked.

'I would prefer not to be,' he smiled.

'I am relieved that you sleep in a double bed,' she said, and smoothly slid under the duvet.

'I promised that I would not misbehave with you, dear one. You must be very careful with temptation.'

'Well, a girl needs a hug every now and again. You seem to be wearing boxers, and I am in a nightie. We are almost prim.'

Edward turned off the light and rolled onto his left side, putting his right arm around Gail and stroking her back. 'Oh, Gail, you are so wonderful.' He gave her a gentle kiss on the lips.

'Mmmm. Keep doing that,' she said, and slid her left leg over him. The kiss became a little more intense. She drew back. 'You seem to have a truncheon in here between us,' she muttered, and moved her hand to stroke the offending weapon. Edward groaned.

'I swear I cannot be held responsible for my actions if you keep on doing that,' he murmured.

'I said over supper a few weeks ago that I had looked inside the packaging but hadn't seen the working parts. All I am trying to do is fulfil the mission.' The laughter was very near the surface. Edward lay there with his imagination running wild. With no apparent effort, Gail slid over him completely and sat firmly on his erection. 'Will you turn the light on, please?' she asked.

Edward reached out one long arm and turned on the light. 'I think, if we are going to get to know each other better,' said Gail, 'we need to see what's on offer.' And with that, she raised herself slightly and pulled off her nightie.

She was all that he had imagined. A smooth, taut body with rounded breasts and small nipples, currently very firm and pointing at him. His gaze wandered down her figure, which curved inwards before reaching her hips, which were trim but entirely feminine. He could see that all of her hair was the same natural colour. 'I need to remove these,' she said, lifting herself again and, with some difficulty because of his physical excitement, slipped his boxer shorts down towards his ankles. He used his feet to complete the exercise. She nestled down again, sitting firmly on him without attempting to join fully. Very slowly and gently, she started to move back and forth.

'Gail, my darling girl, if you keep doing that, I am bound to explode. It could become very messy.'

'If I don't keep doing it, I will explode,' she giggled. 'We have a decision to make, Major Davidson, and I am an equal partner in the process.'

'You know perfectly well that I am longing to make love to you, but I also want to demonstrate that I do not want to treat you as a casual bit of skirt on the side. Gail, I love you, worship you and want to honour you properly.'

Gail paused for thought, then moved off his body, knelt beside him and took him firmly in her right hand. She bent down, kissed the top of his penis, saying, 'Circumcised, I see,' then she licked the length of him until she took him in her mouth.

He closed his eyes, held her head briefly, then gently pulled her upright. 'If you really want me to misbehave, you beautiful woman, I am going to remember this night forever.'

Gail gave a self-satisfied smile as she climbed back onto Edward's body and this time slipped him smoothly into her. They rested unmoving as he used his muscles to make his penis throb. She lay down fully on his chest and he put his hands on her backside, slowly moving one hand down the cheeks, then the other to stroke her lips where he had penetrated her. He tried to push even deeper in, although there was no scope for that. They could not be any closer.

They lay unmoving, both now flexing internal muscles to give exquisite pleasure to the other. Suddenly, Gail's body trembled and she breathed an exhausted breath. 'Stay there,' said Edward. His hands lightly rippled down her back as she pulled her legs tightly together. A second tremor raced the length of her body.

'It's no good. I really do have to move now,' she said, before starting a slow, rhythmic rocking.

The anticipated explosion was not delayed for long. They came together, she for a third time and he for the first. Breathless, they lay entangled, unable to move.

'My God, Edward, you really do excel at everything,' she said. 'I had no idea that making love could be so multiply blessed.'

'Give me twenty minutes and we can try it again.' They held each other tightly, exchanging little kisses for a few minutes. 'It seems that I don't need twenty minutes after all,' he laughed, rolled her on to her back and raised himself above her. 'You can help,' he said.

She pulled him into her a second time and they moved in slow harmony. Edward was desperate to let go, but was determined to help her over the finish line first. As he felt her tremors start again, he developed long penetrating thrusts, repeatedly withdrawing as far as he dared, then pushing hard in to total immersion. As soon as he knew that she had climaxed, he experienced a blinding, surging light, his legs collapsed and he struggled to breathe. They lay, winded, hands gently stroking each other.

'I need a hankie or towel, Edward. You have pumped so much into me that I am going to be like a waterfall. My research has taught me that on the basis of you coming twice, you have given me at least eighty million sperm for my single egg to select.' He reached out and found his hankie, which he gently placed between her legs.

'Is it likely that I have made you pregnant?' he asked.

'No, I have taken the precaution of putting myself on the pill. It is a little early for us to start breeding, don't you think?'

'Well, as long as we can practise first. But I would love to give you babies. Are you going to stay with me tonight?'

'I want to sleep with you all night, my man, but I don't want to be caught out by James and Mary. I don't want them to think ill of me.'

'Well, they are not in a position to be critical, if you think about it. They have enjoyed over thirty years of unmarried sex.'

'I know, but I must maintain the fiction that I am a good girl. Maybe I can slip in here tomorrow night for an all-night stay? If they don't approve, I won't be banished to an outside barn for the next night, because we will be back in London. So, let's have a little snooze. I will leave before dawn.'

The light was just beginning to filter through the curtains, waking Edward, for whom the dawn was an alarm clock. He gently stroked Gail to wake her. She stretched, rubbed her hand down his leg and, with a lingering kiss, she grasped the hankie and got out of bed. Clenching her legs, she slipped on her nightie and quietly opened the door. With a cheeky grin, she blew a kiss and gently closed the door behind her.

Chapter Eighteen

'What a fabulous day,' Gail said, as she picked up another glass that had been washed carefully by Edward, filled with hot water and placed on the drainer.

'You have done brilliantly today, our Gail. It is a long hike up and down those hills, and not made any easier by Hector pulling on the lead like a tractor. Ten brace of grouse is a good day's work for that shoot.'

'Aunt Mary, it was very good of you to ask the Mathesons and Ainscoughs over for dinner. They are utterly reliable guests: amusing, well informed, excellent hosts themselves, and they know exactly when to leave. I won't be staying up much longer.' Edward finished the last glass, dried his hands and watched Gail finish her part of the contract. 'I'll just take the boys out quickly.'

He left. James was in the drawing room, having a quiet kip with a glass of port on a small table beside him. Mary smiled at Gail. 'You have been a marvellous help, Gail. Thank you so much for making sure that we had our dinner on time. Now, you take yourself off to bed. And at the risk of embarrassing you, you don't need to bother with the subterfuge of going to your room.'

Gail blushed. 'Oh, dear. I have been found out.'

'Don't be silly. I am genuinely thrilled for the pair of you. And you wouldn't be able to conceal it from me. Your body language shouts the message that you are enjoying your time together immensely. I was very impressed that you made the effort to go back to your room in the early hours of this morning, but you deserve to wake up in his bed tomorrow. We are pretty open-minded in this house, for obvious reasons. And to reassure you, Edward has not, to my knowledge, ever dragged other girls into his bed here. As we both know, he would regard it as ungentlemanly to invade a female guest's room, so you are the pioneer. Lord, I do hope this all works out for you both.'

They hugged each other and Mary bestowed a loving kiss on Gail's cheek. 'If you hurry, you should give him rather a nice surprise!'

Gail moved swiftly up the stairs, grabbed her toothbrush, a towel and a flannel, then made her way to Edward's room. Five minutes later, she lay naked and snug under the duvet with a warm sense of anticipation.

Edward didn't see her as he walked into the room until he reached to turn on the bedside light. 'Now there's a lovely sight,' he said. 'Clearly you are no longer worried about Aunt Mary's opinion?'

'She is already turning into a wonderful friend. She has known all along and was aware of our adventure last night,' said Gail. 'She told me to hurry up and surprise you.'

Edward laughed, partly at his beautiful girlfriend and partly at his scheming aunt. Quickly, he dropped his clothes on a chair, brushed his teeth and gave himself a quick personal washdown. He slipped into bed and put his arms around his bedmate. 'I need a quick snooze,' she said. 'Wake me.'

She turned around and they formed two spoons. Edward turned off the light and adjusted his position so that his eternal erection rested neatly in the curve at the top of her buttocks. Time clicked by, with Edward contentedly holding one breast and trying to ignore the throbbing of his penis. Twenty minutes later, he could feel a shift in the pattern of Gail's sleep. She carefully moved one hand between her legs and reached back to grab Edward firmly. She pulled him towards her and gently rubbed his tip against her vulva. Then, moving her buttocks very slightly to tilt her hips, she shoved back until he was fully inside her. 'The trick now, Edward, is to see how long you can stay like that. You get a prize if it lasts all night.'

'I've got the prize already. How on earth am I supposed to lie comatose like this?'

'Try it,' she giggled, and then started making miniscule movements while flexing her pelvic muscles.

'That is desperately unfair. Wonderful, but not in the spirit of your challenge.'

'I didn't say that we couldn't move.' She increased the motion. He put one hand on her right hip and held it firmly against his own. She countered by increasing the flexing of her pelvic muscles.

'I am a little lost here, my love. You are going to make me come before I can get anywhere near satisfying you.'

She took his hand off her hip and guided it down to her clitoris. 'Gently stimulate me here. You'll get the hang of it, because the rest of me will give you clues.'

Their bodies barely moved as Edward diligently learned what movements and pressures suited his love. 'Ooh,' she moaned. 'Don't stop. That's absolutely perfect.' The tremor that had presaged her orgasms the previous evening rippled the length of her body. He kept going, more gently, but unrelenting. A second tremor followed seconds later. Then a third.

'It's your turn, my darling man. By all means keep doing what you are doing, but I am now going to destroy your self-control.' And with that, she started to press herself backwards and forwards in short motions. She realised that she was succeeding when the pressure of his hand on her moved back to her hip and she felt the hot rush of his semen pulsing up inside her.

'So much for staying in that position all night,' he said. 'You are a most beautiful and dangerous witch. There is no way that I could have prevented you from winning.'

'Well, we both need a little sleep if we are to be polite to people tomorrow.' She reached under her pillow and removed a large flannel. Carefully, she wiped him as he withdrew and she kept the flannel in place between her legs as she turned to face him. 'Thank you, Edward dearest. You are a wonderful lover. I am going to have some more of that in the morning, please.'

As was his habit, Edward woke as the dawn lightened the edges of the curtains. He breathed deeply, inhaling Gail's scent. Lightly, he stroked her back, but she was deeply asleep. Contented, he snuggled down with one arm across her stomach.

He was lying on his back when he felt the duvet being flung back. The curtains were part open and Gail, naked in all her majesty, was standing at the bottom of the bed, looking at his body. 'Isn't it strange that something as vulnerable as a man's limp penis can convert into such a fearsome and exciting tool?' she asked.

'Thank heavens,' he replied. 'Of course, mine is standard equipment. I knew a man once who had his willy tattooed. His girlfriend was pretty unimpressed because all she could read on the limp member was SNCF. Of course, when he became excited she could read the full message, which said "Societe Nationale des Chemins de Fer".' Gail laughed.

'Please don't try anything stupid like that,' she said. It would be terrible to damage the mechanism that allows it to be such a good friend.' She climbed back onto the bed and they entwined arms and legs, sealing the deal with a long, deep kiss. Edward took a quick look at his bedside clock and said, 'Right, you challenged me to stay in position last night and I failed. Let's see how we both manage now.' He rolled on to her front and moved astride her thighs, leaning forward to kiss her.

He started to make long thrusts into her. 'There is something about angles,' he said, 'but I prefer to look you in the eye. You are such a beautiful, sexy woman.' He raised himself to his knees and lifted her, placing his hands under her bottom. She smiled lazily and went to work with her devastating pelvic muscles. The pressure built in both and Edward feared that he wouldn't be able to hold on. She moved to indicate that she wanted to go on top, so they rolled until she was lying prone along the length of his body. As they had done on the first occasion, his hands moved down to stroke the lips of her vagina, then he ran his hands smoothly up her back to her head, which he took, raised and kissed deeply. 'Now, we don't move.'

They lay motionless, apart from the internal working of highly effective muscles. He stroked her back again as she started to rock. 'No. Please don't move. It will make me lose all control. I am going to make sure that you have some pleasure before I do,' Edward instructed.

The tension increased as Edward's hands paid light touching visits to her body. Both desperately wanted to move, but the deliberate pause heightened their senses exquisitely, until Gail's tell-tale tremor made her body shudder. She emitted a small sigh as a second tremor ran the length of her body. 'I have you, my darling. Just lie on me,' he urged.

They lay, not moving a muscle. Gail said, 'I cannot go on like this. You have made me climax so often that I won't have any energy to stand and be polite to people over lunch.' She pushed herself upright so that she was sitting on him, before she started to move up and down on her knees. He gripped her firmly at the waist, not wanting her to go so high that he fell out, and also to ensure that she spent some time stationary with their bodies pressed together as closely as possible. Finally, with a slight twist of the hips, she virtually sucked the life-blood out of him.

'Oh, my God, how did you do that? It really is all about angles and position. Dear, darling Gail. Thank you.'

They lay entwined as the clock ticked round towards 6.30a.m. 'We had better get up at about eight to eight-fifteen,'

Edward murmured. 'If you're game, let's have a short sleep, and if you can cope with my enthusiasm, we could have enough time for one more session?'

'Where do you get your endurance and energy, Edward?'

'Well, if you think about it, I am now almost as fit as I was at the Montreal Olympics. The fitter you are, the better you perform.'

'Perform! My God, this is a masterclass.'

They lay side by side, with her left leg over him. He moved his hips closer and rubbed himself against her, then slipped smoothly into place. They moved in unison, short, thoughtful thrusts slowly growing in intensity until Edward realised that there was no going back for him. 'I am sorry, my darling, but this can't wait.' Gail grinned contentedly. She realised that she now knew exactly how to distract his perfect self-control and, much as she adored his ability to make her go over the top, it was always good for a girl to understand the key to her man. Edward felt himself going limp, so swiftly reached for a handkerchief on the bedside table, passing it down to help Gail with the aftermath of so much love-making.

They fell into a deep, motionless sleep, still wrapped in each other's arms. With a jerk, Edward came to and saw that the time was already eight-twenty. He stroked Gail's back and her eyes fluttered open. 'Time to get up. Let's have a shower together.'

They rolled off the bed and Edward turned on the shower, checked the temperature, then ushered Gail into the cubicle in front of him. She raised her head to face the water and lifted her hair to let it soak her completely. Edward grabbed a bar of soap and gently started to lather her shoulders, torso, then lower towards her hips, where he gave specific attention to his recent playground, down her legs and then each foot, one by one. She took the soap from him and immediately went for his penis, which was once again rearing its head in an enthusiastic way. 'Edward, down, boy. You have far too much energy, and

I am not at all sure that my female garden can maintain the pace.' She rubbed him firmly so that the lather frothed around her hands. The erection remained firmly in place. 'Do you want me to finish this off?'

'It wouldn't be fair on you,' he said. 'I have had more fun than I deserve. It will go down eventually.' She shook her head with a loving smile, put the soap down and rinsed him thoroughly, before getting down on her knees, gently holding his testicles in one hand and the stem of his manhood in the other. She placed her lips around the glans and started to lick him with an erotic flicking of the tongue. Edward adjusted his legs to stand firmly, and carefully held Gail's head as she added momentum. 'I will give you a clue before I come,' he said. 'I really don't want to ruin your taste buds.' But this was the briefest of their weekend encounters, because Edward was unable to resist the emotional and physical expertise of his lover. As he felt himself coming, he gently pushed Gail's head back, but she pressed her lips firmly around him and continued with the licking motion until he spurted inside her. She looked up at him with sparkling eyes. 'Oh,' he sighed, 'I don't think I can get enough of you.' He lifted her to her feet and kissed her deeply.

By the time that Gail had dried her hair, Edward was starting to make scrambled eggs. James and Mary had greeted him with knowing looks, but refrained from overt references to sleeping well or badly. Gail's arrival was treated in much the same way, although she blushed deeply as she leaned down to give James a peck on the cheek and he grinned at her. Mary got up and gave her another of her famous hugs. 'After we have some of Edward's world-famous scrambled eggs with our local bacon, I am going to push you two out for a walk with the dogs. You might want to take them behind Shellacres and walk down to the Till,' she suggested. 'Then, when you come back, we will lay the dining-room table and get ready for the next invasion.'

The lunch party was noisy. Bill and Suzanne Drake lived a mile away in Etal, while Izzy and George Tufnell farmed over the border in Berwickshire. It turned out that Suzanne had once worked, as she said, for the Ministry of Defence, which Gail and Edward immediately and accurately translated into the Security Service. This gave Gail a little extra support in getting to grips with the personality and culture of North Northumberland and the Scottish borders. By now it was clear to Edward that Gail had formed a special bond of friendship with his aunt. The pair of them laughed at the same things at the same time, and frequently turned to look for confirmation or approval for some small act or statement. James viewed both women with an amused, uncritical air and nodded in with quiet satisfaction at his surrogate son. 'Look after this one, boy. She is very special,' he offered, as they both stood mixing drinks for their guests before lunch.

'I am completely smitten, Uncle James. I have never met anyone with so much vitality, sympathy and humour. She is wildly intelligent, extremely well read and just plain fun to be with. If I thought I could get away with it before meeting her parents, I would ask her to marry me immediately.'

'Well, you are certainly old enough and doing sufficiently well to support a wife. Do you know what her thoughts are?'

'No. We haven't talked about that yet. It is only a matter of weeks since I asked her permission to wage a campaign to win her heart. I daresay that was an unromantic way to start our journey, but she has me down as a military man who plans his strategy and then conducts it. I saw no reason to blur the edges with mythological difficulties. And I can acknowledge my limitations: I told her that I like to win, not for domination, but because I know where I am going.'

James clapped him on the back. 'Go and meet her parents quickly. I judge that you two are in quite a hurry. I do wish I could persuade your dear aunt to tie the knot with me.'

The guests finally left at twenty past four, and Mary told them to forget all the washing-up because they should leave at 4.30p.m. to get to the station for the 5.00p.m. train. In a flurry, Gail slipped upstairs, went to the loo and closed her case. She hadn't seen much of the bedroom she had been allotted, but she loved the house, the farm and its people. She trotted downstairs. James and the dogs were waiting in an orderly line for the departure ceremony, which involved a huge hug for James, much fuss for Hector and Gimli and a leap into the car, which Mary had decided to drive herself. Edward climbed into the back and they set off.

At the station, Mary parked in front of the main door, switched off and got out of the car. She gave Edward his hug and kiss, then took Gail in her arms and said, 'You feel like a daughter and a sister at one and the same time. I pray that you two take this seriously. We want you as part of our lives.' Turning with a sudden tear in her eyes, she got into the car, started it and drove off before she revealed too much emotion.

They didn't talk much on the four-hour journey south. Getting into London at 9.00p.m., Edward insisted on getting a taxi, which took them to Prince of Wales Drive. Asking the driver to hold on for a few moments, Edward took Gail's bag to her front door and turned to give and receive a long, loving kiss. 'I hate to leave you, my love, but I have to be at work pronto in the morning. Moreover, you and I need to do a little thinking and talking about how this develops. I am absolutely your servant. I long to be with you, although I am desperate not to stifle you. Now you have some idea of what we are like at home, where you are already perceived as the most important fixture. It was evident to me that Uncle James and Aunt Mary fell for you as heavily as I have. Will you call me in the next day or two so that we can have a discussion?'

'Dear Edward, you have certainly conducted your campaign in the most forceful military manner.' He stiffened, wondering whether he had been over the top, but she recognised this and said, 'No, don't be an idiot. That was no criticism. It was the acknowledgement of how seriously I take your thinking on how to win my heart. I never thought I would say this to any man in the foreseeable future, but the combination of your loving nature, your ability, intelligence, humour, honour, incredible military record, and exceptional skills as a lover leave me totally defenceless. For the first time in my life, I feel fulfilled as a woman. Edward, let me put it the way that you have done already: I want to have your babies.'

'Ooh!' Edward cried, literally. The tears ran down his face. 'I love you so much. I can't believe that I have persuaded you that I am worthy of you.' She gently wiped his tears and kissed him.

'You are an irresistible force, my man. We need to get you to meet my parents, who will be hugely protective of me. They trust me to make good decisions, but I value their opinion and high regard. I will talk to them, but might it be possible for you to come home next weekend?'

'If that's what suits you and your family, it's a date. And what about your sister? Of all people, I recognise that I need her thumbprint of approval.'

She laughed. 'Oh, yes, you certainly do. I am going to suggest that we meet her for supper before next weekend. Is that OK?'

With that, Edward gave her a lingering kiss, waited until she had gone through the front door of the apartment block, and returned to his taxi.

Jane was out somewhere, so Gail opened the fridge, poured herself a glass of white wine and sat down by the telephone to ring the old folks.

'Hi, Mum, I thought I would give you a call. I am back in the London flat, having had a marvellous weekend in the North.'

She listened as her mother asked a barrage of questions. 'They are the most wonderful, open, warm-hearted and generous people,' she said of James and Mary. 'As you know, they are a little unconventional because they have lived together unmarried for more than thirty years. Mary seems determined that she maintains her independence by being unwed, but the truth is that she is the most loyal, hard-working wife. They make a terrific couple. And Edward is so transparently their loving son. It is very hard to see inside the mind of a man who lost both of his parents as a child. In fact, Mary believes that the loss is a crucial factor in the character and performance of the man we know today. And on that score, I think I have a bone to pick with you and Daddy. I know that he spoke to my dear godfather, so he must have learned that Edward won the Military Cross in Aden in 1967. I wish you had told me, because I only discovered it when I saw a photographic portrait of him in blues and wearing medals.'

'Ah. Yes. Let me quickly put your father on the phone, and we can carry on chatting afterwards.' The phone exchanged hands.

'Darling, I did learn about Edward's MC and I am sorry that I didn't mention it to you. I realise that I was being far too protective of you by checking him out with your godfather. It would have been helpful for you to know, but curiously I think that it may prove to have been a better outcome that you discovered by seeing his family and home. Knowing you, you would probably have thought less of him if he had spilled the beans himself.'

'Too right,' Gail responded, 'but all of the wonderful and glamorous things that he has done have been concealed from me until someone else has publicised them. He is almost taciturn about his achievements.'

'And that matters to you, my darling?'

'Yes, Daddy. It matters a lot. Although I am ringing to report on my wonderful weekend, I am also giving you both the first hint of something more serious. I would very much like to bring Edward home this next weekend. You need to meet him and I need to see him with my family as well as his own.'

Will Ritchie signed off, handing the phone back to Ellie. 'So, you are truly interested in this young man?' she queried.

'I was interested before the weekend, but now I am totally lost. He is… he is just the most fascinating, loving, human being. All that he does, he does extremely well, and spending this brief time with him in his own environment made me feel like a mature woman for the first time in my life.'

Her mother said nothing for a second, reflecting, before asking the sort of question that mothers hesitate to ask their adult daughters. 'And have you…?'

'Mummy, I am twenty-five years old. I have been to university. I have kissed the odd frog, so I wasn't a virgin before this weekend. Edward is so proper and honourable that he clearly wasn't going to take advantage of me. So, I am really pleased that I took the initiative. It was worth every second.'

'So, do you want him in your bedroom next weekend?'

'No. I think not, thank you. He would be embarrassed on his first visit to our home. But you and Daddy are to be uncharacteristically deaf when I make my way to his room!' Her mother spluttered with laughter. 'The diplomat's daughter,' she said.

Chapter Nineteen

Edward arrived at the restaurant a clear twenty minutes before he expected Gail or her sister, Bella, to turn up. Michel greeted him with his customary warmth. 'You are playing the field with two lady friends?' he queried.

'No, Michel. I have as my guests the woman that I hope to make my bride, and you know her well now. But the important person tonight is her sister Bella, who is attending in order to check me out. If she disapproves, my campaign will suffer.'

Michel laughed, delighted that he could observe the theatre of this engaging young man seeking to prove himself. Fifteen minutes later, Gail swept into the restaurant, waved at Michel and gave Edward a smacking kiss and hug. She looked fabulous in a flowery summery skirt with a pearl coloured blouse and a small brooch of a salamander on her left breast. 'Are you nervous?' she asked Edward.

'Terrified. If she disapproves, I have no idea how to overcome the sales objections.'

'Don't worry, you idiot. She is going to love you.'

It took another ten minutes for Bella to make her entrance. The relationship to her elder sister was evident, although she was possibly an inch taller and her hair was darker. Edward and Gail both rose to their feet, Gail to receive a sisterly kiss, while Edward held out a hand for a more formal first greeting. 'Oh, my God, I can see what you mean,' said Bella; 'he is frightfully straight. Come here, you stupid man. I can't shake hands with a potential brother-in-law,' with which she planted warm kisses on his cheeks in a three-course French style.

Edward nodded at Michel, who introduced the menu and wine list. Edward handed the wine list to Gail, and Bella tilted her head, raising an eyebrow as he did so. 'I know about the excellence of your father's tutelage,' he said. 'I would rather bow to the experience of either of you than pretend to be all macho by ordering something you hated.' Bella smiled an acknowledgement, noting this down as the plus point in a man who recognised his companions' skill.

'I have heard endless boring reports about you from this horrid sister of mine, but you can tell me what you are not good at,' she challenged.

'Wow. Straight in with the hacking and slicing,' Edward smiled. 'Are you sure that you don't fence?' Bella shook her head. 'I am not sure that I want to expose all of my frailties, but in the interests of creating fraternal relations, I will own up to a terrible emotional streak. If I hear gorgeous music, say a wonderful hymn with trumpets, drums, and descants, I automatically weep. I cannot help it. Immediate waterworks. Let me admit that when I dropped Gail at her flat on Sunday night, she said something that completely seared my soul and I couldn't stop the tears. She must have realised that I was terminally potty.'

The two girls looked at each other fondly. Gail had reported this to her sister already, and Bella felt deeply reassured that Edward was ready to be so open and honest with her at their very first meeting.

'I am interested that your first example of your softer side was something religious. Are you an evangelist?'

'Oh, Lord, no. I do have a very sincere, deep conviction that there is a benign presence, just as I believe that there is an opposite, dangerous and thoroughly malign force. I would have difficulty in arguing that we are merely an organic accident. Maybe my inner psyche believes that you need to subscribe to an insurance policy. My creed is to do right by all mankind. But you won't find me trying to convert non-believers to follow the faith. They have a right to their opinions; I just happen to think that they are mistaken.'

This philosophical speech was Gail's first real glimpse of Edward's core principles. Bella, who was a wayward communicant, appreciated his stance. 'So, in fact, you have not shared any of your weaknesses. I would argue that a man who is happy to own up to a soft tear duct is actually rather strong emotionally.'

'Oh, dear. Weaknesses. I do have them, but because I have spent a lifetime concealing them, I have difficulty in articulating what they are. Okay...' At that moment, Michel appeared to take their orders. Of course, they hadn't looked at the menu, but Gail said that they had both enjoyed the Chateau Lamartine last time, so they would take that again. To set a lead, Gail went for the snails, followed by a small steak. Bella said she would have the same, so Edward agreed to make the order simple and followed suit. He declined to have the chips, though.

'Let me interrupt your chain of thought,' offered Bella. 'Is your determination to win at everything you do a strength or a weakness?'

'That's a very good question. Let me address the core issue about the determination to win. You know that I was brought up by my aunt and her lover?' Bella nodded. 'I was eight when my parents died, so the move to my aunt's house was a kaleidoscope of physical, emotional and mental challenges. I knew that they were taking me in as their son, but I had the lurking suspicion that they had no choice and that they were under duress. That was quite an adult consideration. I translated it into the understanding that I had to do well in order to earn their approbation. When you are a little boy of eight or nine, you half-fear that a mistake will convert into rejection.' Gail reached across the table and held his hand.

215

'A secondary factor was that although the environment was not new – after all, we had visited many times – it was not home. It wasn't the place that a little boy could leave his books or cards or bicycle or whatever, knowing that mother would indulge the mess. I moved into a house that had not seen a child day to day and was not used to the way that children behave. Nevertheless, thanks to an early introduction to Prep School, I understood how people should behave in an alien environment.

'This may sound like a culture of fear. It was not like that, but I have to accept that I was insecure. History has proven that I had no cause for that. My aunt and uncle have been model parents and I cannot think of anywhere else on earth that I am more content and at home.

'So, to answer your question, the underlying theme is that by virtue of age and disaster, I was weak, but nurture has made me strong.'

'I don't wholly agree,' said Bella. 'I would say that the underlying theme is that you have always been strong. That is your very personal nature. The nurture side of the equation has made you stronger.'

'Gosh, you two, I am getting quite giddy. Darling sis, you have interrogated my man to within an inch of his life. The pair of you have taught me more about Edward than I knew, and this is a reprise of our relationship at every stage so far. He has never volunteered to me any information about his sport, nor his military gallantry, nor his religious beliefs. I have been thoroughly derelict as a friend and lover.'

Edward reached out to take her hand again and kissed it. 'Never derelict. You are the star in the East.'

'There you go, back to religious allusions,' laughed Bella. 'I think you are probably much more holy than you pretend, Major.'

With that, the wine was produced by Michel, followed slightly later by the sizzling snails. 'I think you owe me some answers, Bella. I came tonight to present myself for your approval, but I am now starting the process of learning about – let me say this openly for the first time – my future in-laws.'

'Oh!' Bella rocked backwards. 'Have you actually popped the question?' Gail and Edward looked at each other with unfettered love. If Bella had been in any doubt, that look put an end to it.

'I think that I have an understanding with your sister, based on the last words she uttered to me on Sunday night. But I need to ensure that the whole Ritchie family is signed up to this. If you or your parents reject me, I will have to amend my campaign plan to find a way in. We are going to Sussex on Friday night, as you know. I guess it would be dangerously aggressive to ask your father for Gail's hand on arrival, although that is precisely what I want to do. I hope we will explore the outer ranges of a good relationship over the weekend. I will warmly welcome the wisdom of you two about the timing of that crucial meeting with your father.'

The girls laughed. They laughed at him and at each other. He was so solemn. Clearly, this was his absolute determination to win. He had to lay the plans, organise the environment, create some impetus, then deliver the victory.

'My guess is that Mum and Daddy won't let you leave for London without a formal agreement,' smiled Bella. 'Once they've seen the way that you two behave, they will be looking for legal ways to tie you down.'

The snails were replaced by the steak frites as Bella started to respond to Edward's fair challenge. Edward knew already that there was the strongest possible sibling link, and it seemed that Bella had in some measure adopted the profile and thinking of her elder sister. She loved her work, had good employers, and did what any full-blooded girl should do: she played the field and had no intention of focusing on a single man for some time to come.

'I was like that a few weeks ago,' mourned Gail in mock horror. 'And look what happened there.'

They all laughed briefly. Nobody wanted more wine, and they agreed that they had eaten more than enough. The two girls asked for a cup of coffee and as they were finishing it, Edward paid the bill, adding a generous tip for Michel and his team, who consistently provided the secure environment that Edward sought for his friends.

As they stood to leave, Bella grabbed Edward and gave him a long hug. 'Were you anxious about meeting me?' she asked.

'I told your sister that I was terrified!' he said.

She continued to hold on to him. 'And the result?'

'You tell me. I think that you are an absolute cracker and the men of London need to watch out. Now, I just hope that I passed muster with you.'

She kissed him, saying, 'You pass muster, Edward. Don't waste any time, please.'

Bella declined to catch a lift with them, and they wandered down White Horse Street to Piccadilly, where they caught a cab. When they reached Prince of Wales Drive, Gail grabbed Edward's hand and said, 'You are coming in. No arguments.'

He paid off the taxi and they walked arm in arm to the front door. Upstairs, they found Jane sitting with a glass of wine, watching some television show. She switched it off and got to her feet. 'I hear that you have been chatting up my old school friend,' she said, as she gave him a peck on the cheek.

They chatted for a few minutes until Jane looked at her watch, affecting surprise that it was so late. She disappeared to the bathroom to prepare for bed. The lovers sat down on the sofa, where Gail grasped Edward's hand and asked if he would stay the night. 'Will it upset Jane?' he asked.

'Jane and I have been friends since we were twelve years old. There isn't much that we don't know about each other. I imagine that she would be fearful for our relationship if you didn't stay.'

'Well, that's a deal then. I am extremely happy to accept your invitation, ma'am.'

Once Jane's bedroom door was firmly closed, Gail went to the loo and reappeared in a dressing gown, looking extremely demure. Edward took his cue, went to the loo, gave himself a quick wash, then walked quietly to Gail's room, where he stripped off his clothes as Gail looked on from under her duvet. 'You do have the most magnificent body,' she offered.

'I think that's my line. Yours is the magnificent body. Mine is just skin and muscle.'

For a few minutes they canoodled, both highly conscious of Edward's physical condition. 'I don't want to distract us,' offered Gail, 'but will you tell me something about the engagement that led to your MC?'

'Of course I will, but please not now. It was ferocious, pretty bloody, a number of dead men; truly not the sort of backdrop for a lovely woman in bed with an over-excited man.'

They laughed at each other and gently merged to make slow, passionate love.

Chapter Twenty

The train from Victoria to East Grinstead took an hour. Edward carried a small leather-bound briefcase, which contained all of the shirts, socks, pants and shaving gear that he would need for the weekend. Gail carried a small bag with two changes of clothing and her toothbrush. They exited into the car park, where Gail's father was standing patiently beside the family Ford. Gail hugged her father and turned to grab Edward. 'Daddy, this is Edward Davidson.'

'How do you do, Sir William,' said Edward, holding out his right hand.

'Let's have none of that,' he said. 'I am Will and my wife is Ellie. Welcome to Sussex.'

The journey back to the Ritchie household took no more than fifteen minutes, and Edward sat quietly in the back of the car as Gail gossiped with her father. They arrived at a solid 1930s house, set in semi-woodland on a residential road closer to Forest Row than Colemans Hatch. As they banged shut the car doors, Gail's mother appeared at the door. She hugged her daughter and turned to greet Edward, whose hand was outstretched as he said, 'Good evening, Lady Ritchie.'

She remonstrated. 'I know that Will would have instructed you already. We are Will and Ellie, and I am not going to shake your hand because I need to find out how you kiss old ladies.' They all laughed. Edward dutifully kissed her on each cheek. They stood back to measure each other. This was so obviously Gail's mother. She was a little thicker in the hips, and greyer in the hair, but the same handsome features shone through.

Abruptly, Edward recalled Simon Harker's recommendation that he should meet Gail's mother. That advice was excellent, and if evidence were needed about the way in which the Ritchie women aged, Edward knew he had no fears.

Gail was instructed to show Edward to his room, which sat at one corner of the house with its own small bathroom. He dropped his case and followed Gail back downstairs.

'So, you are working in the Cabinet Office,' offered Will Ritchie as a conversation opener.

'Yes, si... Will,' he replied. 'I understand that my boss was your best man, so I doubt I can tell you any lies about what I do.'

'Let me apologise for being a far too protective parent,' said Will. 'Actually, it was a good excuse to catch up with James, who is as busy today as he was thirty years ago. You obviously get on with him well, and he doesn't tolerate fools. The big question is, are you enjoying it?'

By this time everyone had a drink in their hand – all of it gin. Edward took an appreciative sip, raised his glass in toast to Gail's parents and said, 'Yes. A qualified yes, because it is not anything like the soldiering that I have done over the past twelve years. I command no soldiers, despite doing so for all of my Army career. I have to wangle time to keep up with my sport, and I have been learning the language of Whitehall bureaucracy, which was totally alien when I started. On the other hand, I am seeing the organs of government at close hand. More importantly, my work introduced me to an absolutely lovely woman called Gail Ritchie.' Gail put her glass on a table and walked behind Edward's chair to put her hands on both of his shoulders. She gave him a quick kiss on the forehead, then sat on the arm of the chair to reinforce their closeness.

The Ritchie parents communicated silently together as married couples do. There was no doubt where this was going. 'James spoke very highly of you, Edward.'

'Well, he told me that he had to tell you a load of half-truths!' Edward chuckled. 'I am not sure that I would have wanted to be the fly on the wall. He is a very benign boss, gives me lots of latitude and gently polished instruction. If I knew nothing about our bureaucracy when I started, he has taught me everything I know now. I hesitated with my answer to you about enjoying the job. Truthfully, James Harrington makes it extremely interesting and instructive. If I have any concerns about it, I suppose I can see myself back in the Cabinet Office as a Brigadier in twelve, or fourteen years' time, simply because I have had this insight. It is a mysterious world, as I hardly need to describe to you, but I find it quite bizarre that I have such a large list of people to whom I cannot talk simply because I am privy to such sensitive information.'

'So, you are going to be a Brigadier?' Will twinkled.

'I am not cocky about this, but subject to all of the other factors which direct our lives' – he paused and looked up at Gail's profile – 'I hope to make it somewhat further than that. The Army definitely suits me. I cannot really imagine crossing the floor of the House to become a civil servant or politician. Actually, I affirm that I could never be a politician, although I admit that there is some seduction in the work of Five or Six.'

'Let me ask a much more complex question.' Will hesitated, ducked his head and said, 'Oh my, this is turning into the interview of a prospective son-in-law – sorry. But my question is, what happens if your Uncle James decides to stop farming. It's a family property, is it not?'

'That's the sixty-four-thousand-dollar question,' said Edward. 'My aunt would never run the farm, although she does the book-keeping and general admin. My hunch is that they will keep going until they feel either that I have reached a plateau and need an escape route, or that they have reached the logical end of their stewardship and offer to let me take it over. Uncle James is now sixty. That's not old by any standard. He could go on for another fifteen to twenty years. That would make me forty-four to forty-nine. Of course, that is the key moment in a military career. A good candidate for Major-General can be appointed at forty-seven or forty-eight. Ultimately, my guiding principle is family-oriented. I acknowledge that I may have to abandon ambition for the highest rank in order to become a Northumbrian farmer. I could not imagine selling the property, because there is a generational glue holding us together. But let me return to my earlier proviso that there are other factors which direct our lives.' He leaned his head briefly against Gail's upper arm.

'And you still hope to compete in Moscow?'

Edward sat up straighter. 'I narrowly missed the bronze medal in Montreal. It was entirely my fault; I lost concentration and you perform for only a few seconds in each bout. There is no room for error. My coach, a wonderful man called Les Peters, to whom I hope to introduce Gail in the next week or so, is a fierce, dedicated taskmaster. He has already lifted my fitness to a new high, and we are following the example of another coach and acolyte from the world of ice skating by going back to absolute basics.'

'Who were they?'

'You will remember John Curry? He won the ice-skating gold in Innsbruck two years ago. Carlo Fassi took him on. They went back to the fundamental basics. Curry found that he had almost forgotten the simple things which earn the judges' approval. They say that for a couple of months he was made to skate in a one-metre square of ice, and he kept falling over. But it made him European, World and Olympic champion. Les has taken me back to the very first principles. We are looking at the sport solely through the eyes of the judges. Yes, I have to be technically and practically able to deliver the desired result, but this is probably the first time that I have understood it from the perspective of the judges, rather than the competitive view of a man on the piste.'

'Enough!' said Gail. 'Poor Edward has come into our home and been put through an inquisition.' She turned again towards him and rubbed her hand across his neck and cheek. 'The man needs another drink, even though he rarely drinks at all.'

Edward was happy to yield his glass to Gail's father and received back a full version topped by a fresh slice of lime and more ice. He took a large sip. 'Delicious. The trouble is that when I give up active competition, I will probably want to drink more of it. That's a problem that I am going to ask you to handle, Miss Ritchie.'

'Gail, why don't you and I go and sort out supper,' said her mother. Even Edward recognised this code. 'Let the women go and do something useful while the men focus on the big issues of the day.'

Edward leapt to his feet and Ellie told him that he really shouldn't be on his most formal behaviour. They would all get quite tired if he kept leaping up and down. Will Ritchie, who sat comfortably in a favourite armchair, gestured to a seat close to him on the sofa.

'I am sorry that we haven't met before, but thanks to the reports of James, of Gail and her sister, and Gail's conversations with her mother, I feel I have known you for a long time, Edward. My daughter is very down-to-earth, so her mother and I have been looking at her through a different prism since she met you. She has a new vitality, real sparkle and evidently an extremely tender instinct which is manifest in the way she handles you. Is there anything you want to discuss with me?'

'Yes, sir. Sorry, yes, Will. I didn't expect to be able to have this conversation during this first weekend, let alone the first few hours of meeting you and Ellie. I met Gail only five months ago. I cannot say that it was love at first sight for me, and certainly not for her. But I knew immediately that this was the most fascinating woman and that I wanted to get to know her far better. Fortune favours the brave and circumstances have allowed us to get to know each other better. There is a most alluring common bond between us: our interests, our humour, our outlook on life. It is only a month ago that I asked her permission to wage a campaign to win her heart. I know that could hardly have been a less romantic way of setting out my stall, but I am a common soldier and wanted to be very honest about my intentions. She gave me her consent, so I have tried to deliver the strategy effectively.'

'You know the old saying, marry in haste and repent at leisure?'

'Indeed, I do. I am fortunate that I have only ever known life in a fully harmonious household. My parents seemed to get along well, and my aunt and uncle certainly do. I have the odd friend with a difficult family life. Communication always seems to be the problem. In this, I admit to having been lectured by your lovely daughter, who feels that I have deliberately concealed my few small successes.'

'Not so small, Edward,' Will interjected. 'You have the most impressive CV. A Military Cross, mentioned in despatches and a double Olympian. Moreover, you are an intriguing anomaly in the world of civil servants. Soldiers rarely turn up in the Cabinet Office. That is what I was researching when I telephoned James. What he then told me was the interesting stuff about gallantry and sport. No wonder my daughter's head has been turned.'

'I have never felt that I earned the MC, and the Mention more or less came in with the rations,' Edward protested. 'As to being an Olympian, I concede that is gratifying, but the last thing a man like me would do would be to boast about it when meeting a pretty girl over supper.'

'I accept your rationale. Indeed, I have discussed it with Gail, who claims to be frustrated that you didn't tell her, but applauds the evidence that you considered it unsporting to speak about it.'

'Ah,' said Edward. 'There is the conundrum for a man trying to understand a woman.'

Will laughed with appreciation. 'So, do you want to discuss anything with me?'

Edward drew a deep breath, took a sip of his gin, straightened his shoulders and looked his future father-in-law firmly in the eye. 'Yes. I know that I am being aggressively advanced, but I would like to seek your daughter's hand in marriage. I have not asked her yet, although I have some reason to believe that she will accept me.'

Will thought for a second, having been told by an old friend that the trick to play when being asked this question was to allow an unnatural pause to develop, just to keep the young man on his toes. He felt like asking, 'Which one?', to see how Edward dealt with adversity; but he realised that it would be unkind.

'Yes, that would be very acceptable,' he said, rising to his feet. Edward followed suit and the two men shook hands to mark the cementing of an agreement. 'Now, we have some management issues to deal with,' he went on. 'You haven't asked her. Do you want to get on with that now, or do you want to let the exercise play out over the weekend?'

Edward was very pleased with his host's thoughtful approach to the delivery of the campaign. 'I wonder if you would be content if we kept quiet until Sunday afternoon? My reasoning is that Gail wants to see how I mix with her family. I don't want to undermine her tactics for such a major decision. If I have your consent, I will take her to church on Sunday morning, go for a walk after that and pop the question before we get back for lunch. Although, that said, she may not want to go to church and I don't know where it is anyway!'

'If you suggest going to church, she will fall in line, I assure you. She and her sister are not regular communicants, although Ellie and I are. We will go together, but Ellie and I will give you the chance to walk in the churchyard, or wherever after the service, which begins at 11.00a.m.'

The weekend flew by. On the Saturday, they decided to drive the half hour to Tunbridge Wells, where Edward gave them lunch in a French restaurant which he had researched earlier in the week. Conversation rattled on without any pregnant pauses, and both of Gail's parents naturally spent time getting to know more about Edward and he about them. It worked well and on the Sunday morning Edward realised that his future in-laws must have been given strict instructions by their daughter to ignore her corridor-creeping in the night. Their love-making was more restrained, conscious of the need to be relatively quiet. Edward had no desire to embarrass Will and Ellie, although he assumed that they could not have failed to understand what was happening under their roof.

The church was Holy Trinity in Forest Row, maddeningly isolated in an island of traffic, without a surrounding graveyard. Edward looked ruefully at Will to indicate that the planned walk would have to be transported to the family garden. They understood each other without words, which put a reassuring angle on their relationship.

But the music was excellent, with hymns that amply suited Edward's solid bass voice. Gail stopped singing, merely to listen to this determined man, who delivered a rich undertone to the efforts of the congregation. She gripped him by the elbow after the second hymn. 'Something else you failed to tell me, Edward Davidson. You have an excellent singing voice.'

Edward smiled at her sheepishly. 'The only trouble is that I can't hear it,' he whispered back to her.

The vicar bade individuals farewell at the church door, then the family moved back to the car and slowly drove home. 'Gail, show me the garden,' instructed Edward. Her parents hurried inside, both wanting to survey the next steps without being obvious about it. There was a bench in a small bower sheltered from the house. Edward drew Gail to sit down with him, firmly placing her upon his lap. He gave her a brief kiss and asked, 'So, am I measuring up to your expectations, my love?'

'Yes. Mum is completely besotted with you, and I can see Daddy looking at you with the professional approval that he deployed for favoured embassy staff.'

'So, do you think that I will make the grade?'

For answer, she kissed him fiercely.

'While you and your mother were playing discreet games in the kitchen on Friday night, I had a most serious and candid conversation with your father.' Gail sat quite still. She had not imagined that Edward would go for the kill so quickly.

'He gave me permission to seek your hand in marriage. I am not going down on one knee now, because that will follow when I put a suitable engagement ring on your finger. We will choose that together this week, if only you will accept my proposal.'

'God, you do move quickly. I know that Bella told you not to waste any time, but I thought you would spend this weekend evaluating the whole Ritchie clan.'

'I want you to be my bride. Please say you will.'

A tear appeared in her eye and she allowed a small sob to escape. 'Don't tell me that you are miserable about this,' Edward protested.

'No, you silly, silly man. I am utterly thrilled. I thought you would take time to get all of your ducks in a row, but I should have known better. My tears are joy, something which I know you can understand.'

He allowed his head to rest on her breast as she caressed his neck. The relief was intense. As a soldier, he patted himself on the back for laying an excellent plan and delivering it efficiently. He started to think of all the things that they would have to do to keep the impetus going. They must call Bella, Uncle James and Aunt Mary, a few folks in the regiment, James Harrington; the list stretched out in front of his mind's eye.

'Okay, the future Mrs Davidson. We are going to be a first-class team. Do you think we should go and put your parents out of their misery?'

Gail giggled. 'I guarantee that they are in the snug looking out of the window from behind the curtains. Of course, they cannot see us here. It is tempting to creep up on them, but I love them too much to tease them like that. Come on.'

She slid off his lap, grabbed his hand and they left the bower to appear in the garden and walk decisively to the house. Their joy was abundantly clear in their body language, and inside the house Ellie Ritchie grabbed her husband and gave him a loving kiss. 'Well done, Will. You fixed that very well.'

'It wasn't me,' he said, 'it was young Edward. He had thought it all through. I suggested that there were alternatives to the timing, but he set the agenda. He realised that this weekend was Gail's chance to present her family to her inamorato. She wanted to study him with us, and she wanted him to have the opportunity to work out whether we would all rub along together. The last thing he sought was to undermine that by delivering the *coup de grâce* within an hour of getting here. We have a most intelligent and thoughtful son-in-law, my darling.'

They all met in the hall, each side eager to complete the happy process. 'Mum, Daddy, I think you knew before me that

Edward was going to ask me an important question? Well, I have accepted his proposal of marriage.'

'Hurrah,' shouted Ellie, pushing forward to embrace the happy couple.

'Champagne,' said Will.

Ellie was on fire. 'We must telephone Bella, and James, and your aunt and uncle, Edward. We must make a list, because we mustn't leave out anyone important.' She darted into the kitchen, where Will was confidently uncorking a bottle of cool Pol Roger. 'Darling, you should talk to Bella immediately.'

Gail disagreed. 'I would like Edward to talk to her first. We had supper together on Thursday and she instructed Edward not to waste any time. This came after a really robust interrogation.' She picked up the telephone and dialled the number, before handing it to Edward.

'Hello?' asked Bella, who was standing in her kitchen with three friends who had come for Sunday lunch.

'Bella, this is Edward. Edward Davidson.'

'Oh, Edward, how lovely. I thought you were spending the weekend with my parents.'

'I am, and I am on their telephone in the kitchen. You told me on Thursday evening not to waste any time. Your family has instructed me to tell you that I have not wasted time. Your father agreed to let me press my case on Friday, and today your sister consented to marry me.'

They could hear the scream without the benefit of the telephone. Champagne gurgled into four flutes as Gail took the phone to report to her sister in greater detail. Her parents then followed up with the sort of family narrative that attends an engagement.

'Well, that's the first one. How gratifying. I think you should now phone home, Edward.'

Edward dialled the number, which rang and rang, until a slightly breathless Mary said, 'Sorry, we were out in the garden drinking with visiting chums. Who is this?'

'Aunt Mary, it's me, Edward. I am staying with Gail's parents in Sussex. We just want to let you know that I have done everything in the proper order and Gail has consented to be my bride.'

'Oh, thank God. You have moved very quickly, darling, but I don't think there is anything wrong with that. Your Uncle James will be thrilled. Let me have a quick word with Gail.'

In fact, it took a good ten minutes for the two to stop chatting. Glasses were refilled.

'We have plenty of time to tell everyone else, but I think I would like to tell James Harrington,' said Will. 'You could do it just as well, darling Gail, but James and I go back a long way.'

He went off to the snug, sat in his armchair and dialled the number, appreciating that the Harringtons might well be having lunch. The others stayed in the kitchen and Ellie started to tinker with the stove. Lunch had to go on.

Chapter Twenty-One

For the two young lovers, the pace of life increased immeasurably. The hunt for a suitable engagement ring took them the length of Bond Street and the surrounding area. They found the ideal solution in a shop called Michael Rose in Burlington Arcade, where a simple band crowned with an emerald protected by two diamonds brought dimples to Gail's cheeks. Edward paid for the product, and when it had been put in a velvet-covered box, he placed it in his jacket pocket.

'So, when do I get it?' asked Gail a little peevishly.

'I am not going to complete my presentation in the shop where we bought the ring,' Edward offered. 'We need to be somewhere that we can remember with clarity and joy.'

'Like the train from Waterloo to Cheltenham.'

'Terrific. Great wheeze. Or under the clock at Waterloo station. That should entertain the public. No, why don't we go now to L'Artiste Muscle for a little light lunch. Depending on the number of diners, I intend to put my proposal to you there.'

Michel was not on parade. His colleague, Giles, recognised Edward anyway and was very pleased to offer the table in the corner. Edward asked for two glasses of champagne and warned Giles that he was about to witness a special display. Gail sat, half-turned to watch him give his briefing, then turned fully to look into the small room as Edward went down on one knee, pulled the ring from his pocket and grabbed Gail's hand.

'My most beautiful woman, let me put this ring on your engagement finger. Will you marry me?'

'I never thought I would accept a proposal of marriage in a French restaurant, but it is a lot more romantic than the railway station. My darling Edward, I will love being your wife.' She looked at the ring and leaned forward to kiss him.

Giles and the chef had stood unashamedly watching the performance. They clapped as the happy couple kissed, then offered the two glasses of champagne. 'That is a gift from the house,' said Giles.

They were greatly in demand. Jane Baldwin insisted on organising a drinks party, which was attended by Edward Longstaff, who was very gracious about Edward's swift victory. Henry Rawlings attended, along with four officers of the regiment who happened to be in England on leave or on courses. This was the first time that Gail had the chance to meet Edward's brother officers, and she was intrigued to see how they behaved like siblings. Sir James Harrington invited them both to lunch at The Travellers, before Edward persuaded his aunt and uncle to come to London for lunch at the Cavalry Club with Gail's parents.

The convention in the regiment was that officers should not contemplate marriage under the age of twenty-seven. Moreover, it was the done thing to ask the permission of the Commanding Officer. Edward decided that he should write to Tony Walters, otherwise known to his contemporaries as 'Gloria', who had taken command of the regiment in January. Technically, he did not need to do so since he was at extra-regimental duty, but Edward's innate instinct to do the right things well persuaded him that Tony would be very pleased to be asked.

But both of them still had to work, and Edward had to honour his commitment to Les Peters to achieve and maintain the highest standards of fitness.

One evening, Gail managed to get to the London Fencing Club to observe a full training session. For her pains, Les gave her a thorough grilling about Edward's lifestyle and her responsibility to help him prepare for the Moscow Games.

'You are very fierce, Les,' she said. 'I will do all that I can to support him, but you are his coach, not me.'

Les dropped his head in contrition. 'Forgive me, Gail. I am desperate to get him into the peak of condition physically, technically and mentally. It is most unjust of me to harass you.'

With one of her very sexy giggles, Gail acknowledged that the fitness regime had a very benign impact on other aspects of their joint lives. Les laughed and gave her a quick kiss. 'You look after him properly and we will both be sure that he stays super-fit.'

August folded into September. It was on Wednesday 28th that the Chairman of the JIC told Edward that the Prime Minister had asked for a fuller account of the intelligence about the European summit to be held in Brussels in just over a month's time. 'He wants to hear it from the horse's mouth,' said Sir James.

Edward had done his homework on the Prime Minister. He knew that he had been a sailor, like his father, although the father had been a Petty Officer, while the son was a commissioned Lieutenant. It always helped to have a Prime Minister who had served in the Armed Forces. Soldiers, sailors and airmen never really felt confident that politicians understood them unless they had some sort of track record. Callaghan's three years as a fighting sailor earned some respect.

He was introduced to the PM's office by one of the staff at Number Ten. The PM stood up to greet him. 'Thank you for coming to brief me. Sir James Harrington has given me a rundown on you. Congratulations on your recent engagement.'

'Thank you, Prime Minister. You would expect me to say it, but I am a very lucky man. You may know that Sir James is my bride's godfather, so I have to be on my best behaviour.'

Callaghan laughed. 'This is almost incestuous with you two working for the JIC. Now, they tell me that you were the first person to receive a briefing on the apparent threat to my Brussels visit. I want to hear exactly what you were told and how.'

Edward succinctly related the tale of the *Daily Mirror*'s attempts to persuade Whitehall that there was a threat, Simon Harker's two good lunches, the confirmation of intelligence gathered by 14 Int Company, the identification of the likely perpetrators, and the known and potential capability of the weapons to be deployed.

'Excellent and clear. Thank you, Edward. What do you think I should do?'

'To be honest, Prime Minister, I think the question is more about what the Belgian security authorities should do.'

'Fair point, well made. Some people are trying to persuade me not to attend the conference.'

'Clearly, I cannot make that decision for you, Prime Minister; but I imagine that you need to attend for solid political reasons.'

'Absolutely right, young man. And no British Prime Minister is going to be deterred by threats. So, I am going. You can tell anyone you like, but particularly those Belgian security people,' he smiled.

A week later, Gail and Edward decided to dine at the Italian restaurant in Queenstown Road. L'Artiste Muscle remained their favourite restaurant, but Gail insisted that they should investigate other establishments, if only to provide variety.

'We need to talk about life after the wedding,' submitted Edward. 'I want to support you in your career, but we have never talked about where it might take you, or when.'

'I would give it all up for you, my man.'

'But that would be wrong. When your father asked me what I saw in my own future, it forced me to reflect on the competing

235

tensions in both of our lives. To be honest, up until that conversation with your parents, I hadn't given it too much thought, assuming that if I worked hard and well, I would eventually become General Sir Edward Davidson. Probably not Chief of the General Staff, but certainly on the Army Board. Your father spotted the problem about the farm in a nanosecond.'

'You can probably still do that, surely?'

'Not if Uncle James and Aunt Mary decide to give up. It would break their hearts to sell off the farm. I want to be a good son to reflect their own incredible performance as parents.'

'So, is there an argument for giving up the Army earlier to commit yourself to farming?'

'There is, but I don't think that they would actually want to step back for at least ten more years. At some point, we must have a conversation with them. Ten years would give me the chance to command the regiment. But all of these plans ignore your own career, my darling. So, we have an agreement on honesty. Tell me what you want to do.'

'Culturally, the Service is still behind the pace. Cicely Mayhew was the first woman to join the Diplomatic Service in 1947, and she had to resign when she got married. That rule was overturned only five years ago and it was only two years ago that the first ever female ambassador was appointed. She went to Denmark and is still there today. She is unmarried. Even with the tide turning in favour of women diplomats, I am pretty certain that my options would be severely limited after marriage.'

'But that's terrible. Effectively, I will have brought your ambitions to a halt.'

'No, Edward. You have been the perfect suitor and ultimately, I made the decision to accept your offer of marriage. I wouldn't change that for anything in the world. So, let's just think about the next two to five years. You will go to the Staff College in April 1980. I assume that is just a one-year course?'

'Hmm. Well, you have to do a stint at Shrivenham first. I am not scientifically minded, so I would probably do the three-month course for dumb soldiers, and I think that starts in January. All things being equal, that takes us through to December 1980. Then I have no idea whether it will be back to the regiment, who will still be in Germany, or off on a Staff job anywhere in the world. The top boys get jobs as Brigade Majors.'

'What you are saying is that we have something in the order of two years before you are likely to be posted out of England. That will probably allow me to keep my current job in the Foreign Office. But if you are going to be based away from London, I insist upon being with you. I don't want to leave my husband to stray with temptation.'

'Gail, my darling' – he grabbed her hand – 'you must accept that I am most sincerely monogamous and I simply love you to bits. There isn't a cat's hope in hell of me "straying" anywhere, and my whole being yearns for you to be with me all the time. But I need to say to you that if you want to pursue your career, I would never stand in your way. We would find a way around the difficulties of foreign postings somehow.'

'Let's shelve it for the moment. Thank you for thinking about this, my love, but my priority is my family life, and I have always known that the Foreign Office has difficulty with us girls. Now the one thing we do have to do is make a plan for our wedding.'

'I have been looking at the diary. Would your parents want us to have the ceremony at Holy Trinity in Forest Row, or would they be thinking of London?'

'They have already told me that they think it would work better in London, probably at St Paul's Knightsbridge. Their only concern then is where to hold the reception. So many people go to the Hyde Park Hotel, but I don't want this to be the same old society wedding format.'

'Well, would you be content if we had the reception at the Cavalry Club? It is competitive, convenient, and reliable.'

'That's a really sound idea. Curiously, I think the greater problem is St Paul's Knightsbridge. The church has all sorts of funny rules about who can do what where. I will put Mum on to that. Would you talk to Daddy about the reception?'

'Love to. And because it is my Club, I intend to pay for the booze. I hope your parents would not be offended by that.'

'I can't answer. We haven't had a family wedding since they got married in 1949. But it's a big expense for you. Our traditions all force the bride's parents to pay.'

'I know, but I have saved up more than enough to be able to afford it, and it would give me enormous pleasure. We really ought to have a family conference with your parents to sort it out. But before we do so, may I offer a tentative date and reason?'

'Go on.'

'I propose that we get married on Saturday 5 May, assuming that the church and the Club are available. That weekend is the Cavalry Memorial weekend. There is a regimental dinner at the Club on the Friday night. The Saturday is normally clear, and on the Sunday the regiments march past the Cavalry Memorial with a member of the Royal Family taking the salute. I don't intend that we should be in London on the Sunday, because I hope to have spirited you away to some intimate setting, where I can get to know you better. And on that score, I am going to suggest that we go on honeymoon for no more than a week.'

'A week. I had visions of being in the sun for at least a fortnight.'

'Ah, well, that's the second part of the plan. The World Championships will be held in Melbourne from 12 to 22 July. Assuming I make it into the team, I would like you to come with me and we can then spend ten days in Australia after the Championships.'

'You devious old man. That's an excellent piece of bribery. I have never been to Australia and would love to go. Thinking laterally, is it going to be a wise thing for you to attend the dinner on the night before our wedding? Surely your military pals will try to get you drunk and you will be in a terrible condition the next day.'

'True. They can try, but they all know that I never drink much because of my sport. My thinking was that if convention demands that I do not see you the night before we marry, I might as well be enjoying a good dinner. I imagine that Uncle James will want to go, too. He tends to do so every second or third year, and if he is in London anyway, it makes sense.'

A week later, the whole exercise was set in concrete. The Ritchies were very pleased with the thought that their young had put into it and both St Paul's and the Cavalry Club confirmed the date. Edward spoke to his aunt and uncle, who agreed that the date suited them well, and Uncle James would indeed attend the regimental dinner, if only to keep an eye on Edward, he claimed. Both families agreed to produce their own lists of potential guests, resolving that they should aim for a maximum of two hundred and fifty people. But Edward was very surprised when his aunt and uncle insisted that they would pay for the booze, first because they wanted to do so, and second because they thought that Edward should use the money to make the most of his honeymoon.

Through the weeks of hectic planning and parties, the lovers maintained their own flats. True, they spent most of every week in the bed of one or the other, but they agreed that they should mark their marriage by having one new flat of their own. By doing this, Jane Baldwin had plenty of time to think about her own arrangements, and the young couple could spend time hunting for something to suit their married profile.

239

Chapter Twenty-Two

Tuesday 14 November 1978 marked a change in the pattern of IRA activity. Up until that point, shootings or bombings were sporadic. There was little evidence of an overall strategy. People were still wounded or dying, but an incident might as well happen in Belfast, Armagh or Londonderry. On this Tuesday, however, a co-ordinated campaign of bombs was orchestrated in Armagh, Belfast, Castlederg, Cookstown, Enniskillen and Londonderry. Nobody died, but there were thirty-seven serious casualties. During the following week, more than fifty bombs were exploded around Ulster.

A fortnight later, on 30 November, a repeat campaign hit fourteen towns and villages in Ulster. The next day there were eleven attacks. On 12 December, in Belfast and Lisburn, three women, all the wives of prison officers, were injured by bombs, together with a postman. On 17 December, the campaign moved to mainland England, when bombs exploded in Bristol, Coventry, Liverpool, Manchester and Southampton.

The curious thing was that the intelligence community had not foreseen a change in leadership, and there was little or no evidence that there was a new person in charge. It was as if the years of sporadic and often ineffective terrorism had finally homogenised into a lesson that changed tactics. Edward found that he was attending more long-winded meetings as the Whitehall bureaucracy tried to work out future trends.

Armageddon did not arrive. After the PR success of their co-ordinated bombings, the anticipated months of terror did not materialise. The regular pattern of singular shootings returned until Thursday 22 March, when twenty-four bombs exploded in towns and villages across the North of Ireland. That same day, Richard Sykes, the British ambassador to the Netherlands, was killed, in company with his Dutch valet, in The Hague.

The Government had been in trouble for months. The bureaucracy of Whitehall seemed to be stuck in treacle. Nobody would make decisions, and there was no political energy in the country. At last, on Wednesday 28 March 1979, Margaret Thatcher forced a vote of No Confidence in the Government. The motion was carried by a single vote and the date for a general election was set for Thursday 3 May.

On the afternoon of Friday 30 March, Edward was walking across Whitehall from the MoD to his office when he heard a muffled explosion. To his tutored ear, it seemed to come from his left, near the Houses of Parliament. He picked up the pace and ran upstairs to his office. Jim Shaw was standing at his office window, looking along Whitehall to try to identify where the noise had come from. 'I have a bad feeling that the explosion was actually inside the perimeter of the House,' said Edward. 'We need a radio or television.' Jim went off to find out if anyone had access to a live broadcast. 'The best we can do is go to the Press Office. There's already quite a large crowd, but they'll squeeze us in.'

They locked the office door and went downstairs. The Press Office was bulging with staff, who looked hopefully at the large-screen TV, where a reporter was filling time with fruitless speculation. What did seem clear was that a car exiting the underground car park had exploded. Nobody knew who was in it, nor did they know why the car exploded. Initial reports suggested that there was one casualty, thought to be still alive.

It took almost two hours for the news to determine what had happened. Airey Neave had driven to work in his new

241

Vauxhall Cavalier, which had been parked in the road outside his house overnight. The bomb was placed on the chassis under the driver's seat and was armed by a mercury tilt switch, which only activated when the car went uphill. Going into the House of Commons car park was a downhill manoeuvre, so the bomb activated when he was driving out. The Irish National Liberation Army swiftly claimed responsibility. Up until that moment, few people in mainland Britain ever considered the possibility that they could be the target of personalised bombs.

*****

'It's a good thing that we decided to get married on a Saturday,' joked Edward to his fiancée. We would have been forced to change all the plans if we had opted for the 3rd.'

It was the following Saturday, and they were sitting having a long, late breakfast at Tillview Farm outside Duddo with James and Mary. By curious chance, it was on the Wednesday evening of the No Confidence vote that James had telephoned Edward, wisely guessing that he would be in Gail's flat. 'You won't believe it, my boy. I have managed to persuade your aunt to marry me. It has taken me over thirty years to change her mind, but I think she has decided that, as the "mother of the groom", she ought to be a decent married woman.'

Edward was ecstatic. 'That is the most wonderful news. When are you going to do the deed?' Gail's ears pricked up, realising that it was James on the phone, but not understanding the context. Edward put the phone into his shoulder and made the motion of placing a ring over the third finger of his left hand.

'On Saturday. Short notice, I know, but I don't want her to change her mind. Can you and Gail attend? I would like you to be my best man, and her ladyship wants to ask Gail to be her bridesmaid.'

'I would be honoured to serve. Let Aunt Mary talk to Gail now and we can then carry on the conversation. As your best man, I have questions to ask.'

The women chatted happily for at least twenty minutes.

'The wedding will take place at Norham. I have obtained a special licence and we will have a congregation of only twenty on top of ourselves. If they can attend, all of them will be coming back for lunch, so the help that you and Gail can provide will be physical as well as emotional. And yes, I have presented her with an engagement ring, which I bought over thirty years ago, along with the wedding ring that I planned to put on her finger then. Happily, both still fit!'

The men were in their wedding kit minus jackets, despite Mary's remonstration that one or other of them would dribble egg onto their best clothes. Edward's waistcoat had been bought only a month earlier in anticipation of his own wedding. He was feeling quite the peacock in a bright blue silk waistcoat bedecked with bees and a gold watch chain strapped across his stomach.

The dogs let it be known that someone was coming down the drive. It proved to be Linda Garvey, Mary's hairdresser, who had been commissioned to sort out the hair of both women. 'I think we have time for a quick walk with the dogs while that's going on,' offered James. And, to the intense irritation of their brides, they slipped wellington boots over their dress trousers, put on shooting jackets and made for the back door.

'Why is it that men always wear the wrong clothes for any activity?' asked Mary in a frustrated but affectionate voice.

'I don't think that they perceive any clothes as notably special. Whatever they are wearing suits the moment. That is going to change when I become Mrs Davidson,' said Gail.

'I wouldn't be so sure! I have been trying with James since I first met him, and it has made no difference whatsoever.'

The wedding took place in the Norman church at Norham and, to the surprise of James and Mary, more than fifty people turned up to wish them well. Happily, only the twenty invited guests would move to Tillview for lunch, but at the end of the brief, rather emotional service, James asked everyone to come back to the farm for a drink. 'Have you got enough, Uncle James?' Edward queried.

'They won't all want champagne. We'll get by.'

The noise in the house was deafening. Tumblers of gin seemed to rule the day, and James Wood was never going to be short of that sort of medication. Mary and Gail were joined by three of Mary's oldest chums in the kitchen, where they swiftly put together plates of smoked salmon on brown bread, trying hard not to get in the way of Fiona Bush, who was preparing the lunch for twenty-four people.

The last guests left at half past five. 'My God, I had no idea how tiring it was getting married,' moaned Mary. 'You watch out, my girl. Make sure that you pace yourself.'

'I have been told by countless people that your wedding day flashes by in seconds,' said Edward. 'Was that not the case for you?'

James and Mary looked at each other carefully. 'Actually, that's true. It feels as if we have packed everything into one very short hour. But, without wanting to spoil the fun, I am going to get into something less formal.' James left and could be heard bounding up the stairs.

'And I am going to follow his example,' said Mary. 'I haven't spent this long in a dress for months.'

Edward and Gail exchanged a look which spoke volumes about what they thought the newly-weds might decide to do. They waited a while, wanting to go and do the same things themselves, but not wishing to intrude on their hosts.

They sat gossiping about the new people that Gail had met at the wedding, and after thirty minutes they decided that they could safely creep upstairs to Edward's room. They undressed quickly and leapt under the duvet. Edward was mildly astonished to wake up ninety minutes later, having fallen into a deep and untroubled sleep. He tickled Gail, who came to her senses slowly.

'I will take a shower,' said Gail, 'alone, Major Davidson. I know how excited you get in the shower.'

A disappointed but pragmatic Major decided to slip on some old trousers and a check shirt. He added a pair of brown shoes and quietly let himself out of his room to go downstairs to the kitchen. All was silent. No sign of his aunt and uncle, but the dogs looked at him expectantly, so he put his boots on and his shooting jacket, before wandering out of the back door into the farmyard in the half-dark.

Gail appeared looking rested and content at 7.15 and agreed that she would have a glass of white wine. Fifteen minutes later, Mary appeared. She was clearly mildly embarrassed and decided to brazen it out. 'Well, you two have had all the fun in this house. It's not great for parents to report on their love lives to their children, but I will admit that now that I am a married woman, I have had my first ever legitimate bonk.' They spluttered with laughter.

Chapter Twenty-Three

Edward feared that he would not be able to keep up with events during April because of the competing priorities of his imminent wedding and the potential for chaos caused by Irish terrorists. But for once the terrorists were relatively quiet, although the calm was shattered on 17 April, when the Provisional IRA exploded their largest bomb ever, killing four RUC members as they passed a parked van outside Bessbrook.

The intelligence community largely agreed on their evaluation of Irish terrorism. INLA were suddenly an important ingredient because of their murder of Airey Neave, but the Provos were still the larger force. They were believed to have re-structured to improve their security with a tighter cell system. This ensured that it was harder to work out what they were doing. On the other hand, 14 Company continued to deliver their invaluable insight to the working of the PIRA Council. That, combined with helpful information from GCHQ, started to build the picture of an IRA determined to kill senior government officials. Some reports intimated that they would seek to kill a member of the Royal Family.

It fell to Edward to write the formal brief for Sir James Harrington, who would ensure that the threat to the Royals was conveyed to the Queen as a very serious possibility. Edward soon discovered that the vast majority of the family would be in the United Kingdom for the next nine months, apart from the Queen making a one-day visit to Copenhagen on 16 May. The Royal Protection Group believed that they could cope with any threat in mainland Britain. But there was one significant challenge: Lord Mountbatten had spent many years staying at Classiebawn Castle, overlooking Mullaghmore in County Sligo. The house had been inherited by his late wife, Edwina, from her father, Wilfred William Ashley, later created Baron Mount Temple. After Edwina died in 1960, Lord Mountbatten spent every summer at the Castle with his family.

Edward's briefing paper was presented to Mountbatten by Sir James Harrington. Although he took it seriously, Mountbatten said in a written reply to Sir James that he simply couldn't believe that the Irish would be so stupid as to make an attempt on his life at Mullaghmore, where he was seen pretty much as a local. He knew that the people liked him. He thanked the JIC for giving him such a detailed briefing, nonetheless.

On the wedding front, Gail and Edward spent time with the Revd Donald Harris, who had retired two years earlier but agreed to marry them at St Paul's, where he had been the vicar for twenty-two years. He and the Ritchies had met often during Will's time as a diplomat. Donald Harris looked far younger than his seventy-six years and had been enormously popular with his congregation, amongst whom many of the single women entertained fantasies of capturing this urbane, quite wealthy bachelor. It was said that he had been offered posts as a bishop, but had resolutely preferred to stay at St Paul's Knightsbridge. Now living in Masham Court in Westminster, he entertained the young lovers to tea in order to deliver the excellent stewardship for which he was renowned.

Gail asked Edward if he would consider getting married in uniform, knowing in her heart that he would resist. Her argument was that she had never seen him in military clothing and was unsure whether she was marrying a real soldier. But it did not turn into a bone of contention. Edward would do anything to please his bride, although he felt he had to convince her that it was not a regimental tradition to marry in Blues. Moreover, she had actually helped him to choose the elegant blue waistcoat which he was very much looking forward to wearing again on Saturday 5 May. On the other hand, eight Warrant Officers and Sergeants of the regiment would turn out in Blues to form a Guard of Honour for their exit from the church.

Edward Longstaff and Simon Jones, who was the son of a diplomat and who had known Gail since she was a child, were the only two civilians to be invited to serve as ushers. Longstaff claimed that he was tickled pink to be protected by so many soldiers. Six brother officers played their part, along with Jeremy Unwin, the Best Man. Sir James Harrington, as Gail's godfather, was to give the speech on behalf of the bride.

Donald Harris absolutely made the wedding. His wonderful sonorous voice, deft sense of humour and transparent enjoyment conveyed all of the best messages that the bride and groom could desire, and it was with a sense of wonder that they cantered down the aisle as husband and wife after what seemed like a five-minute service.

The reception was held on the first floor of the Cavalry Club, overlooking Green Park. Half-way along the room, which could accommodate three hundred people quite easily, a small raised platform presented a three-tier cake, alongside which rested Edward's sword. With no shortage of champagne, the noise level had crept upward by many decibels, so it proved to be quite hard for Edward to quieten everyone down, which he achieved by making sure that his ushers placed themselves strategically in the crowd to add local pressure.

'Heavens, you can talk!' The room rumbled with contented laughter. 'Pray silence for Sir James Harrington, who is the godfather of my bride and, more importantly from day to day, my immediate boss.'

There were cheers from the rowdier military folk, but they all subsided as James Harrington moved to the microphone.

'My Lords, ladies and gentlemen, officers of the regiment and other supporters of this happy couple. For you, Edward, the long process of selection is over. After years of fruitless reconnaissance, you have finally and most successfully chosen a suitable bride and supporter. The wonderful thing is that you can now delegate all of those irksome small decisions to someone who will know precisely how to deal with them. She will decide where you live, what cars you drive, how many children to produce and where to educate them. This is marvellous news, because it frees you up to consider the really important questions of the day, like, "Should we really join the European Monetary System?"' The room exploded in laughter.

'Gail, my beautiful [*many cheers*] and hugely intelligent god-daughter, small wonder that you have captured this fierce, competitive man. When you met, neither of you knew that I was the significant natural link between you. In my privileged position, I have watched as Edward completely lost his head and his heart. Once I knew whose favours he sought, I realised that he would never recover, for I have never quite regained my old fire since I first held you in my arms at your christening [*many loud cheers*].

'Of course, the old joke is that every cavalry soldier can speak at least one language! What a relief. Between the two of you, you have English, a fine start; you both have French, and Edward deploys German to Gail's Portuguese. Between you, I believe you can manage Europe.

'Now, I could bang on for hours, but you know the oldest saying that a speaker should be bright, be brief and be gone. I cannot leave without paying enormous tributes to Gail, who is beautiful [*loud cheers*], brilliant [*more loud cheers*] and very funny [*applause*]. I have just the one duty to perform, so I ask you to raise your glasses to toast the bride.'

Edward shook James' hand with great warmth as he stepped back from the microphone. 'Thank you, James. I know well after more than a year working for you that it pays to perform like Samuel Taylor Coleridge's description of an epigram, the body brevity and wit it's soul. One day I aspire to being as cogent and funny as you.

'My honour, duty and considerable pleasure is to thank everybody for their magnificent contribution to today. Will and Ellie Ritchie, together with their younger daughter, Bella, have made an art form of being superlative in-laws. I should say that the hardest interview I have ever undergone was by Bella at L'Artiste Muscle, which is a most agreeable French restaurant just around the corner from here. At our first meeting, I was terrified, because I knew that if I failed to secure her approval, this campaign would not have finished as it has. She grilled me as if I were six pork sausages. But she also told me not to waste any time. Let me thank her for that firm direction, because I asked my father-in-law for Gail's hand only twenty-four hours later!

'I particularly want to thank my aunt and uncle, Mary and James Wood, for their many years of love, affection, support and direction. Without seeking to embarrass them, I ask you now to raise a glass to them, because they got married only five weeks ago.' Loud cheers erupted. 'It is fair to report also that they asked Will and Ellie if they could contribute to the wedding, so they have provided the champagne.' More loud cheers.

'Gail's bridesmaid is her sister Bella, of whom I have already spoken. Bella, take my word for it, do not trust any of my bachelor brother officers. And for you, the brother officers, beware of my new sister-in-law, who will lead you a merry dance. Bella, thank you for all that you have done for Gail and me. You look absolutely stunning.' More cheers.

'I need to make special mention of my fencing coach, Les Peters. Les has driven me to two Olympic Games and is sufficiently soft in the head to be giving it a go for a third time.

With patience, outstanding skill and the clearest trainer's eye, he has taken my sabre skills apart and is reconstructing them with a view to securing the medal I threw away in Montreal.

'I want to thank my regiment, and particularly Sean Lomax, for arranging my military career so that I could spend two years in London. The idea was that I would have more time to train for Moscow. Of course, that was optimistic! But the unexpected consequence was that I met, fell for and have now married this beautiful, intelligent, able, humorous and hard-working woman.' He turned to Gail and gave her a huge hug. The whole room erupted.

With a lingering kiss, Edward turned back to the microphone. 'Let me now ask you to raise your glasses to toast Bella, our bridesmaid.'

With shouts of 'Bella', the whole room drank more champagne.

'And now I introduce one of my oldest friends, Jeremy Unwin, who bravely agreed to be our Best Man. Jeremy is a fine soldier. We have served together for twelve years and been on many escapades. If he elects to publish some of the gory details, you are not to believe him. Jeremy.'

Jeremy Unwin grasped the microphone and held a dramatic pause. Just as the silence was extending people's comfort zones, he laughed and said, 'It is pretty rare for me to be in a room full of regimental colleagues and keep them quiet!

'I have to offer you some hint about the nature and performance of the groom. Gail, I am sorry to admit this to you in public in front of all these fine, upstanding citizens, but I have been to bed with your husband.' There was a ripple of laughter, underpinned by a note of concern. Was Jeremy going to break a taboo by saying something outrageous?

'It is not quite what you imagine. Edward and I went to Luxembourg one weekend after attending a lunch with our affiliated Belgian regiment in Namur. After a longer drive than we intended, we tried to find cheap accommodation. There was nothing available, but we persevered. Eventually, we landed up in an establishment which seemed to be clean and full of laughter. The receptionist gave us a very old-fashioned look when she said that they had a room free, but only with a double bed, and did we want it for the whole night? That was an odd question, but we laughed and asked if they had a bolster, which they duly provided. We said that we fully intended to be there until the following morning. It proved to be a terribly noisy hotel, with people creaking around on the landings throughout the night. It was only when we paid in the morning that we realised that we had been staying in the local brothel!'

The room belched with laughter.

'We have always tried to imagine what the professionals in the brothel thought we were up to. Well, we were clearly complete amateurs. Edward and I enjoyed other marvellous trips. On another weekend, we drove to Copenhagen and quickly found that it was the most expensive city in Europe. Dinner broke us, and we couldn't afford the £12 per head cost of a bed in a cheap hotel. Bear in mind that our pay at that time was £2 per day. Edward owned a lovely, wallowy Citroen DS19, so we made the decision to go out into the countryside, find a quiet field, park up and bunk down for the night in the car. None of that was a problem. By good fortune, Edward wakes with the dawn. He says he can't help it. He came to around 4.40a.m. and sat up to see what was around us. To his deep embarrassment, we were parked on the elegant lawn of a very smart castle. Without disturbing me, he wound up his seat, started the car and drove out as silently as possible. I am still amazed that we got away with that. I imagine the owners would have been rather irritated. He reported to me that it was a most beautiful setting, with a lake, swans, parkland trees and an attractive building. But the weather had been dry for some time, so we didn't do any noticeable damage. I would rather like to go back there and own up. That, I think, they would find amusing. But we weren't using maps, so we have absolutely no idea where we were.'

'Typical cavalry officers,' shouted a wag in the audience.

'Part of my objective is to embarrass my good friend. This is a particularly hard task, largely because he does not do the wicked things that young cavalry officers are prone to do. He is a man who is loyal, trustworthy, good at all that he does and with a military career that the rest of us can only envy. Of course, he won't ever talk about it, and poor Gail has told me that she only discovered the full extent of his gallantry when she went to stay at his home in Northumberland. Actually, I think that was a really clever device, Edward. She was so stunned by your eternal self-abasement that it swung the campaign in your favour. Well done.

'Gail, the regimental family welcomes you with open arms. It's a crying shame that we will not see you in Germany for some time because of Edward's current commitments; but believe me, you are going to be a roaring success. Ladies and gentlemen, I propose a toast to the bride and groom.'

As Big Ben was striking 4.00p.m., Gail and Edward worked their way out of the room and up to the third floor of the Club, where they slipped out of their wedding clothes and into the travelling kit they had planned for their journey to Heathrow and beyond. The wedding finery went into one case, while the dress and Edward's morning coat went into zipped suit covers. A second small case contained all that they would need in the South of France. They took the lift to the ground floor and hung the assorted items in the corridor beside the Field Marshal's Room. Will and Ellie had agreed to take everything home at the end of the day.

As expected, spies had been waiting for the couple to appear, and the vast crowd from upstairs had largely worked its way down into the elegant marbled hall of 127 Piccadilly. Many spilled out onto the road, still armed with champagne flutes. Will and Ellie, together with Mary and James, waited tactfully by the front door. Hugs exchanged, Edward and Gail slid into the waiting limousine, where Jeremy Unwin was holding the door open for them. And they were away.

If the day of the wedding felt like five minutes, the honeymoon seemed to last only a little more than a day. They flew to Nice, where they picked up a hire car and made their way to Villefranche-sur-Mer, where a family friend had most generously lent them a villa by the water. The weather was kind, so for six days they didn't wear many clothes. They ate a huge amount of seafood, both in the villa and in local restaurants. And they made absolutely no attempt to go shopping in the local marche, other than to acquire langoustines, moules, huitres and cheese. They chatted, they slept, they made love, they dreamed of the future and explored the past. They needed nobody else.

Thanks to parental and friends support, Edward and Gail were able to move straight into their new flat on arrival back in England on Saturday 12 May. Edward had given up his old flat and Jane Baldwin had acquired a new flatmate. They had found a large, airy apartment in Lavender Hill, which was chosen as much for its agreeable proportions as for the ease of transport to Whitehall. They had agreed that now that they were sensible married adults, they ought to start trying to find a property to invest in financially. Both agreed that it was madness to carry on renting. It was to be a joint venture in every way.

Chapter Twenty-Four

The 1979 European Parliament Election was held on 7 June. This was the first ever direct election, and fifteen seats were available for Irish representation under a single transferable vote. Fianna Fail led with five seats, followed by Fianna Gael with four, Labour, with four, one independent Fianna Fail and one further independent. There was a 63.6% turnout, of which 3.8% were spoilt votes.

In contrast to this, the UK result was a triumph for the Conservatives, who won sixty of the seventy-eight seats available. Labour took just seventeen and the SNP one. In Northern Ireland, Ian Paisley secured his seat for the DUP, John Hume his for the SDLP and John Taylor a seat for the UUP.

John Taylor was a very lucky man. In 1972, he survived an assassination attempt by the Official IRA. His car was attacked in Armagh and Taylor was shot five times in the head. Edward chortled at the clipped operational report of the shooting, which affirmed that he had not been seriously injured! Five bullets in the head. What did that say about Taylor's brain power? Curiously, Edward had read at least four reports in the past twelve months where victims were shot in the head and reported to be 'not seriously injured'.

In fact, John Taylor proved to be both lucky and resilient. He had extensive facial surgery, notably to his jaw. But he was well enough to re-enter politics and was elected to represent Fermanagh and South Tyrone in the 1973 elections to the Northern Ireland Assembly.

Edward and Gail both agreed from their separate perspectives in the Whitehall circus that there was a new air of urgency about the business of Government. Margaret Thatcher's arrival in power created a surge of sensible policies and actions. As modest desk officers, even they could feel the energy of a good leader.

The impact on terrorism was swift. From a high point of multiple bombings and shootings during 1978, there were very few incidents from May 1979. The intelligence community started to believe that the number of gun-carrying terrorists had dropped to an all-time low. The movement was far from dead, but they seemed to have lost the energy that they had shown over the past eight or nine years.

Edward maintained a close eye on the threat to the Royal Family and raised the issue with his boss at a formal weekly meeting. The frustrating thing was that there was not sufficient evidence to insist that Mountbatten was the most likely prospect. It did not help that for years the Earl had consulted the Cabinet Office annually to confirm that they had no qualms about him visiting Mullaghmore and they had always given him the go-ahead. He made it terribly clear that he was not going to pay any attention unless firm intelligence was produced.

*****

Gail quickly proved to be a patient and highly supportive wife. Edward's training with Les Peters was intense and time-consuming, so the young couple did not have many long evenings together. One way or another, Edward had to be match-fit by 12 July, when the World Champion-ships opened in Melbourne. Edward's selection had been confirmed, and the whole team was scheduled to fly to Australia on 6 July, in order to give them some chance to recover from jet lag. Eight men were selected for the sabre, and four of these would compete in the team event: that included Edward.

Gail was duly booked on the same flight, and they had contrived to secure one of the apartments reserved for the team in St Kilda, only a short walk from the venue where the championships were to take place. On arrival, after a gruelling twenty-two hours of travel, everyone agreed that twenty-four hours of rest were needed. Edward and Gail swiftly surveyed their apartment and went to bed, to fall into an exhausted sleep.

Having known nothing about fencing before, Gail soon became used to the routine of a major fencing tournament. She learned the rules quite quickly, but it took her time to really understand what was happening on the piste. The movements were so swift that the untutored eye could not comprehend the intricacies. Edward found it refreshing and helpful to sit with his bride and explain what he saw that she probably missed.

As the tournament progressed through its pool and knockout stages, Edward grew perceptibly more confident. He admitted that the literal cut and thrust of competition helped to hone his skills and, for the first time, he could feel the impact of Les's strategy. He won more quickly and more cleanly than he had done before. Other contestants noticed it, too. After all, the constituency of the fencing world was not large, and most people knew each other from earlier events. Edward's revised style became one of the subjects that people discussed. At this stage, though, they couldn't do much to interfere with it, because the process of starting from the basics took months of hard work.

On 21 July, Edward achieved his first significant international reward by winning the bronze medal. Les was ecstatic; the Russians were not. They had been winning the sabre with dazzling consistency, and it put their noses out of joint when they failed to clear the board. From Edward's perspective, it was doubly helpful, because it now placed him in the acknowledged top sixteen sabre fencers in the world, which meant that he would not have to compete in pool competitions. Mrs Davidson was absolutely thrilled, and insisted that they telephone the families in England, before she showed her approval in a time-honoured way when they returned to the apartment.

They now had ten days to explore the country, having agreed that they would remain in Melbourne for three days after the competition, then up to a week in Sydney. Distant relatives of Edward's late mother had generously offered to look after them when they left Melbourne.

The Australians were exceptionally open and friendly. Wherever they went, Edward and Gail were treated as long-lost friends. When dining in restaurants, other young couples would make a point of falling into conversation with them. And by virtue of the family links in Sydney, they were entertained in the private homes of half a dozen people that they had never met.

They were lucky that the weather was kind, with sunshine every day and temperatures ranging from 14 to 17 degrees. They sailed in Sydney harbour with family friends, lunched at Doyles in Watson Bay, visited the Opera House, the Fish Market and Governor Phillip's house, which contained a museum of the history of transported convicts. A week proved to be too short, but the time had come to go home. They flew out of Kingsford Smith Airport on 1 August, landing at Hong Kong briefly, before flying on to Heathrow, where they arrived on the morning of 2 August.

Chapter Twenty-Five

The drive from Carrickmacross to Mullaghmore took the two men on the R188 through Carnbane, Tullyvin, Drung and Fairtown, to turn right on to the R212 to pass through Butler's Bridge, Belturbet, Teemore, and Belcoo, where the road passed geographically back into Northern Ireland, until it reached a point half way along Loch Melvin. They reached the coast at Tullaghan and turned left on the N15. Shortly afterwards, they turned right on to the R279 to Mullaghmore.

Tommy McMahon was a married man whose wife, Rose, had given him two sons. He was also an important member of the South Armagh Brigade of the Provisional IRA. He had been trained in Libya and was recognised as a skilled maker of bombs. He had a companion to help lift and drive. It was a little before two-thirty in the morning when the two men arrived at the harbour, where they met the local IRA man, who indicated where the target, a small fishing vessel called *Shadow V*, was tied up. There had been lots of people on the beach up until 2.00a.m., with both the village hotels securing bar extensions for barbecues.

Shadow V was, as the name implies, the fifth in a series of craft called *Shadow* owned by Lord Mountbatten. It was in 1959 that he commissioned the brothers, John and Thomas McCann, to construct a clinker-built cabin cruiser designed on traditional Irish lines, but with modifications to suit the inventive mind of the owner. Not all of the design features were approved of by the professional boat-builders, but their paymaster was a demanding man and they let him have what he wanted. Twenty-eight feet long, she was powered by a thirty-horsepower diesel engine.

McMahon's challenge was to conceal his bomb in such a way that people looking casually into any locker would not recognise it for what it was. With everything already prepared, it took him only minutes to establish the ideal site and fix the bomb in place under loose decking in the cabin. Once back on dry land, he made sure that the weapon was safe, before teaching the local man how to operate the radio-controlled device. The men shared coffee from a flask provided by the local, and at half past three, long before dawn, McMahon set off to return home. He drove a very roundabout route, south to Boyle, then south-east to Strokestown, where he changed cars, before moving north to Granard.

At 9.45a.m., he found himself caught by a Garda road-block. The police were conducting regular roadside checks on tax and insurance papers. They identified two men in the car and when asked where they had been and why, the men in the car were unable to provide convincing answers. It didn't help them that the driver had no idea of the registration number of the car. The policeman's instincts were finely honed, so he called for back-up. The two men were invited to go to the Police Station to clarify their status. They were told that they would not be detained for long, but at 10.45 they were still being held. By now, the Superintendent had established that McMahon was a senior IRA man and, in a moment of inspiration, the Garda understood that they should not allow their captives to wash their hands, because their newly-formed Dublin forensic team would want to take swabs for traces of explosive.

In Mullaghmore, the rain had disappeared and the sun was delivering the warmest of summer days. It was the final day of the school holidays, so the family were determined to make the very most of their lobster fishing. With a great deal of laughter and chatter, Earl Mountbatten of Burma, the last Viceroy of India, was with his daughter Patricia, her husband, John Brabourne, and John's mother, Dorothy, normally known as 'Dodo', who, at 83, was four years older than her host. The younger guests for this adventure were the Brabourne twins, Timothy and Nicholas, who were fourteen. They had made friends with the fifteen-year-old Paul Maxwell, whom Mountbatten paid to help out as a waiter in the castle and to manage the boat when they went fishing. Mountbatten was keen to get the show on the road by 10.15, because of constraints with the tide.

Mountbatten had always loved Classiebawn, but in 1960 his wife, Edwina, died in her sleep during an official visit to Borneo. Death duties would take the vast majority of her fortune and fifteen percent went jointly to her daughters, leaving just five percent for Mountbatten, whose personal wealth was modest. It took him very little time to come to the decision that he would have to sell the castle. This decision had to be reversed quickly, because he was very sensitive to the feelings of the locals at Mullaghmore, who made it absolutely clear how distressed they would be. Curiously, this led to him spending even more time at the castle, rather than less.

The property was a tremendous adventure playground for the Mountbatten family. Every sort of seaside pastime was on the agenda and, as the young grew older, they were able to add riding, golf, salmon and lobster fishing.

But the costs were eating into the Mountbatten finances and in 1975 he sealed a deal with a man called Hugh Tunney, an entrepreneur, who agreed to take on the overhead costs and pay a rent of £3,000 a year, while allowing the Mountbattens to use it in August for the family holiday.

While Mountbatten was convinced that he was invulnerable at Mullaghmore, the Garda felt differently. Starting in 1970, the Irish Government provided security for the Earl. Further constraints were put upon the family movements when Mountbatten wrote to Donal O'Sullivan, the Irish Ambassador in London, in 1972, to point out that there had been a recent kidnapping in nearby Bundoran.

In the complex way that Irish affairs unfold, a hint of vulnerability was revealed when one Liam Carey, who lived in the gatehouse at Classiebawn and who had been a good friend of the family for years, became enamoured of an Irish girl who was closely related to a senior member of the Provisional IRA. At the very least, there was the potential for difficulty.

From the intelligence perspective, Edward was not as convinced as Lord Mountbatten about the goodwill of the locals. He discovered that as far back as 1965, *Shadow V* had been sunk in the harbour. Indeed, it transpired that twice within six weeks the vessel had been damaged in a similar fashion in the same place and roughly at the same time. In 1972, someone had bored holes in the boat to try to cause it to sink. The Garda took it all in their stride, and it seemed that there was little doubt that their guard was down in 1979.

During Hugh Tunney's annual visit to talk to Mountbatten about the estate, the elders of the family discussed the viability of *Shadow V*. After twenty years of loyal service, she was no longer economic to run. Tunney recommended that she should be sold, and his opinion was backed by Lord Brabourne. Mountbatten agreed with a heavy heart and it was resolved that *Shadow V* would be sold when the holiday ended.

There were many boats in the bay, some quite close to *Shadow V*, when, at 11.44a.m. on 27 August 1979, the IRA watcher on the headland above Mullaghmore detonated the bomb. It was as if *Shadow V* had never existed. All that remained were small bits of timber. Mountbatten, his grandson Nicholas and young Paul Maxwell were killed instantly. The Dowager Lady Brabourne appeared to be relatively unscathed, although she was to die of her injuries the following morning.

John and Patricia Brabourne were severely wounded, as was young Timmy, the surviving twin.

The news spread quite slowly and first reached Whitehall at 12.30 when a signal from the British Ambassador to Dublin arrived at the Foreign Office. The information was scant and, in part, wrong, because there was a huge amount of confusion on the ground. It took a long time for people to realise that young Nicholas Knatchbull was missing, let alone dead.

On the first floor of the Cabinet Office, Edward Davidson was inundated with information from all points of the globe. In an intellectual way, he was gratified to observe that the machinery of the intelligence world worked very effectively when there was a crisis. And the whole story started to fall into place when the Security Service reported that two men thought to have been involved in the placing of the bomb had been in custody with the Garda two hours before the bomb exploded. They were still being held, because nobody believed their fictional account of their movements that day.

At 4.00p.m., Edward went with Sir James Harrington to brief the Prime Minister in No 10. They learned that she had been incandescent, raining fury down on all and sundry for allowing this terrible atrocity to occur. But Mrs Thatcher was good with junior staff; she received her visitors without any outburst and invited them to sit in comfortable chairs in her office. Sir James explained that Edward was the desk officer for Ireland, working directly for the Joint Intelligence Committee. He asserted that nobody in England knew more than Edward.

He started with the good news.

'Prime Minister, by a curious quirk of fate, the men who placed the bomb on Lord Mountbatten's boat were in custody when it exploded.' Her eyebrows shot up. 'An alert policeman was manning a checkpoint in the town of Granard, which is about ninety minutes' drive from Mullaghmore. He saw a car in a ropey condition, stopped it and questioned the occupants. Their demeanour and responses were unconvincing, so the policeman called for back-up, who took the car and two men to the police station, which was only a couple of hundred yards away. That was at about 09.45 this morning.

'The men continued to prevaricate, and it took almost two hours for the Garda to work out that they had Thomas McMahon, a very senior PIRA member and well-known bomb maker in custody. In time, they worked out that his colleague was Francis McGirl. It was almost exactly at this time that the man left in charge in Mullaghmore detonated the bomb. Clearly, the police in Granard had no idea about the explosion, but their senses were on high alert and they called for a forensic team from Dublin to come and examine the two suspects. At that point, they were arrested so that they could be legally held.

'We understand that McMahon displayed physical evidence of being involved with explosive recently. The forensic team has taken his clothing, which is said to contain signs of sand and paint. For what it is worth, the Garda are pretty convinced that they have the man who placed the bomb. The trouble now is that we are less likely to identify the man, or men, who assisted in Mullaghmore and actually exploded the device. They say that half of the population in the town are in tears and half are cheering. The Garda are going to have a very hard time trying to piece together who the other culprits are.'

'That is an excellent report. Thank you. I have been trying all day to get someone to tell me what is going on.'

'Well, if I may say so, Prime Minister, the wheels of the intelligence world do work rather well. I haven't had to drag this information out of anybody. It has all been volunteered as soon as the separate sources tidied up the woolly bits.'

Mrs Thatcher looked at Sir James, mentally conveying her acknowledgement that his staff were on top of their game. She thanked them for their time and they strolled back up Downing

Street to Whitehall, turned left and swiftly re-entered the Cabinet Office.

Edward immediately telephoned Gail in her office to give her a rough report on the Mountbatten murder and his briefing of the Prime Minister. He said that he felt he should stay in the office until about 7.00p.m., so she asked if she could come round to his office to wait for him. Delighted with the idea, he agreed, and telephoned reception to say that his wife, who worked for the Foreign Office, would be coming round to sit in his office until he could leave.

She arrived just after five, and Edward dashed downstairs to collect her. She had never been inside the Cabinet Office and was truly gratified to see where her man worked. No sooner had she sat down on a chair by Edward's desk, than the telephone rang. It was Colonel Mark Humphreys in MO4.

'I have just had terrible news from Northern Ireland,' he said. 'Twenty minutes ago, a bomb exploded at Warrenpoint. We have seven confirmed dead. Parachute Regiment on a regular patrol.'

'Oh, my God. As if today weren't bad enough. And it must have been radio-controlled, like the one in Mullaghmore. I wonder if Thomas McMahon was the maker of both bombs?'

'That's lateral thinking. What makes you link them?'

'Well, it is the PIRA South Armagh Brigade area. There is a degree of sophistication in the radio-controlled devices. As we know now, McMahon probably placed the bomb on Mountbatten's boat, but he didn't press the detonator, because he was in police custody at the time it went off. It seems to me that he could have prepared the bomb at Warrenpoint.'

'We will have to follow that through. Are you staying in your office for a while? I will put together a detailed report which you will probably want to share with the JIC tonight.'

'By good fortune, I have my bride sitting in my office, so I don't need to go anywhere.'

Edward quickly explained to Gail what he had just learned, told her to sit still and guard the office while he popped along to talk to her godfather. When Sir James heard Edward's quick summary, his head dropped into his hands. 'What a terrible day,' he said. 'I am sorry to ask you, Edward, but it would be good if you were to stay on the case until we have a clearer picture of what happened. I can't stay past 6.00p.m., I regret, because I have to attend a reception at the Athenaeum. Here is the number. Don't hesitate to call me there up until about 8.00p.m. After that, I will be on my home number.'

'Well, my darling, you wanted to know what my work entailed. I fear you are going to have several hours of it now. James has told me to stay until we have a clear picture of what is going on. I will then draft a brief and call him at his reception or home. If it's OK with you, my love, we will have a quick supper somewhere when this is done.'

Truthfully, Gail was thrilled to have the chance to see Edward at work. Of course, she was equally horrified by the death and destruction that they were assimilating.

Edward neatly sewed two pieces of A4 separated by carbon paper into his typewriter and swiftly started to bang out the key ingredients of his report. He was totally immersed in it, so Gail had the chance to observe him in action. Like every other aspect of his ability, she had no idea that he was an efficient touch-typist. In no time, he ratcheted the first pair of pages out of the typewriter and inserted two replacements. Briefly, he looked at her and said, 'By all means read it.'

The telephone rang again. It was 5.40p.m. 'Mark Humphreys here, Edward. This will be recorded as the blackest day in the Army's history since the last war. I have been talking to Northern Ireland. It seems that the reinforcements who went by road and air to Warrenpoint fell into a well-designed trap by setting up a command post where the IRA thought they would. Another huge bomb was exploded and we have multiple casualties. I can't be firm on the numbers, but it is more than ten dead.'

'I don't have the vocabulary to say what I am thinking, Colonel. Those poor, poor lads. I will be in the office until such time as I can draft a full and detailed report for Sir James.'

With that, he ran out of the office to try to catch his boss before he left for the Athenaeum. He was just in time and quickly sketched out the details that Mark Humphreys had supplied. Sir James shook his head in despair. 'I will be waiting for you to call,' he said.

Edward walked slowly back to the office. Bureaucratic it might be, but he should not really leave Gail alone with all of his papers. 'Darling one, it is going to be a long evening. I cannot leave until I know who wants which reports and when. Do stay if you want to. We will still be able to get a late meal, but equally you may be bored to tears and wish to go home.'

'You're right. I will probably get under your feet here. I think I will go home. Don't think about us going out; we have plenty in the fridge. Just give me a call when you leave the office.' And with that, she gave him a huge hug and kissed him firmly on the lips. 'Tea boy,' she smiled.

Edward realised that his further input would be limited. Once he had the full story, he would phone James Harrington. Just as he was thinking about who would be performing and where, Mark Humphreys called again. 'I will be able to tell you almost everything in the next forty minutes or so. But I am to brief CGS, Dwin Bramall, tomorrow morning at 0830. I would like you to be with me, please, because your thoughts on McMahon may have some resonance. CGS is going to see the Prime Minister at 0930.'

By 7.30p.m., Edward was able to put together a concise, accurate briefing for his boss. He phoned the Athenaeum and asked for Sir James Harrington. The reception staff were fully on the ball and within five minutes he was able to report precisely what had happened. He said that he was aware that CGS was to meet with the Prime Minister at 0930 and that he, Edward, was to attend the briefing of CGS at 0830.

'Right. That's clear. I think it would be a good thing for me to attend the same briefing at 0830, because I am called to the PM's office at 0930, too. Please would you contact CGS's office and fix that? Perhaps you could meet me in my office at 0800 to go through the key points?'

'Of course I will be on parade,' said Edward. He put down the phone and called the MoD, where he was put straight through to the Lieutenant-Colonel who served as CGS's Military Assistant. He immediately saw the wisdom of the Chairman of the JIC attending the full operational briefing and agreed to let CGS know.

Next, he phoned Gail, who had been at home for only twenty minutes. She was relieved to learn that he was coming home immediately and fully understood that he would be on the road at dawn. Edward swiftly packaged the papers together, locked the secure filing cabinet, locked the door to his office and trotted downstairs. Leaving the Cabinet Office, he turned right to walk to Parliament Square, where he managed to catch an 87 bus almost immediately.

Chapter Twenty-Six

Edward guessed that Mark Humphreys would be at work already, so at 0715 the following morning he ran up the steps of the MoD, showed his pass at reception and ran up the four flights of stairs to MO4. His reasoning was sound, and Mark welcomed him with a weary wave. 'Did you manage to get home, Colonel?'

'No. I had a kip on the floor here. But it was worthwhile, because I now have the full story, which I will share with you in a minute. Just let me be trebly sure of my facts about Whitehall guidance to Mountbatten and then can we have a look at your inspired thinking about McMahon?'

'At the risk of overplaying this, Colonel, there has been a history of the Cabinet Office signing off on Lord Mountbatten's trips to Mullaghmore. I discovered several occasions on which his boat was damaged or sunk. We have had consistent reports for several months about the PIRA ambition to have a go at a senior minister or member of the Royal Family, but I concede that we had no specific intelligence about Lord Mountbatten as the target. We put it to him that in the light of historic damage to his vessel, combined with the knowledge that an attack was being planned on a royal, he should consider not going to Ireland this year. He spoke at length to Sir James Harrington and said, "thank you, but no thank you". In his opinion, he was widely liked in Mullaghmore, which was true, even if that did not extend to one hundred percent of the population; and he believed that the IRA would never be stupid enough to attack him there.'

'Good. That's clear. How I wish we had been able to drill down into their thinking a little bit deeper.'

'I agree, but their cell system seems to be working rather well.'

'OK. Now, talk me through your thinking on Tommy McMahon being associated with both Mullaghmore and Warrenpoint.'

'There's nothing terribly complicated about this. Actually, I am mildly surprised that nobody else has been commenting on it. McMahon is commonly accepted to be the leading bomb maker in the South Armagh Brigade. He was well trained in Libya and we have seen his hand in a range of attacks. It is now transparent that he was the person who built the bomb at Mullaghmore. Why would they put a second string onto the task of killing so many of our boys at Warrenpoint? On all occasions, someone else presses the button, but I firmly believe that McMahon manufactures the weaponry.'

'We should feed this through to the Garda for their forensic people to investigate. Good thinking, Edward. Now, I will bring you fully up to date.' And with that, he spoke for ten minutes, with Edward taking notes.

'Colonel, I have to go and brief Sir James. We will be back for the meeting with CGS for 0830. Is the meeting in his office?' Mark nodded, his mind already following another train of thought. Edward left, ran down the stairs out into Whitehall, then across the road to his office.

At five minutes to eight, he tapped on his boss's door. He delivered the full details of the Warrenpoint massacre, summarised the known position on the Mountbatten murder and added his personal thoughts on McMahon's involvement in both. James Harrington reflected on this. 'It is unconfirmed, of course,' he said, 'but who is to say that you are wrong? At the very least, we want to give the Garda the opportunity to check it out with forensics. Right, let us go to the MoD.'

Dwin Bramall, a former Royal Green Jacket, had been in post for only six weeks or so. Edward had met him on many occasions when he had been commanding the 1st Division in Verden. 'Hello, Edward,' he welcomed, 'you turn up in some unusual places.'

'Bad penny, General,' replied Edward.

Mark Humphreys cleared his throat. 'I propose to speak for fifteen minutes, General, leaving half an hour for questions, before your meeting at No 10.

'Let me summarise the Mullaghmore incident first. Sir James is here and will confirm that Lord Mountbatten was encouraged not to go on his family holiday to Classiebawn Castle this year. His Lordship thought that the evidence of a threat was too weak and judged that the IRA would never, and I quote, be so stupid as to attack him there. To put his safety in perspective, the Garda have allotted security staff to provide loose security around the Castle, the family and the boat for several years, although we understand that the intensity has been variable. At no stage has there been a specific threat to Lord Mountbatten.

'We all know now that Tommy McMahon, a recognised leader of the PIRA South Armagh Brigade and its most accomplished bomb maker, was arrested many miles from Mullaghmore some two hours before the bomb exploded. A member of the Garda with a fine nose for trouble stopped and questioned a vehicle containing McMahon and one Francis McGirl, whose whole family has a long association with the IRA. Their suspicions were sufficiently sharp for them to hold on to the two men for over two hours. When they learned of the explosion in Mullaghmore, they arrested the men and subsequently ensured that forensic tests were conducted. Already, it is clear that McMahon made and placed the bomb. The trouble is that we do not know who pressed the button.

271

The Garda have a well-known and effective Superintendent in charge of the investigation, and we now have to support them in their endeavours.

'Let me move now to Warrenpoint. The first point I must make is that the IRA have been studying our movements very carefully for some time. It may be hard to identify this in day-to-day operations, but it seems clear to me that we have become idle about changing our routines.

'At 4.40p.m., a Land Rover and two four tonners of 2nd Battalion the Parachute Regiment passed a parked vehicle on the A2 road at Narrow Water Castle. The 500lb fertiliser bomb was concealed behind straw bales on the lorry. It was detonated by radio command, we believe from the other side of the border. It took out the rear vehicle in the convoy, killing six soldiers. Two others survived, but are severely wounded.

'Soldiers from the first two vehicles believed that they were then engaged by sniper fire from across the water which formed the border at that point. I am sad to report that there were two civilian casualties as a result: one died and one is critically injured. The irony is that one of them lived in London.

'Reinforcements were called and arrived in multiple transports. The first on site was Lieutenant-Colonel David Blair of the Queen's Own Highlanders and his signaller. They flew in a Gazelle. He took command of the site. A Wessex arrived to move the casualties. And on the ground, the Parachute Regiment, supported by a small number of Queen's Own Highlanders, arrived by road. The IRA were clever in their appreciation of where we would place a command post to control the operation. We were far too predictable and therefore took the full thrust of an 800lb bomb placed in milk churns precisely where they anticipated, which was in the castle gatehouse opposite the first explosion. That bomb was detonated thirty-two minutes after the first explosion and killed

272

ten soldiers of the Parachute Regiment and two of the Queen's Own Highlanders. It also completely destroyed the gatehouse. The Wessex was taking off as the bomb exploded. It was damaged, but did not crash. I regret we were unable to recover all of the bodies, because Lieutenant-Colonel Blair was obliterated by the explosion. The only evidence of him being present is one of his epaulettes.'

'And was there any sign of the terrorists who exploded the bombs?' asked CGS.

'No, General. No sign at all. It could all have been done by just one man sitting in woodland by the lough.'

'And is there any gossip on our intelligence networks?' CGS persisted.

Edward responded. 'No, General. You will be aware that the IRA have adopted a cell system which is proving remarkably robust. The Security Service, SIS and Metropolitan Police are as much in the dark as the MoD.'

Mark Humphreys added, 'Edward has come up with the unproven but possible notion that Tommy McMahon was responsible for all of the bombs. He has a reputation, and this all happened in his area of interest. I support Edward's view, so will make it known to the Garda and Northern Ireland police to see if we can prove or disprove it forensically.'

'Very well. Sir James and I had better make a move to Number 10.' Everyone rose to their feet and the two senior men silently left the office.

'I hate to voice this thought,' said Edward, 'but we don't look too good in the face of this surge of terrorism.'

'Too right,' replied Humphreys. 'The IRA will be cock-a-hoop. We had better look out for repeat actions elsewhere.'

Edward was back in his office at 0915, still ahead of his clerk, Jim Shaw. Dutifully, he turned to the newspapers which he had collected on his way from reception. As always, he started with the *Irish Times*, followed by the *Guardian*, the two papers which consistently reported more accurately than any other. He read everything about Mountbatten and Warrenpoint in careful detail, but gained no new knowledge. The other newspapers indulged in some fanciful guesswork, all of it light years from the truth.

At 1045, Sir James popped his head round the door. 'Can you spare me five minutes, please, Edward?'

Immediately, Edward grabbed a notepad and biro and followed his boss to his office. 'Without being indiscreet, I can report that the Prime Minister is not happy. In fact, the CGS told me as we left that he had no idea that she was a "fishwife". For what it is worth, I think that did an injustice to the wives of fishmongers!'

Edward laughed. 'I know that she can be very direct.'

'Direct! Phew. Anyhow, we have to deliver to her by tomorrow a detailed evaluation of the Provisional's current capability. We must leave no stone unturned. And by we, I mean you, Edward.'

Edward almost ran back to his office, where he started to call his opposite numbers. First, he called Edward Longstaff, explained the challenge and asked if he could have SIS input by, say, 4.00p.m. He followed this with calls to Richard Potter in Curzon Street, Harry Martens in Cheltenham and, for good measure, Jack Strong at the Met. Finally, he called Headquarters Northern Ireland and spoke to Christopher Westlake, the G2 Intelligence. They all agreed to deliver, so Edward drafted the skeleton of the report, into which he could drop quotable quotes. At times like this, he wished that he had some form of word processor that could hold all of his written material in a form that could be amended. So much time was consumed loading carbon sheets into a typewriter.

Responses started to flow into his office by lunchtime. Evidently, people had anticipated that the Prime Minister would ask for a total review. He was not surprised that the

Whitehall assessment was little changed from what it had been forty-eight hours earlier. Horrific as the two incidents had been, they did not suggest that the Provisionals had acquired extra men or materials. Indeed, the commonly held opinion was that there were fewer than one hundred gun-carrying terrorists. There was a residual level of popular support in many Catholic communities, and that would take generations to erode, not least because the terrorists maintained their profile and authority through fear.

In summing up the evaluation, Edward observed that the success of their three bombs could only encourage the IRA to develop more attacks along the same lines. He anticipated that vehicles, bridges and culverts would be particular threats to the security forces. He sat back to reflect: should he include that opinion or not? He had been tasked to talk about the IRA capability, not to make recommendations about counter-measures. On balance, he decided to leave it in the paper, because it reflected the view of the intelligence community about likely behaviour.

It was not even 3.00p.m. when Edward walked along to Sir James' office and asked his secretary if he could deliver the report. Grace Evans was a warm and helpful woman who clearly had her boss firmly under control. 'I am sorry, Edward, but he has someone with him.'

'Would you be an angel and give him this paper as soon as he is free? It is for the Prime Minister, and I imagine that Sir James will want to tweak it.'

Thirty minutes later, Grace telephoned. 'Could you pop in, please?'

'Well done, Edward. Contrary to your expectation, I don't want to tweak this report at all. It is absolutely clear and very persuasive. I will get it across to No 10 immediately. I think you ought to clean up and go home to that lovely god-daughter of mine.'

Edward called Gail as soon as he was back in his own office, reporting that he was being sent home early. He was due to have a training session with Les at 6.00p.m., so intended to go to the London Fencing School for an hour of circuit training before Les arrived. He would be done by 7.00p.m. and suggested that he should meet Gail at L'Artiste Muscle at 7.30p.m. She readily agreed and added that she was going to persuade her sister to join them.

By now, Edward's fitness regime was reaching new levels of intensity. He felt more alive than at any time in the past and actively enjoyed the process of honing his body to tackle new extremes. The success in Melbourne had added a permanent confidence that he had lacked before, and Les' sharp eye for detail was delivering increasingly valuable variations to his fighting technique. The trick now would be to time everything so that he was not stale by July 1980.

It was just after 7.30p.m. when he walked into the Davidson family's favourite restaurant. Gail and Bella were chatting away, completely oblivious to his arrival until he kissed the top of Gail's head. 'You two can certainly talk,' he grinned, as he leaned down to bestow a kiss on Bella's cheek.

'Gail was just telling me that you seem to be spending half your time with the Prime Minister.'

'I admit that it has been an unusual thirty hours or so. I had to deliver a detailed evaluation of the IRA to James today. To my surprise, he didn't change a word and sent it around to No 10 immediately. Don't tell anyone else, but I understand that Mrs T is going over to Northern Ireland tomorrow. Well done her. It will do immense good for the morale of the Paras and Queen's Own Highlanders. Now, let's talk about happier things, shall we?'

The two girls had been in the middle of an animated conversation about their parents and how to celebrate their mother's birthday. They recognised that their own preference for a smart lunch or dinner in London would not suit their mum in her current state of mind. She clearly wanted to spend as much time at home as possible, so it seemed that they would have to organise a party there.

Edward was very happy to just sit and watch the sisters gossip. Bella had adopted him as a brother to whom she could talk about anything, and in the three months since his marriage, he had listened gravely to her ideas on life, the relative merits of the many men who chased after her, and how to develop her career. After a lifetime with no siblings or cousins, he found the intimacy of family life totally uplifting.

His mind slipped sideways to think about his imminent Staff College exam. He had already passed the Military Law module, so just had the International Relations and Military papers to complete in a week's time. Very reluctantly, he had concluded that he should not volunteer for any of the other Service or overseas Staff Colleges. It would be wisest to go to Camberley. The first trick was to pass the wretched exam, which he would be sitting in Aldershot on Thursday 6 September, the day after Lord Mountbatten's State funeral.

He realised that the girls had stopped gassing and were looking at him enquiringly. 'What have I done?' he asked.

'Nothing,' said Gail, 'but you weren't with us, so we thought we would give you a chance to join in.'

'I am sorry. I was distracted by thoughts about next week's exam and what would happen if I failed it.'

'Don't be an ass. Of course you'll pass.'

'Nothing is less certain, believe me. I may have plenty of practice in writing bold reports, but I could be caught out by some of the International Relations questions.'

'On the other hand, if you get questions on Ireland, you won't even have to put on a thinking cap,' said Gail.

He smiled. God, he loved this woman, and so many good things had happened for him since he first met her. He would have to pass the exam merely to sustain her confidence in him.

As Edward was paying the bill, Bella turned to her sister and said, 'I see you didn't drink even one sip of wine this evening. Is there something you should be sharing with me?'

Gail looked suddenly very embarrassed. 'I hoped you wouldn't notice. I haven't told Edward yet, so keep quiet, I beg you, sis.'

Bella gave her a hug. 'You clever old thing. When are you going to let him know?'

'Thanks to you, sooner than I anticipated. I guess I should do so this evening when we reach home. I half hoped to let him get the Staff exam out of the way before he started to worry about our lives.'

Bella gave Edward a very fond kiss and hug, before setting off to Piccadilly on her own. 'Wow, what was that for?' asked Edward. 'She's ultra-affectionate tonight.'

'You are a very fine brother-in-law. She laps you up, so she shows it. Don't buck it, my man.'

They ambled down White Horse Street and stood waiting for a taxi, which arrived within a couple of minutes. Half an hour later, they let themselves into their flat. 'I might just watch the news before we go to bed,' said Edward.

Gail turned to him and said, 'Give me a minute. Sit down.' He sat and she parked herself on his lap.

'I could do with this,' he said, nuzzling his face into her neck.

'My darling husband, I ought to tell you something that I have known about for a week. Bella picked up on it this evening and I cannot have her knowing something that affects you without you being aware of it.'

'This sounds very ominous. What have you done, sweetheart?'

'What have you done, more to the point, Major Davidson. You have been far too fertile. I am going to have a baby.'

'Oh, my God!' The tears were instant. 'That is the most stunning news. Am I going to be allowed to keep making love to you?'

'As often as you want, daddy.'

They embraced with deep emotion. 'So how did Bella spot something that I have failed to notice?'

'I wasn't drinking, just nursing a half glass of wine all evening and sipping water.'

'How stupid of me. I never made the link between the drink and the baby. Are you not going to be allowed a drink at all during the pregnancy?'

'It's probably better not to. I don't want to injure the child and, to be honest, I won't miss it. I do love tasting different wines, but I don't really need to do more than that.'

'So, when is it due?'

'I am eight weeks in, which means that we will be parents during the first week of April. I wasn't going to tell you until you had finished your exam, and I would rather not tell anyone else until I have a test at twelve weeks.'

'Not even your parents?'

'Definitely not my parents. All sorts of mishaps can occur, and twelve weeks is generally judged to be a sort of safety point, after which the early gremlins disappear. Assuming all is well, I propose that we stay with my parents over the weekend of 29 and 30 September so that we can tell them face-to-face.'

'My darling, of course. I understand your motives, but you should have shared this momentous news with me as soon as you knew. It must have been so lonely holding on to it. Have you been nervous?'

'I admit to being a little nervous. This is the most enormous step, and our lives will never be the same again. To be honest,

I thought we would have two to three years without children, but your huge sexual appetite, brilliant love-making and energetic body overwhelmed my defences. So much for the pill. What I will say, though, is that when the doctor confirmed my suspicions, I felt as if I had achieved what every woman desires. I am longing to be the mother of your children, Edward.'

They embraced again and the tears coursed down Edward's cheeks in unalloyed joy. 'Why did I want to see the news?' he asked. 'What I want to do is take you to bed and hold you gently in my arms.'

'I am all for that, but first I need to call Bella to tell her what I have done and insist that she keeps quiet.' And with that, she hopped off his lap, went to the telephone and dialled her sister. The conversation was brief, and Bella promised faithfully that she would not breathe a word to anyone, let alone their parents.

Chapter Twenty-Seven

'Ten minutes remaining,' announced the invigilator. One hundred candidates sat in the Aldershot Garrison gym. They had been scribbling for six hours, broken only by the lunch provided for them by the Garrison catering staff. Edward had finished writing fifteen minutes earlier and read carefully through the essays he had written on global affairs. It had been almost too good to be true when he discovered that Ireland had been one of the questions that he could choose. His second essay had been on the strategic and tactical use of Cruise missiles. In his heart, he was pretty confident that he had passed quite comfortably. His writing had been fluent and fulsome, with no pauses to grope for a hidden meaning or elusive word. He had also completed the document which asked him to affirm the order of choice for staff colleges. He had gone for Camberley, Bracknell, then Australia.

He rose from his seat and took his work forward to put on the invigilator's desk. There was no more that he could do. Returning to his desk, he collected his briefcase and walked towards the exit. If he was sharp about it, he could be back in London by 6.30p.m. There was a queue of taxis waiting outside the building, so he climbed into the lead vehicle and asked to go to the station, which was about fifteen minutes away.

The past week had been full of wonder. He couldn't stop thinking about Gail and the baby growing inside her. The whole concept of becoming a father, natural as it was, was also terrifying. They were going to bring into the world a defenceless being that would need years of nourishment, love, care and protection. He was dying to tell Uncle James and Aunt Mary, but knew that Gail's parents must take priority. Only three weeks to go until they could go public.

They were due to spend the weekend with old friends of Gail's in Essex. They had decided to go by train, because the exit from London on a Friday evening would be a nightmare, so they planned to catch a train at 5.20p.m. the next day. The journey would take only forty minutes to Hatfield Peverel, where their hosts would collect them for the fifteen-minute car journey to their house just outside Maldon. Edward had not met Bill and Emma Loftus because they had not been able to get to the wedding. Bill was an accountant and Emma had been a lawyer until she started to produce children. Both had been up at Oxford with Gail and had become 'an item', as they said nowadays in the local vernacular.

He found he was quite weary as he unlocked the door to the flat. There were delicious aromas and soft music wafting around as Gail appeared from the kitchen dressed in a comic pinafore. 'I have got some duck for us tonight. You are to sit down while I wait on you hand and foot. How did the exam go?'

'You won't believe it. One of the main questions was about Ireland. Stunning luck for me. I finished both papers early and had ample time to read through them. I don't want to tempt fate, but I think I will have made it. And I did as we discussed: I listed my priorities for staff college as Camberley, Bracknell, then Australia.'

'Good. Now, a whisky and soda?'

'Yes, please, my slave. You had better be careful. This could turn into a habit.'

They chatted away about the events of the day until Edward had a light-bulb moment. 'My darling, if we are staying with the Loftuses at Maldon, we are bound to be offered oysters. I can have them, but can you?'

'Oh, damn. I hadn't thought of that, and I really do not want to let the cat out of the bag to them at this stage. It would be around our university chums in half an hour, which would mean that Mum and Daddy would be telephoned out of the blue. The trouble is that Emma knows how much I love them. I guess I am going to have to pretend that I have had a funny one recently and am being very cautious. But she is as sharp as Bella and will notice that I am not drinking.'

'OK. I tell you what. I will have just one drink each night. I can honestly put it down to my training regime, and you are following my example out of sympathy. Will that work?'

'I hope so. I will have to drink that one glass of whatever on each occasion. She will see straight through the subterfuge otherwise.'

Liverpool Street station was heaving with weary City workers, most of whom wore no ties and carried jackets under their arms because of the heat. This was England's eternal problem, thought Edward: it is either too hot or too cold. Eventually, the notice board showed that their train would leave from Platform 14, so they joined the shuffling crowd making its way there.

Emma Loftus bounced out of her car when she spotted them coming out of the dirty red-brick building that housed the ticket office. She was a tall, willowy girl, with dark brown hair and a pair of designer jeans below a yellow shirt. Edward could see a child in a special seat in the back. Emma and Gail embraced for several seconds, before Edward was accepted with a kiss to the cheek. 'Very good to meet the man at last,' Emma observed.

Edward climbed in the back beside the child, who was having a quiet snooze. There was not much point in him trying to take part, because the two girls were chatting nineteen to the dozen. In no time at all, they turned into the gateway of a detached property with a small gravel courtyard. Edward tried to leap out to open Gail's door, but he was trapped by a child-lock. The girls kept on nattering, hardly noticing that the man in the back was stuck. Emma opened the rear door to Edward's right and started to unbuckle her child. She laughed. 'Gail, your husband is unable to get out.'

Gail opened the door. She looked happy, relaxed and most amused by her husband's inability to exit the car unaided. He scrambled out, gave her a kiss and leaned back in to grab their one small travelling bag. They all trooped to the front door. 'Bill should be back shortly,' Emma announced. 'I will just show Gail where you are.'

The two girls set off up the stairs, leaving Edward to walk into a sitting room which looked out over the estuary. He spent a few minutes checking out the family photographs and the scattering of stiff invitations on the mantelpiece until he heard the girls coming back downstairs.

'Now, tea or something stiffer?'

'You are going to find us hugely dull,' said Edward. 'I am on a harsh training regime which allows me to have just one alcoholic drink a day. My darling bride has decided to keep me company, which is more than a step beyond the call of duty.'

'Tea, then,' said Emma. They all followed her into the kitchen, which also looked out over the estuary. She flicked on the kettle and reached into a cupboard for a container of tea bags.

They were still sitting in the kitchen when Bill Loftus came back. He was about six feet tall, a little overweight and with a hint that his hair was disappearing already. But he had an engaging personality and immediately offered alcohol. Edward explained that he really was going to be immensely dull and would stick to just one drink per day. 'Well, you can have it now, can't you?'

Edward said he would far prefer to have a glass of wine with supper, so Bill shrugged and went off to find himself a whisky and soda. He came back into the kitchen, slopped down into a chair at the table and joined in the general discussion.

For half an hour, most of the gossip rolled around their friends from university. Emma got up to start cutting vegetables, so Gail joined her, leaving the two men to tentatively learn about each other. Bill suggested that they move to the sitting room so that they wouldn't be in the way; and, as an aside, 'Then we won't be shanghaied into cooking. That would be a disaster for us all.

'I should be congratulating you, Edward. Gail has always had a fleet of interested men lurking around her. It was about ten minutes from the time that we learned about you until you had her walking down the aisle.'

'Thank you. You would expect me to agree with you. It sounds enormously conceited, but when I set my mind on a course of action, I try to deliver. Of course, this time the decision-making was ruled by the heart, rather than the head. In fairness, I made it clear to Gail what I was trying to achieve, so she had a good fifty percent stake in the campaign.'

Bill laughed. 'All she has told us is that you are a soldier and sportsman. Which is more important to you?'

'What a very good question. I don't think that anyone has ever asked me that before. Well, being a soldier gives me a salary. Being a sportsman gives me the fun. The Army is always very generous with time for sport, particularly international sport. Of course, the sport cannot last forever. I am very nearly too old for my game, so the next year will probably see the end of my time on tour. In many ways, that is appropriate. If I have passed the exam which I took yesterday, I should return to very serious soldiering after the next Olympic Games.'

'Olympic Games? We weren't told about that.'

'Ah. Gail is evidently catching my disease. Normally, I try not to talk about it too much, because there is no reason for people to take too much interest.'

'Nonsense. Give me a quick rundown.'

'Very well. I competed in the Munich and Montreal Games in '72 and '76. I intend to do so in Moscow next July. I fence with a sabre.'

'Good Lord. Three Games in a row. That's magnificent.'

'It's not as difficult as you may imagine. But enough of me; tell me something about you and Emma.'

They chatted quietly as the noises and aromas from the kitchen grew in intensity. 'Will you boys lay the table in the dining room, please?' shouted Emma.

'I knew there would be a call to arms,' said Bill. 'We have one other couple coming to supper. Nice people who we have met since we have been here. We thought it would dilute the university memories and save you from total boredom.'

They wandered into the dining room and Bill opened a drawer in a Welsh dresser to pull out knives and forks. 'I'm not sure if we need spoons.' He walked across to the kitchen and took guidance.

'OK. We have the whole nine yards. Two knives, two forks and a spoon.' He handed a fistful of them to Edward, who dutifully started to lay the table. Bill went off to find side plates and a range of glasses. Job done, they retired to the drawing room, where Bill picked up his glass, sniffed it and asked Edward if he would change his mind and have one now.

'Of course, that is very kind. I am sorry to be such a bore, but the drink really does have an impact on fitness, and with the quality of the competition, I cannot afford to lose the plot. But a whisky and soda would be most agreeable. Thank you.'

With patient interrogation, Edward drew Bill out about himself. He had been in his final year at Oxford when he met Emma. They had hit it off immediately and had been living together pretty much consistently ever since. He had been lucky with jobs, because he moved straight into his father's accountancy practice. Emma had gone off to work with a firm of solicitors in London, and that had been the catalyst for them to get married. Their daughter, Sophie, was now eighteen months old.

The weekend proved to be full of laughter, good food and not a lot of grog. Edward managed to have a dozen oysters when they lunched in a fish restaurant on the Saturday, and Emma made no quizzical comments about Gail's lack of oysters and wine. Sunday lunch with roast lamb and delicious roast potatoes brought the break to an end. As they rattled back into Liverpool Street station, they both felt that they had been away for months. Edward quietly stretched out his hand and grabbed Gail's. 'I love you, my beautiful woman,' he said, to the mild amusement of the couple sitting opposite them. They sat contentedly holding hands until the train arrived back at Liverpool Street.

Chapter Twenty-Eight

The train arrived promptly at East Grinstead, where Will Ritchie was waiting patiently in the car park. Gail embraced her father with real tenderness and they stood for a second or two just holding on to each other. A flicker of doubt flashed through Edward's mind that the Ritchies knew or had guessed that there was about to be an announcement, but there was nothing he could do about it. He shook hands firmly with his father-in-law, before they all climbed into the car and set off for home.

Ellie was on her knees in the garden when they arrived, digging away at the new bed they had created on arrival in the house. It was six-thirty in the evening, so Will suggested that they should all have a drink in the garden. Gail looked at her husband, with whom she had agreed the plan. She suggested that they should all troop in together so that nobody was fetching and carrying. Once in the kitchen, Edward drew Gail beside him in front of the Aga and Gail said, 'Mum, Daddy, before you go any further, we need to tell you that you are going to be grandparents.'

Ellie shrieked, putting her hands to her cheeks and surreptitiously wiping an involuntary tear from her right eye. Will instantly moved to shake Edward by the hand, then hugged his daughter again. 'Without doubt, this calls for champagne,' he said.

'It won't surprise you that we have some with us,' countered Edward. He went back into the hall and removed two bottles of Pol Roger from their bag.

'The only trouble,' said Gail, 'is that I am off the booze. But I am very happy to watch you all celebrating.' Edward popped the cork with smooth efficiency, and poured a little fluid into the three champagne flutes that had magically appeared on the kitchen table.

'Well, bring that bottle, Edward. Let's go out into the garden and enjoy the autumn evening.'

Ellie was firing a range of questions at them both, which made them laugh. 'Mum, I can't answer if you keep on questioning me.'

They sat at a garden table, around which were six wooden seats. Edward plonked the champagne on the table as they sat down and Gail started to fill in the gaps in her parents' knowledge.

'So, I am now twelve weeks in. That means that our baby should arrive in early April, which is when Edward will move from Shrivenham to Camberley.'

'Ah, ha,' offered Will, 'so you have had the results?'

'Indeed.' Edward grinned. 'I received the results this week. Thanks to questions that played to my strengths, I passed the exam quite comfortably and was quickly told the plan. I will finish in the Cabinet Office in early December and will have three weeks to manage our household arrangements for the next year.'

'I would think that James will be very sad to lose you,' said Will.

'No sadder than I will be to lose him. He has been the most wonderful boss. I have said to you before that he has taught me absolutely everything I know about the Whitehall machine, and it is bound to be invaluable in the future, even though it paints me as an experienced paper warrior.'

'But come back to your baby,' cried Ellie. 'I cannot wait to be a granny. This is, phew' – she blew out her cheeks – 'simply the most wonderful news, although I don't think we expected it for a couple of years.'

Gail dipped her head. 'You are right, Mum. We thought we might have a couple of years, but – umm – how do I say this? Things got in the way.' The Ritchie family roared with laughter.

'Are you going to let them tell you what sex it is?' asked Ellie.

Edward and Gail looked at each other carefully. 'On balance,' offered Gail, 'we would be happier to let nature take its course and enjoy whatever we are given. In some ways, it stretches the anticipation in a most agreeable fashion, although I concede that my efficient husband and his military planning would prefer to have everything organised well in advance.'

Edward chuckled. 'I can admit that this is the only area of our lives where we have disagreed. No, that's too strong a word. It is the only area in which we have had conflicting opinions. You have to accept that, by instinct and training, I want to be absolutely ready for whatever is on the horizon; but since my darling bride feels that we must wait for the curtain to go up, I am a most willing collaborator.'

Ellie persisted. 'And have you told your sister?'

'I didn't need to,' said Gail. 'We were all having supper together three weeks ago and while Edward was paying the bill she asked me quietly if I had anything to tell her. Clever old stick. She guessed within seconds of us meeting up. I swore her to silence, not to deceive you, but to allow nature the twelve-week margin we needed to be relatively confident that this would probably go to full term.'

'And have you thought of names?' Ellie was on a roll.

'No, Mum. The little squirt has twenty-eight weeks before it appears into our world. We are both enormously content with the notion of a boy or a girl, just so long as it is healthy.'

'Quite right,' said Will. 'Only landed gentry and royalty need to worry about primogeniture. We ordinary mortals can happily rub along with whatever appears. Now, Edward, you are very slow with that champagne.'

Edward leapt to his feet and moved the bottle around the half-empty glasses.

'We were worried only that someone would spring the news before we told you ourselves. We spent a weekend with Bill and Emma Loftus in Maldon, and we had to practise all sorts of tricks to stop Emma guessing. Bill wouldn't have recognised the signs if we had slapped him in the face with an official notice, but Emma is just as sharp as Bella. Still, we got away with it. I knew that if they did guess, it would be around my university friends in a trice, and the parents of any one of them might have telephoned you to enjoy your reaction.'

'On which subject,' said Ellie, 'have you told James and Mary?'

'No. We wanted to see you face-to-face to give you the news. If it is OK with you, we ought to telephone Northumberland shortly.'

'You should do so right now,' said Will. 'Mary will be absolutely ecstatic, and we can all have a happy gossip at the same time.'

Edward emptied the bottle into the three glasses and they rose to go into the kitchen, where Edward swiftly dialled the home number. Mary answered.

'Aunt Mary, I seem to be telephoning you whenever I come down to Sussex to see my in-laws. We arrived an hour ago to tell Will and Ellie that they are going to be grandparents, as are you.'

'Oh, my God, Edward. You really are in a hurry. What marvellous news. I am not going to talk to you about babies. Give me that lovely wife of yours right now.'

Will, Ellie and Edward rolled their eyes as Gail started to chatter nineteen to the dozen. It was going to be some time before she engaged with them again. Edward raised his eyebrows, pointed to his glass and made a bottle-pouring motion. His in-laws nodded happily, so he went to the fridge, pulled out the second bottle of Pol Roger, broke through the foil and untwisted the wire. With an imperceptible 'pop', the cork separated from the bottle and he poured a tiny bit into his glass. They shuffled quietly back into the garden, knowing that Gail would give her mother the opportunity to talk to Mary after the first inquisition.

'Tell me more about the next six months,' said Will.

'Well, first of all, I cannot believe that I have been in Whitehall for almost two years. I think I can safely say that it has been the most interesting job that I have ever done. When I reflect that, but for Sean Lomax's wisdom as Commanding Officer, I would have spent two years at Lulworth barking gunnery commands at students, and never met my bride, my heart quails.

'So I go off to Shrivenham on 6 January. The big question is how we play it. We don't really want to give up the flat in London, and we cannot afford to run one there and another in Wiltshire. Moreover, there is nothing to stop Gail working. It looks as if I am going to have to be a weekly boarder in the Shrivenham Mess. I will take my motorbike down there so that I can get to Swindon station easily, and then it is only an hour's journey into Paddington. This isn't a degree course, just an intelligent look at what scientific innovations will affect warfare in the future, so I am sure that they will give me some latitude as we get closer to Gail's delivery date. After that, though, it would be wrong for us to maintain the London flat, not least because I can secure quarters in Camberley. The military family will support and sustain Gail and the baby if I have to be away.'

'You won't have to worry about Gail while you are at Shrivenham,' said Ellie. 'I can always spend time in London supporting her. But how early can you gain access to the Camberley accommodation?'

'Excellent question. I have put it to the authorities and am waiting for an answer. I don't imagine that it will be too complicated, because this routine has been going on since the end of the war, and there must have been an eternal, but regular turnover of housing. It may be that they offer the quarter in January. After all, the previous Staff Course will leave in December. The only issue is when we actually make the move.'

At that moment, Gail appeared at the front door and asked her mother to talk to Mary. The two women changed places and Gail grinned at her father and husband. 'Mary is such a wonderful friend,' she said. 'I am not sure whether my mother or surrogate mother-in-law is more excited.'

They gossiped cheerfully until Ellie returned. By now it was 7.20p.m., and they agreed that it would be a good time to prepare some supper.

The weekend zipped by. By the time that the young couple reached their flat on Sunday evening, almost everybody had been told the news about a young Davidson, including James Harrington, who visited Edward in his office first thing on Monday morning.

'You are a very fast worker, Edward. I am simply delighted for the pair of you. I am sure that you will be terrific parents. Now, we need to spend a little time working out your handover. I haven't been given the details of candidates for your job yet, but I think the system is going to look for an opportunity for someone from Five or Six to take over from you. Tell me what you think we should be doing to ensure a seamless transfer.'

'I think that two weeks is the absolute maximum handover period that will be needed,' said Edward, 'particularly if the candidate comes from a Civil Service background. I had a huge amount to learn simply because I was a soldier moving into strange territory. That suggests that we should think in terms of them arriving either in the week of the 19th or 26th November. I wish that I had spotted the right candidate during my time here, but the nature of the work has led me to deal with more senior characters in the other services and

293

departments. I simply don't know the potential lower down the scale.'

'I am very content with your judgement. Would you be happy if we waved candidates past you during the selection process?'

'Of course. I would be absolutely thrilled. Presumably, the majority will not have been inducted to HRT, though?'

'That is certainly true. You will be able to tell them the whole story only when one person has been appointed formally.'

Once the Chairman had gone, Edward settled down to the routine that he had established over the previous year and a half. He knew that he would miss the mystique of the business, but he acknowledged how important it was that he should return to the business of being a career soldier. He determined that he would talk to the quartering people in Camberley that day. He had not received a formal posting instruction yet, but he would contact Shrivenham to discuss accommodation for the three months that he would be there.

The telephone rang and he found that James Harrington had been busier than he had anticipated. The Personnel Department asked if they could spend a little time with him going over the job description for his successor. He agreed to visit them on Wednesday. An hour later, Colonel Lewis telephoned him to ask for half an hour of his time to discuss both Edward's plans for Moscow and a review of the HRT induction process so that his successor would receive the full benefit of Edward's own experience. Nobody else chased him on the subject of his departure, but it did alert him to the need for him to draft a timetable for the full induction of the person taking over from him. Putting his daily chores to one side, he turned to his notepad and started to jot down the people and issues that he would have to crystallise.

'Jim,' he called.

Jim Shaw poked his head around the door. 'Take a seat, old friend. I want your help with working out my handover to whoever they choose to take my place. I have suggested that we should start a two-week transfer in the week starting either the 19th or 26th November. I will be seeing the candidates if they want to have a conversation over the next few weeks. I am drafting a programme and would really appreciate you running an eye over it before I offer it to Sir James. But this is also an opportunity for you. You have been in this office for more than three years, which makes you an invaluable resource for the incoming person, but do you want the opportunity to move on yourself?'

Jim sat thinking for a few minutes. 'I enjoy the work here. In fact, I am lucky because you have not been a demanding boss and we have rubbed along rather well. I recognise that at the very least, I will owe the system a duty to support a new person in their early time here.'

'All of this is true and noble. I am concerned for your career prospects, though,' offered Edward.

'You know, I am not a hugely ambitious person. I see myself as a Steady Eddie and I am very happy to accrue seniority by virtue of time. Perhaps I should talk to Personnel about what the future holds.'

'I think you are absolutely right to do that, Jim. To be honest, I think if you allow yourself to stay for, say, five years, you will be left in a time warp and people will be reluctant to give you a chance elsewhere.'

With that, Jim went back to his own small office and Edward determined that he would discuss it with Personnel when he went to see them on Wednesday.

On Wednesday morning, Edward made his way to the Personnel Department, holding his notepad and a biro. He had never actually been to this office in the two years of his stay in Whitehall, so he was agreeably surprised to find an efficient-looking woman in her early forties. She introduced herself as

Margaret Owen. They went into the small meeting room, where Edward made a point of sitting on the same side of the table as his colleague. He preferred to capture body language side-on. It frequently gave him clues that simply weren't visible if the person with him had their legs and feet hidden under a table.

'I have here the job description which was published before your appointment,' she said. 'We will offer it up to the Chairman after you and I have worked it over.'

'Fine,' said Edward. 'But may I raise one other subject at the same time?' She nodded.

'I have a Civil Service clerk called Jim Shaw. He is a quiet, reserved individual who does his job without fanfare and, if I am honest, without flair. He does nothing wrong, he is meticulous, honest and discreet. Clearly, he has the same security clearances that I have, because he handles all of the papers. So, he is utterly trustworthy. But he has been in his role for three years and I am concerned for him that he may miss the boat for promotion or career enhancement. I have had a word with him and that nudged him into reflecting on his future. It gives you something of a clue to his character that he had not, apparently, thought about it until I raised the matter. I did not tell him that I would discuss him with you, but I did encourage him to do so himself.'

'You know, that is rather interesting,' she said. 'We have a number of people at his level who are seemingly happy to bump along doing their daily grind, without thinking about their future. Thank you for raising it. I will dig out his file in order to be ready when he does jerk into action. Now, let's scrutinise this job description. Here is a copy for you, and I have one for myself.'

They read the document quietly to themselves for a few minutes. 'I do remember receiving this when I was nominated for the post, but at that stage I was a soldier with no experience of Civil Service life. At that point, I could not criticise or commend. Now, though, I do have some suggestions, not least because I am aware that the new person will be a Civil Servant with experience in the intelligence community.'

For half an hour, they discussed the document line by line. From time to time, Margaret offered an objection or revision to Edward's ideas, most of which were based upon a Civil Service practice of which he was unaware. By the same token, she nodded with brisk efficiency when Edward made a point about which the Civil Service regime had no experience. This proved to be a good exchange of ideas and customs. The pair of them felt that they had achieved something really useful by the end.

'Thank you, Edward. That has been extremely helpful. I will tidy up the paper and send you a copy. I will also submit it to the Chairman for his approval, and I am sure that he will consult you. We expect to start seeing candidates in the next ten days.'

'Wow. That's crept up on us rather quickly; but now I think about it, there isn't much time, is there? Sir James has asked me to talk to the candidates if they want a briefing before interview, and I am very happy to do that.'

They shook hands and Edward returned to his office.

October started with warm weather and the odd shower. Edward found himself making extensive notes for his successor, whoever that might be. On the 5th he received a list of five people who had been shortlisted to take over his role. Two were from the Security Service and three from SIS. He had not met any of them, but was told that they would call to make separate appointments over the coming week. It was quickly very clear to him which was the best candidate: a female SIS officer with nine years of service to her name, whose confidence was transparent in her very direct gaze, and whose intellect brooked few arguments. She was also very deft in dealing with people, and Edward could see that she would manage the relationships with other services and departments with great skill. He submitted his views to the Chairman.

On 17 October, he was gratified to learn that Sally Wainwright had been accepted for the role and would be joining him for handover work on Monday 19 November. By that time, she would have received her induction on HRT. Edward promptly wrote her a covering letter to the handover notes that he had prepared over the previous weeks, encouraging her to contact him if she had questions before the start date.

And throughout the month of October and into mid-November, it was as if Irish terrorists had gone on holiday. There were a few sporadic incidents in Belfast and Londonderry, but nothing major. This allowed Edward and Jim to ensure that the whole of their operating system was in perfect working order for the new arrival.

Edward confided in his young bride that he felt as if he was on a long, slow train journey to an enjoyable holiday. There was minimum stress and he was able to spend far more time training with Les, or being at home with Gail. They entertained, they ate out, they spent odd weekends with Gail's parents, and they agreed that they would spend a week in Northumberland once he had finally handed over. All the while, Gail's body was changing shape, so that the future parents could see and feel how their world was going to develop.

The handover could not have been easier. Sally Wainwright had spent the past eighteen months in Century House. She understood the Whitehall machine, and she quickly established the basis of a good working relationship with all of the desk officers that Edward had courted so assiduously over the previous two years. The young Davidsons asked her to dine with them, asking other friends from the circuit, like Edward Longstaff, to join them. And Sally was duly grateful. She recognised that Edward could not have made the handover easier. James Harrington felt the same way, and said as much during his final formal interview with Edward on Friday 30 November, before he departed on leave for almost four weeks. Of course, both men expected to see each other often enough in the future, for James would continue to pay godfatherly attention to Gail.

Gail and Edward spent the weekend in their flat, working out how they were going to pack up their possessions for transport to Camberley in early March. The quarter was going to be available from early January, but they agreed that it was better for Gail to keep working, and that meant that she should be in London. Moreover, it was going to be a simpler journey from Swindon to London, and it would be substantially easier for Ellie to visit Gail in London instead of Camberley. All in all, they were happy with the decision.

Edward had the luxury of getting up late on Monday 3 December. Gail had rushed off to Whitehall at her normal departure time, so the post was lying in wait for him at the entrance to the block of flats when he went down to buy a newspaper. There were four envelopes, three addressed to him and one to Gail. He held on to them all, strode down the road to the newsagent, then ambled back to the flat, let himself in and sat down at their kitchen table to open his letters. The first had a look of officialdom, so he opened it to see what else he should be doing before starting at Shrivenham. He was stunned by the contents, which asked him if he would accept his nomination to become a Member of the Most Excellent Order of the British Empire in recognition of his services to the nation. His first thought was, 'That wily old boss of mine.' His second was, 'I really do not deserve this.' His third was, 'Gail might be pleased.'

He put the letter on the kitchen counter, weighing it down with the sugar bowl. He would acknowledge it after discussion with his wife.

Gail, who was going to take leave from Friday night, arrived home at 6.00p.m. Edward was waiting with a hot kettle. He pushed two crumpets down in the toaster as she threw her keys on the table by the front door. She entered the kitchen, gave him a big hug and sat at the table, kicking off her shoes and shaking her hands through her hair.

'So, what have you got up to today, my lord and master?'

They chatted idly while the tea stewed and the crumpets cooked. He slipped both onto the one plate, which he put in front of his beloved so that she could apply the butter and Marmite that she loved with them.

'Oh, I had a funny letter. You had better read it, or you will be accusing me of keeping secrets from you,' muttered Edward, as he handed over the official note.

It took Gail a mini-second to hoist in what the letter was saying. She leapt to her feet, rushed around the table and grabbed her man hard. 'You are amazing, Edward. You have done it again. Not many desk officers get this sort of recognition.'

'Well, let's be honest, it is your godfather's work. I would never have been nominated if he had been someone else.'

'You must not keep on saying these things, Edward. I know, because Daddy has told me, that James thinks the world of you. I concede that he might stretch a point to support me, but he would never interfere with the machinery for honours and awards. You have done a magnificent job and it is entirely right that you should be rewarded. When can we tell everybody?'

'Oh, we can't. We have to wait until the New Year's Honours list is published in the paper.'

'Well, I'm not sure that I can keep it a secret for that long. I must tell my parents, and you must tell James and Mary.'

'Please humour me. The rules are quite clear. It would break all sorts of taboos if we let anyone know before the date of publication. And, my darling, you know that I am not very good at making a fanfare for myself. Will you help me by

300

keeping completely quiet until the due date? I promise that on that date we can telephone our families before they find out by reading the paper.'

'You are a terrible man, Edward Davidson. I can see that in years to come you will acquire more and more honours and I will have to fight you on every occasion to make sure that your nearest and dearest are told properly.' She kissed him lovingly.

Edward, being Edward, completely forgot about the award and had to be reminded by Gail that he had to accept it formally. With poor grace, he wrote an acknowledgement and put it in the post the following day. But after that, it was totally suppressed.

After a conversation with the Mess in Shrivenham, he arranged to take down his military clothing and a range of civilian clothes that week. This would allow him to travel on the day before the course started without the burden of luggage.

On Monday 10 December, they left by train for Berwick, intent upon spending ten days with James and Mary at Tillview Farm. For Gail, it proved to be an idyllic week of relaxing with Mary, who was increasingly like an older sister. Edward and James had two days of shooting, one in Berwickshire, near Greenlaw, and one in Northumberland, down near Scots Gap. Hector was delighted, Gimli furious.

And throughout the ten days, Gail obeyed her husband's stricture to keep quiet.

The happy couple was staying with Will and Ellie when the New Year's Honours were published on Monday 31st December. Gail was actively bouncing with excitement as they got up for breakfast, knowing that she was going to be able to pass the news to her parents before they read it in the newspaper. Edward looked at her fondly, believing still in his heart of hearts that he had no right to this or any other award.

Ellie gave Edward the most enormous bear hug, and Will, ever the solid man of the house, shook him warmly by the hand. Gail kept complaining that she had been forced to total silence for over three weeks. The two men merely nodded at each other, as if to say, 'How do we satisfy the female members of the family?'

'Now, you must telephone James and Mary,' demanded Gail.

'Must I? Surely they will pick it up out of the paper?'

'No, they won't, and nor should they. You have to tell them. Mary reported to me how taciturn you were about your MC and Mention… Now come along, my man. They merit your input.'

With resignation, Edward indicated the phone and received Will's permission to use it. 'Aunt Mary,' he started when she answered the phone, 'Aunt Mary, I have some unexpected news. If you get a newspaper later today, you will find my name in there under the Military honours. Thanks entirely to Gail's godfather, I have been made an MBE.'

'Well, thank goodness for your wonderful wife, darling. Had you not been married, I daresay that the first time we would have discovered would have been if we bumped into you wearing uniform. What a tribute. Well done. Do you know when you will attend an investiture?'

'Absolutely not. Probably some time in the Summer. Would you like a word with my keeper?'

The two women started gossiping, so Edward suggested that he should pop down to the shops to buy the paper. Will agreed, saying that he would go with him. They climbed into the family car, with Will driving. 'I have to tell you that I did know, Edward. James was so pleased that you made it through the filtering system. Of course, he should not have told me. Anything can go wrong between first submission and final publication. But I am really thrilled for you. I know that you are always deeply reserved about public accolades; but believe me, you deserved this.'

'Well, it seems to me that I have picked up the habit of being in the right place at the right time. I sincerely believe that I have not earned any of my medal work. There are so many people who perform greater service with higher skill.'

'Take it from me, the experience of receiving awards will prime you to be a good submitter of proposals on behalf of people who work for you in the future. It is all part of your training.'

The young Davidsons returned to London for New Year's Eve. They had been invited to a small dinner party with six other friends. In accepting, they had warned their hosts that they would not stay to sing in the New Year because Gail had reached a point at which she felt the need for a really good eight hours' sleep every night. As for himself, Edward couldn't really stand staying up drinking too much, when all he really wanted to do was wrap his arms around his darling bride and hold on to her in bed.

On Sunday 6 January, Edward embraced Gail, hugging her hard, then gently stroking her stomach, before giving her a kiss and saying, 'I hope to be back before dark on Friday. I will telephone as soon as I am established in the Mess at Shrivenham.' He left London at 5.10p.m. by train for Swindon. He had with him his trusted Honda 125, for which he paid £3 to put it in the guard's van. On arrival at Swindon, he climbed into his motorcycle overall, kick-started the machine and set off along the A420 towards Shrivenham. He took it steadily through the town, reaching the outskirts near the A419 at 6.30p.m. By now, it was dark and he realised that he would have to do something about securing some high-visibility clothing. He felt really quite vulnerable. A quarter of an hour after leaving the station, he was approaching Longleazes Farm, where Old Vicarage Lane joined the A420 at an angle.

Ernie Winter had enjoyed two evening pints at the Carpenters Arms and was determined to get homes, thinking 'I can't be late for Mabel's tea.' He turned left out of the pub and drove at a modest thirty miles per hour towards Longleazes Farm. It could be a devil joining the main road, so he practised his normal trick of keeping going at about 15mph so that he could accelerate into any gap in the traffic. Briefly, he glanced over his right shoulder and spotted a queue of moving traffic coming towards him from the town. Judging that he had precisely the right momentum, he put his foot down and accelerated onto the main road.

Edward had taken the little car into account, noting that it was travelling slowly. He was confident that the driver would have seen his headlight. But Ernie Winter's abrupt decision to join the main road gave Edward less than half a second and eleven yards to deal with the unexpected appearance of the car directly in his path. Thanks to his fencing, his reactions were always super-fast, but the time and distance were far too short. He hit the rear door on the driver's side at 50mph and was catapulted over the top of Ernie Winter's car at a height of nine feet, following a low parabola for twenty feet to land on his back, half on the grass verge and half on the road. His speed at impact was 32mph, which made his mass 416 stone when he stopped. The pressures were far too great for the human body, so his heart stopped, too.